# THE COUNTERCLOCK PROPHECY

# THE COUNTERCLOCK PROPHECY

Marc Mattson

ISBN: 978-1-7320306-0-2 (Paperback)
       978-1-7320306-1-9 (eBook)

Library of Congress Control Number: 2018902187

Printed in the United States of America.

www.marleygoeste.com

*For Nan,*
*who is probably sad that its not about cats,*

*and Eric*
*who gets me (most of the time).*

# :01 orbits

"It's very flat," Emily Clocke says. It was the first time anyone had spoken since just past Denver. The Clocke family minivan, a tragically abused, boxy, maroon Toyota, is currently limping through Kansas, just on the outskirts of Kansas City.

Sarah, Emily's mother, removes her hand from the steering wheel just long enough to turn down the radio, which wasn't particularly loud to begin with. "I didn't think you were awake," she says, searching for her daughter in the rearview mirror.

Emily pops suddenly into view, her long, narrow, fourteen-year-old head poking up from behind her mother's seat. At the right angle, it might look as if Emily's head had been grafted onto her mother's right shoulder. "I was just...thinking."

"'Bout what?"

"Stuff."

It's the kind of answer a person gives if she's really aching to talk, but not about to speak. It's the kind of answer that says, 'I have so much to say, but you wouldn't like hearing any of it, so let's let it be.'

"Is your brother awake?" her mother asks, astutely changing the subject.

Emily glances behind her. Her older brother Eric is folded into a small nook in the third-row seat, to the left of a stack of boxes, suitcases, and potato-chip crumbs. His face—what there is to see of it under the entirely unnecessary black knit cap that is pulled down almost over his eyes—is pressed up against the driver-side window. Dead to the world. She can even hear very slight snores just above the faint, discordant thumping seeping out of his headphones.

"No," Emily says, answering her mother's question. "Can I poke him in the eye and wake him up?"

"Let him be," Sarah sighs. It is only a half-serious admonition.

Emily slumps back into her seat and resumes pondering her situation. Despite all that had preceded their packing themselves sardine-tight into a lumpy minivan for a trek halfway across the country, the kids—Emily Clocke and her sixteen-year-old brother Eric—had fought the idea with all the respectful ferocity they could muster. "We have friends here," they said, and school, and a neighborhood they understood and were perfectly happy in. Yes, their father was no longer with them, but isn't that all the more reason for them to stay in a familiar and stable environment?

"So be honest with me," Sarah says, deciding against her better judgment to not drop it, "are you going to survive this?"

Emily sits back up at the sound of Sarah's voice, but shrugs at the question. "I guess."

Sarah looks at Emily in the mirror for a long moment. Studies her. The scrutiny makes Emily self-conscious. But then again, what doesn't? She slinks slowly down in her seat again so her mother can't see her in the mirror anymore.

Emily stays awake through the rest of Kansas and is, despite her acute weariness, still awake when they enter Missouri. Restless after nearly two days of watching the sugar-coated mountains of Utah and Colorado morph into the sanded-down flatness of the Midwest, she has nothing left to think about, so she begins to think about irony. She finds it funny that there have been times in her life when she had fantasized about moving. Not for any specific reason, really, but just because.

'Because I'm tired of blending into the background.'

Emily leans her head against the window and lets the running patterns of the highway lane lines hypnotize her. She closes her eyes for—a minute? an hour? When she opens them again (with much effort), she sees a car beside the van, matching their speed. She doesn't think to look at the car itself, because her eyes are drawn exclusively to two men in the car's front- and rear-passenger seats who stare back at her with curious intensity. Yet even when caught staring, they haven't the discretion to stop. Emily doesn't detect malevolence, but their intense faces creep her out anyway. After a moment, the man in the front seat turns and appears to speak to the car's driver. When their conversation ends, he turns again to Emily and looks at her one more time before both men turn forward and the car pulls ahead slightly so that they can ponder Sarah.

"Uh, Mom?"

"What's up?"

Emily is about to answer, but the car suddenly speeds up, breaking away and pulling ahead of the van. Emily follows the car with her eyes for a while, then stops. Do I have 'out-of-towner' tattooed on my forehead? she thinks. There's something romantic about the idea of being a mysterious stranger in a strange new land—a brief respite from her typical anonymity—but now, though…

"What's up?" Sarah asks again.

"Never mind."

"We're in St. Louis, guys," Sarah says. She announces it like they're tourists just passing through. This is partially true, in fact: they are just passing through Missouri. They're heading about another five hours northeast. Difference is, they won't be heading back. They aren't tourists, they're residents-to-be.

"We ain't in Kansas anymore," Eric croaks, not even bothering to open his eyes or lift his head.

"We haven't been in Kansas since seven this morning," Emily says, "You slept right through it."

"Shut up, brainiac."

"I was just sayin'…"

"And do you wonder why you don't have any friends?"

"I have friends!"

"Not anymore!"

"Alright!" Sarah says, "Stop it now before it really starts to annoy me."

And just like that, all is quiet again. The regained silence comes as a blessing. Emily wonders why she had wanted conversation in the first place.

Emily turns back to watch St. Louis pass by, the silvery arch fluttering out from behind the support girders of the steel bridge that takes them over the Mississippi River and into Illinois.

After a while, Eric looks up, his eyes obscured by the forest of matted, jet-black hair that leaks from beneath his cap. "Hey, mom."

"What?"

"I have to pee."

———

Emily presses her head against the window and peers out. She studies Sarah, who leans against the van, one gym-shoed foot kicked back against the wheel, the other stretched out, buttressing her. Dressed in form-fitting jeans and a plain blue t-shirt, her arms folded before her, she looks confident, wholly relaxed and calm, ageless and placeless. But Emily intuits that it's a lie. Her mother is running away from something, and she and Eric are being dragged along for the ride.

She feels nothing until the door of the van slams shut and breaks her concentration. Or lack thereof. Then she sees the ragged, vagabond form of Eric moving away from the van, heading straight for the mini-mart attached to the gas station. As he sulks across the pavement to the door, like a depression-era hobo scrounging for a meal, Sarah yells for him to buy her a Diet Coke. Eric grunts a reply which Emily can't quite make out, but is sure was impolite.

Emily scooches across the bench seat, pulls the door open, and jumps out. She meanders around the back of the van, not entirely sure why she got out. She was perfectly comfortable in the van. She stops and stands on the opposite side of the fuel hose from her mother.

Sarah looks her up and down. "You know, I dread the day when you're going to hate me too," she says.

"What?" Emily asks.

Sarah gives her head a vigorous shake, as if waking herself, which she really is. "Don't mind me," she says, "all this driving is getting to me."

"I'm going into the store. Want anything?"

"We're out of Diet Coke."

"Okay," Emily says, bounding away from the van, deciding not to tell her that she already ordered Eric to get Diet Coke.

"Make Eric pay for it," Sarah yells after her.

"Okay," Emily answers over her shoulder.

Eric is nowhere to be found in the store. Not that Emily really has much desire to find him. Though they are able to find cohesion where necessity dictates (such as explaining to Sarah why they shouldn't move) the one year and two month difference between them is just enough for him to be the antagonistic older brother and her to be the put-upon little sister. Where he seeks her out for his nefarious purposes, she avoids him as an act of self-preservation. Until lately, that is. Now he thankfully avoids her as much as she tries to avoid him.

She finds her way to the wall of beverage coolers at the back of the store and pulls out a six-pack of Diet Coke, then turns to inspect the snack aisle. Eric blows by, grumbling something about Twinkies as he passes out of the store. Emily happily ignores him.

Seeing this, a woman at the end of the aisle smiles and leans conspiratorially toward Emily. "Brothers are a treacherous nuisance, aren't they?" she says.

Emily smiles politely and says only, "Yeah," before turning back to the wall of snacks.

Emboldened by Emily's acknowledgement, the woman takes a tentative step closer. "I presume he's an older brother?"

"Yeah," Emily repeats, adding, "he is," to make her end of the conversation seem a bit more complete. She gives the woman a quick, timid glance. Tall, spindly, middle-aged, slightly older than her mom, the woman is somehow both distinguished yet curiously nondescript, as if at odds with herself about what sort of self-image she wants to convey. Like Emily, her skin is walnut-colored, her ethnicity difficult to determine. Her face is angular and tight but unnaturally smooth, like a stern librarian sculpted by botox. A small-town convenience store is clearly not her milieu. Then again, Emily can picture her fitting in both nowhere and anywhere. A living anachronism.

"Always the provocateurs, older brothers," the woman continues. "He will come to appreciate you in time, I suspect."

Emily smiles and offers a barely perceptible chuckle as a respectful acknowledgement.

The woman stands there, considering Emily. She crosses her arms and cocks her head slightly, as if it might provide a better angle to study Emily. She wears a warm smile, full of a curious recognition that is at odds with her piercing, calculating stare. Finally, after a moment, she says, more to herself than to Emily, "You have a fire in you, do you not? You just do not see yourself."

Emily's eyes widen at this. "Excuse me?" she says.

"No," the woman says, taken aback, "Excuse me. It was nothing."

Emily catches a glimpse of her mother strolling purposefully up the aisle. "What's with you?" Sarah asks, passing the strange woman. "I finished gassing up the van five minutes ago. I was wondering if you fell in the toilet or something."

"Sorry, I was just talking…" Emily says, gesturing to the woman.

Sarah turns to face the woman. Curiously, the woman's smile turns waxy at the sight of Sarah and her eyes widen as if in disbelief. She studies Emily's mother intently, more intently than she had studied Emily, as if memorizing a picture of a long dead relative. Indeed, her face is an odd mixture of wonder and uncertainty and a long simmering melancholy, an unknowable history etched in the lines of her eyes. She says, simply, blankly, "Sayre."

"Sarah, actually," Sarah corrects. "Do I know you?"

This breaks the woman's reverie. She lurches forward and grabs Sarah by the shoulders, her eyes widened in delight, her smile open-mouthed and genuine. "Sayre, it is you!" She glances back and forth between Emily and Sarah. "I had hoped—"

Sarah wriggles free of the woman's grip. "Uh, no," she says, shock and confusion registered all over her face, "I...I think you've got the wrong person."

"But no," the woman says, demands, "You are—" Then she stops and looks carefully, searchingly at Sarah.

Emily shifts her glance between the two of them.

After a moment, the woman's shoulders fall, but she holds her head high and tries not to make it obvious that she is struggling to regain her composure. "I apologize, ma'am," she says. She is conciliatory, but it is obvious that she is nonetheless convinced of her correctness. "Forgive me. You bear a striking resemblance to a former...companion of mine. I thought for a moment you might be her."

"I'm sorry," Sarah says, trying to make light of it, "I'm just...me."

"I daresay you are more than that," the woman says, then catches herself. "I mean, I am sure you are much more than that. I hope I did not startle you." She holds out her hand to Sarah. "Maren," she says.

Sarah tentatively reaches out and takes her hand. She shakes it, lightly and quickly, and withdraws it quickly, not entirely hiding the curiosity on her face. "Sarah—" she says, letting her voice trail off as she decides that a first-name basis is sufficient . "Pleasure to meet you."

"You have a lovely daughter, Sarah, if I may say. I see a spark of ingenuity in her eyes. She must take after her mother."

"She's a chip off the old block all right," Sarah says, lacking for better words. She puts her arm around Emily's shoulder and makes to gently urge her forward. "She just doesn't know the meaning of 'hurry up, we have a lot of driving to do yet.'"

"I'm afraid that is my fault," the woman says, "I have detained her with my silly attempts at conversation."

"Well, that's quite all right," Sarah says, "there's no harm in talking. But we really should be off. We do actually have quite a bit of driving to do yet."

The woman smiles. "Then I shall reiterate my apologies and bid you safe travels. It was very nice to meet you Sarah. Emily."

At that, Sarah leads Emily away.

"Sarah!" the woman suddenly calls out.

Startled, Sarah turns and looks back at Maren, her irritation not particularly well buried.

"Do I not...look familiar to you?"

Sarah narrows her eyes. Her irritation turns into a muted apprehension. "No," she answers after a moment's hesitation, "Should you?"

The woman deflates. She shrugs and shakes her head in reply.

"Well, again, nice to meet you," Sarah says and gently pushes Emily to the double doors of the store.

Emily raises her hands to show the snacks and Cokes she's carrying. "What about this stuff?" she asks.

"Just leave them," Sarah says. She takes the things from Emily's hands and hurriedly stacks them on the counter. She then pushes Emily out the door, leaving the bewildered counter clerk to shrug at the woman they'd just left.

———

"What the hell was that?" Sarah asks, paying less attention to the road than she should. She shakes her right hand vigorously. "She hurt my hand."

"What was what?" Eric asks.

"I'm talking to Emily," Sarah snaps.

"Sore-ee," Eric mumbles before sliding back down into his regular position in the back seat.

"I don't know. She just started talking to me," Emily says.

"About what?" Sarah asks, starting another conversation with Emily's reflection.

"Brothers."

"Brothers."

"Yeah."

"What about brothers?"

"How they're a nuisance. It was just small talk."

"Did she ask about me?"

"No. At least, not until you came in."

Sarah nods, then puts her eyes back on the road.

Emily, who would otherwise have let it drop from her mind, is uneasy about Sarah's anxiousness and thinks more about the woman. She realizes that though she had looked directly at the woman, and could see with crystal clarity the woman's features, clothing, skin color, size, and every conceivable attribute, it was still as if she had viewed her only peripherally. If pressed, Emily could give only the most general of descriptions.

"Do you know her?" Emily asks, meeting her mom's reflection.

"I never saw her before in my life."

"Then that was weird."

"Yes, it was."

———

There is nothing exceptional about their new house. It is an unassuming bi-level in the middle of an unassuming neighborhood that once-upon-a-time was a subdivision for wealthy commuters but has recently fallen to the middle-class. A thick, spidery maple tree grows smack in the middle of their short front yard, just a hop, skip, and jump (not that Eric or Emily do either of those things anymore) from the tiny slab of concrete that serves as their front porch. Though they have neighbors behind them, there are none on either side, so looking up at it from the driveway, there is something deliciously forlorn about the little house standing all by itself, guarded over by a bent old man of a tree.

To be sure, there was nothing exceptional about their old house in California, either, save for the fact that it had all the comforts of familiarity. By contrast, everything in Illinois is alien: the late September air has a palpable Midwest wispiness, the sun shines with a watery sheen, the flat openness is incongruously claustrophobic. Emily feels that she might just as well be walking on the moon for all the relief her new world brings her.

Sarah pops the rear hatch of the van. Eric leans in and begins rooting around in the mess of luggage, probably searching for his own things. Emily wanders up the walkway to the front door of the house and tries the door. It's locked. 'Figures,' Emily thinks.

"I have the key, dufus," Eric says from behind her. "Did you think it would just magically open?" He nudges her aside with his hip and tries to get the key in the lock with one hand while struggling to keep his grip on an oversized box with the other.

"I could help," Emily says.

"Yeah, you could," Eric snaps back, just as the key slides in the lock. He turns it, unlocks the door, swings it open, and marches in. "But I don't see you doing it."

Emily follows hesitantly. Just inside the door, to the right, is a stairway up to the second floor. To the left is an arid, empty desert of a living room, bright with the light of afternoon streaming in. She turns left and just stands, taking in the expanse of room and the view of the front yard through the crosshatched windows.

She has never experienced such emptiness before. This isn't like being home alone in Boulder Creek. This is complete barrenness, not a single piece of furniture to absorb the muffle of her footsteps or the echo of her own breathing. It feels more like a cave than a house. It is definitely not a home.

She walks into the backyard. The shallow, neatly manicured yard slopes downward slightly, which allows a view of the expansive suburb behind them, as well as the newer subdivision just beyond that, where the wealthier people who commute to their jobs in Chicago live. Chicago itself is a faint, hazy promise in the distance to the east. Just down the slope, near the end of their property, before the tall cedar fence that separates their yard from the yards of their only two neighbors, is an old, rickety, weather-beaten wood-framed swing set, presumably built by the previous owners for their kids. Digging it out and dismantling it would have obviously been more trouble than it was worth, so it stayed—a housewarming present for a family whose only use for it was as something to dig up and dismantle.

Emily wonders if the kids who had once played on it miss it yet.

She trudges back inside and climbs up the stairs to the second floor to find her room—or at least what she assumes is her room. It too is bare. She sits down on a pristine patch of green carpet where a dresser or armoire had once been, her back against a wall. Her forefinger absently traces the crater that the missing furniture had created, noting how new that little patch of carpeting looks compared to the rest of the well-trod room. The room is less like a blank canvas than a chore.

She picks at a little piece of carpet lint sticking up on the worn side of the carpeting, and pulls a two-inch piece out. She lays it on the newer portion of carpeting and compares the colors.

'You don't belong there.' She flicks the lint away with her forefinger.

———

They sit on the kitchen floor eating take-out pizza directly from the box, Emily cross-legged in the center of the room and both Eric and Sarah leaning back against kitchen appliances. None of them has an explanation for why the pizza is cut into little squares rather than equal triangles. Then again, none of them would offer an explanation even if they had one: their conversation consists of a deafening silence punctuated by loud chewing. Sarah had earlier made an attempt at talk, telling the kids that things would be better when the furniture arrived, but neither of them dignified the comment with a response.

"Alright, look," Sarah says, rather more firmly than she probably should, "I know you're not happy about this. Neither am I. But I'm trying to make the best of this and I'd appreciate it if you could at least try to yourselves. This silent treatment is getting stale."

At that, Eric throws his pizza down and stands. "You know what? Why should I pretend to be happy? I'm not! I didn't even have a choice." Then he storms away. "And I sure as hell don't believe you're not happy!" he yells over his shoulder.

"Eric!" she yells, but he doesn't stop. "Eric Michael Clocke, get your ass back here!"

When the front door slams behind him, Sarah hops to her feet and stomps toward the door. But halfway across the living room she stops, lowers her head, and pauses. After a moment, she pinions on her heels and spins back around and sits down cross-legged across from Emily, the pizza box between them. She props her elbows on her knees, bows her face into her cupped hands, and exhales noisily.

Emily sits there stone stiff, a little afraid to do much of anything. Eventually, though, the tension even overwhelms her enough to speak.

"Mom?"

"What?" Sarah answers, her face still in her hands, her voice a bit stony.

"Can I be excused?"

Sarah lifts her head and looks at her daughter. She says, theatrically, with very exaggerated facial gestures and a clownish rolling of her head: "Might as well!"

Emily walks out onto the back patio and makes a beeline toward the swing set. The wood beams groan as she sits, and the thick, rubber swing sags greatly under her weight, so much so that the chains presses uncomfortably tight to either side of her hips. But she makes no move to leave. It's better than being in the house with her mother, or in front with her brother.

She scans the dark tableau before her, the faint golden halo that is Chicago hovering over the houses behind theirs. As she looks, she sees that the nighttime sky is much brighter than she'd ever experienced in California, except on those few nights when she'd stayed in L.A., when her parents had to go there for conferences or lectures.

"This sucks," a voice murmurs from behind her. Eric plops into the swing beside her. He drops so hard that Emily is amazed that the beam above then doesn't snap. "Why the hell couldn't we stay in Boulder Creek?"

"'Cause we couldn't afford it, I guess."

"'Cause we couldn't afford it. Nyeh nyeh nyeh," Eric says, parroting Emily in a taunting voice. "Dad left money!"

"Yeah, but I don't think it was enough to pay for the house. At least that's what I overheard mom say. I think she was talking to the real-estate guy."

There was silence after that. Though Emily couldn't entirely believe it, she thought the trip had knocked the fight out of Eric. Oddly enough, under the circumstances, this saddened her. She had hoped for at least some consistency.

After some time gently swinging in silence, Eric asks, "You like it here?"

She looks up. "I can only see six stars. It's too bright here."

"Tammy expects me to text her every day. I don't know what I'm supposed to tell her. I already know it's going to get boring real fast."

Emily thinks his words over. She says the only thing she could think of: "You mean Tammy Dena? You're going out with her?"

Eric blows the air from his lung and stands. "Was," he says and starts to walk away from the swing set.

"What room do you want?" Emily asks after him.

He says, "Whatever," then disappears around the front of the house.

Emily keeps rocking gently back and forth.

———

Emily lies on an air mattress in the bedroom she'd first gone into. There are no shades on the window, so she lies there meditating under the skewed six-pack squares of her bedroom window that are projected onto the ceiling by the streetlight across the street.

She has no clock, so she doesn't know exactly what time it is when she hears the back door slam closed and Eric's footsteps squeak up the stairs. He'd attempted to sleep in the van, and she guesses that he came in because Illinois was colder than he had expected. He'd refused to acknowledge that this house was anything other than temporary.

That's one thing they agree upon.

———

She stood next to her father—right next to him!—and could barely recognize him, which was okay since he didn't even notice at all that she was there. She had made him up from the bits and pieces of memory that she still clung to, the wispy snippets of recollection that she plucked out of the air like so much dandelion fluff. What bits she failed to catch she simply made up with a dash of ingenuity and a dollop of veneration.

His hand hovered over a button, a single button among many on a vast console that stretched before a thick plate of glass that separated them from an immense room. The room, easily the width and depth of an airplane hangar, but about six stories in height, held an enormous steel ball from which protruded a tangle of wires and rods that anchored it to the walls like a Christmas ornament caught by a giant spider.

The button usually resided under a small glass cube that could only be opened by a key, but her father had already unlocked the enclosure and flipped it up, exposing the glowing red button. All he had to do was to push it.

She screamed at him to stop, to not push it, but her voice came out as her mother's. This, she learned, was because her mother was now standing on the other side of her father, looking at him imploringly.

"Daddy, please, don't," Sarah/Emily said. Screamed. Sobbed. Pleaded.

He'd turned his head back to look at the button, his face rendered demonic by the shadows in his cheeks and red glow in his eyes.

And knowing his duty but not the consequences, and despite her and her mother's hysterical pleas, he pushed the button.

———

Emily does not wake from her dream with a melodramatic start, like one might see a character do in a movie, but with a subtle twitch, as if she had been jumping on the mattress and had just fallen back into her body. She finds the sharp, blue numbers of her clock and sees that it's only 5:15 in the morning, not yet time to wake up. So she lies in bed—such as it is—completely wound up by her racing heart, unable to shake the residual emotions of her dream.

Strangely, she finds that tragedy to be more worthy of consideration than the fact that she's lived in Chicago for a full five days already.

In the darkness, she broods on the images that float in her head, trying to piece them back together into a coherent narrative before they dissolve away, like most dreams do. She saw her father in his lab. Or at least what she had remembered of his lab, having only seen it once, long ago, when she was small and the world was larger. She saw the explosion, and the rolling ball of flame that consumed him; both images that existed only in her imagination, but haunted her nonetheless.

What did she really remember about him? He died when she was ten, so she's had nearly five years now to forget what she knew. She's not entirely sure if that bothers her. She can't remember.

She rolls into a sitting position, her body sinking into the sagging mattress, and spins to roll off the edge. She stands and pads into the hall. She pushes open the door to her mother's room and peers into the grayness. Shades are drawn over the bedroom window but the new, morning sun peeks through the edges, trickling enough light in to illuminate the lump in the bedspread that is her mother.

Emily tip-toes to the bed and slides gingerly under the covers. Her mother, facing away from her, moves her head slightly to determine what's amiss. Emily holds her breath and doesn't move a muscle. After a moment, when Emily finally exhales, her mother turns completely over and drapes her arm over Emily.

Emily laughs silently.

"What time is it?" her mother asks, her eyes refusing to open.

"About a quarter to six," Emily answers.

"What are you doing up so early?"

"I had a weird dream."

"A weird dream," Sarah says, purposely emphasizing 'weird.' "About what?"

"Dad."

"Hmm." Sarah rolls onto her back again, awake now, and just looks at the ceiling. Emily watches her for a while, trying to figure out what to say next.

"Why do you work at the lab?" she finally asks.

"Because that's where the work is."

"But—" Emily starts, but decides she doesn't want to continue.

"So what was your dream?"

"Dad was in charge of the lab. In Stanford. And he pushed

this button and the whole thing blew up. We told him not to but he did it anyway."

"We?"

"You and me."

"Was I the Tin Man or the Scarecrow?"

Emily looks at her, confused. "Huh?"

"Nah, it was—" her mother starts to say, sputtering her words. She lays silent for a moment, growing contrite in the quiet. "Sorry, it was...never mind. You know that's not what happened, right?"

"I know," Emily says. Except that she really doesn't know, and she really wants to, but she was already regretting bringing the whole thing up. Because she was ten when he died, the only information she got at the time was that he died in an accident at the lab. Nobody offered any more detail. Apparently grief didn't need any further explanation, so she had to fill in the blanks herself.

They lie a bit in silence, neither knowing what to say.

"I want to go back home." Emily finally says.

"Em, you've been here for all of a week. You've got to give it a little more time than that."

Emily shrugs. "I know, but...I want to go home."

Sarah looks wistful. "Home isn't home anymore."

"Huh?"

Her mother shakes her head. "I know it's hard, Em. It's just as hard for me, believe me. But you can't turn back the clock. My job is here now. Our lives are here now. I made a commitment, and I have to honor it. I didn't know it was going to be as hard on you as it apparently is." Sarah turns on her side to face Emily, draping her arm over her only daughter. "I know it's different, honey, I do. It's not easy on me, either. And Eric's made his feelings rather clear. Has he actually said anything to you, by the way?"

"You think he'd tell me anything?" Emily lies.

Her mother laughs knowingly. "Probably not. Anyway, I just...I just need you to give it more time. Okay?"

"Alright."

They lie there again, unmoving and unspeaking, until Emily hears her mother's breathing get longer and deeper. Emily slowly shifts her feet off the bed and pulls herself up into a sitting position. Let her sleep, she thinks, and moves to stand. Before she's completely upright she catches a glimpse of a picture on the floor next to the bed. She pulls it to her and lays it across her lap, letting her eyes register the image. Two people, happy. In a posed moment, but nonetheless genuinely happy. One is her mother, obviously younger than the snoring woman beside her. The other is a man who, with his rimless round eyeglasses, shallow cheeks and triangle chin, looks less square-jawed, less super heroic than the man in her dream.

Less tragic.

"Dad," Emily says.

She can barely remember. She's not entirely sure if that bothers her.

———

The next morning, Emily is sitting in the waiting room at the front office of the high school, on a bench in a narrow alcove tucked just to the side of the formica counter behind which the school administrators do their work. The room is walled in cinder block painted a glossy, happy, beige-yellow, which she finds oddly tranquil. She waits for the assistant principal, Ms. Marks, to direct her to her first class, which is already the fourth class of the day.

She and her mother had arrived before the first period bell rang, but it took two whole periods to finish off all of the administrative gobbledygook before she could actually start her first class. By the time she was ready to go, it was fifteen minutes into the third period and Ms. Marks decided it would be best to wait out the period so as not to disrupt a class in progress.

So Emily sits quietly. And in her reverie, she lets her mind wander back to her childhood fantasy of being the new kid in school. It always went something like this:

She'd walk into the classroom with a cool, self-assured air of mystery. The teacher would stop what she was doing, the classroom would fall silent, all eyes would be on her.

"Class, this is Emily Clocke," the teacher would announce, "she's come to us all the way from California."

This news would be greeted with subdued curiosity. 'California', the class would collectively murmur, 'How exotic.'

The teacher would tell her to take a seat. She'd purposely ignore the dozens of eyes that would follow her as she walked silently to her desk, and her self-containment throughout the morning would only amplify her mystique.

They'd want to know her. Desperately. Hungrily. They'd want to bask in her aura of celebrity, want to be the first to crack her inscrutability. They'd flock to her at lunch and pepper her with inquiries. "So what's California like? Do you have a boyfriend? Did you know any movie stars? Can we hang with you?" They'd follow her every move, hang on her every whisper like groupies in the shadow of the backstage door.

Oh, she'd be special. The queen. She'd own them...

"Okay, Emily, are you ready?" Ms. Marks pokes her head into the alcove, startling Emily, who hadn't even heard the bell ring. Emily stands and voids her daydream; all of her mental preparation at being the new kid in school is instantly suffocated by a tangle of nerves and circumstance. She forgets that she even had a plan (such as it was), and all she can see now, as she follows Ms. Marks into the hallway, are the eyes of dozens and dozens of other kids staring at her, sizing her up, judging her.

Never mind that the kids, busy with their own concerns and winding their way past each other to get to their next class, barely pay her any notice. She tries to hide behind the books the assistant principal has given her, hugging them to her chest so tightly that her knuckles go white.

"So what do you think of Lederman so far?" Ms. Marks asks, looking over her shoulder at Emily.

"What's Lederman?" Emily asks innocently.

Ms. Marks stops, causing Emily to almost collide with her. "The name of this school," Ms. Marks says wryly, suppressing a laugh and twirling her finger to indicate their surroundings.

"Oh. Sorry," Emily says, chagrined. "It's nice."

Ms. Marks smiles kindly. "It's okay, Emily. You've come a long way. You'll settle in, though. If it's any consolation, your chemistry teacher is new too." She turns to continue down the hall, but stops again abruptly and turns back, narrowing her eyes. "This is going to sound like a strange question, but have we met before?"

Emily gazes up at her, the unbearable burden of new-kid-ness making her eyes the size of Jupiter. "I don't think so," she answers, then unhelpfully adds, "I'm from California."

"I know," Ms. Marks says, "but you look weirdly familiar. And I'm actually not one to remember people too well."

'That's a great quality for a vice-principal,' Emily manages to think.

"Ah well," Ms. Marks finally says. She shrugs, turns, and starts back down the hall. "So yeah, you'll like it here, it's a great school."

They wind a few corners in what Emily initially considers an incomprehensible maze until Ms. Marks strides directly into one of a dozen indistinguishable doorways in the middle of a seemingly endless corridor. "Miss Crana," the assistant principal says upon entering, "this is your new student, Emily Clocke. I'm going to turn her over to you now."

Somehow, over the thunderous pulsing of her heartbeat, Emily hears the assistant principal say something like welcome or good luck or some such other platitude before beating a retreat from the room, leaving Emily alone to face her new teacher and those few students who had arrived already. Great, throw me to the lions. She feels moisture begin to film over her forehead.

The teacher—What was her name? Crana?—smiles a genuine and altogether familiar smile at her, which serves to remove Emily's self-consciousness and replace it with genuine curiosity. Crana? Do I know you?

"Good morning, Emily. It's very nice to see you again," says Ms. Crana, her chemistry teacher.

It is the woman who introduced herself as Maren in the gas station's mini-mart.

# :02 clockwise

"How fast is light?" Ms. Crana asks the class.

Remarkably, not a single hand shoots up. Even more remarkably, no hand ever did.

"Jeez, what an idiot." Connie Booth leans over and whispers to Emily. "She doesn't really expect us to know that, does she?" Connie, whose rounded cheeks and door-knob chin counter her heavy eyelids and constantly pursed lips and draw out a modest sense of geniality, is the closest thing to a friend that Emily has made in the three weeks since arriving at Lederman High School. She and Emily share two classes, which is one more than Emily shares with any other student, so that makes Connie, by default, Emily's new best friend. They live on opposite sides of the city, though, so they never see each other outside of school. This, frankly, is fine by Emily. She's not ready for friends.

"Ms. Booth? Do you know the speed at which light travels?"

"No," Connie answers, "Do I need to?"

"Yes."

"Why?"

"Because I am sure you do not wish to see me again during the summer."

"No, seriously, why do we need to know this stuff? It's all B.S. I'm never going to use it."

"You never know."

"Actually, I do. I'm never going to need it."

"Then you are probably correct. Ms. Clocke…"

Emily slides down her chair into a slouch, imperceptibly shaking her head at Connie's fearless assault on reason. But she is nonetheless caught off guard when Ms. Crana calls her.

"…tell Ms. Booth how fast light is."

Now Connie is looking at her. Emily can't tell if she's laughing or surprised, but either way Connie's grin is stupid.

Emily shrugs and shakes her head in preamble to her answer. "I…don't know," she says abashedly.

"Yes you do," Ms. Crana says. It's not a statement of confidence building, it's a declaration of fact. Ms. Crana seems to be telling Emily definitively that Emily does know how fast light travels. Problem is, Emily really doesn't.

"Um, actually, I don't."

Ms. Crana, unperturbed, fixes a withering stare on Emily. Emily's answer, clearly, is unacceptable.

"Yes. You do," she says. "You all do. We've covered this already."

"No, we haven't," someone says, challenging Ms. Crana's assertion.

"Indeed we have, you just don't realize it. Sometimes knowledge is just a matter of connecting the dots. Everyone get out a writing utensil. You are going to do a little arithmetic."

A collective groan rises like a aural mushroom cloud.

"Why didn't you just answer the question?" Connie whisper-yells.

"Why didn't *you* answer the question?" Emily retorts.

"I did! I said I didn't know!"

Emily shrugs and scrunches her face in reply.

"How long does it take for light to travel from the sun to the Earth?" Ms. Crana asks the class.

Remarkably, nobody answers.

"This is rudimentary knowledge," Ms. Crana scolds.

"This is a chemistry class," an anonymous voice sneers.

Undeterred, Ms. Crana looks directly at Emily. "Ms. Clocke, how long does it take for light to travel from the sun to the Earth?"

Connie kicks her under the table.

"Eight minutes," Emily answers, under protest and annoyed by the bruise she'll likely have on her shin.

"Approximately," Ms. Crana adds. "And how far away is the Earth from the sun?"

Again, nobody answers.

"Ms. Clocke, how far away is the Earth from the sun?"

"93 million miles."

"Approximately," Ms. Crana adds again. "Disregarding aphelion and perihelion. So, now, I ask: how fast is light?"

Nobody is quick to answer. For that matter, very few were even quick to put pencil to paper, their faces betraying their confusion as to just how this obscure problem was supposed to be solved.

Emily, however, is scribbling away. Had she presence of mind to look, she would have noticed that nearly everyone is gazing in her direction, their reliance suddenly on her to get them out of this arithmetical hole. In fact, it's likely that they all believe that she had single-handedly gotten them into this predicament in the first place. In their minds, Ms. Crana and Emily were inextricably linked, both having entered their classroom on the same day. Ms. Crana arrived suddenly and unexpectedly, Emily learned, when their original teacher, Ms. Prybyl, disappeared inexplicably and was replaced without explanation or fanfare. Emily entered literally minutes later, a shrinking violet stick figure in classic black high-top Chuck Taylors, who seemed to have had a passing acquaintance with Ms. Crana, a fact that Ms. Crana exploits mercilessly.

So now they look at the two as a pair: the enigmatic pseudo-hippie who refuses to follow the curriculum but nonetheless trebled the academic expectations that Ms. Prybyl had set, and the clueless pin-cushion of a girl that the teacher continually picks to answer her esoteric questions.

And despite this, and despite herself, Emily puts her pen down and raises her hand, though absently and a bit reluctantly. She notices that everyone is staring at her, including Ms. Crana, and she blushes. Nobody else has his or her hand up.

"Ms. Clocke," Ms. Crana says evenly, "how fast is light?"

"Um...it's," Emily looks away from Ms. Crana and gazes self-consciously around the room. She sees Connie shaking her head slightly, though whether it's in sympathy, apprehension, or rebellious glee, Emily can't tell. "It travels about 193,750 miles per second."

"Using approximations as your source figures, your result is quite accurate. Light, in fact, travels at 299,796 kilometers, or 186,285 miles, per second."

"Okay, so, but, really, why is it important to know this?" Connie asks, "How is knowing the speed of light going to help me become an actress?"

"It is not," Ms. Crana replies matter-of-factly.

The bell rings and the class lets out a collective sigh of relief, pleased that Ms. Crana won't have time for her soapbox. Students begin shuffling out of the room at all manner of speeds, and over the din, Ms. Crana calls to Emily, "Ms. Clocke! Will you stay a moment?"

Emily, in line to exit, slides her book bag from her shoulder and sits down in the nearest chair at the nearest lab table. Connie leans over as she passes by "You gotta stop being teacher's pet," she whispers.

The classroom empties, and Emily fiddles nervously with the spigot of the sink at the end of her lab table. When she finally looks up, she sees Ms. Crana standing behind her desk, her arms folded across her chest, staring imperiously at Emily. Or, as it begins to seem, through Emily.

The silence vaguely disturbs her. After about a full minute of it, Emily works up the courage to speak. "Did you need to talk to me?"

At the question, Ms. Crana raises a finger, commanding Emily to wait. After another full minute, Ms. Crana abruptly adopts a warm, almost motherly smile, and her eyes seem to focus more distinctly on Emily. "Emily," Ms. Crana says, and walks around from behind her desk. "Your friends are Luddites."

"They're not really—"

"They do not recognize the power of knowledge. That will be their downfall."

Emily shivers in response.

"I hope this is not an imposition on your time," Ms. Crana says, "I was hoping to talk to you."

"No," Emily says, "This is my last class before lunch."

"I will not keep you long then," Ms. Crana says, "I have—" and then she stops. The way she'd stretched out the last word makes it seem to Emily as if she'd suddenly forgotten what she had wanted to talk about. Nothing about Ms. Crana seemed ordinary, not even conversation.

"Will your parents be attending the parent/teacher conference this evening?"

"Yes," Emily says, then thinks to add, "well, just...yes." She wants to add that her father would be absent, but it doesn't seem appropriate. Or important.

Ms. Crana seems pleased by this news, though not in any distinct way. Emily just notices something—a brightening of the eyes, perhaps. But she also seems suddenly at a loss for words, and there is another long, uncomfortable pause before she speaks again. "I have been keeping a close eye on your progress in this class," she blurts out, as if relieved to have something to say. "You are doing well, quite well indeed, but there is room for improvement."

Emily isn't quite sure what she is supposed to say, considering that she had only been in class for three weeks so far, which hardly seems like a sufficient amount of time to gauge success or failure. She settles on the simplest and least controversial comment she can think of: "Okay."

"What does your father think of your progress?"

"My father?"

"Yes. He is satisfied? He is not satisfied?"

"He's...dead, actually. He's been dead for about five years."

At this news Ms. Crana's face falls slack and she staggers backward a step. "Five," she says, her voice tapering off as if the wind had been knocked out of her.

Emily looks up at Ms. Crana, confusion drawing over her. "Maybe four."

Ms. Crana regains her composure. "Of course, of course" she says absently. "I am very sorry. How did he die?"

"Huh?"

"How did your father die?"

"Uh—" was about all Emily could muster. What was this? How was this about grades and class progress?

As abruptly as anything that she had done so far, Ms. Crana turns away and faces the whiteboard at the front of the room. She stands looking at it for a good long moment before turning back and once again showing an eerily warm smile.

"I believe that was an inappropriate question," she says, "I apologize for my poor manners. I meant no disrespect."

Emily can neither think nor speak. She sits stock still, not knowing what to do. Ms. Crana had never presented herself as 'typical,' but her behavior in these moments is beyond perplexing.

"Emily, I have something to confess to you," Ms. Crana says, and she waits for Emily to respond. Emily doesn't, so she continues, "I am not, by profession, a teacher."

Emily shakes her head, perplexed as much by the fact of the confession as by what it could possibly mean. She says nothing.

"I am a type of...what you would call, I suppose, a historian."

"Oh."

"Science is my specialty. History is my profession."

"Oh," Emily says again, still searching for something more substantial to say. Or, for that matter, a reason to be there. She desperately wants to get up and leave, bolt, run, but she simply sits there, her nerves frayed.

"Our histories are incomplete. If I were to attempt to teach it I would be exposed as a fraud and my mission would be jeopardized. So I teach science."

Ms. Crana pauses again. Emily senses that she is supposed to continue the conversation somehow, show curiosity perhaps, though she doesn't quite know how. Not that she wants to, anyway. The past five minutes have felt like fifty, and she hasn't a clue what Ms. Crana is talking about.

Ms. Crana eyes her conspicuously. She waits for a response, but Emily has none to give. She is merely baffled.

"I am very interested in your family," Ms. Crana says with clinical detachment, "Who they are and where they come from."

"Why?"

"I find your history interesting. Your parents are—were—scientists, correct?"

"My mother still is."

"Of course."

"My dad…well, you know."

"Yes."

Ms. Crana takes the chair opposite Emily at the lab table.

"I do not mean to be tactless, Ms. Clocke. Sometimes my curiosity blinds me to emotional considerations."

"I guess I just don't understand why you would be so interested in us. We're just…us."

"So says your mother," Ms. Crana says, referring to Sarah's self-deprecatory comment at the gas station. "But she is more than just a 'me,' and together you are more than just an 'us.'"

"How?"

"You knew the speed of light."

"Actually," Emily responds sheepishly, "I didn't."

"But you figured it out."

"Um…actually…" Emily drops her gaze and looked down at the table. "…I didn't."

"How do you mean?"

"Connie showed me the answer."

Ms. Crana eyes Emily searchingly. "I do not believe you."

"She had her book open to the page with the answer and she pointed to it. I just made the number a bit bigger so you'd think I figured it out myself."

Ms. Crana continues to stare at Emily, speechless. She seems infinitely disillusioned. She drops her eyes morosely. "That is rather disappointing. Perhaps I was wrong about you. And if that is indeed the case, I have said too much."

Emily sits stock still, her hands folded in her lap, too anxious to even avert her eyes, though she eventually does anyway.

"I had never considered the possibility of our meeting to be a mere coincidence," Ms. Crana says. "But with your mother there—"

As Emily watches, still frozen by an indistinct fear, she spies a tear stream from Ms. Crana's eye and down her cheek. Ms. Crana notices Emily's gaze.

"You are excused," she tells Emily, absently waving her off.

Emily sits for a moment, then stands and silently exits the room. She isn't sure about anything that happened in the past few minutes, particularly why she lied about not having figured out the speed of light.

Her head spins with explanations. But none of them make sense.

———

Sarah had been on edge even before arriving at the school. She wasn't normally the type to be easily rattled, but Emily could tell that there was something about her science teacher that disturbed her mother. Not that her mother had had any contact with Ms. Crana since the gas station, but the stories that Emily had been feeding her about Ms. Crana—which should have been innocent updates about typical school days— seemed to weigh on her. Emily was perplexed: she herself found Ms. Crana odd but harmless. Her mother, on the other hand, should have been able to write off their brief encounter in the gas station as nothing more than a conversation with an odd woman, something laughed about and forgotten within five minutes. Indeed, Sarah certainly would have done this if Ms. Crana hadn't suddenly shown up as an important figure in her daughter's life. Despite trying to hide it from Emily and Eric, Emily could see that this Crana woman had made a considerable dent in her mother's otherwise unfaltering resolve.

"So she's been…normal…up until this afternoon?" Sarah asks Emily as she swings the van into the school parking lot. "Normal being a relative term, I guess."

"Yeah, she's been okay," Emily answers.

"She's a nutjob," Eric says sharply from the back seat.

"How would you know?" Emily says defensively, "You don't even have her!"

"I've seen her. She walks around talking to herself."

"And she says what?" Sarah says, ignoring her children's side argument, "That she's a history teacher?"

"A historian."

"Well, whatever," Sarah says. "I'm still not happy about her drudging up your father. It's none of her business."

"Mom, don't, like, say anything though, okay? Just talk about school stuff."

"We'll see," Sarah answers vaguely as she pulls the van into a space.

————

Sarah and Emily slip quietly into the science classroom. A smattering of other parents are stuffed uncomfortably into small desks, waiting, their rather aggrieved looks betraying impatience, eyeing the high lab chairs and wondering why they can't sit on them instead. Upon catching sight of Sarah, Ms. Crana abruptly (and rudely) ceases a conversation with another mother and father and approaches Sarah, her face an incongruous mixture of delight and sorrow.

"Sayre," she says, and then adds, with a strange cadence of mourning, "Leeth."

"What?" Sarah says, instantly flashing back to their

encounter at the gas station.

Ms. Crana stops in her tracks and raises her hands in a gesture of apology. Or defeat. She smiles with a thin attempt at chagrin. "Apologies," she says. "I am quite embarrassed. I fear at this rate we will never be able to meet without my reacting so childishly to your resemblance to my...companion."

"Well, I can't say I usually elicit such reactions in people," Sarah says. Her words are strained and apprehensive.

"It is not for you to be concerned, to be sure. It is my error to correct."

"Well," Sarah says, her words coming out with a veneer of calm, "Emily tells me she's enjoying your class."

"She is a very bright young lady. But that is to be expected."

"I was a little afraid that she'd have a bit of a struggle academically, what with the move and a new school and all."

"You have traveled a great distance, indeed," Ms. Crana says, reassuringly. "I wonder how you even know who you are after such stresses."

"I sometimes wonder myself." Sarah looks at Emily. A thought passes between them, projected through Sarah's eyes, and Emily reads every word and blushes. 'Just talking about school stuff!'

"Where did you meet your husband?"

"Excuse me?" Sarah says, caught off guard.

The other parents, though put off by Ms. Crana's sudden decision to ignore them, had been milling about at a polite distance, pretending not to listen, but they quickly shrugged off that courtesy and stared boldly at the two women, leaning in almost comically to hear every word.

"Where—?"

Ms. Crana doesn't give her time to answer. "Where were you born?"

"Why are you—?"

Ms. Crana cocks her head slightly to the side and meets Sarah's gaze, staring at Sarah with a studious ferocity, as if Sarah were the catalyst poured into some sort of experiment and everyone was waiting patiently for the result. "It is quite the coincidence that Emily and I would start here on the same day."

"Is it," Sarah says, a question delivered as a statement. A pause follows. Sarah tries to process the questions, but succeeds only in deciphering that last one. Then her face grows furrowed. "What exactly do you mean by that?"

"I mean nothing other than to comment that she and I happened to begin here on the same day."

"No, you said that you and she share the same DNA."

Emily looks at Sarah, her simmering embarrassment turning to concern. "No she didn't," she whispers to her mother. "She said we started here on the *same* day."

"Same day," Sarah repeats absently. "I think—," then she stops speaking, her face going blank. Clearly, her mind is reeling.

Ms. Crana raises her hands in gesture of surrender. "I have taken too much of your time. I have nothing but praise for your daughter. She is a model student." She holds out her hand to Sarah.

"Thank you," Sarah says dully, taking Crana's hand but not making eye contact. After a brief, light shake, she immediately retreats and turns toward the door, wipes her hand absently on her jeans, and crumples to the floor in an unconscious heap.

————

Emily, Eric, and Ms. Crana hover over Sarah. Emily's face is awash in panic. Eric tries hard to betray no fear, but he is jittery and bouncing on his heels.

"Mom!" Emily yells.

Other people circle around them. Other faces floating impossibly around Emily's periphery. She blocks them.

"What?" Sarah says.

One of the floating heads pulls out a cell phone. Sarah hears a voice say, "I'll call 9-1-1."

"That will not be necessary," Ms. Crana says, concerned but distant. "She will recover. She had a minor seizure. It will correct itself momentarily."

"A minor seizure?" Emily looks at Ms. Crana as if she's crazy. "How do you know that?"

"I theorize that it is a proximal effect of—" She stops suddenly.

"Of what?" Eric asks.

"Stress," Ms. Crana says unconvincingly. "She just needs rest."

Sarah attempts to sit up, against the protests of Emily and the floating heads. After sitting upright for a moment, she rolls onto her knees and attempts to stand. Several people move to lift her, but Ms. Crana holds them off.

"Stand," she tells Sarah.

Sarah stops and looks up at her, her eyes burning with cold fury. "I'm trying! What the hell's the matter with you?" She strains and stumbles but eventually gets to her feet

"You have been dormant too long," Ms. Crana says. "I am drawing the enhancements out of hibernation and they are causing seizures. You need to go home and rest."

"What are you talking abo...Who are you?" Sarah demands.

"I suspect you will figure that out very soon."

"What is that?" Sarah asks defensively. "Some sort of threat?"

Ms. Crana shakes her head. "It is merely a statement of fact."

Sarah is about to argue, Emily can tell, but she stops short. She sets her jaw and nods furiously. "You're damn right I'll figure it out soon!" Then she says to Emily, "We're done," and turns to leave. She adds, "And you can bet your ass that my daughter will not be in your class anymore!" She storms out of the room.

Emily follows sheepishly, leaving behind a room of stunned parents, their heads spinning in unison as they trace Emily's path out the door. Eric, slightly red-faced, shrugs and follows them out.

Ms. Crana doesn't look the least bit concerned.

Emily feels her mattress bounce. It's gentle but the cause is unmistakable. She rolls over to find her mother lying beside her.

"What's up?" Emily says sleepily.

"Nothing. I'm being you for a change."

"What do you mean?"

"Nothing, just…shhh."

Quiet follows. But there is too much swirling in the silence, and it is quickly broken.

"I don't know," Sarah says after a moment, "Maybe this was a mistake. For all of us."

Emily turns her head to look at her mother. Sarah has her head smashed back against a pillow, staring straight up at the ceiling. Emily looks up, barely making out the unmoving ceiling fan in the predawn dark. She traces its faint star shape.

"What do you mean?"

"I don't know what I mean. Hell, I barely know who I am. That woman's got me all rattled."

"Who? Ms. Crana?"

"Yes. And I forbid you to say her name."

"She's not Voldemort. She's actually been okay. A little weird, but not horrible. She picks on me a lot."

Sarah turns to look at Emily, her head crunching the stuffing in the pillow. "What do you mean 'picks on you?'"

"Not picks on me picks on me, like teases me or anything. She picks me. To answer questions in class and stuff. She's testing me."

"Oh. Well, I still don't trust her. I don't trust her at all. In fact, I don't want you setting foot in her class."

"Why?" Emily knew what had happened last night—she was there, after all—but she still didn't understand Sarah's sudden violent reaction to the woman. Or, more to the point, overreaction.

"Because. Because…I say so, okay? Do what I tell you."

It is an odd order coming from Sarah, not the least because it is uncharacteristically vague. Sarah is usually careful to explain a commandment so that Emily and Eric can understand the reasoning behind it. They might not accept it, but they would always respect it. But 'because I say so' is, to Emily, conspicuously undefined. This tells her that Sarah means business.

But it also tells her that her mother isn't thinking clearly. "How am I not supposed to go into her class? I'll fail if I don't show up."

"I'll get you switched."

"Mom, seriously, I don't want my mother rescuing me."

"I don't care. During science period, just go to the lunchroom or something. Go to the library. Go sit under a stairwell. I don't care. Just keep your distance from her."

"But—!"

"Emily, I'm not kidding. I have to figure a few things out. Just do as I say."

"Okay." Emily sighs. "I guess I just don't get it."

"I don't either. That's the problem."

———

Emily stands at her locker, craning her neck to see through the crowd of students making their way to their second-period classes. A person had just walked by—just a glimpse in her peripheral vision—but it caused her to do a double take. It looked like...no, it couldn't be...but is it? It was definitely someone familiar, but the person was gone, swallowed by the waves of commuting ninth, tenth, eleventh, and twelfth graders.

Suddenly convinced by what she saw, Emily pulls her backpack out, slams the locker door shut, and weaves her way through the throng to follow. The pursuit is almost comical, with Emily coming out from behind a student to see the figure duck behind another further up the hallway. Only when they draw closer to the front office does the crowd thin out enough for Emily to confirm who she had seen: her mother.

Emily passes by a connecting hallway. Before she can follow any further, she hears an unwelcome voice.

"Hey, creep!" Eric shouts, racing toward her. "Did I just see Mom?"

Eric swings his head toward the front office just in time to see Sarah disappear into it.

"What's she doing here?" Eric asks.

"I have no idea," Emily lies. She immediately thinks of Ms. Crana, and feels a pang of guilt, though she really doesn't know why.

In tandem, they both creep slowly down the hall. The principal's office is to the right of the front office, walled by an 8-foot wide by 5-foot tall window that allows the principal, if she so wishes, an unobstructed view of the hallway. When Emily and Eric get closer to the office, they approach cautiously and peek slowly around the edge of the glass. Their view is obstructed by window-length blinds, left open slightly and angled such that anybody looking in can only just make out the principal and whomever she might be talking to. Thankfully, this arrangement also offers a bit of anonymity to whoever might be peeking in from outside.

"What's she doing?" Eric asks after confirming that it was, in fact, their mother in the office talking to the principal.

"I don't know," Emily answers lamely.

"You two need to be moving along," a voice calls from their left, making them both jump. Ms. Marks stands in the doorway of the front office, glaring at them. At the sound of Ms. Marks' voice, Sarah turns back to look out the window.

It is doubtful, though, that she sees Emily and Eric, who are already halfway down the hall and safely submerged into the roiling sea of students.

———

Emily defied her mother's orders, though not willfully. Well, not entirely willfully, anyway. She was so used to the routine of going to the science lab at fourth period that she found herself halfway to the classroom before she remembered what her mother had said. She decided to go anyway, convinced that her mother was way overreacting.

She enters the classroom to find Ms. Crana behind her desk as usual. Connie is in her seat. As usual. The usual gamut of classmates—from feeble-minded to fairly adept—shuffle in lazily. As usual.

"Dude, what happened last night?" Connie asks excitedly.

"Dude?" Emily says, amused by the masculine colloquialism.

"Whatever! I heard your mom freaked out or something."

"She didn't freak out," Emily says, but then thinks better of her response, "Well, yeah, I guess she freaked out. But it was nothing." She glances nervously at Ms. Crana, terrified of being overheard, but Ms. Crana is busy at the whiteboard.

"How can freaking out be nothing?" Connie asks, "I heard she, like, fainted. That's what Leanne Heard heard…er…said. She said her dad was in the room when it happened."

"Yeah, but she's 'kay."

"Man, that must have been embarrassing. What were they fighting about?"

"They weren't fighting!" Emily protests a bit too loudly.

Ms. Crana ends their conversation. "All right, settle down. Let us get started." She comes out from behind her desk and proceeds to ignore Emily. She usually began class by challenging Emily with a question. Ostensibly, she was quizzing the class as a whole, but she always looked at Emily when she asked the question, and it was clear that she had expected Emily to answer it. Sometimes Emily did, sometimes she didn't. In any case, nobody else in the class ever did, and on the occasions that no answer was forthcoming, Ms. Crana devoted the day to that problem.

Today, she looks squarely at Connie and begins with a statement.

"Yesterday, Ms. Booth asked why the speed of light was so important; how knowing it would help her become an actress.

And I told her it would not." She surveys the class to see if she had intrigued anybody. Most of the students are glancing furtively at Emily, their looks searching, wondering about her reaction to suddenly being ignored. Ms. Crana continues, "My assessment of that matter has not changed. However, my original query was not necessarily about knowing the speed of light, it was about determining the speed of light by using previously gained knowledge, as Ms. Clocke was able to do." She still doesn't look at Emily.

"Enrico Fermi stood in a desert bunker in Los Alamos, New Mexico, waiting for the first atomic bomb to be detonated. He stood there tearing a sheet of paper into small bits of confetti, which he then patiently held in his hand until it was time to put on the blast goggles. When the bomb went off and the shockwave hit the bunker, Dr. Fermi threw up the bits of paper and watched them scatter into the air, carried backwards by the shockwave. When everything had settled down, he measured the distance between where he stood and where the confetti dropped, and from that was able to make a relatively accurate estimate about the power of the blast."

"Who's Enrico Fermi?" someone asks.

"Later," Ms. Crana says. "I relate this story to indicate that it is not always about the answer, but about how you arrive at it. Everything you learn teaches you not only about a particular subject, but also about how to think in new and different ways. How to attack problems from different angles, how to find solutions in places that would otherwise be unthinkable. How to see the world in four dimensions. Science and math are foremost among those subjects."

"Three dimensions," someone interjects with a chuckle, then adds tentatively, "Right?"

Ms. Crana ignores the comment. "We often do not know what bits of knowledge are going to help us in the future, and sometimes we are unjustifiably confident that the things we learn will have no bearing at all on our lives. But that does not mean it is not important to try to learn them."

Now she looks as Emily.

"Knowledge is cheap. Ignorance is expensive."

Ms. Crana surveys the room. Surprisingly, she has their rapt attention. The kids groan about her soapbox rants—which are common—but they usually listen despite themselves. This one has them glued, but the expectant looks on their faces indicate less an interest in the subject than a gleeful hope that Ms. Crana is going to melt down. Indeed, Emily spots three students surreptitiously holding up their smartphones, camera lenses pointed right at Ms. Crana.

There is a collective twitch when the silence is shattered by a sharp knock on the glass of the classroom door.

The principal, Ms. Griffey, pokes her head into the classroom. She smiles blandly at the class, and then looks gravely at Ms. Crana. "Ms. Crana, I hate to interrupt your class," she says in strained, tentative tones, "but may I speak to you in the hallway?"

Ms. Crana nods and follows. Ms. Griffey smiles again at the class and retreats into the hallway, closing the door behind her.

Just before the door swings completely shut, Emily hears a strange squeal, familiar yet difficult to place, which she recognizes just as someone in the room says, "That sounded like a police walkie-talkie."

Emily suddenly has a bad feeling. The statement energizes the class, and several students begin making their way to the door to see what's happening, Emily among them. But they have barely taken more than a few steps when Ms. Marks peers through the door, sees them approaching, and gestures impatiently for them to sit back down.

Everyone scrambles back to their seats. Except Emily. She freezes at the sight of Ms. Marks, but stands her ground. She has a sinking feeling about what she thinks is happening and needs confirmation. When Ms. Marks turns away from the doorway, Emily creeps forward.

"You're gonna get busted," Connie whispers loudly.

Emily waves her off. Her perspective of the scene in the

hallway shifts slowly as she approaches the door. She sees Ms. Crana, her back to the classroom. Ms. Griffey is facing her, a very severe—perhaps angry—look on her face. From where she stands, Ms. Griffey should clearly see Emily, but she's too involved in her discussion with Ms. Crana.

Emily suddenly senses the presence of more students behind her, but ignores them. She sees Ms. Marks, standing slightly back from the other two women, threatening to turn to check on the class again. The other students flee again, but Emily holds her ground, desperate to get a better view of the scene, knowing full well what the police walkie-talkie means.

"Is it the cops?" someone asks.

It is. But Emily doesn't answer.

She sees the blue of their uniforms, the gold of their badges. Two of them stand opposite the women, their faces respectful but alert. One of them nods and reaches gently for Ms. Crana's arm, appearing to want to lead her away. But Ms. Crana jerks her arm backward, then shoots it out like lightning toward the officer's chest. It doesn't seem to be a malicious move, more instinctive and defensive, but it's enough for the two officers to move to restrain her. Ms. Griffey and Ms. Marks stumble backward to move out of the way. One of the officers grabs and spins Ms. Crana by the shoulder, while the other reaches to his belt and pulls off a pair of handcuffs. Ms. Crana moves again to shrug off the officers, but a glimpse of Emily looking out at her appears to momentarily distract her and the officers pull her arms behind her and slip the cuffs on.

Despite everything, Ms. Crana does not appear particularly flustered. She merely nods at Emily.

Ms. Marks recovers her senses and follows Ms. Crana's gaze back to Emily. Annoyance plays across her face. She strides over and opens the classroom door. "Ms. Clocke, this doesn't concern you."

'Actually, I think it does,' Emily thinks, not unreasonably.

"Get back to your seat, please." Ms. Marks enters and moves to close the door behind her.

Ms. Crana looks at Emily again and says, slowly and calmly, "Emily." But Ms. Marks closes the door before she can say anything else.

Still looking at Emily through the glass, Ms. Crana raises her voice to be heard. "I will protect you," she says.

The hairs on Emily's neck stand on end.

And then the police lead her science teacher away.

It would be the last day Ms. Crana ever sets foot in the classroom.

Emily's too.

# :03 falling

"I'm driving you both to school this morning," Sarah announces. "In fact, I'm going to drive you to school every morning from now on."

"Mom, she's a nutjob and she's in custody," Eric protests, understanding without having to be told that this was all about keeping Emily safe from Ms. Crana. "And by the way, she's in custody for lying about being a teacher. I wouldn't call that being America's Most Wanted."

"Yeah, but just lying about being a teacher is not grounds for bringing in police and locking down the school. Or for putting her in custody. Clearly, there was something more going on."

Eric tilts his head back and rolls his eyes. "God, Mom, you're like all paranoid all of a sudden and I can't do anything!"

Sarah ignores Eric's whiny protest. "Get your stuff. We have to get moving or I'm going to be late."

In the van, Eric resumes his usual brooding silence in the far back. Emily, in the middle row, is quiet too, but not because she's upset about missing the walk to school this morning. What had happened to Ms. Crana the day before was still foremost in her mind, and there is something about it—beyond a fragment of guilt—that weighs on her.

Emily, in her own little reverie, doesn't notice that the van is slowly veering over into the oncoming lane. That is, not until she hears the blare of a car horn and feels the van careen violently back into the correct lane.

"Jeez Mom, what the hell?" Eric snaps, sitting himself back upright after having been knocked over in his seat by the force of the van's sudden lurch.

Sarah is shaken. "Ohmygod!" She slows the van and brings it to a stop against the curb. She turns and glances quickly, almost wildly, at Emily and Eric. "Are you two okay?"

"I'm good," Emily responds, "I guess. My stomach is in a knot…"

"I'm so sorry," Sarah says, almost pleading. "Eric?"

"What?"

"Are you okay?"

"Fine," he snaps.

Sarah turns forward and grips the steering wheel. She sighs so deeply her entire body shudders.

"What happened?" Emily asks.

"I don't know. I had double vision for a second. For an instant I—" she pauses, clearly unsure whether she should continue. "I didn't know where or who I was. Just for an instant."

"Should I drive?" Eric asks. Emily can't tell if it's sincere or sarcastic.

"Uh, no," Sarah says, slamming that discussion down. "I'm fine, and I have to get to work."

"And you're worried about us?" Eric sneers, any sense of benevolence—sincere or not—gone is a flash, "We're not the ones fainting all the time."

Sarah hits the steering wheel. "I am not fainting all the time!" She sighs deeply again. After a moment, she turns halfway and whispers, "Em, come here."

Emily leans forward.

Sarah turns on the radio and asks, "Have we had this conversation before?"

"I can hear you," Eric answers, "and yes, all the time. 'You never listen blah blah blah…'"

Sarah closes her eyes in an attempt to wipe away the pained expression. She takes a deep breath, opens her eyes again, and says to Emily, "Does this— Have we done this before?"

"What do you mean?" Emily asks.

"This. Have we...did this?" Sarah shakes her head as if to clear it. "I'm having a really really strong sense of déjà vu. It feels like I've done all of this before."

"Well, yeah. You have had this same conversation with Eric many times," Emily says with a little trace of irony. "In the past few weeks, anyway."

Sarah considers it, then nods and turns forward. "Yeah," she says, starting the van moving again. "I guess that's it."

———

The van rolls up to the front of the school. The side door slides open and Eric launches out, tromping off in a surly funk without even a wave goodbye. Emily stays behind.

"What?" Sarah asks.

"Are you sure you're okay?" Emily asks.

"Why wouldn't I be?"

"Oh, I don't know. Fainting, déjà vu, almost getting us into an accident!"

"Don't you start, too," Sarah says impatiently, "Why is everybody trying to save me? I'm fine. You're fine. We're all fine, Now go go go. I'm going to be late and so are you."

Emily slips out of the van and presses the button to close the door. As it slides shut, she realizes that she doesn't have her backpack. A quick glance inside before the door shuts confirms that it is not in the van. She'd left it at home.

She steps forward to come even with the passenger window and looks at her mother, her mouth open to speak. The window rolls down.

Sarah barks out, "What?"

"Nothing," Emily lies, "just saying bye."

"Okay. Be good, honey. See you tonight."

Emily watches the van pull away.

She watches it for longer than she needs to, then turns in the opposite direction and starts walking, in her own newly created little funk. The sky is an intensely sharp blue, and perhaps because of that she finds herself squinting excessively. It is an annoyance on top of an annoyance. And because of it she barely registers, in her peripheral vision, the nondescript white car about a half-block behind her that begins moving just as soon as she does.

Twelve minutes later she is standing in front of her house, the one that doesn't seem like hers. The one that, in her cookie-cutter neighborhood, she still sometimes mistakes as someone else's. She stares at it a moment, willing it to be familiar, until a passing car breaks her meditation and she walks up to the front stoop.

She remembers exactly where she had left her backpack, so retrieving it is only a matter of opening the front door, reaching inside and to the right, and swinging it onto her shoulder. But there is still something unsettling about the new old house. She unlocks and opens the door and takes a step inside, pausing for a moment to get her bearings. Why, exactly she has to get her bearings is at first a mystery, but she realizes suddenly that after almost a month living in the house, this is really the first time she has been inside alone, and it still fits like a stiff new pair of jeans that haven't worn to her body yet.

"Hello?" she announces, self-consciously. It's a whim; she hoped she'd laugh at herself for saying it, but she actually feels something beyond silly.

She stands a moment longer as if waiting for an answer, then reaches down and lifts her ridiculously overstuffed backpack up onto her shoulder and slips back outside. The door slams with a certain finality, harder and faster than she'd intended. 'Ghosts in there,' she thinks, knowing full well it wasn't true. But still…

There is something familiar about the nondescript white car that is parked across the street from the house. Even though there is a mammoth maple tree between the car and the house, it isn't hard for Emily to spot it. It isn't the car itself that is so noticeable, but the fact of it. Emily has never seen a car parked there before (cars stuck to driveways in this neighborhood), so it's presence is instantly noticeable.

She keeps a casual, curious eye on the car as she ambles down the front walk, crunching over the newly fallen leaves dropped from the tree in the front yard. Maybe it's some utility workmen waiting for a work truck before beginning on the phone lines or something. When she clears the tree and can get a good look, she sees two men staring intently at her, one in the front passenger seat and one in the back. Clearly, they are not workmen of any kind. Their manner of dress is sparse and drab, vaguely military. The men obscure her view of the car's driver.

Emily is extremely put off by their staring, which she simply dismisses as rude. But then it hits her that she has seen both the car and the men before. True, she could remember neither with any detail, but their position and the unnatural concentration on their faces raises the hair on her neck and arms. It looks exactly like the car she had seen when they were still on the road to Chicago from California, just before meeting Ms. Crana at the mini mart.

'Monsters out here,' she thinks. She's not entirely sure she's being ironic or not.

She decides not to press her luck and moves quickly back up to the stoop and unlocks the front door again. As it swings open, she glances over her shoulder. The car inches forward, presumably to get a better vantage point of her house. Or of her.

She closes the door and steps back. There are no curtains on the front windows, only shades. She paces along the windows and pulls each shade down quickly, then retreats a few steps into the room. There is enough morning sun slicing through the vertical slits between the shades and the window frames that the room is cast in a dull, smoky gray. Emily positions herself so that she can peek through one or two of the slits from as far away as the middle of the room but still get a sense of what is happening outside. They are fragments of the outside world, a prism reflection in reverse. She holds her breath to steady herself, to focus on movements.

Dust motes dance in the beams of light that cut through the slits, making them sparkle like a laser light show. The front tree dances in the wind, cutting through the gaps a fluid green pattern like a narrow waterfall. A bird zooms past, a zoetrope dot flitting across successive slits.

She exhales, unable to hold her breath anymore. She slides the backpack off her back and swings it around, plopping it on the floor at her feet. She unzips a front pocket and rummages through it, frustrated that she can't find what she's looking for.

A white blur moves across, jumping from slit to slit. The car?

A sense of dread wells up and she pulls her hand out of her backpack and desperately pats both her pockets. She groans and pulls her cellphone out of one of the pockets and presses the shortcut to dial Sarah.

The ringing drags on. The room grows more oppressive. Finally the phone connects. Her mother's voice states her name and commands Emily to leave a message. Emily hangs up before the beep.

She prepares to dial 911, but then thinks better of it. She studies the slits again, and when she detects no movement, she tentatively approaches the windows. She stops at a slit then takes a deep breath again and holds it. She peels back a side of the shade and peeks out. The tree. The space across the street. No car.

She moves to another shade and peeks out the other side. The front yard. Another neighbor's house across the street. No car.

She pulls the shade out and walks behind it, positioning herself between the shade and the window. She examines the scene in front of her fully. Tree. Front yard. Neighbors.

No car.

She exhales again, then walks out from behind the shade.

She swings her backpack up over her shoulder and shuffles to the front door. She pauses, then opens it, stepping slowly out onto the stoop and peeking around both sides of the entranceway. Still no car.

Emily closes the door behind her and slowly makes her way down the walkway. She is all the way to the front sidewalk when the car rounds the corner and positions itself in her view. The distance between the car and her is now half that of the distance between her and the house. Whatever their intent, the people in the car could overtake her long before she makes it back to the front door.

She isn't quite sure what to do, though she knows that the most sensible solution would be to try to go back into the house anyway and call the police. But the house is, to her, still cavernous and unfamiliar…and empty. She doesn't relish the idea of bolting back into an empty house to wait the interminable length of time it would take for the police to arrive. So she makes to bolt for a neighbor's instead.

But then the driver leans forward, apparently to get a better view of Emily. It is fast, this action, and seems to pass in only a moment, but the figure leans into the light enough for Emily to perceive a face. And the face she perceives stops Emily from doing anything. Her goose bumps flare up again, as do her most immediate fears, but are joined by a confused curiosity. And now she leans slightly to the side, her head cocked even further in an attempt to see the driver again.

"Ms. Crana?" she says.

"Do you see the sky, Ms. Clocke?" Ms. Crana asks.

Emily looks up at the sky for a moment, doesn't see anything unusual save for the sharp blue, then looks back at the car.

"We believe it is going to begin soon. The end. We think you should come with us."

Emily bolts in the opposite direction, toward the school. She runs so hard her backpack bounces off her shoulders and slides down her back. After a block and a half, her lungs begin to burn and a knife-sharp pain pinches her right side. She abandons the backpack, letting it slide off her shoulders and crash onto someone's lawn, and runs unhindered, discovering that if she holds her breath for a few paces, she can relieve the stitch in her side. But that, of course, only makes her more breathless, and when she flies into the school and bursts right into the principal's office, it takes the two office aides, the school nurse, and the principal to calm her down enough to tell her story.

————

Emily is again sitting in the waiting room at the front office of the school, on the same bench in the narrow yellow alcove tucked just to the side of the formica counter. Her foot taps furiously on the floor, and she feels the salty lines on her cheeks where the tears have dried.

When she'd stormed in, she'd babbled streams of unconnected words between huge breathy sobs, and it took Ms. Griffey about 30 full seconds before she could coax out enough information to make sense of the narrative. When Ms. Griffey had put the puzzle together, she immediately ordered the aides to announce a lockdown and ran into her office to call the police. Emily had tried calling her mother from her cell phone several times, but Sarah never answered. That only compounded Emily's anxiety.

The door to Ms. Marks' office opens and she steps out. Her face is friendly, but it is a clumsy attempt to look reassuring. Emily detects the gravity behind the facade. Ms. Marks takes a seat next to Emily and places gentle pressure on Emily's knee to stop her foot tapping. She does this with a warm, knowing chuckle, which helps put Emily at ease. Slightly.

"Ms. Griffey has called the police," Ms. Marks says, "and they're on their way. We're having a little bit of trouble getting a hold of your mother, though. Is there anybody else we can call? We want to make sure that somebody knows you're okay."

Emily shakes her head. "Just my brother."

"Well, he's in his home room and we're going to leave him where he is. He's safer just staying there."

Emily feels on the verge of tears again. "I'm sorry, Ms. Marks. I didn't mean…"

Ms. Marks puts an arm around Emily's shoulder and draws her close. She waves a finger in front of Emily's eyes in mock scolding. "No, no, no. Emily, this is not your fault. Don't you worry. It's going to be okay."

Ms. Marks stands up. "Now I have to go…"

At that moment, the lights in the office flicker, and then go out. Emily clenches every muscle she can, then releases her pent up nerves in a massive full body shiver.

"Ah, great," one of the office aides groans. "Because the day couldn't get any better."

Ms. Marks laughs. "She's quite the optimist, isn't she?" she says to Emily. She then calls out to the aide: "Call Mr. Bakke and make sure he knows. Maybe he just has to reset a circuit."

As the aides scurry about to fulfill this new duty, Ms. Marks turns her attention back to Emily, who seems about ready to fold into herself. Ms. Marks sits down again. "I'll tell you what," she says to Emily, "I'll stay and hang out here with you for a few minutes. At least until Mr. Bakke gets the lights back on."

"Ms. Marks," one of the aides says, "I can't reach Mr. Bakke. I think the phones are dead."

"Lovely," Ms. Marks says sarcastically. She pulls a cell phone from her pocket, an older style flip phone. But when she flips it open, she notices that it doesn't have a signal. "That's weird," she says more to herself than to Emily. "The signal in the school is usually pretty good. Service must be down." She powers the phone down then fires it up again but nothing happens. "Check yours," she says to Emily.

Emily pulls hers out. She rolls it over in her hands and looks at the face. There are no bars displayed, and the data icon is missing. "Nothing," she says.

"What is going on?" Ms. Marks asks nobody in particular.

"What the hell is that?" one of the aides suddenly says, forgetting propriety. She is looking through the window at the sky.

Emily looks over sees nothing. She stands up and takes a few tentative steps toward the windows.

"Emily." Ms. Marks warns, "I think you should stay where you are. Don't go by the windows, please."

Emily stops and looks back at Ms. Marks. Without a word or protest, she sits back down.

"It looks like the northern lights," the other aide says.

"In Illinois?" the first aide says incredulously, "And during the day?"

"I didn't say it was the northern lights," the second aide explains, "I says it looked like the northern lights."

Ms. Marks glances at Emily then walks to the window to see for herself. Emily follows tentatively.

"The sky looks green to the north," Ms. Marks says. "Wow, it really does look like the northern lights."

Outside, a kinetic mobile of emerald light dances in the sky. It washes in in waves from the north, as if gravity has given up its fight and is letting Lake Michigan pour into the sky to crash into a retreating shoreline of pure cloud.

Emily turns back and sits down on the bench, sure that this is somehow her fault.

She's partially right.

---

"There is something very weird going on," Ms. Marks says, moving back toward Emily. "You just sit tight. The police are here."

Several uniformed police enter the office. Ms. Marks consults with them briefly—and quietly. Emily notices them stealing quick glances at her before Ms. Marks invites them into the principal's office. One officer, a short, powerful looking woman with impossibly blonde hair tucked up neatly under her police hat, doesn't follow. She instead walks up to Emily.

"Hi," she says. "You're Emily?"

"Uh huh," Emily nods.

"I'm Officer Letts," she says. "Tracy." Emily takes her offered hand and shakes it twice. "Mind if I sit?"

"No."

Officer Letts sits beside Emily. She is less intimidating when sitting, and she relaxes her hard stare enough to give Emily a warm smile. "Crazy day, huh?"

Emily nods. "Yep," she says weakly.

"So I hear you saw your science teacher in front of your house this morning?"

Emily leans forward, resting her elbows on her calves. She stares at her feet as she answers. "Yeah," she says.

"Hey now," Office Letts says. She puts her hand under Emily's chin and gently lifts her head until she can see Emily's eyes again. "Don't go feeling all guilty about this. You didn't do anything wrong."

"Okay," Emily responds, unconvinced.

"We're not here to arrest you, Emily, if that's what you think. We're here to help."

"I know," Emily says, "it's just…" She trails off.

"What?"

"I don't know," Emily says. She's right: she doesn't know. She doesn't understand anything that's happening. It's bad enough that she's the new kid in school—the new kid in town, for that matter—but now she's caused enough drama in the past two days for an entire year. And she's only been in town for a little over a month.

As if on cue, Emily hears the principal's voice drifting out of the office. Ms. Griffey is usually one for diplomacy with respect to official conversations, but her voice rose uncharacteristically while in conversation with the police. Emily hears her say, "This is not good news. Is she here for that young lady? Emily Clocke? We can't seem to get a hold of her mother."

This makes Emily look back up at Officer Letts. Her face is etched with concern, if not outright panic.

"Apparently discretion is not your principal's middle name," Office Letts comments wryly. She glances conspiratorially at the officers standing in the principal's office, who at that moment realize that their voices are carrying and shut the door. Letts takes a deep breath and looks at Emily. "Alright. I guess there's no point in my not telling you, since you've gotten an earful already. But don't tell anyone I told you. Ms. Crana was in custody for questioning as of last night, but somehow wrangled herself free sometime early this morning. No one is sure how, exactly. She just wasn't there anymore."

"So she's coming after me?"

"I didn't say that. We have no idea what she's up to. But there's no reason to think she's coming after you. Did she say anything to you when you saw her this morning?"

"Something about something starting today. Or soon."

"What's starting soon?"

"I don't know. The end, or something."

The principal's door swings open and one of the other officers sticks his head out. A bulky, gruff-looking man wearing his police hat high on his forehead and his belt conspicuously tight, he addresses Officer Letts rather brusquely, with no concern about interrupting her and Emily's conversation. "Hey, you gettin' through to the station?" he asks, tugging on the walkie-talkie clipped to his shoulder.

Letts presses the transmit button on her walkie-talkie. "Dispatch, this is one-two-one, do you read?"

Her question is answered by static. She tries again but gets the same response. She shrugs at the other officer, who re-enters the principal's office grumbling under his breath.

"Emily, could you excuse me for a moment?" Officer Letts asks. She stands and walks to the principal's office door, gently opening it. As she passes into the room, she gives Emily a short, concerned glance before closing the door behind her.

Emily slumps back against the wall. Of all the anxieties of the day, it's suddenly the 'we can't seem to get a hold of her mother' that rings in Emily's ears like a portent.

So Emily reaches down into her backpack and pulls out her cell phone.

It rings, startling her. Service has obviously been restored. "Hello?" Emily whispers into it.

"Emily?" a breathless but familiar voice says. "What's the matter? I'm almost done!"

"What?"

"I'm almost done! I'll be right up!"

"Where are you?"

"I'm in the tunnel. I'll be right up!"

"What are you talking about? Mom, Ms. Crana's here!"

"Ms. Cra—!" Sarah's voice stops suddenly. Then: "Oh."

"Oh? Oh what? Mom?"

"Yes! Em! I'm here." Her voice carries a note of confusion, but is nonetheless reassuring. "Where are you?"

"At school."

"At school. Yes! Where at school?"

"In the office."

"Is Eric with you?"

"No, I'm by myself. Mom, what's going—?"

"Em," Sarah interrupts, "You need to go find Eric."

"The police are here!"

"They're here too. You need to go find Eric and the both of you need to..." squuueeee!

Emily jerks the phone away from her ear. A piercing whistle suddenly replaces the voice of her mother. "Mom? Mom!"

Squuueeeaaauuurreee "—Emily!—" squuueeesshh "—Emily, I can't hold the frequency, so just listen—" squuueeerrreee "—find Eric then—" squuuee "—Ms. Crana. Emily—" squuueee "—you hear that? Em—" squuueeerrraaaaffft.

Emily stares at her phone in disbelief. It was dead again. Completely dead, out of power.

That conversation—if it can be called that—did little to give Emily any reassurance. In fact, it did just the opposite. How should Emily reconcile years of overprotection with the voice of her mother telling her to leave the safety of the office and police protection to venture out into the school to find her brother? Does she know the school is on lockdown? Does she know Ms. Crana is looking for her?

She sits back down on the bench and stares at the door to the principal's office, willing it to open, desperate for Officer Letts to walk out and tell her what to do.

Just then, Eric runs by the office door and stops, takes a fast glance in, looks right at Emily, and turns to run off again. Moments later, before Emily can even react, he's back in the doorway again yelling her name.

He thrusts his hand out to her. "Come on, we have to go!"

———

Eric grips her hand so tightly that despite every other thought and feeling that is running through Emily's head, she actually has a moment to spare to consider how much it is hurting.

He is dragging her along through the darkened hallways, quickly and with such force that Emily dare not stumble or Eric might accidentally rip her arm out.

"What are you doing?" she asks breathlessly. "Let me go! That hurts!"

"We need to get out of here!" he yells back. "She's here for us!"

"Eric, the police are—" and before she can finish she does stumble, her knees buckling until she falls forward and her legs fall out behind her. Eric's hand holds tight to hers, but the cell phone whips out of her free hand and slides across the floor.

"Leave it," he says, and tries with  brute force to lift her back to her feet. She grunts in pain, the unexpected force of Eric's pull making it feel as if her arm was being ripped from her shoulder.

"But mom might—"

"Mom won't," he says, matter-of-factly. "She can't."

Emily scrambles back to her feet, but resists Eric's continued tug. At the sign of resistance, he relaxes his grip and turns to look at her.

And then the phone rings.

They both freeze.

They both turn and look at the phone, neither moving a muscle because, for their own reasons, neither had expected it to ring.

Emily breaks the moment: "It's mom!" She bolts for the phone.

"Wait, Em!" Eric lunges after her but doesn't manage to catch her. Emily scoops up the phone, slides the answer button, and presses it to her ear.

"Mom?"

"Emily!" her mother says.

"Mom. Ms. Crana's here! She's…!"

Eric tries to grab the phone from Emily's hands, but Emily spins away and puts the phone back to her ear.

"Emily, listen to me. Listen to me! Is Eric there?"

"Yes, he—"

Eric pulls at the phone again and this time manages to pull it from Emily's hand. It goes sailing down the hall, landing with a crash and sliding across to rest at the foot of a locker.

Emily stares at him in disbelief. Why would Eric grab her phone and throw it when she was talking to their mother? A rage unlike anything she'd ever felt builds up inside of her and she just stares at him through narrowed eyes. She resists the urge to do what she really wanted to do.

Eric stares at her wide eyed. "It slipped!" he blurts out, his face full of surprise. "It slipped out of my hands!"

She can't resist anymore. WHAP! She smacks him in the jaw, open handed, with as much power as her boiling emotions would allow her, sending him sailing into the lockers, stunned as much by the sting of the blow as by the fact that she had even delivered it.

He rights himself, and they face off again, she heaving from anger and the unsettling and unfamiliar feeling of adrenaline, he looking shocked at her power and sudden brutality.

When the shock wears off, Eric shoves her away with an equal force, making her stumble backward. "Fine!" he yells. "Get the hell away from me then! I don't give a damn what happens to you!" He spins away and stalks off down the hall.

She watches after him a moment, trying to summon the willpower to think clearly and piece the day together. Failing miserably at that, she remembers the cell phone and turns back to find it.

It starts ringing again as she picks it up. The case is chipped and the face bears a spiderweb crack. She swipes it gingerly to answer.

"Mom?"

"Emily, what's going on?"

"Eric threw the phone away."

"Is…" *squueeeee* "…there?"

"Who?"

*Squueeeee* "…are you with her?"

"Mom, you're breaking up again!"

"Ms. Crana. Is Ms. Crana there?"

"She's in the school! She's looking for me!"

"You and Eric need to go…" *squueeee squeeeeeeerrrraaaaffftt* "…police!"

"Mom, I can't hear you!"

Frustrated, Emily holds the phone out in front of her, studying the signal indicator on the phone's display. The bars suddenly go flat. She begins to wander aimlessly, searching for a spot that will get a stronger signal. The instant a bar appears, she redials her mother's number.

*Squeeeeeeeerrrraaaaffftt*

"Hello, Emily," says a familiar voice.

It's only then that Emily realizes that she'd wandered into an empty classroom. She assesses her surroundings quickly before she turns to see who spoke. Six columns of desks and as many rows. A door at the back of the room that she knows leads into the storage closet. Shatterproof Plexiglas windows that slide open a mere six inches. There's no way out of the room other than through the single doorway, which Ms. Crana is now standing in.

"Hello," Emily says—squeaks really—her mind too cluttered to find anything more appropriate to say. Completely robbed of the power and fury that overcame her only moments before, she is now completely frozen, unable to move. Of course, even if she could move, she's not sure where she'd move to.

"Did Eric find you?" Ms. Crana asks. Her voice is gentle, friendly, deceptive.

Emily nods. "Yes."

"Did he update you as to the situation?"

Emily meekly shakes her head. "No."

"Ah," Ms. Crana says, moving slowly into the room. "I feared that would be the case. Where is he now?"

"I don't know," Emily mutters, hoping a better answer than the truth will reveal itself. Despite what had just happened between them, Emily has no desire to get Eric any deeper into this danger. She suddenly blurts out, "He went to get the police," hoping it would come out with some conviction.

It didn't.

"Emily, are you aware of what is happening outside right now?"

Emily hesitates, jerks her head slightly to check out the window, then thinks better of it and looks back at Ms. Crana.

"No," she says.

"The world is ending." Ms. Crana says, still in that eerily composed voice.

There is a very long pause. Emily, as usual, has no response other than to blink. And even that she does reluctantly, unwilling to take her eyes off Ms. Crana for even that small of an instant.

"That doesn't trouble you?" Ms. Crana asks.

Emily shrugs.

"Ah," Ms. Crana says, as if it is a eureka moment. "You don't believe me."

Emily does not answer.

"That is understandable," Ms. Crana says. She lets out a small sigh. "Wait," she says, raising a finger as if to stop Emily from doing…anything. She stiffens her back and looks up and over Emily's head.

Emily braves a fast glance behind her, sees nothing, then spins her head back to lock eyes again with Ms. Crana. But that is not quite possible: Ms. Crana's eyes jerk rapidly back and forth, as if she were reading something on the wall behind Emily. Emily takes another fast look, sees a white board on the wall, but sees nothing written on it. She begins to consider that Ms. Crana might be having some sort of seizure, and entertains the idea that this may be a good chance for her to slip by her former teacher unnoticed.

But just as the idea forms, Ms. Crana snaps her attention back on Emily, her eyes now betraying a wild impatience. "I'm afraid, Emily, I now lack the time for friendly persuasions," she says, the calmness in her voice now seeming a bit more… malevolent. "You need to come with me." She pulls a small black cylinder from her pocket and presses down on the top. It releases a gentle but menacing hiss.

As Ms. Crana takes a step forward, Emily backs down between two rows of desks, sliding them out of the way as she bumps past them.

"What do you want?" Emily screams, her panic finally allowing her a voice. "Why are you doing this to me?"

"I'm saving your life," Ms. Crana says, then lunges at the girl, pressing the cylinder to Emily's neck.

Its hiss explodes in Emily's ears, and she falls limp to the floor.

# :04 shockwave

Ms. Crana enters the hallway backwards, dragging Emily's rag doll body by the arms. As Emily's powder-blue Skechers thump across the wood threshold, Ms. Crana swings her former student around and begins backing down the hall, preparing to heft the dead weight onto her shoulder.

"Oh god! Put her down! Put her down!" commands a voice full of cold fury. Fifty meters down the hall, just past an intersecting hallway, Officer Letts stands with her gun drawn, pointed squarely at Ms. Crana.

Ms. Crana freezes, but does not let go of Emily. She stares at Officer Letts, her eyes wide like a kid with her hand in a cookie jar, less nervous about being caught than intent on concocting an acceptable excuse.

"I said let her go," Letts says slowly, lowering her voice an octave. "Step back and put your hands on your head!"

"You would have me just drop her to the floor like any old piece of refuse?"

"I would have you lower her to the floor gently, then step back and put your hands on your head." Letts motions with her head for Ms. Crana to look behind her.

Slowly, deliberately, showing no deference to Letts, Ms. Crana does just that, and sees three police officers approaching with guns drawn. Turning back, she sees two more officers coming up behind Letts. Without argument, Ms. Crana gently lowers Emily until she is lying face up on the floor

"Now step back and put your hands on your head," Letts commands again, a palpable relief in her voice.

But Ms. Crana only turns slowly so that her side is to Letts, and raises both arms out and away, hands palm up. She looks slowly, menacingly, between Letts and the two officers opposite her.

Eric suddenly pops out from the intersecting hallway, his gait naively purposeful, almost predatory. He blinks and surveys the situation, not sure where to start. Seeing the police with their guns drawn, he gulps and raises his hands. But after a moment, he notices Ms. Crana…and Emily's prostrate body lying at the woman's feet.

"What the hell did you do?" he yells, dropping his hands and falling to his knees beside Emily.

"Eric? You're Eric? Eric, I need you to back away." Officer Letts raises her gun again and moves forward slowly, cautiously, her eyes darting quickly from Emily's limp body to Eric and back to Ms. Crana.

"But—" Eric begins to protest, but is instantly shut down by Letts.

"Eric, this isn't the time for heroics. We'll take care of Emily, but I need you to move aside so you don't get hurt."

All during this exchange, Ms. Crana stands serenely, arms still spread outward, looking from Letts to the officers who creep closer from the other side. The idea of being intimidated by the police surrounding her never seems to enter her mind.

"I'm not going to tell you again to step back," Letts commands Ms. Crana, continuing her slow march forward. "Put your hands over your head and get down on your knees."

"The constable is right, Eric," Ms. Crana calmly interjects, "you should step away. I don't want you to get hurt."

Eric looks up at her, his eyes pleading.

At that moment, one of the officers behind Ms. Crana

springs forward, grabbing for her arms to pull them behind her and push her to the ground. Ms. Crana pulls her hands free with little effort and sidesteps the officer's approach, forcing him to grab at thin air. His momentum sends him stumbling forward, and Ms. Crana grabs him by the belt buckle and spins him head over heels, throwing him effortlessly into the lockers.

Ms. Crana stumbles and falls backward, a victim of the opposing force of the throw. Eric, at that moment, springs to his feet, his reflexes a split second too late in their attempt to dodge the flying police officer. He's on his feet just in time to recoil from the deafening POP of a gun. A gun discharging a bullet meant for Ms. Crana, who is no longer in the line of fire.

Though Eric is. He drops to the ground like a rag doll tossed from a speeding car.

The other officers begin to fire, seemingly indiscriminately, bullets aimed directly at Ms. Crana.

"Don't shoot! Don't shoot!" somebody yells. It's probably Letts. She's thrust her hands out, gesticulating frantically for everyone to stop. But her pleas are ignored amidst the blur of violence and fury. Deafening pops of gunfire echo down the hallway, and Letts drops her shoulders to stand defeated by a situation she fought desperately to avoid.

It was out of her control before it even began, and five seconds later it's over. Five seconds; a heartbeat by anyone's watch, but an eternity to those in the hallway. The world could end in less time.

A ringing silence overcomes them as the echoes die down. The proverbial dust settles into a horrible, confusing calm, and Letts is left standing, horror stricken, over a prostrate Eric and a prone Emily.

The other officers stare ahead, taking stock in themselves, stunned. Stunned at what had just happened, and stunned in their knee-jerk participation in it. But mostly stunned at Ms. Crana, who is down on one knee, her arms still outstretched in both directions, palms upward, the ground around her peppered by a few dozen spent bullet shells.

With not a scratch on her.

That fact barely registers when another ringing pierces the crashing silence. It's Emily's phone, frantically calling to its owner from down the hallway. Its gentle, tuneful tinkling is an odd contrast to the heaving, breathless sighs of the officers whose guns are still drawn; and the tense glare of the woman who by all rights should be a dead heap on the hallway floor.

"Eric, answer the phone please," Ms. Crana says with the controlled authority of a teacher.

Letts stutters at Ms. Crana, words caught in her throat. She can't decide whether to ask Ms. Crana why she's not dead, or why she's commanding Eric, who is dead, to answer the phone.

But she chokes it all back, stopped by the fact that Eric slowly raises his head and looks at Ms. Crana. He blinks wistfully. "What?" he says.

"Answer the phone, please," Ms. Crana says again. "I suspect it's your mother. I'll need to speak to her."

Eric pushes himself slowly up and to his knees. "What?" he says again, more incredulous than confused.

Before he can move, Emily sits bolt upright. She pauses in that position, a feral terror tensing her body, until she hears the phone ring again. Then she jumps to her feet and lunges toward the phone.

"Em!" Eric yells to her, jumping to his feet to follow.

"Let her go," Ms. Crana calmly tells him. "She needs to hear it."

"Hear what?" Letts yells, her voice a mixture of fear, adrenaline, and confusion.

Ms. Crana responds in the same calm tone: "That her life, as she knows it, is over."

———

Emily sprints frantically down the hallway, uncontrollable tears streaming down her face. A potent mixture of fear, relief, and adrenaline has her moving, and the only thing keeping her from a full run is the fact that she's trying desperately to keep the phone to her ear.

"Mom, she tried to kill me!" she sobs into the phone, almost choking on the air she's heaving.

"No, no! She wasn't trying to kill you, Emily." Sarah's voice is a fair approximation of rational. To anyone else who would be listening, there is a clear note of desperation masquerading as calm. Flush with her own panic, though, Emily is all but relieved to hear her mother's voice again.

"I don't have much time," Sarah says, distracted. "Em, I need you to stop and take a breath."

Emily slows, her legs wobbly like Jello. She leans sideways, banging her shoulder into a locker, then slides down to the floor in a ragdoll heap, her legs folded under her. "Mom, I want to come home," she sobs.

"Emily, there's nobody at home, honey."

"I want to go home, back to California."

"Sssshhh. Em, it will be alright." Sarah's voice becomes a lullaby. "Everything will be alright, I promise you. But you need to listen carefully. Can you do that?"

Emily tries desperately to compose herself, but can muster only a half-hearted nod and barely perceptible "uh-huh" followed by a sniffle.

"Okay, good. I need you to go find Ms. Crana and do everything she tells you, okay? Do you understand?"

Eric appears from around a corner, halting his full-on run when he sees Emily sitting against the lockers. Emily looks up at him, pleading. Eric looks directly back at her, his face set in a serious, parentally worried look. He nods at her. "We have to go."

"Emily," her mother's voice chirps from the phone, "did you hear me? Find Ms. Crana and do exactly what she tells you to do. Everything! Do you understand me?"

Emily shakes her head.

"She can't see you," Eric tells her.

"No. Mom, she tried to kill me," Emily says into the phone.

"Emily, honey, she didn't—"

In the background, Emily can hear a loud, adamant voice. It is strangely familiar, though she can't make out what the voice is saying. In response, she hears Sarah respond in a distant, muffled voice: "You and I might have slightly different thoughts on that. Go back and strap in, I'm right behind you!"

"Mom?"

"GO!" Sarah's voice returns to normal clarity. "I'm here, honey."

"Who are you talking to?"

"Don't worry about it, it's not important…"

"Mom, I'm scared."

"I know, honey, I know. Everything's going to be alright, though. Is Eric with you?"

"Yes."

"Okay, good. I need you to go with Eric and find Ms. Crana. Can you do that?"

"I…I don't know."

Ms. Crana appears from around the same corner as Eric, but stops several paces behind him.

Emily scrambles to her feet. "She's here!" she shouts into the phone.

"No, no, it's okay," Eric says, spinning frantically, trying to both assure Emily and stop Ms. Crana from advancing. "She's not trying to hurt us!"

At the same time, Sarah tries to reassure Emily from the phone. "Emily, Emily! It's okay!" Sarah says, "It's going to be okay.

"And Emily?"

"Yeah?"

"I love you. You know that, right?"

"Mom?"

There was no answer. Dumbstruck, Emily stares at her cell phone, then tries calling her back. But a cautious hand slowly removes the phone from Emily's hand.

Furious, Emily claws at Eric, ready to fight for her phone.

She stops when she sees the tears streaming down her brother's face. "She called me earlier," he says quietly.

"What's it mean?" Emily asks.

"I don't know," Eric says. He turns and looks at Ms. Crana, then back to Emily. "But I think she's right. We have to go with her."

———

They're running across the field at the back of the school; a utility easement, a wide, weed-strewn alley for high-tension electrical towers. Rows of houses butt up against the side opposite the school, and a high chain-link fence borders each side, ostensibly preventing students from using it as a shortcut to their classes.

Emily is running because Eric is running. As she crosses the field in his wake, her wide gallop crunching the tall dry grass beneath her feet, she realizes that she has absolutely no idea how she came to be there. Events were a cross-eyed blur even before Ms. Crana did whatever she did to knock Emily unconscious. That sensation now is amplified by everything that happened after she regained consciousness.

She barely recalls standing up after cutting off the phone call with her mother, or Eric's tugging at her arm when Ms. Crana prompted her to run. She doesn't remember at all scaling the chain-link fence to get to the field. And she certainly doesn't know why they are running and where they are going.

She regains a semblance of awareness just in time to prevent herself from tripping over Eric's prone body. He had been running with a sense of dire purpose only moments before, but he suddenly and violently fell backward, his feet swept out from underneath him, as if hit in the forehead by some unseen baseball bat.

His mouth warps into a tight grimace, and he grits his teeth as he smashes his palms against his forehead, as if trying to drive a pain away by pushing it down into his body. Emily stands over him uselessly, struggling to figure out what to do…or even what happened.

Eric begins rocking back and forth and moaning piercingly, trying mightily to prevent himself from appearing weak by crying. There is no doubt that whatever happened was incomprehensibly painful.

"What's the matter?" she asks, moving around to the side of him. And then her head hits something. She recoils instantly then spins to see what she hit.

"Nobody told me it was invisible," Eric says, eyes still shut tight.

Emily sees nothing, though; nothing but the field she had been running in and the fence that she had been running toward. But she puts her hand up and it stops in mid air, pressed against something that to all of her other senses is not there. She presses hard but her hand does not move but to flatten harder against whatever invisible object she is touching. She reaches her other hand up and begins to feel along the object, running both hands over it as if spelling out some semaphore code. Somebody observing from across the field, with Eric coiled at her feet and her hands waving wildly in midair, might mistake her probing motions as a call for help.

The object is warm and smooth and vaguely pliable, like a thin aluminum can. She can't tell by touch alone whether it's metal, plastic, or some other substance, but it's feel is both familiar and foreign. As she ponders that notion, Emily realizes that she's not as surprised as she probably should be that an object associated with Ms. Crana would be described that way.

It's then that she notices the undulating green sky.

Ribbons of emerald phosphorescence shimmer above her like thousands of green flashlights pointed up at a blue ceiling. She rotates slowly as she cranes her head upward, her mouth dropped open in awe. She almost feels as if she's at the bottom of a pool looking up at the sun, and all she can hear is the sound of her own heartbeat in her ears.

Then, as if emerging from a dark, silent cavern, the world

suddenly rushes toward her and she becomes acutely aware of her surroundings. There's the wide, cut hole in the fence that they must have run through to get onto the easement. Beyond the fence are the police cars that surround them, forming a distant and wide arc, their lights curiously dark. The police officers themselves press up against...something...some unseen barrier, looking in at them helplessly and confusedly. And all the people drawn to the spectacle—students, teachers, neighbors—stand cordoned off at a further distance behind the police, looking in with great awe and curiosity, wondering what the danger is and why those people were running through the field.

And then she turns and sees Ms. Crana, standing in something yet in nothing. She floats about two meters off the ground, though her feet seem firmly planted on a solid surface. Behind her is a pulsing glow, and the faint outlines of a wall and a floor, set inside some sort of borderless box or window. She speaks, but above the overload of sound and image Emily cannot focus, cannot discern the words coming from her mouth.

"Get in!" Ms. Crana yells, and she gestures for Emily to approach, "Come on! Grab your brother and get in!"

"What is happening?" she screams back, wide-eyed, stepping slowly backward, retreating from everything she is seeing...and not seeing.

"I don't..."Ms. Crana begins to say, beginning a dispassionate plea. But she pauses, and it's obvious from her weary exasperation that she's done explaining and is instead going to take action.

Suddenly, silently, the space around Ms. Crana fills in. A blue glow radiates outward from where she stands, like a neon ink stain spreading across an invisible cloth. In its wake appears a flat white material, smooth and glossy like fiberglass, but as thin and flimsy looking as wax paper. The glowing stain spreads and disappears in seconds and Emily finds herself standing before some sort of airplane. It is bulkier than one of those private jets rich people travel in; about as long—20 meters or so—but stubbier, wider. Its wings begin almost at the transparent, bullet-nosed cockpit and extend all the way back, angled out such that its width is very nearly equal to its length. They taper up and across to form the cabin, making the entire vehicle appear is if it were a blunt arrow tip.

The whole vehicle looks to Emily like a squat, stocky cousin of the old American space shuttle that she once saw at the Smithsonian in Washington D.C. when she was younger.

Ms. Crana emerges from a doorway set near the back of the spacecraft and walks purposefully down a narrow gangplank extended outward from the wing. Toward Emily. She carries the black cylinder, pressing down on the top to release the menacing hiss.

Emily's eyes widen with terror and she stumbles as she tries to back away. She immediately props herself up and kicks outwards, trying furiously to continue backwards in an awkward crabwalk.

"Wait!" Eric yells, peering out from behind a palm that he still presses hard against his forehead. "Wait! Don't, don't!" he says to Ms. Crana. "She'll go! She'll go! Emily, get on board!"

As if accentuating his plea, a bright flash splits the sky open and the thunderous roar of supersonic electricity pierces Emily's ears. She falls to her back with a scream and wraps her arms around her head.

The sky is now alight in a crackling grid of white energy. A hot wind whips along the easement and the support coils that bind the high tension wires above them begin to spit out fountains of sparks. The people lined up outside the fence are rushing to and fro, some fleeing, some searching, some praying, and a few just standing frozen in terrified awe.

As if pushed, Eric runs up the gangplank and in through the doorway. He spins around and yells: "Emily, come on!"

Emily looks at him tearfully, pleadingly. She shakes her head.

In a blindingly swift move, Ms. Crana presses the cylinder

to Emily's neck. The hiss is barely audible over the noise as Emily falls limp once again.

"No, dammit!" Eric yells, "Why did you have to do that?"

Ms. Crana lifts Emily into her arms and runs up the gangplank. "You do not try to reason with a drowning woman."

"She wasn't drowning!"

"No, but that might be preferable to what's coming. We have to leave now!"

The door shushes shut behind them.

————

They're in a narrow, oblong cabin, approximately the width of a commercial passenger jet, and with similar beige plastic walls, but considerably shorter. Immediately inside the hatch are two sets of two transparent half-cylinders stacked vertically across from each other, each covering a recess as wide, as tall, and nearly as deep as the half-cylinders themselves. Four glass sarcophagi. Just past the cylinders, forward toward the cockpit, are two sets of two passenger chairs, also across from each other. Ms. Crana gently eases Emily's limp body into one of the chairs, and pulls a series of straps and buckles around her, securing her in.

"You take that chair," Ms. Crana commands Eric, gesturing to the chair opposite Emily. He climbs onto the chair and awkwardly contorts himself until he is in the proper sitting position. Ms. Crana straps him in as well. "She'll be awake in a moment," she says, then takes the seat in front of him.

Eric looks over at Emily. She is staring upward with drunken, half-closed eyes.

Before he can say anything, he feels a sudden, immense pressure push on him, as if a ton of bricks were thrown flat onto his chest. His whole body is pushed back so hard he feels is if he's going to fuse into the chair.

Eric ekes out a few shallow breaths, struggling so hard to bring air into his lungs that he doesn't even notice the severe shaking, or the intense flashes streaming through the portholes. He's being pushed back so hard into his chair by the force of upward momentum that he can barely even lift his head. He lets it flop back and fall to the right so he can peek at Emily.

Emily's eyes are wide open now, crazed saucers spinning in their sockets. She's panting hard and gripping the armrests of her seat so tightly her knuckles are white from the strain. An intense flash and powerful quake dissolve her thoughts. The ship rattles around so severely the whole interior becomes a whirling blur. Then, just as suddenly as it began, the rattling stops and she's jerked forward off her seat, her chest and neck straining against her safety straps, the breath knocked completely out of her lungs. It feels like her whole body is going to come shooting out of her mouth.

The vehicle is now falling in almost as straight a course backwards as it had previously traveled forwards.

"Engines offline!" a foreign, masculine voice shouts from somewhere in front. When Emily clears her head enough to notice, she sees two additional seats in front of Ms. Crana, occupied by two men. They're sitting in a cockpit, or at least what Emily thinks should be a cockpit. It's small and tight like those she's seen in an airplane, but there seems to be no flight control panel at all. In fact, from her perspective the two men appear to be floating in the sky, protected from the elements by a huge, curved windshield that slopes down in front of them.

Emily turns and locks eyes with Eric who, despite his previous bravado, looks as scared and confused as she feels. She looks at him and she's no longer sure what to feel; whatever anger she had toward him has melted away and her eyes cling to his face as if it's the only grasp on sanity she has left. Somehow, she thinks he may even be the only link to life she has left.

All at once the cabin roars back to life and Emily is again pushed back hard into her chair. They ride upward again, and as they climb, Emily shifts her focus to look past Eric and out the porthole next to him. Through it she sees the white wisps of clouds giving way to increasingly bright green strands, and the entire cabin is now aglow in neon emerald. She turns away from Eric to look out her own portal. The green begins to fade and Emily can see Earth curving away. In her narrow field of vision, it appears to be covered by a fierce, undulating blanket of energy.

The pressure that's pushing her back into her seat begins to ease up. At the same time she feels a disorienting rotation. Though she's sure the ship itself is moving forward, the sensation of pointing upward begins to spiral away until she feels as though she is sitting straight up. She looks at Eric and sees him staring back. She has the unsettling feeling that he is about to cry.

Emily herself has exhausted her repertoire of emotions in the last three hours, and every one that she's burned through has been tied somehow to this strange woman in the seat in front of her, this alleged science teacher. She turns to look again out the portal. She can see Earth clearly below her, it's familiar blues and beiges and whites shrouded in a gauzy green blanket. She leans her head over and presses it against the portal, studying North America. Her eyes wander over it, gazing from the rippled mountains of the West to the printed circuit grays of the Midwest and East coast. She stops to focus on the rather featureless center, her eyes boring down to find something. Anything. She wonders why, if Earth is so curved, Kansas is so flat.

"Is your brother awake?" her mother asks.

Her...mother?

Emily spins her head to look at Eric. No, Emily wants to say, I want to poke him in the eye to wake him up.

But Eric is looking out his own portal and paying no attention. She looks forward and sees her mother in the seat in front of her, yelling something.

"What?" Emily yells back.

But not to her mother.

"Hold on tight," Ms. Crana yells, "We're not at a safe distance yet!"

"But…!" Emily starts to object, but sees Eric still resolutely refusing to look at her. What about Mom?

She's suddenly pushed back into her seat again, though it's not as crushing as their initial escape from Earth's gravitational pull. She hears chatter coming from in front of her, though over the engine noise she can't make out much. She eyes the two men in the cockpit, sees their bodies animated, tense. Ms. Crana nods and shifts in her chair in reaction to them.

"What's happening?" she yells at Ms. Crana.

Ms. Crana addresses both her and Eric. Her words are calm, but her tone betrays a false security. She explains herself swiftly, as if her words are outrunning something. "Aft sensors are indicating a massive gravitational pulse emanating from a region just beyond Earth's orbit. But we haven't yet achieved a sufficient velocity to—"

Emily is buffeted violently back and forth and side-to-side, her seatbelt straining to keep her in place. There's a vague sense of spinning, tumbling uncontrollably, like a rickety boat on rough seas. The electrical system begins to flicker, the lights strobe, turning the experience into a carnival horror ride.

And just as suddenly, it stops.

And there is absolute silence in the nearly absolute darkness.

"What's happening?" Emily asks.

Ms. Crana leans over and cups her hands against the portal and looks out. She studies the blackness for a few moments, then pulls back. She thinks on it a moment, then looks out again. When she pulls back once more, her face is steeled with determination.

"What's happening?" Emily asks again.

"I'll be right back," Ms. Crana says, unbuckling herself from her restraints.

Though she can't see, she can sense Ms. Crana floating out of her seat and to the back of the cabin.

"What the hell happened?" Eric asks.

One of the men begins to answer from the cockpit, and as soon as she hears him say 'extinction level event,' Emily turns off the conversation. She folds back into herself, exhausted by the running and the fear and the uncertainty and the yo-yoing of her emotions. She stares out her portal at a tableau of more stars than she's ever seen in her life, but she doesn't even actually see them. She doesn't care now whether home is California or Minnesota, she only knows that she wants to be there. Except apparently there isn't there anymore.

With her eyes and ears effectively switched off, she starts to become vaguely aware that she can't feel her own weight. It's an odd sensation: though securely bound by them, she feels she is neither sitting in her chair nor pressed up against her seat restraints, but is floating somewhere in between.

Heh. Kansas is in between California and Minnesota. Yeah, she'll even take flat Kansas now to call home. Wherever her mother wants to take her.

The feeling becomes more acute, and she discovers to her dismay that without the constant buffeting of her senses, she can no longer ignore the intense nausea she feels. Weightless or not, the fluids churn up from her stomach and burn her throat as they violently make their escape. In many ways, the heaving rocks her body far worse than their bruising escape from Earth's gravity. The sharp pains in her chest, the indignity, and stinging sadness of loss… The tears well up in her eyes and turn quickly into wrenching, pitiable sobs. She begins to cry unrestrained and unapologetically.

"Em."

A gasping, breathless blubbering, there is no catharsis in it, no cleansing. Her cries morph slowly into a formless, uncontrolled moaning…

"Emily."

…which then eventually coalesces into barely comprehensible mutterings of home and mother and I want to go I want to go I want to go.

"Em, it's going to be okay."

What the hell? The shock of so ignorant and impossible a platitude silences her. She turns in the general direction of

74

her brother and attempts to pierce the darkness with a glaring anger. The sudden and acute quiet, though, calms her ravaged nerves, and she sees him, in her mind's eye, looking back at her with genuine concern.

That's a bigger shock.

"How can you say that?"

"Emily, we have listen to her," Eric interjects. His voice is not so calm, but he puts on a brave front. "Ms. Crana. She's..."

"Why?" Emily screams, interrupting Eric. "Why should we listen to her? What is she doing to us?"

"She's helping us!"

"How do you know?"

"Because...mom told me!"

Emily pauses. The answer doesn't quite compute, and it takes her a moment to figure out why. "And when's the last time you listened to mom?" she says, delivering the retort with a sting of venom. As scared as she is, she's equally angry at Eric's veneer of calm. He knows something that she doesn't and she resents it. Resents that her mom shared with him some kind of secret that somehow explained every fantastical facet of this nightmare but chose not to share it with her.

"Mom is dead."

There is another silence. "Yeah," he finally says, so whisper quiet that she can't actually hear him. It was clearly not the answer he wanted to give and she only understood it by the nearly imperceptible nod that accompanied it.

"The Earth is...dead."

"Yeah, I guess."

A silence consumes them. It brings a voice to what they both thought.

Moments later cabin lights come back on, though they're much weaker, casting an eerie glow throughout. But Emily can see Eric. He struggles to appear nonchalant, but Emily can make out tear streaks down his cheeks. She finds this gratifying. He's not the stoic, unfeeling jerk she always thought he was.

Ms. Crana reappears between her and Eric. She pauses

momentarily to study Emily's face. She reaches out a tender hand and gently wipes the tears from Emily's cheek with her thumb. "You are certainly your father's daughter. Adversity brings out the best in you."

Then there is a flash, and the power goes out again.

There is silence for a moment, then Ms. Crana says, "Understood."

Emily tries to find her face in the darkness. "Understood? What's understood?"

A bright white flash lights up the cabin and fades. A few small, dull emergency lights cast pale yellow circles, just enough light to barely illuminate the ship.

Ms. Crana passes an indulgent glance between Eric and Emily, then pauses to look at the floor, appearing to collect her thoughts. "Indeed," she says, sounding as if she were answering an unasked question. "Then initiate emergency return procedures." Moments later, Vernon and Algate, the two men from the cockpit, float past, heading to the back of the ship. Ms. Crana turns, grabs the back of Emily's and Eric's seats, and pulls herself away from them.

"Follow me," Ms. Crana says, beckoning them to follow.

Emily and Eric look at each other, trying to determine what to do, what the other will do. Finally, Eric begins unstrapping himself and Emily follows suit. They awkwardly float into the aisle, nearly colliding with each other as they struggle to master weightlessness. Ms. Crana shepherds them toward the back of the ship, to the cylinders they'd seen when they first boarded. Looking at them now it is clear that they are meant as chambers for people.

Vernon and Algate are already occupying two of the chambers, the transparent half-cylinders hissing shut to cover them, sealing them in. Ms. Crana points to the two adjacent chambers and orders Emily and Eric into them.

Emily eyes her warily. "What are these for?"

"They're protection for the journey forward."

"What do they do?" Eric asks.

"They protect you for the journey forward."

"You said that already," Emily says.

"As with many things this day, I lack the time to provide lengthy explanations. You'll have to trust me."

Eric ponders a moment. "Is this cryogenic freezing?"

"It is exactly cryogenic freezing, Mr. Clocke. Well done."

"Does it hurt?"

"Not a bit."

Eric studies her warily. After a moment, he says "Okay" then enters the chamber. The cover closes over him, hissing to indicate an airtight seal.

"You too," Ms. Crana say to Emily.

Emily makes no move, just fixes on Ms. Crana with an inscrutable stare.

"I haven't hurt you so far," Ms. Crana offers.

"You've hurt me plenty," Emily counters.

"Temporarily, and with justification," Ms. Crana explains without a trace of defensiveness.

"My mother is dead and my home is gone. The entire planet! That's not temporary!"

"I share your loss," Ms. Crana says, clearly pained.

"Don't patronize me," Emily hisses. "I've lost everything!"

Ms. Crana chews on her response. "Indeed," she finally says. "But you should know that your mother…" she pauses, wondering on the wisdom of continuing.

"You don't know anything about my mother!"

"Your mother was my sister."

———

"I don't believe you," Emily says.

"I know you don't," Ms. Crana says. She stares at Emily, searching for something more to say. When it comes, it comes without warning. "Forgive me," she blurts out, suddenly and deftly pushing on Emily's arm so that the young woman spins into the chamber. The chamber lid snaps shut, sealing out the cabin's environment.

"Please trust me," Ms. Crana pleads.

Emily is too surprised at first to be enraged. But whatever anger boils up is repressed by the immediate sense of confusion she feels when a viscous liquid begins gushing up from the bottom of the chamber. She is, at first, curious: the liquid is yellowish and slightly foamy, like watery honey, and large ribbons of it float up from the gushing stream and reach out to her like undulating tentacles. Some break off into quivery, free-floating blobs, slowly coalescing into near perfect spheres, like opaque bubbles. She reaches out and pokes one and the liquid mostly wraps around her finger, but a slight wiggle of the finger breaks the sphere into two equal bubbles.

For a few brief seconds, Emily's curiosity leads her into a dreamy, almost childlike fugue as she swats at the globules and they break into liquid confetti, bouncing around the chamber and re-adhering into larger globules. But the pressure of the liquid amassing around her legs makes her realize that it's not going to stop until it completely fills the chamber.

Panic wells up. She begins smashing her hands against the chamber cover, desperate to open it. She barely notices Eric's identical panic, or that the same thing is happening in the other occupied chambers as well. But she sees Ms. Crana. She sees the sinister, tormenting pleasure etched on her face, the sneer of a bully enjoying the act of pulling wings off butterflies.

"Listen to me!" Ms. Crana screams, directing her voice at both her and Eric.

But desperation and hatred burn in her, and Emily refuses to listen. In zero-g, the liquid doesn't fill the chamber in an orderly top-to-bottom manner. It swirls around her so that she has no sense of the chamber's capacity, but the pressure is mostly on her legs, and she can feel it on her hips as it crawls up her body. She pounds on the transparent cover. "Let me out! Let me out!" she screams, the acute fear distorting her mouth into a cracked smile.

"Listen to me!" Ms. Crana screams again. "It's a protective fluid! It acts like a cocoon!"

The weight of it presses on her with varying degrees, but it's now compressing her chest. She gasps short, shallow, panicked breaths and her head begins to swirl from the lack of oxygen. She continues to throw blows against the cover, but her strength is drained and her hands barely connect with enough pressure to even make a thud. She presses her face against the transparent door and looks pleadingly at Ms. Crana.

The slimy solution is starting to trickle into her mouth.

"Let it in!" she hears Ms. Crana scream again. "Breathe it in!"

Emily is now completely submerged, the liquid gushes completely into her mouth and nose, choking any further attempts to talk. She stops fighting. And the liquid fills her completely.

# :05 arrival

Emily shudders involuntarily. Her muscles twitch reflexively in an attempt to generate body heat to relieve her chill and restore her core body temperature. Unfortunately, this purely physiological attempt to restore homeostasis triggers an overwhelming urge to yawn, which is painfully stifled by the sheer amount of liquid in her lungs and throat. Perversely, the desperate choking sends a burning hot flash through her body, which helps dramatically to warm her and reduce the shivering. But none of this registers consciously. Her body is on automatic as she heaves forward, crashes her head against the transparent covering, and spews out what seems to be gallons of yellow, mucus-like fluid.

It comes out in seemingly unending tidal waves, the disgorged fluid sucked into vacuum nozzles in the wall behind her before the floating liquid can be recaptured by her mouth and nose. Her lungs burn desperately to suck in oxygen but her spasming abdominal muscles overrule them until they're satisfied that she's relatively empty.

Then the inward heaving begins as she sucks in mouthfuls of air. Her torso is so wracked she feels as if she'd been continuously hammered by steel fists, and her expanding lungs feel like steel daggers trying to push their way out of her chest.

Even worse, heaving while in a weightless environment causes her to bounce violently off the walls and floor and ceiling of the cramped chamber.

Eventually, the vicious shuddering stops. She arches her back and presses her forehead against the chamber lid, closing her eyes to shut out stimulus and concentrate only on breathing. To see her now, someone might mistake her pose as peaceful contemplation, but the tears that carve lightning-streak tracks down her cheeks betray her. The tears, too, get sucked off her skin and into the vacuum nozzles.

The chamber door gently clicks open and Emily pitches forward slightly.

"Circumstances always seem to ensure that I do right by you in entirely the wrong way," her mother says. And then her mother's warm arms wrap around her, engulfing her in a welcome sense of peace and safety. But the peace is short lived as the spark of an idea forms. An unwanted thought butts its way into her head and she jerks back, realizing suddenly that she is not in her mother's arms.

"Where am I?" She pushes away so forcefully that the recoil carries her right back into the chamber. Tall and wiry, matted by a sheen of silky liquid, Ms. Crana looks ghostly and stern, and for a split second Emily considers locking herself safely back into the chamber, until she gathers her wits and realizes that there is no safety in the chamber. Yet she's not entirely sure why. She has a memory of drowning, but it's vague and hazy yet distinct and clear. And close but far. It seems as if it happened in the distant past but only moments ago.

She grabs hold of the chamber's edge and swings herself out into the hall, spinning herself back around 180° as fast as possible so as to keep her eyes squarely on her tormentor. "What did you do to me?"

"That which was necessary."

"I was drowning." It was as much a question as a statement.

"You were in suspended animation." Ms. Crana shifts slightly so that Emily can see the chamber behind her. It is misty with condensation. Tendrils of smoke pour off the surface and curl away in all directions, eventually dissipating into invisibility as it mixes with the air around it. "I flooded the suspension chamber with oxygenated fluorocarbon vitrification liquid, and once it completely permeated your body, I flash froze it to induce cryopreservation. It is perfectly safe and perfectly common."

"Maybe where you come from it is, but I was drowning!"

"In point of fact, you were not drowning," Ms. Crana explains. "Oxygenated fluorocarbon fluid is breathable. However, taking fluid into the lungs goes against your instincts, so you fought it, and the panic you felt during those moments led you to feel as if you were drowning. I do regret that. I apologize for making the last thing you remember so traumatic."

"Why did you do all this?"

"So I could bring you home."

"What do you mean home?"

"Caelestis."

Emily stares at Ms. Crana, her face inscrutable. "What is Caelestis?" she asks, but after chewing over a thought, she spins and propels herself toward the cockpit. Through the glass, looming large in her field of vision is a pale orange and beige sphere streaked with overlapping bands of cottony white, like a layered sand sculpture in a circular bottle. Its size is overwhelming, almost inconceivable, and it appears so close that it seems almost flat, like a disc rather than a sphere. A flaming red blemish peeks angrily through the slowly swirling mists of the lower right-hand corner of the sphere—the Leviathan's eye studying Emily as Emily studies it. This, she realizes, is Jupiter, the fifth and largest planet of the solar system (or is it the fourth?) and Emily is seeing it up close and personal, unaided by a telescope.

"That's Jupiter," Emily says, her awe rendering her voice toneless and flat.

"Isn't it freakin' awesome?" Eric says, his voice full of unabated excitement.

Emily is incredulous. "Why are we at Jupiter?"

"That is the location of Caelestis," Ms. Crana answers.

"What is Cael...?" Emily suddenly jerks her head away from the view to follow the sound of Eric's voice. She sees Eric sitting in the pilot's seat. "What are you doing here?"

"She brought me," Eric smiles, thumbing back at Ms. Crana.

Emily spins to look back at Ms. Crana. "He flew us to Jupiter?"

Ms. Crana smiles. "No, not exactly. Mr. Clocke has merely been observing. Autopilot is bringing us into a docking vector around Caelestis."

"WHAT THE HELL IS CAELESTIS?" Emily screams, her wits losing the battle to frustration.

"Sit," Ms. Crana commands, gesturing to the empty co-pilot's seat.

"I...no—!" Emily stammers. "I just want you to tell me what's going on!"

"Sit," Ms. Crana says adamantly, "and I will attempt to do so."

Emily glares at her and refuses to budge.

"Alternatively," Ms. Crana adds, "we can return to the cabin seats and leave your brother to his own devices."

Emily stares out the portal at the gas giant before them, unconsciously shaking her head as if it were an involuntary twitch of her neck. She can't even process her thoughts to be able to form questions. Maybe I really shouldn't know what's going on.

Emily, despite herself, looks to Eric for guidance. He just shrugs and nods toward the co-pilot's chair. Reluctantly, Emily positions herself to slip into the seat.

"Why do you know so much?" she asks him.

"I don't," he answers, "I just go with the flow."

"You're so full of crap," Emily says, sliding into the seat next to him. She turns to look out the portal. A small part of the narrow furrows that crease her forehead is caused by the reluctant belief that there is really nothing left to surprise her. But there it is, the largest planet in the solar system, so close she feels as though she could reach out and touch it. "Why Jupiter?" she asks.

"Jupiter itself is not our destination." Ms. Crana points out the window to a black dot floating serenely along Jupiter's equatorial plane, looking like a dust mote locked in a perpetual slog through a sandstorm. Emily empathizes with the dot's frustrating lack of progress, but she shares none of its seeming tranquility.

"That's Caelestis?" Emily asks. "That little dot?"

"That's Europa, the fourth largest Jovian moon."

As she watches it, Emily notices the dot get slowly larger, more distinct and spherical, appearing to approach the ship. "It looks like it's coming right at us," she says.

"Actually," Ms. Crana corrects, "We are moving toward it. It only looks like it's coming toward us because Jupiter takes up so much space in our field of vision that we can't perceive our motion toward it. Europa is so small relative to the planet that our motion toward it makes it appear as if it is instead moving toward us."

"So if that's not Caelestis, then what is?" Emily asks with mounting impatience.

As they move forward, Europa slowly begins to command the foreground. The Jovian moon now seems close enough to reach out and pluck from the sky; to be able to hold the pale, scarred marble between two fingers. The swirling maelstrom clouds of Jupiter frame the moon as the ship floats toward it. As she watches, Emily spots a slight, wispy ring appearing to halo the moon.

"Do you see that ring around Europa?" Ms. Crana asks, pointing at the ring.

"Kind of."

"That is Caelestis."

"And again, *what* is Caelestis?" Emily asks, waving her arms to release the frustration of having to ask again.

"Caelestis is a ringed space station in orbit around Europa," Ms. Crana says. "It is where Misters Verton and Algate, as well your mother and father and I were born."

"What!? No, I—that's not—," Emily stammers, then something Ms. Crana said comes running back to the forefront of her mind. "You said my mother was your sister!"

"I did."

"What did—what did you mean by that?"

"Precisely that. Your mother was my sister. I am your aunt."

———

Emily rises from her seat and propels herself to the back of the cabin, tears welling in her eyes, turning Jupiter to a wavy, glowing blur. Ms. Crana reaches out to stop her, but Emily bats her hand away. "Leave me alone!" she growls as she floats past.

"I think you should let her be," Eric whispers to Ms. Crana.

The ship falls to silence. Emily floats between the last row of seats, wanting to curl up and lay her head against the portal ledge and just cry and then sleep. But she can't bring herself to do anything other than sob pathetically, suspended two feet off the floor. Her mind swims with the idea that she doesn't want to lose, she can't lose, even though she doesn't even know what game she's playing. Or what war she's fighting. Regardless, she steels herself to the fact that she won't let herself lose, so she fights back more tears and straightens her body.

She wipes her eyes on her shoulder sleeves, and looks at the back of the ship, checking the quality of her vision. The ship is still a shimmery blur, but she makes out the empty cryo-tube that she just exited, and the one across from it that last held Eric. Then she notices the two tubes behind them. She floats toward them, momentarily startled by the pallid, stupefied stares of their occupants: the two pilots. They are encased in columns of pale yellow ice, their faces fragmented by webs of fine cracks. She is reminded, for some reason, of the waxy, zombie-like statues of Neanderthals she's seen in the natural history museum back in California.

Then the truth of the cryotubes hits her, and she spins and propels herself purposely back to the cockpit.

"Can I talk to Eric?" she asks Ms Crana.

Ms. Crana nods and floats to the back of the ship.

Emily sits back down in the pilot's seat. "There are only four tubes."

"What?"

"There are only four tubes."

"So?"

"There are *five* of us. We took two, the pilots are still in the other two. Where did Ms. Crana sleep?"

Eric cranes his neck back and silently counts the tubes. He looks back at Emily and shrugs. "I don't know."

"Do you even care?" Emily asks, shocked by his nonchalance.

"Yeah, I care!" Eric responds swiftly and defensively.

"But you just blindly believe everything she says?"

Eric pauses, then squeaks out, "Yeah, actually."

"Why?"

"Because—" Eric pauses, something on his tongue. Finally he says, "Mom told me to."

Emily nods, heartbroken. Then she says, "Since when did you start doing what she told you to?" It was swift and savage and the fact that she said it surprised even her.

Strangely, Eric doesn't react with the fury Emily expected. She apparently pinched a nerve she didn't know he had, and she regrets saying it. Maybe he does actually have feelings...

"She didn't tell me anything," Emily says with a sliver of resentment.

"She didn't have time to tell us both. She barely told *me* anything, really."

Emily sniffles and wipes her eyes with her wrists. "You look like you're having fun." She says it lightly, but her tone clearly masks offense.

"I don't know that fun is exactly the right word."

"Well, you don't seem all cracked up, anyway."

"Trust me—," Eric starts to say, but lets it drop. By

the sound of it, Emily realizes that he was about to confess something, but decided instead to keep up the appearance of masculine confidence.

"So…Caelestis is home?" Emily calls to the back of the cabin in as friendly a voice as she can muster, signaling that her conversation with Eric is done.

"Yes," Ms. Crana says, floating forward, a note of regret in her voice. "And it is now your home as well."

"It's like *Halo*!" Eric says, pointing at the silvery ring.

'Pardon?" Ms. Crana asks.

"It's like *Halo*," Eric explains. "The video game. We're going to live on *Halo*!"

"I see," Ms. Crana says, clearly not seeing.

"How did it get there? Emily asks.

"We don't actually know," Ms. Crana answers ruefully.

"You don't know?" Emily asks, incredulous. "How could you not know? You live on a space station that wraps around an entire moon and you don't know how it got there? I mean, we can hardly keep the International Space Sta—" A thought hits her and she pauses to let it form. It comes in pieces, and she fights to create a picture. "How could—" she begins tentatively, piecing the strands of her thought together. "How could a space station that size be built around a Jupiter moon and nobody know it? For that matter, how could a space station that size even be built at all and nobody know it?"

Eric suddenly catches the drift of her argument. "Wait a minute, yeah! We never went to Jupiter. I mean, like astronauts. NASA astronauts never went. NASA never even got past the moon. Except for satellites and robots. They say it'll be like 30 years before man even gets to Mars."

"Where are we?" Emily asks, twisting in her chair to look back at Ms. Crana.

"You are exactly where your senses tell you you are," Ms. Crana answers matter-of-factly. "You are on a spacecraft on an approach vector to a space station in an orbit around the Jovian moon Europa."

"Okay, but how?" Emily demands. "How is it here?"

"How indeed?" Ms. Crana asks enigmatically.

Exasperated with Ms. Crana, Emily and Eric look at each other. After a moment, they both crane their heads to look past Ms. Crana, to the back of the cabin, to the cryo chambers. Then they both look back at Ms. Crana.

"How long were we popsicles, exactly?" Eric asks.

Ms. Crana fidgets for a moment, then says, "I do not understand 'popsicles.'"

"How long were we frozen?" Emily impatiently clarifies.

"525 years."

————

Emily and Eric are stunned by this revelation. But after only a few seconds of absorbing the information, the wheel of Emily's mind begins spinning. "Okay, so, wait a minute," she says. "If this is the 25th century—"

"26th," Eric corrects, then he suddenly sits bolt upright, his face beaming. "You can travel through time!"

"Yes," Ms. Crana says reluctantly.

"So...we go back!" Eric says excitedly, his head spinning from Ms. Crana to Emily to Ms. Crana again. "We can go back! Back to yesterday morning! We can go back to yesterday morning and save Mom!"

Ms. Crana shakes her head. "It does not work that way. Time is—"

"We have to go back!" Emily says emphatically.

"No, no, listen," Ms. Crana implores, "the energies required for reversing time are enormous."

"But you're time travelers!" Eric interrupts, exasperated. "This is a time machine, for chrissake, right?"

"Mr. Clocke!" Ms. Crana shouts, a sliver of anger slipping into her voice, and both Eric and Emily are shocked into silence. Immediately chagrined, Ms. Crana composes herself and resumes in a steady voice. "Mr. Clocke. I understand your enthusiasm for wanting to reset the events that have transpired.

As I made clear earlier, I too have an emotional stake in what has happened and would do anything in my power to right them. But it is not within my power to do so. Time travel is an enormously complex endeavor and requires energy levels that are orders of magnitude higher than this ship is capable of generating on its own. I'm sorry, but we can't go back." She emphasizes the finality of the last three words. The discussion is over. "We are now on a docking approach vector. You will need to strap in."

"No, no, no, no," Emily protests. "You can't tell us...you can't just tell us that—" She jabs a finger at the gas giant outside the windshield. "You owe us an explanation!"

"I agree. But at the moment, there are more pressing concerns. We are approaching the station and need to prepare for docking." Ms. Crana waves her hand in the air in front of them. As she does, the joystick arms automatically slide to an upright position and the cockpit windshield lights up with colorful raster images of maps, power meters, virtual buttons, and dozens of other indicators.

"Pay attention," Ms. Crana says, pointing to an image of a spherical grid projected on the windshield directly in front of Eric. "See that control there?" she asks him. "That's called a celestial sphere. It depicts the attitude of our flight path with respect to everything that's around us within a 125,000 kilometer range. The arrow that appears to be floating in the center represents us. Sensors are still calibrating, so the sphere isn't registering anything in the range. However..." she pauses and flicks her fingers wide open, causing the sphere to enlarge and center on the windshield. At the same time, an overlay of dots appears, seeming to wrap around the spherical grid. Ms. Crana continues: "Using our forward visual array, we can capture an image of the astronomical objects before us, extrapolate from it a full radius of objects, and wrap that around the spherical grid. From that, we can pinpoint where any known astronomical body should be with respect to our present direction..."—a tiny representation of Europa pops onto the grid, appearing in a position to the lower right of the center arrow—"...and orient ourselves so that we're facing it."

"Why are you telling us this?" Emily asks petulantly.

"So you can dock the ship."

"US?" Emily replies, surprised.

"Mr. Clocke specifically," Ms. Crana answers calmly, as if it were a straightforward question.

"*ME?*" Eric exclaims. "I don't know how to fly this thing!"

"Where are the pilots?" Emily asks.

"Hmm," Ms. Crana says to Eric, perplexed. "I took it for granted that you would know."

"How would I possibly know?" Eric says, prompting a terrified look from Emily.

"*Where*...are the pilots?" Emily asks again, her voice a rising panic.

"Still in stasis," Ms. Crana answers her abruptly, then turns back to Eric. "You're an early-21st century adolescent American male. I was to understand that military training was compulsory during your era."

"What? No! Not until we're 18!"

"Why are they still in stasis?" Emily continues, not noticing the fact that she's being ignored. "Shouldn't they be flying?"

"Very odd," Ms. Crana says to herself. "Clearly my knowledge of your culture's military structure is incomplete..."

Emily looks out the portal. Europa is now prominent, clear and distinct. Streaked with so many cracks and fissures, it looks like a ball of tightly wound, pale yarn, beaten and scratched by a cat with razor sharp claws. Yet it seems as smooth as polished glass. Caelestis, in contrast, is not so much a smooth, polished ring anymore as it is a knobby, reticulated chrome bracelet. And it's approaching rather quickly.

"Side thrusters are live," Ms. Crana announces, "so we can still spin." She points to the representation of Europa on the celestial sphere. "I want you to manipulate the controller arm until Europa spins around to align with the point of the arrow. Do you think you can do that?"

"I don't know!" Eric stammers.

"Oh for...!" Emily yells at Eric. "*Halo*, dummy! Just play *Halo*!"

"What?" Eric asks.

"Halo! You said yourself this is like *Halo*!"

"I said the station was like *Halo*!" Eric replies. "I don't know anything about flying a spaceship! This isn't a video game!"

"You've played enough that you should be able to!"

"Yeah, but...why?" Eric asks.

"Just do it!" Emily screams at him.

Eric grasps the joystick and gently moves it toward him and to the left. The ship spins in answer to his moves, though much faster than he'd expected, so both he and Emily are whipped to the right.

"Do it better!" Emily yells miserably.

Eric puts the joystick back into the default position, stopping the spin. On the celestial sphere, Europa is now almost opposite to its original position. The ship had spun approximately 180 degrees.

"So now you have an idea of the sensitivity of the controls," Ms. Crana says. "Give it another try."

Eric moves the joystick again, directing it away and to the right, but with a far gentler pressure than earlier. The celestial sphere spins Europa toward alignment with the point as the ship itself spins on its center axis. After a few misses, he finally gets the grid to align close to the point. "Almost there," he says.

"Actually, that is quite good," Ms. Crana tells him encouragingly. "Your halo trainer has done an effective job. Now apply forward thrusters."

Eric pushes the joystick forward gently. Emily feels the backwards tug as the ship moves forward. From a distance, the station was a gleaming silvery ribbon. Up close, it's a haphazard collection of shiny boxes strewn across a landscape about 400 meters in width. Emily feels as if she could just as easily be flying over a moonlit suburban neighborhood in an airplane. There are no lights or windows visible anywhere across the surface of the station, so what detail she sees comes from the illumination provided by Jupiter.

"We're now going to have to roll the ship to align with the spin of the station," Ms. Crana says.

"The what?"

"The spin of the station creates a centrifugal effect equal to 1G," Ms. Crana explains. "That's the equivalent of Earth's gravity. Our approach vector brought us into a position that is counter to the spin of the station. We have to roll 180° to align the ship at a right angle to the axis of the spin; otherwise, we'll find ourselves upside down when we dock. Are you ready to perform the maneuver?"

"Uh...no," Eric answers.

"I believe you are," Ms. Crana responds. She begins manipulating the holographic controls projected in the cockpit. A vector grid perfectly overlays the view, accentuating the ring that is Caelestis. The overlay of Caelestis makes visible the parts of the station that, without the added visual, would otherwise be invisible behind the curve of Europa. She points to a tiny, subtly glowing dot that appears on the ring far behind the moon. "That's where we're docking," she explains. "You need to line up with the ring so that you're flying above and parallel to it."

Eric tilts his joystick and, after first overshooting the target then over-correcting, he begins to position the ship over the ring. As Emily feels the sideways pull of the ship beginning to roll, she leans into it and looks up through the cockpit window.

As they move, the ship begins to align vertically with the ring so that it becomes like a giant curved runway beneath them, the glowing dot sliding closer and closer to them. The landscape begins to arc up across and around the cockpit until it's suspended above, the unlit boxes dotting the upside-down horizon and rolling effortlessly over them. Emily sees that the dot projected on the cockpit window indicates the docking area is rapidly approaching. Once the roll is complete, she notices that she's beginning to feel heavy. Centrifugal force, she thinks, remembering what her father explained to her when she got stuck to the wall of the rotor ride at the amusement park. In fact, she's amazed she remembers that incident considering that she spent most of the ride concentrating on not throwing up, which she did anyway minutes after getting off it.

The dot projected onto the cockpit windshield morphs into a rather prominent rectangle, now clearly in front of the rolling horizon. Behind the glow of the projection, Emily can see the docking bay itself, a glowing white opening on the tip of a particularly tall and long outbuilding along the edge of the ring.

"Now position the arrow so that it aligns with the docking bay," Ms. Crana tells Eric. He moves the joystick until the arrow is centered over the glowing triangle. Once that happens, Ms. Crana waves her hand and the overlay grid disappears and the joystick arms slide back down to their original positions, giving Emily and Eric a full, unobstructed view of the station.

"Very nicely done," Ms. Crana tells Eric. "Now please excuse me for a moment." She spins and floats to the back of the ship, disappearing behind a service door.

"Where the hell is she going?" Emily says, panicked. "She's, she's...we're—!"

"Oh my God, we're going into the Death Star," Eric squeals breathlessly, interrupting Emily.

The ship slides effortlessly through the opening into a polished white hangar. The walls have the same fragile, plastic-y sheen as that of the ship itself. Ahead of them, opposite the hangar opening, a transparent wall separates the hangar from an entirely white control room in which three technicians sit. Behind the technicians, lined up shoulder to shoulder, are eight rather tall, wiry, and somewhat bald people, dressed in form-fitting light gray tunics, their arms clasped behind them. To a person they stand displaying the same grim demeanor, like a group of irritated parents displeased with the quality of boyfriend an errant daughter has brought home.

"Look at me," Ms. Crana says, suddenly appearing beside

them again. She gently grabs hold of Emily's chin and turns her head sideways. With her other hand, she touches her forefinger just behind Emily's ear.

Emily winces. "Ow! What the hell was that?"

"Just a small static shock," Ms. Crana says.

"Yeah, I felt it! But why?"

"The Prime Minister heads the debrief team," Ms. Crana says, a note of anxiety in her voice. She indicates a particularly reedy, aquiline, stern-looking woman with skin the texture of pale tree bark who stares inscrutably back at her. At them.

"What's that got to do with shocking me?" Emily asks, fingering a small lump behind her ear.

"Passengers are a violation of protocol," Ms. Crana explains. "Strictly speaking, you two are contraband." Ms. Crana pulls her gaze away from them and looks at Emily. "Be very careful about what you say. I'll explain later," Ms. Crana says.

"Of course you will," Emily says sarcastically. "Why start now?"

————

Ms. Crana pushes the airlock hatch open and finds herself face to face with a phalanx of unwelcoming bureaucrats lined up in a V shape, like bowling pins. At the apex, the Prime Minister stares inscrutably at Ms. Crana. Several moments of silence pass between them, and then Ms. Crana says suddenly: "I wonder if we might communicate verbally, Prime Minister. The children, I'm sure you understand, do not have the capacity for cyte transmission."

Another moment of silence passes, during which the woman's narrow eyes drift slowly over brother and sister, assessing them with all the dispassion of a haughty school marm. "I am unaccustomed to verbal communication," the Prime Minister finally says, her eyes falling back onto Ms. Crana. Her voice defies expectation; it is a lispy, slow, cottony drawl, as if her thick tongue can't quite roll correctly to form the necessary consonants for speech. "And I am not convinced that it is advisable to have the children present for this debrief."

This exchange is followed by yet another silence. Emily can't quite understand the scene playing out before her, but she does detect an underlying tension, as if the two women are locked in a passive-aggressive battle of wills. Of course, that could also be a projection of her own nerves...

"We shall determine that," the Prime Minister says suddenly. "Let us continue this debrief in my office."

"Will you allow the children to be present?"

The Prime Minister pauses and eyes the siblings. "As you wish." She turns on her heel and glides quickly back through the crowd. "But we will not verbalize," she conveys over her shoulder.

As their words fade from her consciousness, Emily realizes that though she heard them perfectly and clearly, she didn't actually notice either woman's lips move.

"Um...what just happened?" Eric asks.

"We are continuing the debrief in her office," Ms. Crana says, starting to herd the two teenagers toward the doors. "Come along." Ms. Crana directs her two unwilling passengers forward. As they step forward and pass through the phalanx of gray tunics, each person on either side of them turns on their heels and follows, maintaining the same V formation as they retreat from the hangar.

"Who are they?" Eric says.

"They are the Prime Minister's cabinet," Ms. Crana tells him.

"They're kinda creeping me out."

"Firstly, they can hear you," Ms. Crana says. "Secondly, you are 'creeping them out' as well."

"What did I do?" Eric asks.

They progress down a wide hallway, glaring white like everything else, but banded with more welcoming earth tones like beige, light gray, and peach. The walls seem like they're covered with microfiber cloth, capped with concave wainscoting that makes the low, paneled ceiling somehow less threatening. The floor is a single unbroken sheet of a strong, polished beige material—fiberglass perhaps?—that despite its toughness, seems to absorb their footfalls like a thin cushion.

Emily leans over to Eric and whispers: "Hey, did you hear either of them talking?"

"Who?" Eric asks.

"Ms. Crana and the Prime Minister lady. Just now, before we got off the ship."

"No. They just stared at each other, then the Prime Minister walked away."

"Okay, good," Emily says, relieved but not sure why.

"Good? Why good? What was that about?" Eric asks.

Emily shakes her head. "I have no idea."

As Emily absorbs her surroundings, she captures, in her peripheral vision, glimpses of the gray-suited people fanned out behind her. When she turns to glance at her companions they all, in turn, snap their heads forward from what was, she is sure, a curious examination of her. Moderately amused, she turns to look in the other direction and the men and women on that side snap their heads forward as well.

Except for one.

A striking man, absurdly thin like the rest, but with a smooth, velvety, equally-proportioned face, as if it had been manufactured. Unlike the others, he hides himself under the hood of his gray cloak. His wide eyes are of such piercing green that they seem to glow, though perhaps that is because they are such a contrast to the cloak hood. He stares unblinkingly at Emily with what she could only describe, dichotomously, as dispassionate curiosity. Neither his gaze nor his stance wavers for the entire march to…wherever.

'Ok, I'm sort of creeped out now, too,' she thinks.

Though they pass narrow, two-paneled doors that dot the walls at equidistant points, the group walks toward the wider doorway at the end of the hall. The room they enter is, not surprisingly, white. Emily had half expected to walk into a throne room, except that the room is considerably smaller—about 30 feet long and about as wide—and is furnished with nothing more than a single chair at the far end. At the first glimpse of the chair, her first thought—God help her—is that it looks like the captain's chair on the bridge of the U.S.S. Enterprise, though more skeletal, like a decked-out high-end ergonomic office chair. Then she realizes that she's seen it before, as twin seats in the cockpit of the ship.

Unlike the varied earth tones in the hallway, the room is a pure, brilliant white. There are no hard corners anywhere in the room, making it not only difficult to tell where floor, ceiling, and walls meet, but also to tell where the walls exactly are. Emily would be afraid to walk forward for fear of smacking her face, Eric-style, on an unnoticed wall, except for the spatial reference that the lone chair provided.

The Prime Minister takes the seat and bids Ms. Crana to come forward. Emily and Eric step forward as well, but Ms. Crana spins and thrusts her arm out to stop them. "This will not take long," she says. "Do not approach. Just stand in the corner and pay attention." She looks directly at Emily as she stresses the last two words.

Ms. Crana moves forward and is joined by the cabinet members, who fan out to form an arc around the Prime Minister. As soon as they're in position, their backs to Emily and Eric, a stillness falls over the room.

Suddenly, a deafening roar fills Emily's ear. She winces in pain, clasping her hands to her ears.

"What's the matter?" Eric asks her.

"Sssshh sshhhh!" She straightens up slowly and tentatively removes her hands from her ears and looks at Eric, a look of surprise crossing her face.

"What?" He asks again.

"Don't you hear that?" She whispers.

"Hear what?"

"Those voices?"

Eric raises an eyebrow. "You're hearing voices?"

"You don't hear them?"

"I don't hear any…"

"Wait wait!" She says, cutting him off. "I just heard our names." She waves a hand in his face to silence him, then closes her eyes and presses her hands against her ears. She hears voices, but they are indistinct and layered, like a strange brew of Emily's own inner voice mixed with an echo of other, foreign voices; a chorus of thoughts crowding in from her subconscious. She's able to understand words and phrases when only one person is 'speaking,' but it becomes impossibly cacophonous when more than one person tries to communicate at a time.

Her body tenses with concentration. Slowly, she finds she is able to sift through the layers and recognize distinct voices. Ms. Crana's is already familiar, though it is odd to hear her own voice threaded through Ms. Crana's words. The other voices she cannot recognize.

> "So you understand who they are."
>
> "I understand who you think they are."
>
> "With respect, Prime Minister, there is no question of their identities."
>
> "Correction. There is no question of their lineage. Of that I concede. As to their identities…we shall determine that."

"I think it's them," Emily whispers to Eric, subtly pointing at the group. "I think I can hear them."

"They're not saying anything," Eric points out dryly.

"I know, except…I think maybe they are."

> "Have the children been made aware of their link to this station?"
>
> "They are aware of who their parents are, yes."
>
> "And have you informed them of their alleged identities with respect to Prophecy?"
>
> "Not as yet, no."
>
> "And do you believe they are the two referred

to in Prophecy?"

"You're fully aware of my views of Prophecy. They have not altered."

"What are they saying?" Eric asks.
"Something about a prophecy."
"What prophecy?"
"Shhh! I don't know! Let me listen!"

"Did we detect a momentary failure of the time ship's proximity protocols?"
"It's possible."

Despite no words being spoken, the people nod and gesticulate as if in full conversation. Emily tries to sync the words she is hearing with the subtle body language of each person and deduce who is 'speaking.'

"The cataclysmic shockwave knocked all systems out and we were floating dead for a number of minutes. Portions of the system were still rebooting as we approached the station."
"I've never known a system to take 500 years to reboot."

Emily shakes her head. "I can hear them somehow, but they're not making any sense." She turns back to face the group, but is met by Ms. Crana, and the voices suddenly stop. "The Prime Minister would like to meet you officially," she says, ushering Emily and Eric forward. "Prime Minister, may I introduce Mr. Eric Clocke and Ms. Emily Clocke, children of Earth."

Emily and Eric both utter a shy "hello."

The Prime Minister nods imperiously. "Welcome to Caelestis station, children of Remnant."

———

The conversation with the Prime Minister and her council is brief and perfunctory. Eric and Emily learn nothing new of the where, what, how, and why of their presence or of the events that occurred to bring them there. Any questions they ask are deflected with promises of explanations at a later date. Ms. Crana affects a maternal, protective stance near Emily and Eric as they field questions from the council. Indeed, she acts as defense for some questions that they couldn't possibly answer without sufficient knowledge and context. Questions that only add to their own long list of questions.

As the conversation draws to a close, the man with the hood breaks quickly from the group and strides purposely toward Emily and Eric. "Commander Maren," he conveys to Ms. Crana, "Please introduce me." His conveyed 'voice' is as smooth and velvety as his skin.

"Deacon," Ms. Crana reluctantly complies, "this is Mr. Eric Clocke and Ms. Emily Clocke. Eric and Emily, this is Deacon, the Minister of Spiritual Affairs for Caelestis station."

"The Minister of Spiritual Affairs," Eric dictates back, making the statement a question. He uses all of his willpower to not rudely look away from the man's unnervingly perfect face.

"You are captivated by my appearance," Deacon conveys flatly. From anyone else the observation might come off as arrogant. From this man, however, it is merely fact. "That is understandable. Indeed, you must have many questions."

"Hello," Eric says dubiously, holding out his hand, completely unaware of Deacon's greeting.

Deacon looks at it with curiosity.

Emily opens her mouth to speak, but Ms. Crana intercedes before any words come out. There is an undercurrent of cold bitterness in her voice. "The children are not enhanced with aprocytes. As such, they cannot receive cyte transmissions. You of all people should understand that."

"Indeed," Deacon responds, looking away from Eric's outstretched hand. "An oversight born of exuberance. I'm sure you understand: this is a great day."

"For some," Ms. Crana says coolly.

"I am prepared." Deacon gestures behind him and a young man steps forward. About Eric's age, tall, narrow, with smooth skin the color of an autumn leaf but wearing a hooded cloak that marks him like Deacon, the young man stands before them with legs locked straight and hands cupped before him, as if part soldier, part butler. His head is slightly bowed, his eyes downcast, though whether this is the practiced humility of a servant or the trained reverence of a divinity student, Emily cannot tell.

"This is my acolyte," the young man says.

Emily and Eric cast furtive glances at each other. They have no idea what he means or how to respond.

"This young man is a student of Deacon's," Ms. Crana explains, "studying to be a First Disciple. He will act as translator."

"Hello," Eric says, holding out his hand.

The young acolyte looks at it with curiosity.

"Does anybody know how this works?" Eric says, examining his own hand.

"There is plenty of time to share cultural niceties," Ms. Crana continues. "The first thing is for you two to get some rest. We have prepared a room for you." She slides open the doors and steps aside, gesturing for Emily and Eric to exit.

"I beg pardon for my encroachment," the acolyte says, bowing. Next to him, Deacon bows as well.

"Your what?" Eric asks, but Ms. Crana gently pushes him into the hallway before anyone can answer.

As the group steps into the hallway, they see that both sides are lined with people. Unlike the council, the people before them are a variety of builds and a multitude of ages. Instead of the simple gray cloaks, they wear a rich tapestry of styles and colors, some vivid, some muted, some contrasted by the pale browns of their skin. A village stands before them, a culture. But it is a dissonant image: distinct individuals gathered into a crowd, but all in utter silence, and all with faces of respectful awe, like a colony of humbled puppies patiently awaiting recognition from their masters.

Ms. Crana prods Emily and Eric—who stare before them with barely concealed anxiety—to move. They begin to take tentative steps forward. As they walk, the people immediately to either side of them bow their heads and drop to one knee.

"Deacon," Ms. Crana says, "your encroachment may be unpardonable."

"I have no doubt it was necessary," he answers silkily.

He steps around Ms. Crana and maneuvers beside Emily. He stops and raises his hands high in grandiose reverence. The people before them drop to their knees and the people behind them follow suit, rippling in a wave down each line. She knows his next words were not given voice, but they reverberate through her ear nonetheless:

"Welcome to Caelestis, Saviors of Remnant!"

# :06 station

"The Remnant was violently cast out of the Motherland," Deacon preaches, "to wander through the cold, empty vastness of space for over 400 years before establishing a permanent home in the shadow of Jove! But Unification is promised! The Saviors of Remnant have been delivered!"

"What's he doing?" Eric asks.

"I don't know," Emily answers. "I don't understand what he means. What's 'unification?'"

"What are you talking about? Are you hearing voices again?"

Emily turns to look at Deacon and notices that indeed, though his oratory is booming, his arms are waving wildly, and his face is dramatically contorting with emotion, his mouth is not moving. Then she looks at his eyes and see tears streaming down his polished cheeks in thick rivulets. But his face betrays no fear or sadness. In fact, he is beyond happy; his entire being is permeated with ecstasy. They are tears of unadulterated joy.

"I guess I am," Emily concedes.

Ms. Crana scowls and pushes Emily and Eric forward, guiding them down the hallway, through the silent, reverent crowd. As the people gape at them, a mixture of fear and joy washing over them, Emily feels as if she is being paraded, though it is apparent that it isn't Ms. Crana's intention to do so. It is clear, however, that it is Deacon's, though she can't even begin to imagine why.

What's Unification? And what is Remnant?

More questions. More questions likely to go unanswered.

Emily is too stunned by the rows of nearly prostrated people to resume questioning Ms. Crana. She knows she wouldn't get answers anyway. Ms. Crana is purposely being cagey, pointedly redirecting the conversation every time a question is asked.

They walk for some time through twisting corridors that go from narrow to wide to narrow and take seemingly purposeless turns. Finally, Ms. Crana directs them to a set of double doors recessed into a small vestibule. As they come upon the entrance, Ms. Crana moves aside and gestures to Eric and Emily to proceed through. Eric takes the cue and BAM—smacks face first into the closed doors. He recoils, pressing his hands once again against his forehead.

Ms. Crana, stunned, looks him over. "Why did you do that?"

"Why did I do that? Why didn't the damned doors open?"

"Because you didn't open them." Ms. Crana places her hands into the recessed handles of each door and pulls them apart so that each half recedes into the respective sides of the wall.

"I thought they were supposed to open automatically!"

"Why would they do that?"

"To let people in, like on *Star Trek*."

"I do not know *Star Trek*."

"The doors open automatically on *Star Trek*. They go shhwweeesshh and open. Why don't they do that here?"

"Some doors do," Ms. Crana offers, "when there is a practical reason for them to do so, such as on the automated conveyor tubes or at the farming-module docks. Otherwise it would be impractical to require every door to open automatically. Unnecessary mechanisms increases the number of things that can malfunction, reducing the operational efficiency of this station. We are perfectly capable of opening doors ourselves."

Her lecture over, Ms. Crana steps into the room. Eric follows, and Emily follows him, a wicked grin forming on her face. "Nice job, Captain Kirk."

"Shut up!" Eric snaps.

It is a sparse, narrow room, which comes as no surprise to Emily. Nor is it a surprise that it is overly white and almost blindingly clean. Despite this, it has a rather military feel, with two stacked bunks recessed into the wall and two tall, narrow lockers recessed side by side into the opposite wall. It reminds Emily of the bunk rooms on the aircraft carrier that she'd toured on her fifth-grade field trip. This room is equally spare, equally utilitarian, but slightly more inviting. Shiny white plastic rather than cold gunmetal iron.

"What is this?" She asks.

"Your quarters for the night," Ms. Crana answers.

"We're going to live here?" Eric asks incredulously.

"For the night, yes." Ms. Crana reiterates. "You will be given permanent, separate quarters adjacent to mine, but for the night you will be perfectly comfortable here."

"No, no, no!" Emily says, angrily waving a finger at Ms. Crana. "I want to know what all that was! All that bowing and that Deacon guy! And what the hell we're doing here! You promised us you'd explain everything!"

"Indeed I did," Ms. Crana says coolly. "And I shall. However, you are depleted. In your present state you do not have cognitive capacity to process the amount of expository information required to paint a complete picture of your situation. You must rest. When you have slept and are appropriately rejuvenated, I will continue explanations. Not—"

"We've been asleep for 525 years!" Emily interjects. "We're not tired!"

"I'm a little tired," Eric adds incidentally.

Ms. Crana makes a show of thinking it over then strides fully into the room. She gestures to the lower bunk. "Sit. Both of you."

Emily and Eric do as they're told.

"It is against my better judgment to do so, but I will tell you what is most relevant at the moment, nothing more. Do you understand?"

They both shrug.

"There is a lot you need to understand, and it will not serve you to be given all of the information all at once. You do not, as I believe the adage goes, quench a thirst with a fire hose.

"The scholars—and preachers—call us, our culture, the Remnant. To the best of our knowledge, we are the sole remaining members of the human race. We have no knowledge of how the Remnant came to be. Our history was lost at some indeterminate time in the past—our past, not yours—as the result of a systemic virus or some event that completely wiped out the station's data. Thus, what I am about to tell you is little more than a mix of myth, legend, theory, and educated conjecture based on our research. It is, in short, unreliable and open to interpretation. But what has otherwise been codified into record is that at some time in the past—again, your era's future—a group of pioneers would colonize a space station, break from Earth's orbit by some unknown means, and spend some number of years drifting outward until being captured by the gravitational pull of Jupiter. Then by some means, also unknown, the station would settle into an orbit around Europa."

"But I guess I still don't understand where the station came from." Emily says. "I mean, there was no station like this built 500 years ago. Just the International Space Station. And if the Earth was just destroyed—"

"To be clear, the Earth was not destroyed," Ms. Crana explains.

Emily and Eric perk up at this statement, their faces suddenly expectant.

Ms. Crana continues: "It is still where it should be. It is, however, devoid of life."

They both exhale, crestfallen again.

"Nonetheless," Ms. Crana says, "you broach an important

point. One of the enigmas we're tasked with solving is: where did the Remnant originate, and how did we get here?"

"Who's 'we?'" Eric asks, confused. "Us? Me and Emily?"

"No," Ms. Crana says. "Your mother, father, and I. And misters Algate and Verton. And three others. We are what are called chronographers. Historians, you could say. Historical anthropologists. We are members of a corps of researchers that travel from our era back to various points in Earth's history to collect as much intelligence as possible so that we can recreate the records of both human history and our own culture's specific history. The history of Caelestis, of how it came to be, what its purpose is, what it was intended to be and to become...

"Our population apparently included enough technical and scientific expertise to recover and rebuild the systems and sustain the station, but all of the historical records were completely eliminated. We are trying to rebuild the knowledge of our past so we can understand where and how we came to be, as well as determine when and how our records were erased."

"And how Earth was destroyed," Emily says dully. "Or whatever."

"Yes...well—" Ms. Crana sighs, not knowing what else to say to that.

"Guess we know now," Eric says to fill the silence.

"So...our mother was a historian?" Emily asks. "A time traveler?"

"And your father, yes."

"Why didn't they ever tell us?"

"I hypothesize that they did not know," Ms. Crana answers.

"How...huh?" Emily and Eric reply in unison. Then Emily continues, "How could they not know something like that?"

"When your mother and I met at the fuel terminal several weeks ago—excuse me—gas. Gas station!—when we met at the gas station, she did not recognize me. I deduce that she didn't actually know who she was. Our aprocytes are programmed to calibrate our speech and behavior patterns—"

"Wait, your what?" Eric asks.

"Aprocytes. Artificial progenitor cells," Ms. Crana says as if it were common knowledge.

Eric shrugs melodramatically. 'And that is supposed to make sense to me how?' he thinks.

"Aprocytes," Ms. Crana explains, "are artificial robotic progenitor cells that can differentiate on command into any cell type necessary in a particular circumstance. They enhance the natural functions of the human body and can, among other things, give us nearly five times our normal strength, swiftly repair all but the most severe physical damage, and retrieve and process information stored in external electronic data repositories."

"That's how you stopped the bullets!" Eric shrieks excitedly.

"That is partially correct," Ms. Crana says. "My aprocytes signaled to my epicytes to create a countermeasure shield which neutralized the bullets before they could contact my skin."

"What are epicytes?" Eric asks, now getting a little flustered by all the new information.

"Never mind!" Emily says impatiently, then pointedly asks Ms. Crana, "So what does that have to do with our parents forgetting that they're time travelers?"

"When we reach a destination," Ms. Crana explains, "the first thing we do is to scan for broadcasts, conversations, or anything that can provide a thorough indication of local cultural norms. Our ship's knowledge base analyzes the data, constructs an ethnological model, then transmits that model to our aprocytes, allowing us to instantly adopt the language, speech patterns, sociopolitical sensibilities, and behaviors of our location. We can instantly assimilate into any given culture and adopt appropriate and plausible identities. And depending upon the technological level of the era, we can create and plant false records of our identities in the various bureaucratic systems to provide us with a traceable history.

"For instance, on Caelestis we do not have surnames. My actual name is Maren. However, while on Earth, I was able to create a full identity and traceable electronic records indicating that my name was Maren Galilea Crana. With that I obtained all of the credentials required to drive, vote, and perform other legal functions in your society."

"Then why were you arrested for not having a teaching license?" Emily asks.

"Our false identities are thorough but nonetheless imperfect. Indeed, for the duration of our stay in any era, we endeavor to avoid any actions that may bring undue scrutiny of our backgrounds, such as becoming teachers. In this instance, however, I found adopting that profession to be a necessary risk. Unfortunately, certain details of my teaching license appear to have triggered a more thorough background check than what was initially done, and those details were found to be falsified. As a result, other aspects of my identity were determined to be false as well.

"Which brings me to my original point: on occasion, when we arrive at a destination, our aprocytes are unable to calibrate to the cultural standards, so all of our assimilation techniques fail, and we become like chameleons unable to change colors. I posit that something similar may have happened to your mother and father, only with an inverse effect. Instead of the aprocytes switching the assumed identities off, they instead embedded those identities into your parents' consciousness. Their actual identities were suppressed and they knew themselves only as their assumed personalities."

"So...I'm not getting any of this," Emily says, trying to steer the conversation back to things she hopes she'll understand. "What does any of that have to do with all this 'unification' and savior stuff?"

"Actually, what's with Deacon in general?" Eric adds. "That guy is weird."

Ms. Crana raises her eyebrows, clearly wishing she didn't have to pursue those questions. "Our society is governed by a social covenant deeply rooted in Testament, the codified words believed to be those of the founder—or founders—of Caelestis."

"You mean like the Bible?" Eric asks.

"Similar to your Bible, yes. And your Quran, and any of the sacred canonical texts that are foundational to spiritual faith. Many of these texts contain folkloric tales of a savior—one who will guide or deliver an errant society to salvation. In this regard, Testament is no different. One of its central tenets involves the introduction of a savior, or saviors, that will help reunite the Remnant with the lost progenitor race."

"What's the progenitor race?" Eric asks.

"You, essentially," Ms. Crana answers. "The human race. The originators of Caelestis."

"So why don't you all just go back in time and reunite, then?" Eric asks. "Problem solved."

"Or problem created. That may be the catalyst that ultimately destroys humanity and creates the Remnant."

"But we know what destroyed Earth—er, humanity—we just lived through it."

"Perhaps. But where is Remnant?"

"Okay, I think you were right," Emily announces. "This is a bit much."

"Indeed. I will leave you to get settled now. I will come to collect you in the morning." With that Ms. Crana stands and marches unceremoniously to the door. "Say goodnight to Vocks," she says, then shuts the door gently behind her.

Emily and Eric stand there, mouths agape, their minds a flurry of frustrated anxiety.

Then Eric blinks. "What's Vocks?"

———

*It is one hundred fifty-one minutes past the night cycle, Ms. Emily Clocke,* a shrill, oddly familiar voice screams in Emily's ear. It jolts her awake, and she shoots up into a sitting position, nearly banging her head on the underside of the top bunk. Her body suddenly feels constricted, as if she has somehow been mummified.

After a moment, her senses return, and she realises that the constriction is, in fact, her blanket, which had probably wrapped itself around her as she flailed blindly upon being startled awake.

By that voice.

That familiar voice that sounded...not unlike herself.

"Who's there?" Emily asks into the darkness, but there is no answer. Her startled drowsiness makes her heart thump noticeably in her chest. Her breath is labored and uncomfortable. "Who's there?" she asks again. "Ms. Crana?"

"There's nobody there," Eric's drowsy voice responds from somewhere above her. Though he claimed the top bunk, the acoustics of the room make it sound like his voice is coming from somewhere across from her. "You were talking in your sleep."

"I was?"

"Yeah. You were talking in that twittery, moan-y sleep voice. You said 'goodnight, Vocks' and then kinda screamed and asked who was there."

"Goodnight, Vocks?" Emily asks.

*It is one hundred fifty-two minutes past the night cycle, Ms. Emily Clocke,* the loud voice says again.

"What the hell is that?' Emily asks.

"What is what?" Eric counters.

"That voice. It said 'it is one hundred something minutes past...whatever, Ms. Emily Clocke' really loudly."

"You're hearing the voices again?"

Emily touches behind her right ear and feels the thin disk that Ms. Crana had attached earlier. "Well it's...yeah...it's the same voice," Emily says. "I think it's the thing behind my ear."

"Tell it to shut up. I'm trying to sleep."

"Vocks, shut up," Emily says.

*Please clarify directive.*

"Shut up."

"I didn't say anything," Eric responds.

"Not you," Emily says, "Vocks!"

*I am at your service, Ms. Emily Clocke.*

"Shut up."

"What'd it say?" Eric asks.

"Shut up!" Emily says.

"Is that what it said or what...?"

"Shhh! How do I address you?" Emily asks.

There is silence for a moment until Eric's perplexed voice cuts through it. "Who, me?" he asks.

"Not you!" Emily says to Eric. "Vocks!"

*I am at your service, Ms. Emily Clocke.*

"Vocks what?" Eric asks at the same time.

"Shut up!" Emily says again.

"Who, me?" Eric asks again.

"Yes, you!" Emily answers.

"Me Eric?"

"Yes, you Eric! Shut up! I'm trying to talk to Vocks!"

*You have but to ask a question, and I shall endeavor to answer it to the best of my ability.*

"What are you?" Emily asks, but is again met by silence.

"What'd it say?" Eric asks after a moment.

"Nothing," Emily says.

"Are you talking to me?" Eric asks.

"Oh for...! Don't start that again. Yes, I'm talking to you... Eric! It didn't say anything."

"Maybe it thinks you're talking to me."

"Because I am talking to you! Oh wait..." Emily stops to consider Eric's comment. Perhaps it wasn't another dig at the 'who's on first routine.' Maybe it was an actual insight. "Vocks!" she announces, then lets it float out there for a minute.

*I am at your service, Ms. Emily Clocke.*

"Is that how I speak to you?" Emily asks, chagrined when she's met by silence yet again. "Vocks, is that how I speak to you?"

*I do not understand your question, Ms. Emily Clocke.*

"Stop calling me Ms. Emily Clocke." Silence again. "Vocks, stop calling me Ms. Emily Clocke."

*As you wish. Is there another appellation by which you prefer to be addressed?*

"Another what?" Emily asks, but is glad to be met by silence. "Vocks, what are you?"

*I am your personal assistant.*

"How do you work? Eh, I've got to get used to that. Vocks, how do you work?"

"Please refine and specify your query."

"How do you...Vocks, how do you...get your information? How do I hear other conversations through you?"

*I retrieve information from the Caelestis station knowledge interchange and relay it to this unit, which makes it audible by means of bone conduction. I can also relay external conversations via the same means, provided at least one of the parties involved cytecasts the conversation.*

"What is cyte...Vocks, what does cytecaste mean?"

"What is that, like Simon says?" Eric comments.

Emily shushes him before Vocks answers.

*Cytecasting is the broadcasting of conversations between two or more citizens via aprocyte relays at a frequency range of 2.4-2.5 gigahertz. While this inhibits...*

"It's like wifi beaming the internet straight to my head," Emily says. Met with silence, she calls out, "Eric!"

"Yes, what?" Eric's startled, disembodied voice answers.

"Were you sleeping?"

"I was just...yes," Eric says defensively.

"This thing is basically beaming the internet straight into my head."

"Why didn't I get one?"

"I don't know. Ms. Crana just popped it on my neck right before we got off the ship. She must have wanted me to hear the council. But you can ask it stuff and it just taps into the station's database."

"Like Siri."

"Pretty much, yeah. Are you tired?"

"Yes and no. What time is it?"

"Vocks, what time is it?"

*It is one hundred fifty-six minutes past the night cycle.*

"What does that mean?" Emily asks.

"What does what mean?" Eric asks her.

"Okay, can we not go there again? Vocks, what does one hundred fifty-six minutes past the night period mean?"

*Caelestis station is broken down into two light cycles which loosely mimic Earth's day-night cycles. The light cycle consists of a two-hour drawing up period followed by a ten-hour cycle of full light followed by a three-hour drawing down period. The night cycle consists of nine hours of semi-darkness. It is currently one hundred fifty-seven minutes past the night cycle, or ninety-seven minutes past the conclusion of the drawing up cycle.*

"What did it say?" Eric asks.

"It's morning. At least I think that's what it said. Vocks, how long have we been asleep?"

*Eleven hours thirty-two minutes.*

"Geez!"

"What?"

"We've been asleep for eleven and a half hours!"

"Give or take a couple hundred years," Eric comments wryly.

"So what do we do now?"

"I thought Ms. Crana was supposed to come get us."

"Me too," Emily says, then adds mischievously, "Wanna go for a walk?"

———

Emily and Eric emerge from their room into a wall of silent people. In an instant, the horde animates, forming, with eerie, orderly precision, a small arc around them, blocking off the rest of the corridor. Rows and rows of expectant faces gaze at them, eyes smiling rapturously, mouths open into beatific caverns. Tears run jagged rivers down some pale, lined cheeks.

Emily and Eric are struck speechless, a reaction that is becoming annoyingly common of late. Within seconds, a murmur rises slowly from the silence, a susurration of staticky, breathy voices reverently chanting the words "saviors" and "unification" and "deliver us," lapping and overlapping them until they become nothing but a scraping white noise ringing in Emily's head.

To Eric, they are silent movie zombies. "What are you doing?" he asks them, trying to stifle a growing panic as they tighten in around him and his sister.

"Part!" Emily hears a light but forceful voice yell. She's certain Eric doesn't. At the sound, the arc of people parts in half with eerie, mechanical precision, revealing Deacon's young acolyte.

"They are guests!" he conveys, spreading his arms out in welcome. The people recede slightly as if chastised, but mill about, affecting nonchalant poses that do nothing to mask their intent to listen in. With an annoyed huff, the acolyte says, "Disperse!"

The crowd slowly and haphazardly breaks off into groups that retreat down the corridor in either direction.

The acolyte approaches Emily, head bowed, eyes cast downward, his robes dripping off his impossibly thin frame like black waterfalls. The hood of his cloak is pulled back and resting atop his head like a black rooster's comb, providing Emily with a view of his golden brown eyes. Bright and full of youthful curiosity, they glow of their own accord, not lit by artificial power. Unlike Deacon, his coffee skin is marbled with the minute imperfections of real skin, but is otherwise free of any type of blemish or follicle.

But Emily can't tell what they see when they look at her.

"I have come to escort you to your new quarters."

"I thought Ms. Crana was coming."

The acolyte puzzles over this information. "I do not know Ms. Crana," he finally admits.

"What do you mean you don't know Ms. Crana?" Emily

says, "You saw her yesterday. She's the one who brought us here!"

"Ah, Maren," the acolyte acknowledges. "Yes. Forgiveness. I did not initially recognize her by her mission alias. Unfortunately, she was detained and unable to call on you at the designated hour. I was asked to escort you in her stead."

"Can we get breakfast somewhere?" Eric asks. "I'm starving."

"Sustenance can be arranged, yes."

"Then lead on, brother!"

———

They are in a monorail car, gliding so effortlessly that the only way Emily and Eric even know they're moving is that the stanchions of the tunnel they're traveling through appear as a gray whirlwind outside the windows. The tunnel itself is virtually transparent, looking out upon—depending upon where you look—outer space, Jupiter, and the icy scars of the moon above them. Eric, who is slack-jawed at the sight, predictably remarks on their transport's similarity to a certain people mover at a certain California amusement park. "Except Disneyland doesn't have a view of Jupiter." Then, thinking a moment, he adds, "*Didn't* have a view of Jupiter, I guess."

Passing support beams give their ride an occasional strobe, and when Eric lets his surroundings fade to his peripheral vision, he can almost imagine he's riding through town on a California school bus, the early morning sun punctured occasionally by the shadow of a streetlight or telephone pole. But when he catches himself drifting there, he looks out into the eye of the mighty red storm and pulls himself back to now. Best not to go back. They are here now. This is home. There is no bus, no California. And the early morning sun is Jupiter...or artificial.

"Do you guys do crepes?" Eric asks.

"Crepes? Forgiveness. I do not know crepes," the acolyte says.

"Crepes. You know, like really thin pancakes. And you fill them with melted chocolate."

The acolyte hesitates in responding. Eric registers minute facial expressions that lead him to a depressing conclusion: "Oh god! You don't know chocolate?"

"Yes!" The acolyte's face lights up, suddenly happy that he can please Eric. "I do know chocolate! The cocoa bean, while not a staple crop, is placed into rotation on special occasions. I'm sure your arrival will be considered as such. Regrets, however, that I do not know crepes."

"I guess I'll just have to teach you how to make them."

"That would be pleasant. Any artifact from your culture that is currently unknown would be welcomed on Caelestis."

"Yeah, I'd love to see that," Emily taunts. "He has no idea how to make pancakes unless it's already mixed in a squirt bottle."

"Shut up," Eric say dismissively. He turns suddenly to the acolyte with a sense of urgency. "Hey, what's your name, anyway?"

"Brin," the acolyte says.

"Brin what?"

"Just Brin," Brin says.

"Pleasure to meet you, Brin," Eric says breezily, "I'm Eric." He holds out his right hand.

Emily rolls her eyes. Where did this Eric come from?

"Yes," Brin says, "I am aware of your designation, Mr. Clocke." Brin says this earnestly with no trace of irony.

"Oh jeez, don't call me Mr. Clocke! It's Eric!" He pushes his hand forward a bit, reminding Brin that it's still there.

"Why do you hold your hand out at such an angle?" Brin asks.

"So you can shake it," Eric answers.

"Shake it?"

"It's a customary greeting," Emily interjects.

Eric reaches out with his left hand, grabs Brin's right hand, places it into his own right hand, then shakes it.

"I can't believe you guys don't know shaking hands," Eric says, shaking his head.

"Information is not distributed equally," Brin explains. "If the customs of your period were not entered into the knowledge interchange or were registered as classified or faith sensitive, it would not be disseminated to me."

Eric nods, neither understanding nor really caring to pursue the conversation further.

The breezy blur of support stanchions suddenly gives way to darkness, the dull peach glow of Jupiter is snuffed out as they enter some sort of access tunnel. Before them, another glow begins to define the walls, whiter, livelier, crawling toward them as they move toward it, then...

Whoosh!

They are floating over a city. A stretched, gleaming patchwork of chrome and glass and white towers, unsullied green-blanket parks, and immaculate rowhouses. The rowhouses run the entire length of the city and are stacked asymmetrically against either side, sloping upward from the ground floor, creating the appearance of a channel made of jagged cliff walls, within which sits the rest of the city.

The city itself flows organically, threaded together by meandering ribbons of water and narrow, tree-lined alleys thrown down like pick-up-sticks, as if Frank Lloyd Wright had turned Falling Water into the cliff dwellings of Mesa Verde. It is a meld of polished urbanity and contented suburbanity; an artist's depiction of planned randomness in crisp lines and bold colors, sunnily lit by rows of blindingly bright lights that hang from the transparent ceiling.

"Wow," Emily says under her breath. She finally allows herself to be awestruck.

She is transfixed by the way the landscape rolls and bobs beneath them, as if the town were built upon a long stretch of wrinkled carpeting. Tiny birds (birds!), the species of which is unfamiliar to her, flit from tree to tree, and some fly parallel to their monorail car, flapping their wings in welcome, then zooming away to alight on motionless branches and the roofs of nearby buildings. People dot the landscape, walking and laboring amongst the tableau, going about their business with purpose and determination. A few people recline in the open park areas, some grouped around large gazebos that are perfectly centered to allow for congregating. Emily wonders at the possibility that the gazebos are meant for concerts, like the ones she attended with her mom and dad on some Sunday evenings back in California. She grows wistful at the thought, but not maudlin, still taken in by the idyllic nature of the landscape below them.

"Is this where we'll live?" Eric asks, barely filtering the hope from his voice.

"Not this habitat, no," Brin says, "but one like it."

"You mean there's more?"

"This is one of eighteen habitation modules. There are…"

"Eighteen!?" Eric blurts out in disbelief, interrupting Brin. "There are eighteen of these things?"

"Eighteen, yes," Brin says. "With two more under construction. Each with a similar urban plan, each containing an average of five thousand residents. The station also consists of eight agricultural modules, four waste treatment modules, four water filtration and reclamation modules, three manufacturing modules, two engineering modules, two medical modules…"

"Yeah, I get it," Eric interrupts again. "It's huge."

"Only 60 percent of the station is currently in use, but current projections indicate that we'll reach capacity within 50 years. After that, life will become unsustainable without implementing austerity and population control measures. That's why unification is so important."

Emily searches Brin's face for more information.

"That's why you're so important," he says.

She turns from him to look out the window again. "I'm not sure I see my importance here," she says to herself.

Out the window, she sees that many of the people below them have suddenly stopped their activities and are turning toward their soaring monorail. They stand at loose attention, heads bowed, very similar to the manner in which…

She looks up at the acolyte. He too is standing at loose attention, head bowed. Emily shifts to the other side of the monorail. The people on that side are the same. Not all, but most.

"What are they doing?" Emily asks. She looks to Brin for explanation. "Why were those people outside our room doing that?" Threads of disparate conversations begin to weave together in her head. "The unifiers," she mumbles to herself, remembering Deacon's words from when they'd first arrived. "What does all that mean? The Saviors of Remnant?"

"You will receive an explanation shortly," Brin says cryptically.

The monorail begins descending in a wide loop, arcing around a central tower that rises imperiously in the center of the habitat module. It reaches up the entire 20 story height of the module, a thin silver spire tapering to a wider base, touching the ceiling with the tip of its finger. It is, from what Emily can see, the tallest building in the module.

At the 180 position of the loop, they notice that the track terminates into a transportation hub that bears a resemblance to a late nineteenth-century train station, built of rough-hewn beige limestone and paved with sienna cobblestone bricks. A track emerges from the other end of the station, arcing up and back around, continuing on in their original direction of travel, traversing the other end of the station.

As they slide into the station, Eric remarks, "This looks just like…" He leaves the remainder unsaid: the train station back home.

They exit the monorail and take a slight ramp down to a wide walkway, which continues the cobblestone paving. Meter-high gray brick walls line either side of the walkway, holding back trees and lush vegetation. Dried rainbow colored leaves rustle past their feet, swept along by the slight autumn morning breeze.

"Um…" Eric says and leaves it hanging for a moment, his face scrunched up as if his mind is processing a huge thought.

120

He points absently down at the sidewalk. "Why are there leaves on the ground...and why do I feel a breeze?"

"The station's life support systems mimic Earth's orbital and rotational periods in order to maintain physiological equilibrium. Though humans are quite adaptable, hundreds of thousands of years of acclimation to Earth's circadian and perennial patterns cannot be completely reoriented within a few dozen generations, thus the lighting systems maintain a 24 hour day and the environmental conditioning units mimic the seasonal changes of a 365 day year, as if measured in a stable, temperate environment."

Eric shrugs. "Why do I always ask questions when I know I won't understand the answers?"

"The breeze you feel," Brin continues, "is caused by a combination of the environmental conditioning units and the minute air movements generated by everyday activities. The living modules are large enough that they actually have their own microclimates. Indeed, the environmental conditioning units do as much to regulate the natural climates as they do to actually influence them."

The pathway they are on widens and eventually opens to overlook a broad, grassy area ringing the wide base of the spire. The entire area is perfectly manicured, utterly pristine and picture perfect, as if Norman Rockwell had only just put the finishing touches to a vibrant, photo-realistic painting of his ideal future.

Eric takes it all in with guarded awe, a tincture of hope invading his newly acquired vigilance. A number of people meander around the area, engaged in various activities. Both Emily and Eric look at them warily. To their surprise, each person shows uniqueness, a definite sense of individuality expressed in a wide variety of wardrobe styles, which offset the much narrower range of physical distinctions. Sizes and shapes vary from tall to slightly less tall, lithe to strapping. Short and stout appear to be in short supply. So too is there little in the way of skin variation, with each person being a shade of watery coffee. Their faces maintain certain racial and regional traits from Emily's Earth, but are otherwise eerily smooth and blemish-free, not a trace of acne, freckles, or moles.

But what is most unique is that there is no fawning, no servile bowing, no overwrought crowd surrounding them. Instead, as soon as Emily and Eric emerge from the pathway into the open area, the people turn as one to look upon them with an immediate, intense, but not unfriendly curiosity, then almost as immediately regain control of their senses and turn back to go about their business, as if having been castigated for peeking at something they shouldn't.

"They seem friendly enough, at least," Eric says, not sure if he's being sarcastic or not. "Well, now they do, anyway."

"Yes. You'll forgive their inquisitiveness. It is an expected reaction to such visitors as you."

They continue on along a path that meanders around the spire, bright and clean and pleasant, encountering more people, themselves bright and clean and pleasant, if not a little awestruck. Their glances are surreptitious and inquisitive, but they remain distant and respectful.

It does not make Emily and Eric any less wary. They don't so much feel like animals on display as animals on parade.

They walk across small, sturdy wooden bridges that look like they were just built over streams that were just channeled. There are people walking dogs, people sitting on small patios in front of their living units stroking cats that sit upon their laps. Birds flit happily from tree to tree. A pleasant stroll through a pleasant park in a small pleasant town on a pleasant autumn day.

Yet Emily feels none of the pleasantness. She looks at Eric and sees in his face—in the unconscious, coiled tension of his frame and the cautious gait—a mixture of excitement and anxiety.

Emily wonders at Eric's variability. One moment he was enraged by his inability to understand the very things happening before him, the next he's cracking jokes and staring in wonder at every new sci-fi marvel within view. But then, she realizes, that's her lot too. She hasn't had a moment to process what is happening to her since she was stunned and dragged aboard the spaceship in the lot behind her school.

The invisible spaceship.

That brought her 500 years into the future.

To a giant ring space station orbiting a moon of Jupiter.

Because these things are coming so fast, they can only deal with things as they come. Maybe Ms. Crana was right. Maybe it is too much to process at once. Maybe she should have just stayed in her room and slept and wondered and taken things slowly. Maybe...

Emily notices that the path they're on is drawing closer to the spire. As they round to the point where the path meets the base, she sees a short, wide entranceway leading into the structure. They enter and pass through a long, sterile, but brightly lit tunnel.

They emerge from the tunnel into a large, circular room; bright and immaculate, painted bright gold by the faux sunlight streaming in from outside the structure. The polished granite floor is inlaid with pale tiles that form concentric circles, the outermost of which is ringed by tall decorative arches that reach up about four stories to support an intricate ring which appears to be a representation of the station itself. Through the ring the entire inside of the spire is visible, tapering upward into an elongated cone at the distant top point. In all, the room has the appearance of the nave of a lively baroque church or the rotunda of a state capitol building.

"What's going on?" Emily asks, startled. "Where are we?"

"Where's Ms. Crana?" Eric adds.

"She is detained, as I explained previously," Brin says, moving behind them.

It's only then that they notice the imperious, shadowy figure approaching them.

"It is a rare privilege," Deacon conveys, gesticulating wildly, "that outsiders get to visit a sacellum.

123

He bows fawningly, then straightens and holds his arms outward. "Of course," he conveys, "you are no ordinary outsiders."

The he takes a single step backward and begins floating.

Like a dark angel.

# :07 prophecy

Emily hears her name.

"Emily."

She whips around to see...nothing. She scans all around her and cannot see the person whose ethereal voice bounced through her head. "Where is she?" she asks out loud.

"Where is who?" Eric responds.

"Ms. Crana."

"Emily, do not be frightened," Ms. Crana conveys.

"Where are you?" Emily asks.

"I'm right...Oh come on, really?" Eric says, recognizing that he's being cut out of the conversation yet again. "The guy is floating and I don't get to hear why?"

"Emily," Ms. Crana conveys to Emily, "attend to your brother. Step away from Deacon so that you can speak for both of us."

"Um...Deacon is floating at the moment!"

"He's on the ascension point. He's going to the sacellum. Where is Brin?"

"Right next to me."

"Follow Brin's direction and do exactly as he says. You will not be harmed.."

"Can you clue me in?' Eric asks impatiently. "What are we talking about? Where are we?"

"The sacellum," Brin says, "A place of reflection and meditation. Open only to those who have devoted their lives to preserving the Word and the words. It is my favorite place."

"So how come we get to go?" Eric asks.

"You are the Word," Brin answers.

"Might as well just keep talking to myself," Eric says. He turns to Emily. "So where is she?"

"Where are you?" Emily asks Ms. Crana. "Are you not coming?"

"I am not. I am not invited. The sacellum is for keepers of the words and the Word."

"But I'm not…"

"But you are. Invited."

"Why do you say that like it's a bad thing?" Emily squints, then looks up at Deacon, ascending even higher. "None of this makes any sense. It's not wrong to want to know what's happening."

"I agree."

"Then why are you treating me like I'm the bad guy?"

"I too am navigating new territory," she says with an air of apology. "And none of it makes sense. Do as Brin says."

"What do we do?" Eric asks her.

"I don't get her." Emily shakes her head and looks at Brin. "What do we do?"

"Step onto the ascension point," Brin replies.

"Which is?"

"The innermost circle."

Emily looks at the floor. She follows the concentric circles to the innermost circle and realizes that Deacon had stepped backward into it. "Why?' she asks.

"It will take you to the sacellum. There you will know the Word."

Emily looks into Brin's eyes. "I'm supposed to trust you," she tells him, learning at once that the practice of trying to read truth in someone's eyes is complete bunk.

"By Maren?"

"By...Crana, yes. I was told to trust her too."

"And do you?" Brin asks.

"Vocks," Emily says, not taking her eyes off Brin, "what is the ascension point?"

*It is an inverse gravitation column that suppresses the centrifugal effect of the station's spin. It allows the gravitational pull of Europa to guide you up to the sacellum, which is at the spire of the cathedral.*

"Is it safe?"

*Perfectly.*

"What'd it say?" Eric asks.

"It's apparently safe."

"It is safe, provided you remain steady and relatively motionless," Brin says.

Eric steps to the edge of the circle and studies it. He looks back at Brin for reassurance, finds none. "I ask for crepes, I get indoor skydiving." He steps forward and instantly begins floating. "Holy crap! Okay! Okay!" he yells, panicked at first. "Okay! Okay, this is...this is actually kinda cool!"

When he's about five meters up, Emily steps forward. Mirroring Eric's approach she looks first at the circle and then at Brin. "I have to float...all the way up there!?" She looks up at the top of the cathedral. Deacon is just a dot, a dark star burning on the bright ceiling.

"Relatively motionless," she says wryly. She steps forward and suddenly feels as though her center of gravity has shifted, as if she were suddenly falling...upward. It's a completely different sensation than the weightlessness she experienced on the ship. She doesn't feel the instinctive jolt of panic that accompanies a fall, nor the need to reorient herself to a landing position. Instead of the absence of gravity, it's the presence of opposing gravities of nearly equal strength.

She peeks down to see Brin step into the circle below her and begin to rise. She checks her progress and looks up to see Eric, about 4 stories above her, rigidly straight with his arms pressed to his sides. She feels a freedom in the distance between them. She makes the sudden decision to enjoy the experience. She lifts her head as if to bask in sunlight and raises her arms.

"Don't…!" she hears from beneath her.

The weight of her right hand pulls on her and she inexplicably finds herself falling. Not falling up, and not with control, but headfirst, downward, with the full force of gravity and the accompanying involuntary frenzy. And then she finds herself rolling end over end, a 180 degree roll punctuated by a vice-clamp to her right wrist and knife-like jolt in that shoulder.

And then she's dangling, her descent slowed but not arrested.

With surprising ease, Brin reaches down and grabs her left wrist—the one he doesn't already have in his grasp—and pulls her up to him, face to face. "Hold on," he says, and wraps her arms around his neck. They descend slowly for a few moments and then their descent stops.

"Forgiveness, Ms. Clocke," he says as Emily, craning her neck back to prevent her face from touching his, nonetheless blushes. "In explaining the safety of the gravitational columns, I had not considered your inability to see its boundaries. The slightest breach of its confines can alter the balance of forces and pull you back into the gravity of the station."

"Good to know," she says, her voice a mix of irony and annoyance.

"Are you ready?"

"For what?" Emily asks. She gets her answer not from Brin but from the fact that the ground begins to slowly drop from them again.

Emily looks up, concerned that Eric may suffer her mistake, but he is nowhere to be seen. "Where'd he go?" she says, then looks down and scans the ground in a fit of panic.

"Mr. Clocke has successfully reached the sacellum."

"Thank god," she says. Then, after an uncomfortably long silence, "Um…can I let go now?"

"Do you wish to?"

She peeks over his shoulder and sees that they are passing

through the ring. The ground is now about five stories beneath them. "No!" she says and, despite herself, tightens her hold around his neck.

"Be prepared to disengage in a moment," Brin says.

Her eyes shoot open. She hadn't even noticed that she'd closed them. They approach a narrow hole in the ceiling above them only just large enough for the both of them to fit through. An alarm goes off in her head but subsides as they pass through into a small circular chamber approximately 10 meters in diameter. As soon as their feet pass through the hole, Brin gently pushes Emily away from him, just enough to ensure that she steps safely onto the landing. Once he's sure she's securely on firm ground, he maneuvers backward and drops to the landing on the other side of the hole.

He bows slightly.

"Uh...thank you," she says, distractedly brushing her hands down over her jeans as if straightening an invisible skirt. Then she adds, quietly and with a complete lack of irony, "Superman."

"I beg your pardon?" Brin says.

Emily blushes. Her features soften and she looks down. "No, nothing. I'm just...I'm sorry, I was just...he's a—"

"Superhero," Eric says, drawing Emily's attention into the room. He is seated in one of several chairs that ring the room's circumference. The chairs lean back at approximately 45 degrees, like plush Adirondack chairs, and Eric sits with his hands behind his head, smiling smugly at the uncomfortable drama playing out in front of him.

Long windowless portals ring the room, opening it up to a view of the entire module. Warm light from the outside streams in to illuminate the patterns on the pale walls, an aesthetic strangely familiar to Emily. Dozens and dozens of compartments, ports, access hatches, switches, buttons, LED lights, handles, and cubby holes, arranged in a seemingly haphazard fashion, run all the way around and up to the tapered ceiling, which itself frames another large, windowed portal that looks out onto the scarred surface of their host moon.

Sensing her discomfort, Brin gestures to a seat behind her as he himself turns to take one behind him. She walks glumly to the chair beside Eric, whose grin grows wider at her approach. She plops into the chair and turns to see him beaming. Without missing a beat, she stands and plops into the next chair, crossing her hands as she does so.

Which only makes his grin wider.

She turns her head up at him. "Shut up," she says tartly.

Deacon and Brin recline with their eyes closed, their hands draped over their chests, fingers linked as if in prayer. As Emily scans the room, she is drawn back to Eric, who waves and points frantically to the wall just behind the left side of his head. She can't tell by the look on his face whether it is the excitement of discovery... or fear. But it doesn't matter, for as soon as she is in her seat, a hatch raises to close the floor and the portals hiss with the hermetic seal of opaque windows, leaving the room in near complete darkness.

"In the beginning," the acolyte announces, his voice deep and theatrical, "there was Earth." Immediately, the room flashes and a perfect, three-dimensional representation of Earth appears in the center, floating about two meters off the floor.

"Wow," Eric says under his breath. Though he knows intuitively it's a holographic projection, it appears so solid and tangible that he has to suppress the urge to stand and pick it up, shrug it onto his shoulders and protect it like Atlas.

But it begins to change. The white wisps dissipate, the green turns orange and the blue turns green.

Then a dramatic, instantaneous fire ravages the entire surface, an orange and yellow bloom like a bursting, wilting sunflower.

Emily winces.

When the fire and dust settle, all that is left is a desiccated, shriveled, scorched brown rock floating alone in outer space. Behind it is a fine, lonely mist of stars, floating like glitter sprinkled on a dark canvas.

Bits of the glitter begin to shimmer and jitter, as if Emily and the other observers were in motion. Bits of rock flit by, then larger boulders, then jagged asteroids.

Mars zooms past.

A pale star in the distance grows.

A large, unruly object floats in from behind the observer's position. Metallic, man-made, vaguely familiar.

Eric slides down in his seat and swings his foot toward Emily, trying to connect with her outstretched leg. He manages to brush the cuff of her jeans, startling her but drawing her attention. He mouths something to her, but in the dim light thrown off by the hologram, she can't make it out.

She shrugs in answer.

He tries again, trying to clarify by exaggerating and slowing his mouth movements.

She rolls her eyes shrugs again. "Just say it," she tells him.

"What are you hearing?" he asks.

"Nothing."

The object seems to grow as it floats toward the pale ball, pieces adding onto it like links attaching themselves to a chain.

The pale ball becomes recognizable as Jupiter, its bands of gas becoming distinct, the red maelstrom menacing.

The view zooms downward, toward a beige marble floating under the gas giant's protective gaze.

As the object approaches the small orb, it coils and uncoils like a writhing snake, then whips its length around, one end connecting to the other until it is has securely belted in the moon.

As the moon draws closer, details appear on the station that rings it. Small details fill in, unfinished sections suddenly pop into existence.

Eric recognizes it. It is a view he had seen only hours before from the spaceship's cockpit.

Suddenly they seem to be inside the station, in a cavernous expanse. Grass appears, spreading across the vast floor like a green sea rolling to shore. Trees sprout up. People pick. People plow. People harvest.

A giant mechanical wall assembles itself and begins to rumble forward.

Through the wall into another cavern. People build. Decks, corridors, rooms. People live. Hospitals, infirmaries. People die.

Through the wall again, into another expanse. Corkscrews spin up to the ceiling, vegetation begins to drip off them. Little wheeled boxes scurry about. Train cars full of fruit and vegetables.

Then into another cavern. Like the others, this cavern springs to life. Grass, trees, buildings. People. A spire grows in the distance, in the center. In a taller building, babies are born. In an adjacent room, small transparent capsules are filled with liquid. Babies are incubated.

Eric sits up. "Are you hearing anything yet?" he whispers.

"No. It's completely silent."

Out of the module. In outer space. Steel girders jut forward into the distance, curving, meeting with another module far ahead. Robots fly and weld and stretch a long, thin sheet of white material over the framework, encasing it.

It is a cavern now. Walls spring up. Robots scurry about, building things. Engines. Spaceships. Holes are cut into the walls, the spaceships are lined up and shot outward.

Their view follows one. Away from the station, away from Jupiter, back where they started.

Earth.

And then away again. To Jupiter. To the moon that orbits it, over the ring, in through the hangar.

"You know," Eric whispers, "If they'd've just brought us here in the first place it would have saved us a lot of trouble."

Emily shushes him.

Into another expanse. Following a monorail, gliding over a city, through the eye of the needle in its center, into a small room. A capsule. Four people seated.

Focus on two. Teenagers. A boy and a girl.

And the acolyte's voice, in Emily's ear:

"From before the beginning, two shall arrive. Speak unto them the words so that they may carry them forth, and the beginning shall become the end. The tribe untied shall be the tribe united. Ten zero eleven zero zero by zero two eight five eight six three by two one."

Suddenly the image disappears and the room is unsealed with a whoosh that pops Eric's ears. Artificial sunlight pours in, blinding them. Their sight eventually recovers, leaving their sensibilities adrift. They both stare up at the empty space above them where the images had just hung.

And the questions still hang.

Slowly, Eric's senses return and he looks at Emily. It's almost comedic, the faces they throw at each other as they fight for control of a middle ground between polite disbelief and downright scorn. Eric shrugs and throws up his hands in disbelief, but then the memory of his unfinished business breaks through and he excitedly resumes pointing to the spot on the wall next to his head, the spot he was desperately trying to draw her attention to before the holographic presentation began. He leans aside to let Emily see.

An American flag.

————

Emily grips tightly to Brin, her arms wrapped around his neck as they float down. She is exhilirated—gripped by a curious mix of fear, reticence, and animal longing. When their feet finally come to rest on the floor at the bottom of the spire, Emily quickly unwraps herself from Brin's neck and takes a step backward. "Thank you again," she says shyly, her eyes locked on the center circle on the floor.

"Superman?" Brin says, causing Emily to blush again.

Brin looks up to see Eric's progress, noting that he is still several stories up.

"Forgiveness, Ms. Clocke. It appears I have caused you discomfort, but I am afraid I do not understand the cause."

"No," she lies, "I'm just...it's just..."

"The vasodilation of your facial capillaries suggests embarrassment."

Emily stares at Brin, now entirely unsure if she's truly embarrassed or annoyed by his presumptuousness. She decides it's both.

Brin notices. "I believe I have furthered your discomfort." He bows slightly. "Forgiveness. It was not my intention. I fear I do not yet know the appropriate protocols for engagement with someone from your culture."

Emily continues to stare at him. Her annoyance begins to turn to amusement as Brin attempts to spin his explanation.

"Now who's embarrassed?" she says with a slight grin.

Flummoxed, Brin just stares back. Then he recovers. "Indeed. I too find myself to be...embarrassed." He says it as if it were a foreign word. "I confess that I am unaccustomed to the sensation, and I fear my adverse reaction to it may have caused you further discomfort."

"Never mind. How about we just start over?" Emily asks, raising her hand again. "Hi, I'm Emily."

"I am aware of your identity," Brin says. Then his eyes instantly light up in recognition: "Ah! I see! Forgiveness, Mr. Clocke...Eric...has explained this."

He reaches forward, grabs Emily's hand, and shakes it vigorously, as if her arm were merely a rubbery appendage. She drops his hand after only a few shakes for fear of throwing her shoulder.

"Okay, that's good," she says, "Now you're supposed to say, 'Hi, I'm Brin.'"

"But you already know my designation," Brin says, confused.

"Ah," Emily mutters, "I guess I have a lot to learn about this place."

Emily feels a light slap on her shoulder. "Thanks for that!" Eric whispers angrily. "You left me with the guy who doesn't know how to talk!"

"I didn't even see you land!" she says with surprise.

"I landed right in front of you, for cry-eye!" Eric says with exasperation. "Get your eyes out of his! I don't have a thingy on my neck and I have questions!"

Deacon touches down and steps beside the acolyte. Immediately, the acolyte bows in subservience, his expression drawn blank. "What questions do you have?" Deacon conveys, looking at Eric.

But Eric, of course, doesn't hear, and the ensuing silence rattles him. "What?" he says, unnerved by Deacon's stare. Then it dawns on him: "Are you trying to tell me something? Could you, you know, it's pretty damned rude when people start having silent conversations!"

"Forgiveness Mr. Clocke," Brin says, his head dropping lower, "I am failing at my mandate."

"I don't know what that means, but would you please stop calling me Mr. Clocke? And get me an ear thing! He's apparently talking to me and I can't hear him! I couldn't hear any of that," he says pointedly, gesturing up to the sacellum. "It didn't make any sense."

"He couldn't hear the ending," Emily says to Brin.

"The end words are the gospel," Brin says. "It is the Word we preserve. The silence preceding it represents the grueling 400-year journey of the Word, enduring through the vast, soundless, unforgiving environment of outer space to illuminate us and give us hope."

"So, what, I get to experience the grueling silent part and she gets the words? Do you not understand that I couldn't hear anything?"

"I again beg forgiveness, Mr.—" Brin says, halting before he finishes the name. He nods to sheepishly acknowledge his near miss, then continues, "Allow me to recite. 'From before the beginning, two shall arrive. Speak unto them the words so that they may carry them forth, and the beginning shall become the end. The tribe untied shall become the tribe united. Ten zero eleven zero ten by two eight five eight six three by two one.'"

Eric just stares at him in disbelief. "And what the hell does that mean?"

"'From before the beginning two shall arrive,'" Brin repeats. "You are the two. 'Speak unto them the words so that they may carry them forth, and the beginning shall become the end.' We have given you the Word, and now you are bound by destiny to implement it. 'The tribe untied shall be the tribe united.' You and your sister shall reunite the Remnant with the Mother Tribe. You are the Saviors of Remnant."

"You are their salvation!" Deacon conveys with his typical theatrical flair. "The fulfillment of prophecy! The Saviors of Remnant!"

At the first sign of Deacon's movement, Eric realizes he's conveying once again. "Are you kidding me?" he yells, and turns in a huff. He stalks away, heading to the exit tunnel. "There better not be any bowing people out there!" he yells over his shoulder as he enters the tunnel.

Emily, torn between her own frustrations and a baffling need to apologize for Eric's, looks to Brin with apologetic eyes.

"Ms. Clocke—" Deacon begins to convey, a plaintive note coming through.

"Don't follow us," she interrupts, and turns to run into the tunnel.

———

Instead of the fawning crowd she had feared, Emily notices that the area around the spire is completely deserted. Eric makes his way along the path unaccosted. She wonders if Brin has somehow shooed everyone away.

"Where are you going?" Emily calls out to him. She jogs to try to catch up to him.

"Wherever! Anywhere but here!"

"Why are you so angry all of a sudden?"

"All of a sudden?" He stops and turns. "What do you mean all of a sudden? Do you think I want to be here?"

"Yes, actually I do. Why wouldn't you? It's like a playground for sci-fi geeks." She doesn't say it with malice, but she realizes instantly how it will come across and she braces for the inevitable impact. It doesn't quite come the way she expects.

"Why are you so happy all of a sudden? Oh yeah," he adds venomously, "you have a boyfriend now!"

And again, as has happened so many times over the past few days, a dark blue silence descends between them, a gulf of wildly inconsistent, constantly vacillating emotions. Eric turns his back to her and stomps away, heaving in blind frustration. Emily stands there, deflated, watching him retreat. She realizes now that ever since arriving at the station, she feared this very scenario. His leaving, her being alone. But at the moment she welcomes it, prefers to test her resolve against it.

When he is out of sight, she sighs and begins to walk. Wander. Her senses are on high alert, expecting Deacon or Brin to suddenly appear out of nowhere and begin proselytizing. She moves away from the spire, toward the edge of the open area that rings it. She's essentially aimless, save for her desire to move in the opposite direction of the transportation hub that she's sure Eric is heading for.

She finds a park bench nestled in a small cove created by a tall hedgerow. Sitting on it she can view the entire parkland surrounding the spire, though there really isn't much to see. Trees tremble almost imperceptibly, driven by the slight breeze. An occasional bird scores a line across her field of vision. The lawn under her feet is the most perfectly modulated green she's ever seen, save for the golf course her father once took her and Eric to in his short-lived attempt to introduce them to sports.

The sensory disconnect is a welcome relief, but it does nothing to settle her mind. She can close her eyes and think real hard but even her imagination can't remove her from this place. Can't remove her from a world the imagination is, under normal circumstances, supposed to conceive, not relieve. How does she go home?

Suddenly there is a child standing before her, a young

girl of about six or seven years of age. The child looks out at Emily over the tops of watery eyes, a picture-book drawing of innocence but with a serious expression bordering on doleful.

"Are you the savior?" the child asks.

Emily just stares at her, no answer coming to mind. No thoughts at all, really, except self-doubt and the fate of an entire world—as it were—weighing on her shoulders.

"Are you going to save us?" the child asks.

A man appears beside her, breathing heavily, his face ruddy and sheepish. "Forgiveness. Come along, Teece," he conveys, gently tugging on the child's shoulder, "They told us not to disturb the young lady." The man nods apologetically and escorts the young girl away.

"But I just wanted to know," the child conveys, plaintive and frustrated. She twists around to try to address Emily again, but the man pushes her back into place and they walk off down the path, the girl's protests growing fainter.

'I want to know too,' Emily thinks. 'Except, maybe I don't.'

People slowly begin to trickle out onto the spire field, inspired, perhaps, by the young girl's boldness. They move stiffly, self-consciously, making a concerted effort to get from here to there without either crossing into Emily's direct view or making eye contact with her.

"Vocks," Emily says.

*Emily.*

"Do all these people believe?"

*Please clarify. Believe what?*

"That I am some sort of savior?"

*Many do, but not all.*

Emily ponders Vocks's answer. Oddly—perhaps happily—she finds herself struck more by the inexact nature of Vocks's response than by the content of it. It didn't know the context of her question, but knew enough to answer concisely, and not overload Emily with data.

Maybe that's what I need, Emily thinks, just the bullet points. I'll figure out the details myself.

Emily feels the bench quake, and turns to see Eric slouched in the opposite corner. "Where the hell did you come from?"

Eric folds his arms. "Really? You're going to start with that again? I walked right in freakin' front of you!"

"Well, I don't know!" Emily responds, exasperated. "Everyone's a blur. Everything's a blur!

"It's all a blur."

"Well, at least you have...!" Eric says as he stands and pushes away in a huff. But he stops before completing his sentence, and stands hunched, his back to Emily. He lets out a deep sigh and turns back around.

Emily wipes her eyes with the back of her hand. "I just can't figure out this place. I thought I had it—"

"Tell me about it," Eric says with a slight sneer. "I can't hear anything and you hear everything. Either we get too little or we get too much. It's going to be frustrating either way."

"Yeah, but you can't blame them, though," Emily says, gesturing in the general direction of the spire. "It's not really their fault. You can't be angry at them that you can't speak their language."

"It's not about language, though. Brin speaks English, but half the time he doesn't speak at all! That's why I'm frustrated. I have no choice in the matter: I can't learn to hear silence."

They fall into a silence, both just staring blankly at the anonymous people walking back and forth before them.

"So what are we to them?" Eric asks. "The Chosen One?"

"The chosen ones. The chosen two!" Emily says.

"No," Eric says with a touch of irony, "there is no chosen two. There's only a chosen one."

"And it's never a girl," Emily says with mock indignation. 'Luke Skywalker, Harry Potter, the Matrix guy...'"

"That's because we're better at everything," Eric taunts, grinning.

Emily shakes her head and smiles, letting a little laugh escape her lips. "If you're so great at everything, why did you come back? You couldn't get the monorail to work, could you?"

"Shit!" Eric exclaims, eyes wide in surprise, then explodes with laughter. "How could you possibly have known that?"

Emily stares at Eric in surprise and begins to laugh herself. "It's a good thing we're in the same boat" she says between fits of giggles, "because if we weren't I'd really hate you right now!"

And with the subsequent giggles this elicits, the people stop their conscious avoidance and turn to stare, not knowing whether to be amused or frightened.

————

A few minutes later, they are aboard a monorail, gliding effortlessly away from the transport station and climbing back up and around the spire, eventually zooming onto a straight track and away. It exits through a tunnel at the end of the living module, opposite the one they'd entered through. The tunnel is at first deep black, unlit, but eventually enters into another transparent one with a view of the station and of outer space. They can see along either side of the station now, noting how some sections further along appear to be steely, unfinished infrastructure, like the skeletal ribs of a gigantic, long dead whale. These stretches reattach to more solid station before the remainder of its expanse is lost behind the horizon of its host moon.

"Sixty percent, huh?" Eric says, allowing the comment to float in silence for a moment before adding, "The station's not even finished but they expect to run out of room."

Emily watches the approach of a finished module, the wall facing her consisting mostly of windows. At a distance, the windows glow with a slight green tint, but as they draw closer, she can tell that the green is actually vegetation. Within yards, she sees that they're some sort of tall, perfectly straight trees, the branches of which appear to be configured into a perfect corkscrew.

As they pass through into the module, they are offered a view of the complete module. Emily sees instantly that she was wrong. They are not trees.

"What the hell is it?" Eric asks.

The monorail track is positioned at the upper corner of the module, looking down over an inconceivably vast room that stretches the 200 meter width of the station, hundreds of meters in length, and at least six decks down below them. The ceiling one deck above them illuminates the room with an approximation of midday sunlight, revealing rows and rows of corkscrew columns, like giant spiral staircases, stretching floor to ceiling, each one teeming with lush vegetation. Water slowly drips from the tops of the corkscrews, trickling down onto the plants, eventually falling through a grid floor and into a graded channel, creating rivulet streams that flow into intermittently spaced drains.

"It's a farm," Emily says.

"It doesn't look like a farm to me," Eric says. "Unless it's a Willy Wonka farm. Where are the cows?"

"Look closer. All those plants are vegetables."

Indeed, as he looks, he notices that the growth on one spiral is corn, and on another is tomatoes, and yet another contains what he suspects is green beans. Each spiral contains a different vegetable, making an enormous variety. They now notice that the spirals are wide and tall enough to comfortably allow several people to walk arm and arm through the vegetation all the way around and up.

"So then it's a garden," Eric says, taking the opportunity to correct her.

"How does this work?" Emily asks.

"How should I know? I didn't even know it was a farm."

Emily frowns at him, then says, "Vocks, how does this work?"

As Vocks answers, she relays the information to Eric.

*This farm complex is one of eight throughout the station, two in each quadrant. It works on the principle of vertical hydroponics, which is a technique first attempted in your era in which vegetation is bathed in a mineral-rich solution on a vertically inclined surface. Each column contains a single type of vegetable and produces enough each day to feed approximately one thousand two-hundred people.*

"Produces enough each day?"

*It is an accelerated growth and harvesting process. Plant maturity is achieved within five hours of seeding, depending upon the plant. Harvesting, waste disposal, column preparation, and seeding take approximately another two hours. The process is repeated continuously, with crops rotated every cycle.*

"It sure looks like it can feed more than twelve-hundred people."

*Nearly 60 percent of the crop is dedicated to producing Glycine max derivatives, which are a primary component of the resins used to develop this station.*

"The station is made out of plastic," Emily says, a nervous lilt in her voice.

They see large boxes are on some of the spirals, similar in size to freight cars, attached to tracks on the inner-support columns, rolling slowly down and around, apparently harvesting the crops. Further behind those boxes, attached to the same track, are other boxes that seem to churn up and quickly compost the vegetation that remains from the first pass.

At the bottom of the corkscrew, the harvesting boxes slide off the track and lock into grooves on the floor. They are then routed through a complex maze, twisting and turning around corkscrews and other harvester boxes until they are positioned parallel to the outer wall, where they all converge and run along the wall, in a single, unconnected line.

Their monorail continues on until they reach the other end of the module, taking a full five minutes to ride its length. They see nothing but rows of hydroponic corkscrews from one end to the other. Emily has to fight to suppress the urge to address Vocks with more questions. She rather needs the silence to counter the visual overstimulation.

At its terminus, the corridor opens out upon another expanse, but instead of a farm they see before them a vast orchard, or what they assume is an orchard, trailing off as far as they can see down the length of the station. About twenty rows of trees span the width, but the rows stretch out so long that they are lost to the horizon of the station itself.

"You know," Eric says, "Seeing all this food makes me realize that we still haven't eaten."

"Yeah. You know, we haven't actually eaten for several hundred years," Emily comments.

Eric looks at her, stunned. "Did you just make a joke? Nice. Shall we venture downward?"

"Vocks," Emily calls, "how do we get down there?"

In answer, the monorail stops and begins to move backwards. After about 20 seconds, the car stops and the doors swish open, revealing a short, narrow room. Emily and Eric look at each other for support. "Elevator?" they say in unison, then laugh nervously before stepping into it. The doors swish shut behind them and the elevator begins to fall at a stomach-dropping rate.

The elevator stops as abruptly as it started and the doors swish open. The siblings remain steadfastly glued into place. Finally, Eric, regaining a slight sense of balance, carefully shuffles a foot forward, planting it firmly before attempting to move the other. He then slowly pushes himself out of the elevator. When he fully regains his equilibrium, he makes a beeline for an apple tree, the sight of food instantly dispelling the giddiness of the elevator ride. He plucks an apple, makes a perfunctory effort at wiping it on his shirt, then takes a large crunch, tearing off a piece that's probably too large for his mouth. But he makes a go of it, his cheeks puffing out to hold it all in but his lips unable to stem the tide as rivulets of juice stream down his chin, dripping dots onto his shirt. He plops to the ground, landing cross legged and leaning his back against the tree, forgetting for a moment where he actually is.

Despite her growling stomach, Emily is more tentative in leaving the elevator. She takes a step out, planting both feet firmly onto grass. Or what appears to be grass, anyway. It's a strange reveal, turning from the bland, monochromatic elevator to the vivid colors of a verdant orchard on what passes for terra firma. Despite everything that is hitting her senses, her mind has room to draw the obvious parallel to Dorothy emerging from the black-and-white house to the vibrancy of a lush Oz. She refrains, however, from speaking of Kansas.

Emily takes another step forward and positions herself so that neither her direct nor her peripheral vision can perceive the artificial elements of the scene before her. Focusing on one spot, one tree, the trees in the foreground and the trees in the background blur into one, so there that is only that one tree. That one tree, in the grove two hours north of their California house, where her father put her eight-year-old self on his shoulders on the brisk day in late September and pointed to that one apple, the monstrous one just above the one with the brown dent, the one that she has to stretch to reach, that she has to grab with both hands to pull hard, and pop…!

But it was more than a pop. It was a wheezing, rasping mechanical groan, like the rusty-chain-link staccato of a long freight train snapping to attention at the initial tug of an engine, and it dissolved the massive apple she held in her hand and wiped from her consciousness the long-gone trees of California.

To her left, she notices the wall that divides the spiral garden from the orchard starting to rumble and quake. Subtle at first, the quaking increases in intensity as she watches. Within seconds, the whole lower portion of the wall, a section about ten meters high and stretching the whole width of the room, detaches and pushes away from the remaining structure. As it moves forward, a series of doors on the forward portion of the wall slide open, gaping maws that line up perfectly with the rows of trees.

What she thought was a wall is in fact a worn, oily, metal behemoth, a foreign contrast to the stark, white plasticity of the rest of the station. Emily realizes what it is: a harvester. And then she realizes that it is coming right at her.

As the harvester-wall comes within five meters of her, she springs backward into the still open elevator, pressing herself flat against the back wall. The harvester passes, immediately closing her in and filling the transparent enclosure with a hazy spray of moist heat and the acrid smell of burnt oil. After a few moments, it is gone, and the elevator entrance is clear again. Emily peeks out quickly to her left to see if anything else is coming, then to her right to follow the long harvester as it moves forward, trailing behind it a flat, open field of leaf and wood-pulp detritus.

And no Eric.

# :08 harvest

No Eric.

Emily takes off running after the wall-length harvester, an instinct seizing hold of her body and taking command. Her conscious mind furiously churns through options, determining what she's going to do when (if) she catches up to the moving wall. The ground beneath her is spongy and pliant, like the mulch floor of the playgrounds she played on as a kid, and ribbed like a washboard so that she has to traverse small valleys and hills, making it difficult to maintain a consistent stride or speed. As she closes in on the harvester, it releases a particularly large mound of mulched apple tree. She leaps over the pulpy mound, making her lose ground.

But it's right there, slightly more than an arm's length away, this moving wall, this gigantic machine. She just has to push harder, that extra little bit. Her arm outstretched in front of her, it's so tantalizingly close that the determination to just reach out and grab hold is enough to distract her from the fact that her lungs are burning so badly it actually makes her jaw ache and her legs feel like splintering matchsticks. It's right there, right there, the rungs of a ladder that climb to the top of the wall, just another inch, don't stop…

She grabs it, her right hand clasping onto a rung and gripping so tight it cuts into the pads of her fingers. But the fact of grabbing it loosens her concentration and she suddenly feels her body weighing her down. Her legs slip out from under her and she lurches downward, twisting her fingers painfully in the thin metal rung as she falls to drag behind the wall. Mulch and debris fill her dragging shoes, digging painful channels into the tops of her feet.

Emily flails with her left hand, attempting to grab onto another rung. She swings up and misses, swings up and misses, then wisely chooses to make her goal the same rung that is biting into her right hand. Swings and connects. The pressure on her right hand now considerably reduced, she loosens her grip just enough to return some sensation to her cramped fingers. Then she lets go completely and swings her arm upward just enough to grab onto the rung above it, slipping her fingers behind the metal bar to gain more leverage to pull. She pulls upward and follows suit with her left hand, grabbing onto the next rung. Straining muscles in her arms that she never even knew she had, she continues in this fashion until she pulls herself high enough to be able to swing her leg onto a rung, then lift herself completely onto the ladder.

After maneuvering both arms behind the rung closest to her face, she braces her elbows against the wall and the back of her wrists against the metal of the rung. She leans back slightly and use her own weight to relieve the pressure on her arms and fingers. It's not much, but God it still feels good!

Okay, enough of that. She flexes her fingers several times, then squeezes her arms out from behind the ladder. She starts climbing, even though the muscles in her arms and legs are screaming, and the mulch in her shoes are like daggers sticking into the bottoms of her feet.

Emily makes it to the top and peers over the lip. A rolling river of perfectly formed red apples rolls by her, pushed through a five-meter-wide channel toward the far wall of the orchard room by an unseen conveyor. More apples are pushed onto the stream, spit out of chutes embedded at equal points along the short walls that form the channel.

Emily groans. To get to the front of the harvester, she'll have to somehow traverse this red torrent. She pushes herself up, her arms trembling with the strain, and balances herself on the lip of the channel. She can see the orchard in front of her, the unstoppable behemoth rolling over and consuming the seemingly endless rows of trees. That view, combined with the roiling flow of apples rushing past her perpendicular to the motion of the wall, brings forth a now all-too-familiar sensation of vertigo. She has to move fast or she'll never make it across.

"Vocks, how deep is this?"

*To what does the word 'this' refer?*

"The apples! This river of apples!"

*Unknown.*

"What's underneath it?"

*Unknown.*

"Great."

She knows instinctively that trying to walk across through a landslide of fruit would be like trying to wade through white water rapids. It can't be done. So she leaps forward into the torrent, pushing off the edge with as much energy as she can muster, hoping she can fly far enough to at least grab hold of the opposite edge of the channel.

She belly-flops smack into middle of the channel and is immediately spun lengthwise and carried along by the current of solid, ripe fruit. The solid ripples lift her along the surface but batter her body raw, like being raked over smooth rocks in a shallow but powerful stream. She pushes her arms down, trying to find a solid surface to lift herself, but her hands just slip down among and through the crush of apples.

With a mighty effort, she rolls herself over onto her back. She lifts her head to get a bearing on her surroundings. The edge of the channel is about a meter away, tantalizingly close. She pulls her arms in and begins to rock back and forth. After a silent count of three, she spins herself and rolls across the distance, right to the edge, and immediately grabs hold of the first ledge she can find. She stops abruptly, nearly yanking her arms from her shoulders, and the apples now begin to pelt her in the head. She's now a point of resistance to the flow, so apples begin to pile in front of her, creating a great strain on her grip, starting to bury her. She pulls hard. Up and over, she straddles the other lip, but falls immediately off the other end, over the front of the moving wall...

She crashes with a thud onto a metal covering. An awning over one of the inlets where trees are pushed into the harvester. Looking over the lip, Emily sees leafy greenery channeled, compressed, and sucked in beneath her, the wispy crunching and snapping of leaves and branches sounding almost like a rolling tide pushed onto a windy shore.

She's nearly content to just lie there and try to stop feeling her own body, the noise and steamy rumble of the massive machine be damned. She could turn it into white noise, pretend she's lying on the roof of the old station wagon that time they went to the drive-in theater and her father cranked the engine on so he could run the air conditioning. She could just lie there and pretend she's back with her family...

She suddenly remembers why she just endured what she endured. Her actions are swift and sudden. She rolls into a crouch, orienting herself forward and making the awning she's on into a lookout. "Eric!" she yells, and then mutters, "Where the hell is he?" to herself when she gets no response.

*Unknown.*

"I'm not talking to you!" she says irritably. She cups her hands to her mouth and yells again. "Eric!"

She hears a muffled, breathless wail and spots movement in her peripheral vision. It's Eric, running along between a row of trees about twenty meters to her right. Though she can barely make him out as he darts in and out among the trees, she can tell that he's running with all the strength he can muster. But he's ragged, bone-weary, losing ground.

With barely a thought, Emily darts across the awning and leaps the three-meter gap to the neighboring awning. A reserve of adrenaline courses through her, giving her lift and determination, allowing her to lose track of her own pain and exhaustion. She vaults the next gap and skitters across that next awning. Eric is coming into line. Hurtle a gap, streak across an awning, lithe and nimble, outside her own body. Leap, dash, leap, dash. Eric is in sight; one more leap. Now she crashes, belly-flopping onto the awning, sprawls out and leans over the outside lip of the mulching chute, leaves and branches tearing into her face and back and arms as she reaches down and...

He's just within reach. Like everything today, just within reach but miles away. Just a little further and maybe she can grab his collar, pull him up.

"Eric! Take my hand!"

At the sound of her voice, Eric turns his head. The distraction makes him falter. He loses his stride and crashes down onto one knee, but recovers almost instantly. He takes two more steps, but his legs bow and he pitches sideways, crashing down on his shoulder. The wall—the sprawling, hulking harvester—overcomes him, consumes him. Emily sees it roll right over his body and suddenly the whizzing grind of the mulching isn't white noise anymore.

And before she can scream, before she can even react or feel much of anything, the wall lurches to a stop, throwing her forward into the spindly, unforgiving branches of an apple tree. She careens down through the branches as if she's being shoved from person to person through an angry crowd, then flops with a thud onto the ground at the base of the tree, the wind completely knocked out of her.

Whatever residual adrenaline she had has been drained from her body, and she lies there jittering as if she's being pumped through with electricity. Her body slowly sheds its numbness in favor of rather acute aches, so it is with great struggle that she reluctantly drags herself around to see what became of Eric.

Eric. Emily spots him through a meter-tall gap between the ground and the bottom of the wheezing harvester. Battered and bruised but apparently intact, he lies spread-eagled, half-buried in the mulch...on the other side of the wall. Dirt and churned up wood cover his sweat-streaked face, giving his skin the appearance of bloody, pulpy tree bark. Slowly Emily crawls hand-over-hand to the harvester, pausing momentarily to determine how she wants to proceed. Or if she wants to proceed.

She crawls forward and drags herself under the harvester and over to Eric. She grabs his hand, pushing her fingers down on the veins on the inside of his wrist. Feeling nothing, she moves to the side of his neck and presses down. She still feels nothing. A sweaty panic begins to tighten within her as she moves the back of her hand to within a few centimeters of his nose.

"Please be breathing, please be breathing," she mutters, blowing tiny plumes of dirt up from the ground with each strained exhale.

The muscles of his body tense, then loosen and his whole body trembles as he shakes loose a very big, wet sneeze onto the back on Emily's hand.

"Eeeuuuwww," Emily moans, wiping her hand across her shirt.

"What were you trying to do to my neck?" Eric asks in between gulps of air.

"I was checking your pulse."

"Do you even know CPR?"

"Yeah, kind of."

"The carotid artery is closer to the jaw. You were pressing on my ear cavity."

Emily is momentarily astonished. "That's a very obscure fact coming from you."

"I was a lifeguard at scout camp last summer, dumbass. I learned CPR!"

"What happened?"

"They taught me CPR! What do you mean what happened?"

"No, I mean just now! What happened to you? With the huge...mulcher thing?"

"I don't know," Eric says soberly, sitting up on the third try.

"The machine just caught up to me. I fell and it pretty much just rolled right over me. I mean, it rolled me over a couple of times, but no blood and guts. At least, I don't think." He gives himself a cursory check.

The harvester rumbles and spews forth a shot of steam, startling them both. Then, with a percussive clank that seems to roll down its length, it lurches forward again and starts rambling away, spewing up a cloud of dust and wood pulp. When they see that the harvester is moving away from them, they both fall backwards and lie in the mulch and detritus, spitting out the dust that settles over them.

"When did you become such a badass?" Eric asks, his lungs still burning. He smiles to himself, partially in gratitude for still being alive, partially because he's damned impressed with his sister right now.

Emily doesn't smile. She hadn't heard him. She lies staring at the ceiling, fascinated because she hadn't noticed it before. But who notices a ceiling? Long plastic-looking arches reach across the width of the module, curving upward and in, spaced at roughly 100 meter intervals and braced by a center beam that spans the module's length, itself curving slightly to conform to the arc of the station. Emily allows herself the whimsical thought of having been swallowed by a giant metal snake, albeit one with transparent skin. Beyond the windows is the pocked and scarred paleness of Europa, lit by the orange glow of Jupiter, which must be just out of sight beyond the walls of the station.

Jupiter.

And beyond that a vast, black void.

————

The black is muddied by a pale, ruddy, watery light. Emily blinks and the water swirls and settles, the light still pale and indistinct. She blinks again then rubs her eyes and sees that the ceiling is dotted—almost consumed—with wavy speckles. Blinking rapidly again to clear her eyes, she notices that the wavy speckles are, in fact, leaves.

They are lying in an orchard.

She turns to look at Eric, lying face up several meters away, his legs parted and partially lifted by a tree trunk. A comically timed apple lands, with an equally comic hollow thud, squarely on his forehead.

"I didn't! What!?" Eric stammers, startled to consciousness.

"You were sleeping?"

"No. Wait, was I?"

Emily lifts her head and props herself up, leaning back on her elbows to look up again. "Was *I*?"

"What the hell...?" Eric exclaims, finally noticing the trees.

"How did we get here?" Emily asks no one.

After a beat, Eric asks, "What did it say?"

"What did what say?"

"Your neck, dummkopf."

Emily scrunches her forehead, looking at him as if he's crazy.

"The thing on your neck. What did it say? About the trees?"

"Oh! I didn't ask!" Emily admits sheepishly. "Vocks, how did we get here?"

*Through means of self-generated bipedal locomotion.*

"Really?" Em says with dripping sarcasm.

"Hey Em..." Eric says, trying to interrupt.

Ignoring Eric, Emily continues her conversation with Vocks. "No. How did we get here? Into this orchard?"

*This is the same orchard. You have not moved.*

"Really?" she asks, now with genuine curiosity.

"Em!"

*Yes.*

"It's the same orchard," Emily tells Eric. "Vocks, how is it possible? All of the trees were mulched."

*As explained previously, food production relies on an accelerated growth and harvesting process. Plant maturity is achieved within five hours of seeding, depending upon the plant. Harvesting...*

"EM!"

"It's an accelerated growth process," Emily explains. "We haven't moved, the trees grew around us."

"I kinda figured that," Eric says and gestures to the tree he's under. His foot is planted inside the tree, buried past the ankle, consumed by the tree's trunk. He tugs and tugs, gripping his shins with both hands and pulling madly, but the leg won't budge. The tree has grown around his foot and ankle.

"Aw jeez!" Emily yelps. "Vocks, how long have we been here?"

*4.89 hours.*

Emily runs over to Eric and tugs on his leg too. No movement. She plants her feet in a wide, tug-of-war stance and pulls hard, succeeding only in making Eric grunt and grimace.

"Can you pull your foot out of your shoe?"

"No. It's grown around my ankle pretty tight."

Emily spins around wildly, quickly surveying the surroundings for something she can use to extract his leg. An axe, a crowbar...

"A lightsaber would be nice," Eric says.

"Well, use the force and get yourself one!" Emily screams, throwing up her arms in frustration at his blithe tone.

Eric is astonished by her reaction. "What are you yelling at me for?"

"This isn't funny! We've got to get you out of there!"

"No shit, Sherlock! You think I'm enjoying this?"

A tremor rumbles beneath them.

"You're sitting there making jokes while I'm..."

"First of all, I'm not sitting. I'm laying..."

"See? You can't take this seriously! Do you even know what's going on?"

"No, I don't, as a matter of fact! I'm not hooked into the internet like some people! And forgive me for using humor to diffuse tension! I guess it would be better if I just screamed like a girl!"

They hear a loud rumble, and another apple falls next to Eric's head. He turns to look at the downed fruit.

"Oh! Scream like a girl?" Emily yells, "From the guy who's been whining like a baby..." She continues an angry, stream of consciousness rant, completely unaware that Eric is not paying attention anymore.

Eric picks up the apple and examines it, his eyes scrunched in dawning realization. It's not the apple that's the problem...

It's the tremor.

He drops the apple, puts both hands on the ground palms down. He feels it.

"Hey, Em..."

"I felt it," she says, having been jarred out of her rant.

They look toward the far wall, in the direction that the harvester had gone earlier. In the distance, a thick mist rolls toward them, obscuring the behemoth that is making the trees tremble like frightened children. Then the mist—a shot of steam that pushes a wave of humid air at them—dissipates, revealing the familiar maws of the tree-swallowing harvester.

"It harvests in both directions," Emily says for no reason at all.

"Get me out, get me out!" Eric screams.

"What are you panicking about? Just lie there like last time."

"I'm stuck! In the tree! That thing is going to pull me up with it and mulch me!"

Emily processes his words. When it dawns on her that Eric may be right, she springs to his side. She grips his leg again, bracing one foot on the tree trunk next to Eric's foot, and pushes with her leg while she pulls with her arms. Eric screams in pain and fear and desperation, but the foot is stuck fast, as if it's a thick, low branch of the tree itself.

"Vocks!" Emily yells, "What can I do?"

*Define parameters.*

"His foot is stuck!"

*Please provide context for the removal of the foot. In what is the foot stuck?*

"Oh for...! In a tree! His foot is stuck in a tree! And a harvester is coming! Wait...can you stop the harvester?"

*No. I cannot transmit command lines to the harvester. It is of a design that preceded cytecaste telemetry. It is designed for a single purpose and thus operates independently of the core intelligence.*

"Jeez! Vocks, what are my options then?"

*I have taken the liberty of cytecasting an emergency signal to the nearest ag-mechs. They are enroute to our location.*

Emily looks at the harvester bearing down on them. It is about seventy-five meters away and closing in.

"Vocks, when will the ag-mechs get here?" Emily asks, continuing to pull mightily on Eric's leg. Eric screams panicked queries to Emily, which she ignores to focus on Vocks's words.

*4.25 minutes.*

"And when will the…"

*1.87 minutes.*

"That's not enough time. Vocks, what can I do now?"

*Duck.*

Emily stops pulling. She presses her fingers into her ears to remove the external noise. "Vocks, what did you say?"

*Duck.*

"Duck? Are you kidding me?"

*I am incapable of humorous repartee.*

"EMILEEEE…!" Eric's screams merge with the wheezing mechanical noise generated by the giant, deadly wall that is bearing down on them.

She turns, sees the harvester only inches away, and falls face down into the dirt next to Eric, covering him with one arm. She's barely on the ground when the lip of the harvester passes over her. Almost immediately, Eric is pulled out and up from under her arm, then instantly plopped back down again beside her, landing with a grunt.

As before, the harvester passes over then stops with a lurch and a resonant clank. It spits a wide, flat spray of steam upward, which falls as a warm, drenching downpour, then falls silent.

"Eric?"

"Yeah?"

"You alive?"

"Yeah."

"You intact?"

"Yeah."

"No more apples."

———

A ragged, grimy, motley pair limp slowly away from the harvester. Mud and mulch tattoo jagged lines down their sweat-soaked faces, their constant eye-wiping creating dark craters around their eyes.

"No more apples," Eric says, trying to playfully mock Emily, but the statement comes out tired and flat and more sincere than ironic. He growls: "I don't need apples, I need a shower."

Behind them, the harvester shudders and clanks. Another drenching spray of steam rains down over them.

Eric stops walking, stands still. He adopts the wan, droopy-eyed face of a dour sitcom straight man suffering one too many degradations.

"I really want to find that funny," Emily says, stopping beside him.

Eric nods absently then starts shuffling forward again. Emily follows.

*Damaged biological matter detected.*

Emily stops. "What?"

"What what?" Eric says.

"No, not you. Vocks, what do you mean damaged biological matter?"

Eric stops now too. "Damaged what now?"

*That statement did not originate from me. I am relaying cyte transmissions from an ag-mech in the vicinity.*

"A what?"

"An ag-mech..."

Eric turns slowly to see movement over Emily's shoulder. "Uh, Em?" Eric says, his eyes going wide.

Emily turns to see a small machine rolling toward them at breakneck speed. It is a crude, industrial robot, about the size of a refrigerator. Its upper body consists of a bulky white trunk, nearly approximating the torso of a human body but without a head. Instead, its 'shoulders' arch upwards to form two multi-directional turrets from which sprout four long, narrow articulated arms, two from each shoulder, at the end of which are three-fingered claws. The torso rests upon a narrow stalk that gradually tapers down and spreads out to form two arches that jut out forward, like the wheel wells of an automobile. It has the same worn, oily, mechanical look as the harvester.

*Damaged biological matter detected.*

"Oh."

"Is that the thing that's supposed to be coming for us?" Eric asks with masked calm.

"Vocks…?"

*Yes.*

"Should we wait for it?"

As it draws nearer, the robot raises all four of its arms. *Damaged biological matter detected.* The claws open with an unforgiving clank.

Eric blows the air from his lungs. "Okay," he says, then spins in place, flailing slightly, scanning to find a path to safety. "Look!" Eric points to the far side wall. A line of what appears to be trams is running parallel to the wall, intersecting with the end of the harvester, which is now as far away from them as the far wall. "I think maybe we should…"

"Let's go!"

They tear off running in two different directions toward the trams; Eric moves diagonal to the wall, jumping rows and dodging trees, while Emily makes a straight line along a row. The robot pauses, momentarily confused, but adjusts course and moves to pursue Emily.

"How do we get on?" Emily yells.

"How should I know?" Eric yells back, his voice trailing off as he moves further away from Emily.

Emily stops in her tracks and watches him recede. "Where are you going?"

"I'm going...!" Eric stops too, suddenly confused by why Emily is so far away from him. When he sees the robot on an intercept course for Emily, he tears off in her direction. "He'll catch you on a straight line!" Eric yells back. "Use the trees as cover!"

*Damaged biological matter detected.*

The robot's flat voice drones again in her ear, spurring her to action. As she turns to run again, moving in a zigzag route toward Eric, she notices that the line of tram cars is ending, and, though not moving particularly fast, the last car may reach the end of the orchard module before she can reach it. She swerves a few degrees to her right and increases her angle toward the exit. She frantically points ahead and barks orders at Eric. "Eric! That way! That way! Toward the exit"

"That's where I'm going!" he yells back.

They race forward, lungs burning more and more with each increasingly difficult step. Their speed now seems to sync with the train, and the point where the trams exit the module approaches, but neither is sure they can sustain the speed required to meet the tram at the point.

Or can they? They seem to have a large margin of safety, maybe four whole tram cars now. If they angle out toward it a bit more, they should meet the tram well before the last car passes through the exit...

Within meters of the intersection, Emily realizes that she's still moving too fast. She loses her footing trying to slow down before she smacks into the train and pitches forward, landing chest down, feebly jutting her arms out to break the impact before she breaks her ribs. She slides forward, scraping her palms. Eric's legs get tangled with hers, and he too pitches forward, squirming his body like a falling cat to orient himself so he can land on his side, away from Emily.

Suddenly, Eric spots the robot drawing quickly upon them, all four claws outstretched and open, and bounces back up almost immediately. He grabs and pulls on Emily's arm and lifts her to her feet with surprising force and speed, then races forward to match the train's speed. Grabbing hold of a hand railing at the back end of a tram car, he pulls himself up and swings onto the coupling gear between trams, not noticing until it's too late that Emily never regained her footing and simply crumpled back to the ground.

Emily, sprawled on the ground, looks up to see the tram car pass through the exit, Eric's head peeking out the side. "Hey, wait!" she yells uselessly.

"Come on!" he responds in the only way he can.

*Damaged biological matter detected.*

"Yeah yeah! Shut up!"

The robot bears down on her. Emily picks herself up and sprints beside the third to the last tram car, reaching for and missing the hand railing. She can't match the train's speed, and it is moving too fast to grab hold from a stationary position, so she continues moving forward. "Emily, stop!" Eric yells, but, working more on automatic now, she passes through the narrow opening between the train and the edge of the exit, eyes fixed on Eric's receding head and not on the tight space that is squeezing her between the exit wall and the tram that is swishing past within inches of her body.

But she does feel the tug on her shirt as the robot's claw tightens around her collar.

Her breath is ripped from her lungs as the tightened collar bunches against her throat. She jerks back, her feet nearly slipping out from under her, and grabs at her collar just as the robot smacks into the side of the entrance and rebounds into the moving tram cars. Freed from the pull of the robot's claw, Emily pitches forward again and just barely avoids falling into the side of the moving tram.

Sparks burn the back of her neck as the robot is spun and scraped between the wall of the exit corridor and the train. Twisted and torn into a flailing mass of metal and wire, it falls under the train and all but disintegrates.

After several meters, Emily emerges from the exit corridor to discover herself running along a service grate that runs parallel to the train, closed in on the other side by a transparent wall that looks out upon…

Jupiter.

The service grate appears to connect the orchard module to another unfinished piece of the station. Above her again is Europa, beneath her empty space. Dizziness and nausea well up inside her, and her pace slackens. The tram races by her, the air pressure of each passing car pushing her more and more off balance.

"Look at the train!" Eric yells, his voice barely discernible as it fades into the distance. "Em! Look at the train!"

Realizing his tactic, Emily focuses on the tram cars and begins moving forward again, trying her best to ignore what is around the other three sides of her. She reaches out for another passing handrail and grabs hold. The speed of the tram jerks her forward and lifts her off her feet, making it feel as if her arms have been ripped from her shoulders.

Her fingers are locked around the handrail so tightly she couldn't let go if she wanted to, but her arms burn so powerfully that she can't pull herself up. Her feet lose traction and she loses her footing, her legs dragging along the grate, swaying violently back and forth, threatening to swing under the tram itself.

Despite her focus, her peripheral vision detects the end of the service grate approaching swiftly, several meters ahead. Adrenaline (how much more adrenaline does she have?) shuts all conscious thoughts down and focuses her body onto two things: her arms and the service grate. She pulls mightily and, without even noticing how she got there, watches from a perch on the car coupling as the service grate disappears beneath her.

As her conscious thoughts return, she begins to focus on determining how she'll unhinge her fingers from the handrail. With great effort, she pries open the fingers of her left hand and, after flexing them to relieve the stiffness, uses them to pry open her right hand. "I really hate ladders," she wheezes.

Now, how to get to Eric? She slides her entire arm around behind the handrail and crooks it at her elbow, swinging her body around to peek around the side of the car, looking forward to determine how far ahead Eric is. She sees the top of his head sticking out three cars ahead.

"Vocks?"

*At your service.*

"Next time I want to take a walk, tell me to shut up."

*Define 'shut up.'*

"Never mind." Emily swings herself back between the cars, pressing herself back against one. "How long till this train stops?"

*This train does not stop.*

"Ever?"

*As part of the continuous farming process, the delivery tram cycles the entire station, loading and unloading—*

"Okay, okay. How long till we reach a part of the station where I can get off?"

*We will reach the quadrant 3 ag processing module in 13.35 minutes.*

"I really don't feel like standing here that long."

Though barely able to raise her arms, Emily crooks her hands around the upper lip of the tram car. Sliding her foot into an indentation in the car's wall, she simultaneously pulls and pushes herself up until she can see over the top edge and into the car's bed, which is about three quarters filled with apples.

With about two meters of clearance between the ceiling of the tram tube and the top of the car, Emily squeezes herself over the top until she's straddling the edge on her belly. She wriggles forward, then pitches face first into the car, sinking down onto a bumpy bed of apples. Struggling to stay on top of the apples, she crawls hand over hand to the front of the car. Exhausted, she crawls over the front lip of the car, swinging herself around on her belly to pitch over legs first, trying to find purchase on the coupling. Satisfied, she puts all her weight on her feet, spins slowly, and grabs onto the railing of the car opposite her.

Two more to go.

She repeats the process on the next car, crawling through more apples, then finishes by making her way on her hands and knees through even more apples. With barely strength left to think, she swings her legs over into the next car, only to hear Eric's muffled voice. "Em, no! Go back!"

She drops over the lip but instead of falling onto apples, she falls about two meters and smacks down onto hard floor. Dazed, she shakes her head and tries to stand, only to walk right into a cloaked figure, her head smacking hard against the person's chest. She looks up to meet Deacon's green eyes burning malevolently at her from behind the shadow of his hood. A hand darts out to grab her wrist. It is not the velvety flesh she had expected, but a pliable plastic not unlike what she felt when pressing her hands against the outside of Ms. Crana's ship. The other hand darts and out grabs Emily's other wrist. Pliable or not, the pressure of the grip becomes uncomfortable, and then downright painful.

"Okay, that hurts!" Emily cries out.

The voice that responds, however, is not that strange mix of Deacon's and her own, but is flat, electronic, and emotionless. And like all voices on this station, it rings in her head, emanating from no direction. "You are damaged hominid."

"Deacon?" Emily asks, confused. "What are you doing?"

In answer, the hood slips down to reveal a smooth, featureless, ovular head with dramatic etched striations drawing upwards from the chin to the bottoms of the eyes, as if it were wearing war paint. It is not Deacon. It is an android, sterile and white.

*You are damaged hominid,* it conveys  into her head. *You must be rehabilitated.*

"I'm Emily Clocke!" Emily screams. "I'm Emily Clocke!"

*You are damaged hominid. You must be rehabilitated.*

"I'm Emily Clocke!" She squirms and wiggles to try to get away from the android's crushing grip, but in this battle of man versus machine, machine has the upper hand.

Emily is held fast.

*You must be rehabilitated.*

"What do you mean rehabilitated?"

"What do you mean rehabilitated?" asks a voice cracking in fear. "What are they doing to us?"

Emily contorts her body to peek behind the android. She catches a glimpse of Eric being held fast by another, identical android.

———

"You are damaged. You must be rehabilitated." Deacon—the real Deacon—conveys this without a trace of menace. That he does so while tightening the bindings that hold Emily and Eric secure to the medical tables upon which they lie only makes it all the more menacing. To Emily anyway. To Eric, Deacon's silence is even more menacing.

The room they are in is vast, dark, and stale. Vaguely medical, in a not-very-antiseptic, assembly-line industrial way. Rows of perfectly spaced medical tables stretch off into the shadows, cold, silent, and empty, telling horror stories of grisly Nazi-like experiments. It's a vaguely dichotomous room—at once both ancient, dusty, and rusted yet beyond modern by early 21st century standards. Its starkly hi-tech utility gives Emily a surer feeling of being the future's past.

The tables they are on form an outline around their bodies. Within the outline a rubbery tubing slowly inflates with air and wraps over them, lightly pushing them downward and further securing them to the tables.

"What are you doing to us?" Emily screams.

"Rehabilitating you." His face is stony, his lips still refuse to move. His voice rings in her head.

# :09 time

"We didn't mean to leave," Eric pleads, furiously trying to worm his hands through the straps that bind his wrists to the arms of the gurney. "We were just going for a walk. We didn't mean to hurt anything!"

In response, Deacon's green eyes bore through him.

"What did he say?"

"He said 'I understand,'" Emily tells him.

"What does that mean?"

"Yoo weel note bee hahrmid," Deacon verbalizes. Or tries to. His voice is laborious and thick, a sonorous croak, the words peeling slowly off his untrained vocal chords, sounding almost like a hokey Eastern European accent to ears that have listened to too many spy movies. It was not reassuring.

Suddenly, the interior of the tables sink slowly downward, relieving the pressure of the air-filled restraints. A wet sensation caresses Emily's back, and by the sound of Eric's huffy exhortations, she figures he's feeling it too. A distant panic rises in her, inching up slowly at the same speed as the liquid filling the crevice she's wedged into.

"Is this the same stuff? Is this the same stuff?" Eric yells, quickly losing the calm he was already fighting to control.

Emily chooses to assume it is the same 'stuff' they were

frozen into on the ship, though this is purely an intellectual exercise. Her slow burn is threatening to spill over as the liquid forms around and covers her, inching up her cheeks, preparing to cover her mouth and nose.

She pulls into her lungs and closes her mouth, just as the liquid rises above her lips, holding her breath as she is completely submerged. She feels a vague electrically charged tickle, then whoosh—the liquid completely spills off her, leaving her completely soaked and gasping.

And feeling surprisingly unhurt. She feels none of the burning, none of the wiry, jittery exhaustion she felt only moments before. She sits up as the table begins to rise and the straps release, and by the time the table clicks back into place, she's completely dry. She sees Eric flop over the side of his table and crash to the floor, an arc of dense liquid trailing behind him as if he'd just fallen through a thick, wet, spider web. His speed and motion betray an angry desperation. He is dripping wet, obviously having jumped off the table before the drying process had started.

"Yoo arhe re-hhabeelitateed." Deacon says.

"I am not rehabilitated!" Eric screams, pushing himself back to his feet. "I'm tired of this place! I'm slimy and cold and I can't hear and I don't know what the hell is going on!" He sees Emily sitting up on the table examining him with an infuriating calm. "What the hell are you looking at?"

"How do you feel physically?" she asks with an infuriatingly calm curiosity.

"How do I...what?"

"How do you feel? Physically?"

"I'm pissed off!"

"Fizz-ick-lee!" Emily says, stressing every syllable.

"Are you kidding me?"

"No, how do you feel?"

Eric glares, fuming like an angry bull. Unconsciously, however, he takes stock. After a moment, the fuming stops and the angry creases in his forehead begin to smooth. He considers it consciously. "Actually," he says, surprised at himself, "I feel kind of okay." He rolls his shoulders and bends his knees and does a series of odd stretches in a sort of ritual self-assessment.

He studies Emily. "Why are you so calm all of a sudden?"

"I'm starting to figure this place out."

"Are you two okay?" Ms. Crana asks, bursting from the shadows, betraying the first sign of fear that Emily has seen in her.

"We're fine," Emily tells her. Her reassurance is confident, almost to the point of nonchalance. "Just tired."

Ms. Crana grabs hold of her shoulders and leans over to look into her eyes. Emily sees genuine concern, tenderness. And, for a moment, her mother.

"Really, we're fine," Emily says and looks away, blushing.

"I'm not!" Eric says.

"Duh rehhabeelitaeshun is..." Deacon says—or tries to say—before Ms. Crana silences him with a stony glare and a raised finger.

"They are rehabilitated," he conveys.

Ms. Crana spins to face Deacon. "I suppose I should thank you?"

"That is not necessary. However, I do believe that, under the circumstances, ill temper would be inappropriate."

"You'll forgive me for questioning your timely presence."

"It is purely coincidental."

"I've no doubt."

"What are they saying?" Eric asks Emily.

"They're fighting."

Eric shrugs. "Quietest fight I ever saw. Just like...hey, do you remember mom and dad ever fighting?"

"No," Emily says.

"Yeah," Eric says absently, growing thoughtful.

"I apologize for this...," a familiar voice says. Looking past Deacon and Ms. Crana, Emily and Eric see Brin.

"How long has he been here?" Eric asks, then shakes his head. "You guys are like creepy ninjas."

167

The young acolyte walks between Deacon and Ms. Crana, who continue waging their silent battle. Gesturing back to Deacon, Brin seems to be searching for a word to finish his apology for their tete-a-tete, but the sentence is never finished. Instead, he stammers: "It is unbecoming of both of them to act in this manner before you."

At that, both Deacon and Ms. Crana spin to look at him.

"You forget your place!" Deacon conveys, eyes glowing. Literally.

The acolyte snaps to attention, his face flushing, then hangs his head again shamefully. "I apologize, father," he says, then to Emily and Eric: "Forgive my insolence."

"That's okay," Emily says reassuringly.

"Wait, he's your father?" Eric asks the young acolyte.

"Figuratively speaking. He is my spiritual advisor."

"Oh, so like 'father' as in priest."

The acolyte is silent for a moment before becoming suddenly animated. He raises his head and beams broadly at Eric. "The head of the ancient cath-ollick church! Yes, yes!"

"Catholic," Eric helpfully pronounces.

"We are in possession of several cath-ollick antiquities," the acolyte says with interest. "Would you like to see them? Does cath-ollick represent your form of worship?"

"Well, not mine, no," Eric says. "We were...well, actually, we didn't really go to church."

"I see," the acolyte says, his interest suddenly waning.

"Are you cath-ollick...Catholic?" Eric asks, before catching himself.

"No, cath-ollick is an ancient religion, suitable for cultures living in the pre-remnant cycle. I am a keeper of the Word and of the words," he says to Eric. He then suddenly stiffens, stands at attention and bows his head again. "Indeed he is," he says flatly.

"Huh?" Eric says, confused.

Deacon suddenly appears beside his acolyte. He places his hand on Eric's shoulder, an awkward attempt at cordiality, but still appears cold and imperious. "My young acolyte is a testament to true faith," the acolyte says for Deacon. There is a long dramatic pause, as if Deacon is expecting a follow up question.

Eric leans over toward the acolyte. "So how come you talk but he doesn't?"

The acolyte leans in to Eric as if trying to be covert. "All on Caelestis have the capacity for speech, but not the necessity."

"And you have the necessity?"

"Yes, but…" the acolyte begins, but stops and, apparently chastened, stiffens and bows his head again. "I fear that the responsibilities of office have left me less time than I'd thought to practice the duties of faith," the acolyte says, resuming his channeling of Deacon. "I must now defer to those I have taught with the hope that I have taught them well."

"I don't…" Eric starts to say, before Ms. Crana steps between him and Deacon.

"The children are wet and tired and undoubtedly hungry," she says, addressing Deacon, "and while I am sure they appreciate your restorative efforts, they require something with alimentary value."

"What does that mean?" Emily asks.

"Food."

"Yes! Food!' Eric wails, "If I don't eat soon, I'm going to crash!"

"In the parlance of your time, yes, that is accurate," Ms. Crana confirms.

"Ms. Crana," Emily asks, "is it possible for you to always speak in the parlance of our time?"

"I can adjust my diction to accommodate any cultural or colloquial dialect."

"So that's a yes?"

"That is a yes," Ms. Crana says, then quickly corrects, "*That's* a yes."

---

They are in a more luxurious car of the monorail, though that luxury is only relative to the utilitarian car they arrived in. This car is not dissimilar, but it contains padded benches for them to sit on. Eric sits on the edge of one, hunched over with his elbows on his knees, head down, coiled tightly like a football player benched for the other team's foul. Across from him, Ms. Crana sits unassumingly next to Emily, a rag doll slumped in her seat, head against the glass of the cabin, eyes to the semi-transparent ceiling, arms draped lazily beside her and her gangly legs sprawled out in front of her, feet turned awkwardly inward.

"So where are we going?" Eric asks.

"I am escorting you to a nutrition square," Ms. Crana answers.

"Sounds delightful," Eric says with dripping sarcasm.

"Perhaps, in the parlance, I should call it a 'food court?'"

"That's only slightly better."

The monorail enters the transition tunnel in silence, then emerges into the transparent service tunnel, the amber glow of Jupiter nicely matching the simulated waning sun of the living module. The three passengers remain somber and unmoving, like weary commuters on the late bus home.

Emily lifts her head. "Where were you?"

"Pardon?"

"You let Deacon rehabilitate us. Where were you? Why weren't you there?"

"For that matter," Eric chimes in, "why didn't you stop the machines in the orchard?"

"I didn't know you were in the orchard," Ms. Crana answers.

Emily in incredulous. "How? How could you not? Deacon and Brin found us!"

"Deacon and Brin followed you."

"Why?"

"Because they felt it necessary, I presume."

"And you didn't?"

Ms. Crana leans forward and clasps her hands together. "I

allowed them to direct you to the sacellum. It was against my better judgement, but I felt it necessary for you to understand how some citizens view your presence on this station. I chose, for my own reasons, not to accompany you there. That, in retrospect, was a mistake. The message presented to you triggered a response that ultimately led to you getting severely injured. You needed further context in order to make sense of it and I failed to provide it.

"I'm sorry I was not there for you."

Neither Emily nor Eric responds.

"On Caelestis," Ms. Crana says, "there is context for every decision. Change is not the struggle it was in your time. Social change, I mean. Procedural change. Our synaptic interconnectedness means there is no decline in efficiency when a change is initiated."

"So your minds are all interconnected?" Eric asks. "Like bees and ants?"

"Only in a manner of speaking. We do have free will. We do have our own minds and opinions, disagreements. There is still bureaucracy. But once a change is agreed upon, instantaneous communication allows us to bypass the adaptation curve. We are in a constant state of data confirmation."

"So how come you didn't know where we were?" Eric asks.

"Because I'm not connected to you."

This riles Eric. "That's because…!"

"I'm not connected to your sister, either," Ms. Crana interjects. "Not in the way you think I am, anyway. I can communicate with her, but I can't tell where she is at any given moment. You see, Caelestis was developed in two distinct eras utilizing two distinct technologies. The first was, we believe, built ad hoc, as needed, presumably in response to constantly changing situations. It uses technology standards like radio-based interconnectedness, semi-invasive medicine, and directed automation, like the harvester you encountered.

"The second was a direct result of the advent and successful assimilation of aprocytes with our bodies. The aprocytes completely changed the manner in which we interacted, not only as a society, but how we interact with our machines. With aprocytes, technology is not externalized; all of the tools available to us are extensions of our minds and bodies. We don't just use them, we are essentially merged with them. This allows us to be very deliberate in the development of the modules on this station. The entire infrastructure of second-phase development is built upon that interconnectedness."

Ms. Crana stops, leaving the thought hanging.

"And?" Emily finally asks.

"It means that I couldn't find you because you're not connected. The infrastructure relies entirely upon aprocyte interaction to function. This monorail, the station's citizenry, the knowledge database... We are all interconnected by aprocytes. But neither of you have aprocytes, so the station doesn't recognize you." She points at Emily. "You have a slight connection because of your device, but its control is limited to some minor station functions, social communications, and a connection to the knowledge interchange. Otherwise, as far as the station is concerned, you two don't exist."

Emily silently laughs at this. 'I don't want to not exist,' she thinks, the imprecise, hesitant phrasing perfectly capturing her confusion. It was exactly how she felt arriving in Chicago: the newness, the unfamiliarity, the feeling of being an animal on parade before a whole new audience who doesn't see who you are but what they want you to be. New kid, savior. Same judgement, slightly different conclusion.

The car passes into a new module. It's a bit darker, more contained, full of small, glass-walled rooms that stretch along its length. Each room is built around a small glass box, each of which is connected to the ceiling by an intricate array of wires and tubes. Though they move through the module rather quickly, Emily notices that a number of those glass boxes contain—or at least seem to contain—babies. And the babies appear to be floating in a thick, amber-tinted fluid.

"What the hell is that?" Eric exclaims, his shock mixed with a morbid curiosity. "Are they...dead?"

Ms. Crana looks up. "No. This is the postnatal unit. The incubator, if you will. All newborns are transferred to this unit immediately after birth to appropriately acclimate to their aprocytes."

Eric stares wide-eyed at the incubators, his imagination captured. "So, like, how are the babies born? Do they like grow in those things?"

"No. Of course not. Do you not know how babies are born?"

"Of course I know how babies are born!" Eric yells rather too quickly, his face flushed.

Ms. Crana smiles knowingly. "The process is no different than it was in your time. Sexual intercourse leads to fertilization; nine months of gestation in the mother's womb results in birth. The difference is, during the gestational period, the mother's aprocytes are integrated into the fetus via the umbilical cord."

"So this is where they get aprocytes implanted?" Eric asks, barely hiding his excitement.

"In a manner of speaking. Aprocytes are artificial cells for which the human body has natural defenses. A non-acclimated body would fight them as it would an infection. During the gestational period, there is a balance whereby the mother, though supplying the aprocytes, conversely also acts as the defense against them. By the time of birth, most children have acclimated to the point where the aprocytes are stabilized within the body. There are, however, exceptions. The children you see here are the exceptions."

"Will they live?"

"They will be fine. The incubators are filled with chemical stabilizers which help the body achieve equilibrium. We have a zero percent mortality rate."

Eric stares out, intrigued. He appears reengaged, reenergized, flush with the possibilities.

He smiles.

"Pancakes!" Eric yells at the sight of the stack placed before him. "I haven't had pancakes in a week...or, well, a couple hundred years, I guess. However that works."

The four of them sit at a long banquet table, one of dozens that are spread out in a subsection of the living module that feels more like a giant, tree-lined atrium. It's a mall food court writ large, but more spacious, open, orderly, clean. The four of them are the only ones at their table, with Ms. Crana and Brin sitting across from Emily and Eric. Other people sit at tables around them, grouped in concentric circles, conspicuously busy at being inconspicuous.

"How does that work anyway?" Eric asks before shoving a fork full of dripping pancake into his mouth. "How old am I...?" He swallows hard. "Am I 16 or am I like 580 or something?"

"That depends upon your point of view. Do you measure your life chronologically or as a sum total of experiences?"

Eric looks at Emily, who shrugs. "Uhhh...I don't know?"

"Look at it this way," Ms. Crana says, "If you were to measure my life as a linear chronology, from the day of my birth until this moment and including all of the time I've been cryo dormant, I am nearly eight thousand years old. However, I've only accumulated empirical knowledge for fifty-two of them."

"Eight thousand YEARS OLD!" Eric shrieks. Moist flecks of pancake come flying out of his mouth. "How can you be eight thousand years old? How many times have you travelled back into the past?"

"Seven times."

Emily does the math. "But that's only about 3,500 years. Seven times 500 is 3,500."

"The duration of travel depends entirely upon to when we are travelling. A trip to 2015 and a trip to 1720 are of different durations. And those durations are doubled because we have to get there and back."

"So...wait a minute," Emily says, "why would it take five-hundred years to go back in time? Isn't it, like, instantaneous?"

"No," Ms. Crana. Her face then turns grave and she studies them for a moment. She leans in toward them and continues portentously, "Pay very close attention."

"Okay," they both respond.

"Time travel is not as it is portrayed in your fictions. Just as we cannot instantaneously travel from your era to this one, we cannot travel from this era to yours. The travel durations are relatively identical."

"I'm not following," Emily says. Eric seconds that.

"That is why I said pay attention."

"Okay," they both respond.

Ms. Crana continues: "Time is a dimension, just like height, width, and depth." She places her index finger on the table in front of Emily and pushes it toward her, drawing a short vertical line. "So let us represent this as height."

"Oooohhhh, now that's cool," Eric says, amazed by the line that appears from under Ms. Crana's finger. "How do I do that?"

Emily shushes him.

Ms. Crana continues. "And this is width." Beginning from the bottom of the vertical line, she draws a short horizontal line to the right.

"And then this is depth." She squares off the two lines, then adds more lines to create an image of a cube.

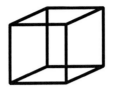

"The next component is time. It is attached to and inseparable from the first three dimensions, and is often portrayed as a cubed cube—a cube within a cube. However, for the purposes of our discussion, we'll portray the dimensions as such." She draws a long horizontal line, at the left end of which draws the letter A. At the right end she draws the letter B.

**A** _____ **B**

"The line represents the direction of motion, through all four dimensions. With respect to time, that direction is past—" she points to the A and traces quickly to the B at the end of the line, "—to future.

"Now, momentum dictates we expend no undue energy simply floating from past to future. It is the direction the universe forces us to go as a condition of existence." She points at the letter A at the left end of the line. "Cause," she says, tracing her finger across the line again to the letter B, "—becomes result.

"But things get a little complicated when we try to define this direction of motion as 'forward.'" She runs her finger from A to B again. "The complication is that there is no such thing as 'backward.'" She runs her finger back to the A.

"'Backward' is a term humans developed to differentiate motion counter to the direction that one's eyes happen to be looking. But the physical universe doesn't differentiate—momentum is always forward, regardless of which direction you happen to be looking."

She notices the quizzical looks on her proteges' faces. She draws a small arrow on the line, next to the A, pointing toward the B.

"Okay, pretend this arrow is a boat and you're in it travelling across the ocean." The little arrow begins to move along the length of the line toward the B at the right end.

**A** →                                             **B**

"When you get halfway across the ocean you decide it's time to go back to where you came from." The little arrow stops at the center point of the line. "How do you do that?"

"You turn the boat around," Eric answers.

Ms. Crana taps the arrow and it spins to point in the opposite direction, back toward the A.

**A**                       ←                           **B**

"And when you turn the boat around, in which direction are you travelling?"

"Forward."

The little arrow starts moving along the line again, back toward the A.

"Are you sure?" Ms. Crana asks. "You're moving in the opposite direction that you were originally travelling."

"Yeah, but you spun the boat around, so you're still moving forward..."

"Correct. Even though you're going to your starting point, you're not actually travelling backward, you're still travelling forward."

"I think I get it," Emily says, "but it doesn't explain how you get back to where you started. I mean, back to where you actually started from. How do you actually go back in time?"

"In a manner of speaking, you don't," Ms. Crana explains. "You have to do this:" The arrow image appears next to the A again and begins travelling along the line toward the B.

**A**                      →                      **B**

When it hits the center point of the line, the entire line

appears to spin along the axis that the boat has made so that the B is on the left and the A in on the right.

**B** $\longrightarrow$ **A**

"You don't turn the boat," Ms. Crana says, pointing to the arrow, which continues on its original trajectory but is now heading toward the A. "You turn the ocean."

"So...that part I don't get."

"You have to redefine what forward actually means. The process of time travel requires us to completely spin the universe 180° so that 'forward' means that future flows to past, result flows to cause. B flows to A. But where turning a boat on the ocean requires little more energy than normal, turning the ocean requires an enormous amount of energy, much, much more than our craft is capable of generating on its own. Thus, the energy is generated by the station and released as our initial means of propulsion, much as a slingshot propels a stone. However, once we actually succeed in spinning the ocean, so to speak, temporal speed equalizes, and the new forward becomes, for us, the norm. So the energy we expend moving from future to past is no different than when moving from past to future. So in terms of duration, a five-hundred-year trip, whether forwards or backwards, takes five-hundred years."

"Which means we have to be popsicles no matter what direction we're going," Eric says.

"Correct."

"But if energy returns to normal," Emily asks, "how do you turn the ocean again when you get to your destination? You don't have the station to generate the energy..."

"That's a very astute question," Ms. Crana says, clearly impressed. "And not easily answered. For the most part, energy is transferred from the station and stored on the craft until we reach our intended destination. Its release becomes the equivalent of the stone hitting the target, and the energy dispersal spins the universe again."

"What if the stone doesn't hit the target?" Eric asks. "What happens then?"

"We don't know," Ms. Crana answers gravely.

———

"This," Ms. Crana says, gesturing to the multi-unit building that stands before them, "is our residence."

"Our? We'll be living with you?" Emily asks.

"Not with me, no. Adjacent to me. You will take the chambers across from mine."

"Chambers," Eric says, accenting the syllables with a sonorous Darth Vader voice. He looks up and down the row of houses. From his perspective, they stretch from horizon to horizon, and though the architecture creates a distinctness from section to section, those distinctions are basically white noise to his eyes. "How are we supposed to tell which one is ours?"

Ms. Crana studies the houses. "Ah," she says, understanding dawning on her, "I see your concern."

"Maybe we could move to one at the end of the module?" Emily suggests. "That would make it easier for us to find."

"I have specific reasons for your residing here," Ms. Crana says, pointing up at a specific apartment. She offers no more.

"We could paint it purple," Eric says. Emily frowns at this.

"We will make appropriate accommodations for you to be able to find it," Ms. Crana says impatiently. "Let us go in. I'd like you to see it."

They walk through the entrance closest to them. Like the entrance to the spire, it does not have a door. This makes Emily double back outside and glance around at the structures within view. She hadn't noticed before, but with few exceptions, "There are no doors or windows on any of the buildings," she says as she re-enters the building.

"There are windows, actually, to cut out ambient station sounds," Ms. Crana says while striding through the vestibule, which Emily notes is not dissimilar to the lobby of a small hotel, if the small hotel were extremely white. "They are non-reflective so you don't notice them. Each entrance is equipped with an emergency shield in case the station's environment is compromised. Which has never happened. Otherwise, we generally have no need for doors."

Appropriately, she strides right up to a door.

"I thought you said…" Eric starts, but is immediately cut off.

"This is the lift. This door is a safety requirement." The lift doors slide open and Ms. Crana enters and bids Emily and Eric to follow.

"And, yes," Ms. Crana says as the doors slide closed, "each chamber—excuse me, apartment—does have doors. We do recognize the need for privacy."

She barely has the sentence finished when the lift doors slide open again revealing a long hallway. Ms. Crana leads them forward several hundred meters before turning down one of many junction hallways, each of which are on the same side of the hall. Opposite them a long row of portals looks out upon outer space, framed at the top by the pale, curved horizon of Europa. The secondary hallway is only a few meters long and opens back up to the central module.

"We walked all this way only to go back out…?" Eric starts to say, but his mouth drops in awe when he sees the vista before him. The hallway opens up to a wide, shared balcony, which juts out in front of the chambers on either side of it. At the railing, he sees that they are actually on the top floor of the structure and can see down upon the whole station. It is not quite the view from the height of the highest point of the monorail, but it is an expansive panorama that allows them to observe life on the station.

"Is this us?" he asks. "I mean, where we live?"

Ms. Crana points to a door—an actual door—to one side of the balcony. "That, specifically, is where you live. That—" she points to a door on the opposite side "—is where I live."

Emily walks to the door then stops. "Can we go in?"

"Of course. It is your home now." Ms. Crana says it warmly. Neither Emily nor Eric are sure yet whether to agree with her or not.

Emily pushes the door open and enters. The room is not the sterile, white cell she'd expected. It is warm and spacious and lived-in, full of earth tones and fabrics, carpeting and comfortable furniture and soft, golden lighting. The living area is open to a small kitchenette, or what Emily presumes is a kitchenette, as it is stocked with sleek, unfamiliar equipment alongside the more familiar cabinetry. Emily follows a hallway beside the kitchenette and finds two bedrooms, sparsely furnished, waiting for individual touches. She emerges back into the living area, astonished at the familiarity, the similarities to apartments in her own world.

"It's like a rich person's condo," she says, "or a really nice hotel room."

"Except for the bedrooms, it is still furnished to your parents' tastes." There is a conspiratorial lilt to Ms. Crana's voice, but she does not follow up. The comment hangs in the air between her and Emily.

It doesn't register at first; Emily's attention is too divided. Scanning the room, her eyes come to rest on a photo propped up on a side table next to the couch. A simple, flat, black-and-white photo behind glass in a simple, flat, black wood frame. Her curiosity is piqued more by the fact of the photograph than by the subject matter, which she can't quite make out at a distance.

"You still have photography?" Emily asks, moving toward the photo for a closer look.

"That was not taken on the station," Ms. Crana says.

Emily pauses momentarily in her stride, thrown off by the note of gravity in Ms. Crana's voice. 'Why so serious?' she thinks. 'It's just a photograph.' When she resumes her approach, it is with greater purpose: 'But of what?' When she's a few feet away, she makes out her mother's face. She is in the foreground of the picture, simultaneously familiar and foreign: eyes smiling, mouth in a toothy, unguarded grin. She is younger—younger even than the picture she'd seen in her mother's room that morning so long ago—more self-assured, happier.

Emily grabs and lifts the frame with a swift urgency, almost covetously, as if it were something stolen and then found. She draws it close for examination, like an art curator appraising a forgery.

In the photo, over her mother's shoulder, wearing a more devilish grin, is her father. He looks nothing like she remembers. His face is fuller, less sallow, his eyes wide and alive. His hair is disheveled and his chin sports a day's growth. He is rakish and carefree, not worn down by the apprehensions that she sensed through the happy-go-lucky persona he adopted for her and Eric.

Further behind him, melding into the out-of-focus background, is a woman. Tall and lithe, straight-backed, caught in the act of trying to avoid the camera, wearing a polite rather than genuine smile. Ms. Crana.

Emily looks up at her, the real her.

Ms. Crana looks back plaintively. "I do see the resemblance to your mother," she says quietly, studying Emily, "particularly in the eyes and mouth. Eric, however..." She shakes her head. It is not what she had wanted to say.

Emily studies her father's image. It is uncanny, the resemblance between her father and Eric, and Emily suffers a twinge of embarrassment that she didn't notice it earlier.

"Where did you get this?" Emily asks. It almost came out accusatory, but Emily caught herself. She made it an innocent inquiry.

"It was taken on our last mission together. Before...well." She smiles emptily. "I've since led two more with Misters Verton and Algate."

"But where was it taken?"

"July twenty-three of 1955. The coast of southern France. We were investigating the high-energy research facility known as CERN, which was then in its infancy. Your parents were always exuberant about our missions. The novelty of Earth never wore off. They liked to immerse themselves in the culture by taking frequent holidays. I indulged their flights of fancy because they were exceptional historians and scientists, and because rest is a necessary component of any productive mission. It also afforded a better assimilation into the culture. On that particular holiday, I did happen to accompany them, and they had some sort of camera appropriate to that era. I believe it was one that used a light-sensitive silver halide emulsion to capture the image. Your father, being prone to whimsy, turned the camera on himself and took what I believe in your era would be called a 'selfie.'"

At that moment, Eric emerges from the bedroom hallway carrying a dark plastic box. "Emily, look!" he says. "Can you believe this? Pong!"

"What?" Emily says, annoyed by the interruption.

"Pong, the old video game. I mean old old. Like, from the 50's or 60's."

"1975," Ms. Crana corrects. "It actually belonged to your parents. Your father had planned to fabricate the equipment necessary to make it operational."

Emily holds the picture out toward Eric. "Look," she says.

"What?" Eric says, bothered. Despite himself, he looks, though it's too far away for him to see the details. "It's a picture. So what?"

Emily huffs and moves toward him, forces it into his free hand. "Oh," he says, and absently puts the Pong box down on a couch "Wow."

"Yeah," Emily adds.

"They look young."

"Yeah."

Eric takes the picture from Emily, walks to a couch and sits. He stares at the photo. "What were their names? Like, their real names? Their names here?"

"Your mother was called Sayra and your father was called Leeth."

"So what are our real names?" Emily asks.

"Emily Clocke and Eric Clocke," Ms. Crana answers matter-of-factly. "You were not born prior to your parents' last departure. You are children of Remnant, but born on Earth. As such, you have forenames common to the current cultural standard and you share the surname of your parents' assumed identities."

Emily takes another glance around the apartment. It is an orderly, elegant mish-mash of eras, but it flows with a decorator's style and appears cohesive. And then it dawns on her: "What did you mean that it's still furnished to our parents' tastes? Was this their apartment?"

"It was."

She looks at Eric, who is still staring at the picture. She sits beside him. "Would you mind...?" She asks Ms. Crana. "Could we...?"

"I'll leave you to get settled," Ms. Crana says, then exits the apartment.

Emily leans over, her shoulder touching Eric's, and looks at the photo again.

"You know," Eric says, "I actually...you know..." He can't finish. He forces the picture into Emily's hands and stands. He tries to surreptitiously wipe his eyes, but Emily sees it.

He turns to face her. "We're the only two left." He gestures at the picture. "That's all we've got left. This is it, I guess."

Emily ponders this for a moment. Slowly, her edge erodes, but she still remains tense.

"I'm not going to say it's going to be like home," Eric says. "Like Earth. But I know for a fact that this is what mom wanted. She told us to go with Ms. Crana. She told you, too. I heard it when you were talking to her on the phone. She must have had a reason."

'She must have had a reason.' Everything Emily has learned in the last few days—everything Ms. Crana has told her—collides with that statement, builds upon it, begins to connect and coalesce. Into a vision.

"Do you want to stay here?" Emily asks Eric.

"What? No!" Eric's denial is half-hearted.

"Are you sure?"

"Well, I mean, there are some cool things, but…" Eric plops back down onto the couch. He is not ambivalent, he is defeated. "I'm just trying to make the best of it. It's what mom wanted."

"Are you sure?" Emily asks again.

"Sure about what? It doesn't really make any difference anyway. We're, like, here now. This is home."

Everything connects and coalesces into a reason.

"Mom had a reason, we just don't know what it was. But I think Ms. Crana did."

"Did what?" Eric asks.

"Have a reason."

Everything coalesces into a plan.

Emily stands, turns to Eric and thrusts the picture out at him. "Don't get settled," she says defiantly, "we're going home!"

# :10 launch

A vague scribble of cityscape is all they can see from the window of their apartment. Earlier, when the lights began to wane into the night period, the view of the module bore a slight resemblance to the classic view of Los Angeles from the Griffith Observatory...if the L.A. horizon had ended after several hundred meters. Pale discs of luminescence dotted the landscape like strings of Christmas lights thrown haphazardly over a cliff. Eventually, the 'ground stars,' which is what Emily called the L.A. lights when she was younger, winked off one by one, leaving the module bathed in black.

"Man, it is dark." Eric says. "Why are there no streetlights?"

"They probably don't need them. Apparently there is little night activity on the station."

"How much more time, do you think?" Eric asks.

"I don't know," Emily answers without commitment. "What do you think?"

"It's been night for about four hours, I guess. I really didn't pay attention to when the lights actually went off."

Eric steps on his tiptoes and tries to see further over the balcony railing, which juts out from the window just far enough to block a significant portion of the view directly below their apartment. They'd watched the module lights dim from the balcony, but decided it would be better to wait inside, away from Ms. Crana's prying. Or anybody else's prying, for that matter.

"I don't see any kind of movement out there," Eric says. "I guess there's only one way to find out." He plants both feet back on the floor and steps away from the window. Without hesitation he goes straight for the apartment door and opens it.

"Wait, wait!" Emily says, just loudly enough to cause Eric to slam the door closed. Loudly.

"What did you do that for? You'll wake up the neighborhood!" Emily says.

"So you wouldn't wake up the neighborhood? This is your plan, genius, what's the hold up?"

"I just...I don't know. Are you sure we should go now?"

Eric throws up his arms. "What difference does it make at this point? So what if we get caught? What are they going to do, flush us out an airlock? We're the Saviors of Remnant, remember?"

Emily is not entirely sure what that argument means, but it's persuasive nonetheless, and she exits the apartment behind Eric. They walk immediately into a massive wall of darkness.

"I can't see a thing," Eric whispers.

"Wait for your eyes to adjust."

Eventually, they are able to make out the vague shapes of walls and hallways. They pad slowly past Ms. Crana's apartment, Eric in the lead, holding his hands out before him, each step a deliberation. Emily is behind him, her hand on his shoulder, matching him step for step. After a time, they make it through the corridors and to the lift.

"Okay, so now what?" Eric asks, his hands gliding down the walls on either side of the lift doors, trying to find buttons or controls of some sort. "How do we make this thing go?"

"I don't know. There's no button?"

"I can't find one. Why don't you ask your ear wart?"

"My what? Oh. Vocks, how do get the elevator to work?" In answer, they hear the lift doors open and a blinding light pours out. "Oh jeez! Vocks, can you turn the light down?" The light dims to a point where they can both stop shielding their eyes, and they step in.

*Where would you like to go?*

"Down. To the first floor."

The lift drops to the first floor and Emily and Eric step out. The hallway they step into is slightly illuminated, just enough for them to be able to navigate.

"At least there's some light," Eric says.

*I've taken the liberty of providing illumination commensurate to your current level of ocular sensitivity.*

"It's Vocks. She's controlling the lighting."

"Good to know there are actually lights," Eric says. "Won't that attract attention?"

"I thought it didn't matter."

"It *won't* matter if we get caught. But the idea is still not to!"

"Vocks, is anybody outside?"

*The public space of this module is currently unoccupied.*

"We're good," Emily says.

They emerge onto the walkway in front of their apartment building, stopping for a moment to get their bearings, looking around for any signs of life in the low light. A flutter above them knocks Emily out of her skin. It's a bird flitting from the tree next to them, flying off to be swallowed up by the darkness.

"Chill, jumpy!" Eric says, suppressing a laugh.

"It's still too dark to see where we're going," Emily says. "And I'm not even sure I could find my way in the daylight. Or, whatever light."

"Ask Vocks."

"Vocks, where is the monorail station?"

*Follow the illuminated path.*

The walkway suddenly flashes to life. A series of dull, amber lights frames the walkway that stretches and twists before them, the lights decreasing in strength as they progress several meters ahead.

"Vocks, that's not a very long path," Emily says.

*In deference to your desire for stealth, the lights only illuminate a small percentage of the pathway. They will progress in sync with your pace, and likewise diminish behind you.*

"That is too cool," Emily says.

"What?" Eric asks.

"The path is being lit for us."

"I really need one of those," Eric says resolutely, referring to Vocks.

"If this all works out, it won't matter," Emily says.

After a few minutes, they reach the transport terminal, and with Vocks's help they board a monorail. Emily sits quietly, contemplatively. Eric paces, eyes concentrating on the floor. They feel a thrill of confidence, of having a purpose, of knowing their destination.

But when they reach their stop, they exit the monorail to the realization that they have no clue how to get there.

"We haven't really thought this through, have we?" Eric comments, staring at the next hurdle they have to face in order to get home.

A timeship. Docked quietly, illuminated by a faint cone of white light.

"I have," Emily says with a touch of bravado.

"Oh, listen to you," Eric says, "all brave now that we made it here. Ten minutes ago you couldn't take a step without worrying that we'd get caught."

"And that's the point," Emily says. "I don't think the station even knows we're here."

"How could it not? You used Vocks to do everything."

"I think Vocks is tied into the station but the station isn't tied into it. Not entirely, anyway."

"Why wouldn't it be?"

"I have no idea," Emily answer, "but I'm going to take advantage of it. Vocks, open the ship's door."

*Unable to comply. It is a manually operated door.*

Emily scans the side of the timeship, searching. Finding what she's looking for, she steps forward and presses a barely visible latch in the side of the ship. The latch depresses inward, creating a handhold, which Emily pulls to swing open the hatch.

"Really? No *Star Trek* doors?" Eric asks.

"Will you shut up about *Star Trek* doors?" Emily fumes. "I guess it makes sense. Cut down on automation—at least in the newer sections—to conserve as much energy as possible for time travel."

They enter and work their way into the dark interior of the ship.

"They just leave it unlocked like that?" Eric asks.

"Why not? The newer technologies are based on the aprocytes, like Ms. Crana said. The ship would know if a resident of the station was nearby. But we don't have aprocytes so the ship has no idea we're here. Vocks, turn on the lights."

*Unable to comply. I have no command access to the ship.*

"No lights," Emily tells Eric. "We'll have to feel our way to the front."

"Jeez. Do these people see in the dark, too?"

"Probably," Emily answers.

"Great. Now I'm going to be the one worried about having been seen."

They work their way up the aisle, occasionally banging their knees on the backs of seats. Eventually, they make it to the cockpit, which they can just about make out from the residual light coming in through the windshield from outside. They carefully make their way into the pilot's seats.

"Okay, so now what?" Emily asks once they're settled.

"How would I know? I thought you knew."

"I have no idea. You're the one who flew this thing!"

"You're kidding me, right? I just docked it! I don't know anything about launching it! You're the one connected to Vocks! You tell me what to do!"

Emily sighs. She'd made too many assumptions. She'd counted on Eric knowing how to launch. "Vocks, how do we launch the ship?"

*Launch coordinates are input via cyte control. Launch occurs one minute after crew has been secured.*

"Vocks, we don't have cytes."

*Coordinates can be manually engaged, but that will require powering up the temporal navigation processor.*

"Okay, so do that."

*Unable to comply. I have no command access to the ship.*

"So how do we power up the...whatever your said?"

*Engage manual pilot by pulling up the navigational levers.*

"The navigational levers? What are...?"

Eric preempts her question by reaching down between his legs and pulling up the joystick stowed under his seat.

The manual joysticks pop up from underneath them, and the projected raster graphic interface controls splash across the inside of the windshield. A small representation of a keyboard is projected at the bottom of the window, with a blinking cursor appearing on the first of four lines spread horizontally above it.

*You have approximately thirty-three seconds to input the temporal coordinates before the navigation processor consumes the allotted power.*

"Thirty-three seconds!" Emily yells.

"What?' Eric asks.

"We have thirty-three seconds to input the coordinates."

"Well, what are they?"

"I DON'T KNOW!"

"You don't—? Jeez, Em, you really didn't think this through! Ask Vocks!"

"Vocks, what are the coordinates?"

*What is your destination?*

"Earth."

*Earth is the standard spatial coordinate and is determined by and irrevocably linked to the temporal coordinates. Please input an appropriate temporal coordinate.*

Emily begins to stammer. "Uh, uh, twenty, twenty, twenty... twenty-sixteen!"

"What is it asking?" Eric asks. Emily ignores him.

*You must provide a month, day, and time to Jovian standard.*

"What is Jovian standard...screw it! Vocks, just tell me what I need to input to go back to 9:00 a.m. central standard time, September 30th, 2016!"

*Confirm Gregorian standard.*

"What? Yes! September 30th, 2016!"

Vocks calculates coordinates then recites them to Emily, who pounds them so hard on the glass that each contact of her finger shoots a jarring pain up her arm. When she presses Enter, the entire display disappears from the windshield and everything goes dark.

"Now what?" Eric asks.

"I don't know. Vocks, now what?"

*You have seventy-six seconds to enter the cryo-chambers before launch.*

"Why can't you just tell me these things up front?" she exclaims, standing up from her chair and moving herself back into the cabin. "Come on," she says to Eric, "we need to go into hibernation."

"But..."

"No! We need to go now!"

She opens a chamber and clambers in, shutting the hatch behind her as if she knew what she were doing. A dull light illuminates the interior just enough for her to see Eric enter the chamber immediately opposite hers. Judging by his face, he is not pleased by the prospect of complete immersion in the cryo-fluid. Truthfully, neither is she.

When both chamber hatches are closed... Nothing happens.

"Vocks, why isn't anything happening?"

*Have you entered the cryo chambers?*

"YES!"

*The ship is unaware of your presence. Please depress the manual activation button that is immediately below the number at the top rim of each cryo-chamber that is to be used.*

Emily opens her chamber and looks at the top of Eric's chamber. The number 1 is printed at the top rim of the chamber, and just below it, barely perceptible, is an ovular indentation. Emily puts her fingers into the indentation and presses inward. Eric's chamber immediately begins filling with the thick yellowy liquid. She turns and looks up at her chamber and presses the button below the number 2. The button immediately begins flashing red.

"Vocks, what's wrong with my chamber? The button is flashing!"

*The chamber must be sealed.*

"What do you mean sealed?" Emily yells, near panic. "Is my chamber not sealed?"

*Close the chamber door.*

Emily slams the door and the chamber immediately begins filling. She looks over at Eric and sees that the liquid is now to his elbows. He is trying his best to smile at her, but his grimace betrays his terror. She doesn't blame him. Despite having gone through this—twice, if you count the medical module—she can't wrap her mind around the idea of allowing the liquid into her lungs. But that moment comes, and despite her resistance, the pressure of the liquid on her face and the searing burn of her lungs desperate for air finally makes her relent, and the liquid pours in.

And then she finds herself regurgitating it. A heave of her lungs and she instinctively tips her head to allow a stream of liquid to shoot out of her mouth. The force of the discharge pushes her body upward and she smacks into the ceiling of her cryo chamber. Strangely, the chamber is empty, the only liquid left—besides what's flowing from her lungs—is a thin sheen covering the inside walls. 'Where did it all go?' she has the presence of mind to think in-between heaves. It takes a few seconds for her to find the presence of mind to wonder why she's floating.

Across from her, Eric is suffering through the same degradation. She can hear his flagrant whimpering in-between heaves and see his body whipping back and forth and up and down the walls of his chamber. He was never good at being sick.

"What the hell happened?" he says, after spitting out the last of the fluid. "Why did it empty all of a sudden?" He positions his feet at the bottom of the back wall and braces himself against the transparent door, his head pressed forward, his wet hair wild and matted, his shoulders heaving as he noisily sucks in mouthfuls of air.

"I think I know," Emily says as she pushes open the chamber door and peeks around to the cabin. Her eyes go wide as her suspicion is confirmed. She pushes her feet against the back wall and propels herself out of the chamber, using the door to pull herself around and position herself to float toward the cockpit. "Come on," she yells back at Eric. As she approaches, the view outside the cockpit begins to loom larger and larger, the piercing blue and white and green and beige overwhelming her eyes.

Earth. From orbit. The blue sphere consumes their entire field of vision.

"Holy shit!" she hears from behind her. "How did we... how are we... we're here already! How did we get here so fast?"

"We didn't get here fast," Emily says, situating herself into the co-pilot's chair. "It took us 500 years. Backwards years."

"I don't even remember getting frozen!"

"It's weird," Emily says, becoming contemplative at the view, "how looking at that—how that view—actually feels like home. I mean, it is home, but you never think of the entire planet that way."

"So now what?" Eric asks, settled in as pilot. "How do we get down? How do we land?"

"Vocks," Emily says, "how do we land?"

*Input coordinates.*

The coordinate screen flickers up on the windshield again.

"What would the coordinates be? I don't know how to..."

"Latitude and longitude," Eric adds helpfully.

"I know that, dufus. But how do I get the latitude and longitude?"

"Ask…"

"Shhh!" Emily raises a finger to Eric.

*Provide an approximate location based on hemisphere and continent.*

"Northern hemisphere, United States."

*United States is a politically designated boundary. Continent is identified as North America.* Emily shakes her head, embarrassed at her mistake. *Please narrow location. You may use state and city designations appropriate to the era. Or access a location on the map.*

A wireframe globe appears on the windshield. The globe is quickly covered by dozens of shades of colors until it looks like a smaller version of the Earth that they see outside. Intuiting the controls, Eric raises his hands to the image and begins gesturing so that the globe spins. When he spins it so that the Great Lakes are directly in sight, he draws his hands apart to zoom in to the southwestern tip of Lake Michigan, to Chicago.

"Thank you, Google Earth!" he mutters. He grins at Emily. "Some things just work!"

He continues zooming in and zooming in until he finds their city, their street, then their house. He points a finger at the backyard and a glowing red dot appears on the map, some text dropping down under it.

"Vocks, can we land there?"

*Please read disclaimers on chosen location.*

Emily leans in and silently reads the text under the dot. "Insufficient area for landing," she reads aloud. "Area is not sufficiently remote. Landing would cause significant disruption to surrounding community. Ship would be compromised."

*The selected location is not suitable for landing.*

"Thanks, I figured that. What would be a suitable location?"

"The school, probably," Eric says, preempting any answer from Vocks. He begins gesturing to find the school on the map. "I mean, Ms. Crana landed there, so it obviously works."

He points to the map, indicating the same easement behind the school from which they took off a few days earlier. "Right there."

"Vocks, land us in that spot."

*Please confirm coordinates and depress the button marked Engage.*

Emily reads the coordinates from the map. She looks at Eric and motions for him to press the flashing button below the coordinates on the map.

"Really? That's it?" he says, incredulous. "That's all we have to do?"

"That's it, apparently."

"I don't understand why I needed to learn to fly this thing, then" he says, the phrase 'learn to fly this thing' coming out in a frustrated, mocking tone. "It's all automated."

*Please fasten safety harnesses for descent and landing.*

They barely get their safety belts hooked when their stomachs lurch and their view suddenly turns to churning gray wisps of cloud. Cottony tendrils quickly give way to a swiftly skewing profile of Lake Michigan's southwestern tip, and the ground zooms up until they find themselves hovering over their school.

*Please refine and confirm coordinates.*

"Wait," Emily says, "something is weird."

"What?" Eric says, looking from Emily to the view of the school below them. His brow furrows in confusion. "Where's the pool building?"

"I don't know," Emily says, just as confused. "I mean, I didn't know every inch of the school, but it did have a whole other section to the back there, right?"

"Yeah, the pool," Eric confirms. "I had swimming in gym this semester, so yeah, that was definitely where the pool was. Or is. Or should be or whatever."

"Okay, well I say we land and check it out, anyway."

———

They stand at the edge of the airlock, staring down at the ten-foot drop to the dry, weedy grass beneath them.

"The ramp is invisible, I'm telling you!" Eric says adamantly. "Just like the rest of the ship."

Emily looks at Eric skeptically.

"I'm telling you!" Eric reiterates.

Emily braces herself against either side of the hatch and tentatively puts her left foot forward, lowering it slowly, unconsciously bobbing downward like a blind man's cane. When it finds purchase, she lets go of the hatch and leans out, moving her right foot in front of her left.

She is standing in midair.

"Man, that is weird looking!" Eric exclaims.

"It's weird feeling, too," Emily says.

"Well, I'm glad you didn't fall," Eric says, "'cause I really wasn't sure about the ramp."

Emily turns and glares at him.

Eric grins. "I'm kidding."

"Come on!" Emily says, moving carefully down the ramp and into the dry grass. "There's no fence there, either. We can walk right up to the back of the school."

They do just that, peering into classroom windows as they walk along and finding them empty.

"Hey, does it feel like October to you?" Eric asks.

"No. It's more like summer."

"And it's gotta be like noon," Eric says. "Where is everybody?"

"Uh oh," Emily says. "I have a bad feeling this isn't Kansas... Vocks, what year is it?"

There is no response.

"What did it say?" Eric asks.

"Nothing. Vocks, what year is it?"

Again, no response.

"Maybe we're too far away from the ship for it to connect," Eric reasons.

"We're only a hundred yards away!"

"Well I don't know! Bad wifi I guess!" Eric stops at a window. "Hey wait! There's somebody in there." He cups his hands against the window. "Hey Em, there's a class in here!" He begins tapping at the window. He sees the teacher, a burly fellow with a gentle face and a scraggly orange beard sitting on the edge of his desk, look at them with annoyance. He waves a hand, trying to shoo them away. Eric waves back, trying to draw him over. The teacher stands and moves to the window. He yells something, but Emily and Eric can't make him out through the glass.

Eric shrugs.

The teacher rolls his eyes and reaches for the window crank. The bottom pane pushes outward slightly, and the man leans over so his mouth is to the crack. "You'll have to go around the front. The ladies in the front office will let you in."

"We're not here for class, actually," Emily says.

"We need to know what year it is," Eric adds.

The teacher grunts impatiently and closes the window, a smattering of giggles escapes before it completely seals shut. Eric can see the students in the classroom all facing the windows, smiling and waving and pointing and laughing. One greasy-haired student flips him the bird.

"That class is only half full," Eric says. "It's like a summer-school class. It is summer!"

"And the pool hasn't been built yet," Emily adds. "We've got to be way early. Like, years early."

"Yeah. Too many things are different."

"Excuse me!" a voice cries out, snapping Eric's and Emily's heads toward the corner of the building. A woman, tall, slim, barely out of college and slightly on edge, steps around the corner and approaches them. She walks with clear intent, someone with something to prove. "You two shouldn't be there! Are you supposed to be in class?"

Emily squints to confirm her recognition. Unconsciously, she walks a few steps toward the woman and says her name without thinking. "Ms. Marks?"

"Do I know you?" Ms. Marks says, slowing, betraying a slight apprehension before squaring her shoulders back up and continuing forward like a sheriff in a B western.

"Yeah, it's…"

Eric hits her in the arm.

"What?" Emily says crossly, turning to glare at him. Eric opens his eyes wide, almost comically wide, a sign that he is trying to indicate something without speaking. Then it dawns on her. "Oh," she says. She suddenly recalls her brief conversation with Ms. Marks in the hallway only a few short weeks ago—and nearly 20 years in the future.

"No," she says to Ms. Marks, entirely unconvincingly. "At least, not yet."

"Then I suggest you two move along," Ms. Marks says.

"Let's move along," Eric suggests.

"Moving along," Emily says, looking over her shoulder as they retreat. Ms. Marks looks back at her with the same intense scrutiny she exhibited in the hallway that morning of Emily's first day at school. It is as if she had recognized a perfect stranger.

"Do you think Mom and Dad are here yet?" Eric asks when they're out of earshot.

"I don't know. Let's go find out. Is she still watching us?"

Eric looks back at the school. "No, she's gone."

"Good. Let's get back into the ship."

They're barely up the ramp and through the hatch before she's asking Vocks the date.

*By the Gregorian standard it is Wednesday, June 18, 1997.*

"Did it answer?" Eric asks.

"Yeah. It's 1997."

"Holy hell! That's definitely early," Eric says. "Like, twenty years too early! We weren't even born yet. Did you input the coordinates correctly?"

"I thought I did. Maybe I transposed a number or something."

"Ask it if Mom and Dad are here."

"Vocks, are our mom and dad here? On Earth right now?"

*Unknown. I do not have sufficient information on the identities of your parents.*

"Sarah Clocke and Lee Clocke."

*Unknown.*

"It doesn't know," Emily tells Eric.

"So what do we do now?"

"I don't know," Emily answers. "I guess we wait."

"Wait? Wait how?"

She looks at the cryo-chambers. "I think that's probably how. Vocks, can we enter the cryo-chambers while we're still on the ground?"

*Yes.*

"For how long?"

*Please clarify query.*

"How long can we stay in stasis if we're on the ground?"

*Given all potential variables you have sufficient energy and an appropriate store of cryo-fluid to maintain three cryo-chambers in stasis mode for approximately 323 years and still successfully effect revival.*

"Wait, what do you mean an 'appropriate store of cryo-fluid?' How much is there?"

*There is an appropriate store of cryo-fluid to to fill three cryo-chambers.*

Her face drops. "Fill three cryo-chambers how many times?"

"What is it saying?" Eric asks. Emily waves him silent.

*There is sufficient store to fill three cryo-chambers one time or one cryo-chamber three times.*

She looks at Eric. Her words are directed to both him and Emily. "Vocks, are you saying that we only have enough cryo-fluid to put the two of us into statis only one more time?"

*Correct.*

Eric does the math then shrugs. "So what? We freeze ourselves now, wake up in twenty years and go stop whatever the hell happened—or is going to happen or whatever—and we won't have to freeze ourselves again."

Emily begins to protest. "Yeah, but what if—"

"No what if's," Eric says decisively, pointing a finger at her. "We're going to freeze ourselves now and wake up in twenty years and go stop whatever the hell happened." To emphasize the decision, he walks to the cockpit and sits himself down in the pilot's seat.

Emily stares at the back of his head, processing the statement, running all of the variables through her head. She had come to the same conclusion as he, but still has to hold the decision up to the light of day to make sure she's seeing it clearly enough.

She is. It was decided.

"Okay, I agree," she says, walking to the cockpit and sitting in the co-pilot's seat. She looks out at the school. The tall, parched grasses between them and the building jitter in the lonely breeze, waving like the surface of a golden lake. "But we can't stay here, though. Can we? In the field, I mean. Right next to the school?"

Eric eyes the window of the school through which he spotted the class. He can just make out movement within the room. Probably the unhelpful teacher strutting up and down the aisles, keeping his unruly summer students in line. He remembers the kid who flipped him off.

"Probably not. There's too many people, right? Someone will run into the ship."

"Vocks, what are the odds of us being discovered if we go into stasis right here next to the school?"

*100%.*

"Vocks agrees with you," Emily tells Eric. "So where do we go?"

"We've got to find a cave somewhere. Or a deserted island. Or what about, like, the Yukon or somewhere remote?"

Emily watches puffs of dust swirl up from the arid ground. Occasionally, a minute cloud puffs up against the windshield and disperses. "It would have to be somewhere where dirt or rain or snow couldn't give us—"

Eric snorts. "I don't think rain or snow are going to damage a spaceship."

"Not damage, dumbass, give us away. The ship is invisible, but it's really just an optical illusion. It still takes up space. Rain will pelt off it and snow will land on it and then people will see it. We need to go somewhere where nothing can affect it like that."

Eric concedes. "That's actually a good point. So, then, a cave on a deserted island. Or wait—how about the moon?"

"That's not a bad idea. Vocks, how much would flying to the moon change how much energy we have to stay in cryo?"

*You have sufficient energy and an appropriate store of cryo-fluid to maintain three cryo-chambers in stasis mode for 979 years and still successfully affect revival.*

"Wait—979?" Emily exclaims, surprised by the extreme uptick in years. "How could it be 979 years when it was only 120-something if we stayed here? Don't we expend a lot of energy going to the moon?"

*Yes. However, cryo-freeze takes advantage of the vacuum of space to maintain appropriate temperatures. On Earth, the spacecraft must expend energy to maintain the frozen state.*

"Jesus, this is just too much..." Emily says, exasperated. She turns to Eric. "The moon's actually better because it's cold."

"So then let's go."

A few minutes and bouts of nausea later they are skimming above the mottled gray surface of the moon. The angled sunlight reflecting off the blanket of regolith that covers the surface gives it a mesmerizing, translucent quality, an almost gauzy, white glow. The long shadows of ridges and craters run from their approach but are easily overcome. Despite their incredible speed, the effect is of a slow, tranquil glide, like a casual drive through the desert at dusk (albeit fifty meters above the ground). The idea flits quickly through both Eric's and Emily's minds that the moon would be a nice place to...

"Where are we going?" Eric asks. He alternates his focus between the achingly lonely landscape and the projected vector grid that mimics it. Thrown up across the windshield, the ship projects information about each natural landmark they pass.

"I don't really know," Emily answers, coming out of her own fugue. "Vocks, where would be a good place to land and enter cryo-sleep?"

*Recommend an area in the Aitken Basin near the south pole. Coordinates 89.9°S 0.0°E.*

Emily recites the coordinates and Eric keys them in. Their stomachs sink as the ship almost immediately tilts, banking in a tight curve in response to the new directions. Within minutes they find themselves in darkness, the ship having settled in a deep crater. Only the rusty hue of the data being projected onto the windshield provides any illumination. It is an appropriate reading of their mood. They are both slouched in their chairs, limp, immobile, tied down by safety straps and the greater force of inertia.

Eric looks wearily at Emily. "I had a thought," he says, as if almost reluctant to mention what's on his mind. "What if we woke ourselves up some time before Dad died? Maybe we could, you know, save him?"

"Okay, Marty McFly," Emily says, more derisively than she'd intended.

"No, I'm serious!"

"Uh-huh. When did Dad die?"

"I think I was probably nine or ten…" he falls into a silence, making a rough equation.

"You know," Emily says, "I don't think this is such a good idea. We don't know exactly when we're going. If we get it wrong we could end up having to wait years before we can see Mom."

"Uh, no! We can see Mom right away!" Eric says, clinging tenaciously to the idea like a dog to a bone. "If we're too early, we talk to both of them. If we're too late, we talk to just Mom. Obviously. I don't think we look so different now than we did five years ago that they won't recognize us."

Emily ponders his logic. Even if they do get the wrong date, they'll have more than enough time to ponder a solution. And he's right, all they have to do is convince their mother of their story, and that shouldn't be too hard. She hopes.

"He died in the spring," Eric says, "if that helps. That much I remember."

"Vocks, what do I need to input to go into cryo-freeze until March 1st, 2012?"

Vocks tells her and she inputs the data.

"Wait wait wait!" Eric says emphatically. "Read it to back to me. I want to double check."

Emily stares at him.

"What?" Eric says, "You got us here twenty years too early last time, I just want to make sure!"

"Vocks," she huffs, "what do I need to input to go into cryo-freeze until March 1st, 2012?"

She repeats to Eric the numbers Vocks calls to her. He reads the numbers off the windshield display, then murmurs his agreement. She hits Enter.

*You have seventy-five seconds to enter the cryo-chambers before the ship enters hibernation.*

"Okay, let's move!" Emily says.

They unstrap and stumble back to the cryo-chambers, unused to the moon's lower gravity. At the chamber, Eric finds the manual switch above the door, presses it, and scrambles into it. Emily does the same. They experience the same moment of diluted terror when they can no longer hold their breath and the fluid rushes down their throats.

After what seems only moments later, they once more purge themselves of fluid and shake off the effects of hibernation.

Then they realize they are again weightless.

"Um," Eric says, opening his chamber door, "why are we floating again? The moon has gravity."

"I don't know. But I don't like it."

They both float to the cockpit, checking out the portals on either side of them as they move forward.

Stars.

A sense of dread weighs on them, but still they remain weightless.

From out the front windshield they see stars. No cave. No moon. No Earth. No planets at all that they can make out.

Just stars.

And then Emily hits her head on something.

And an alarm starts blaring.

# :11 zeroes

Emily winces. The sharp squeal pierces her eardrum like an icepick.

Eric floats forward, staring out at the stars, ignorant of the fact that Emily is pressing her hands against her ears, her face scrunched up into a grimace. He lowers himself into the pilot's chair.

"Turn off the alarm!" Emily screams above the din.

"What alarm?" Eric says with surprising calmness. "And why are you yelling?"

"The alarm! Can't you hear the alarm?"

"I don't hear anyth—" Eric says, then points to the windshield. "Oh. I guess there is something flashing. Look." He motions to a blinking icon on the windshield. It is a simple graphic showing two arrows pointing to a pill-shaped icon within concentric half-circles. It reminds Eric a little bit of the speaker icon on his laptop.

"Yeah, that would be an alarm!" Emily yells.

"Will you stop yelling? There is no alarm!"

"Vocks, stop the proximity alarm!"

The alarm continues blaring.

*The proximity alarm is not active.*

"Then stop whatever alarm is on!" she screams.

Emily is instantly bathed in blissful silence. She breathes in deeply and blows the air out of her lungs, grateful for the quiet and hoping the residual ringing in her ear will stop soon.

"You seriously didn't hear that?" she asks Eric.

"I didn't hear anything," Eric says with a tone of annoyance.

"It wasn't the proximity alarm," Emily says. "Vocks, what was that alarm?"

*An active telemetry transceiver capsule of unknown origin is converged with this position.*

"It's some kind of—oh." Emily turns to look at whatever she'd hit her head on. About a meter away from her, tumbling slowly toward the back of the ship, is a white, pill-shaped capsule about the size of a shoe. "It's some kind of capsule," she says, reaching out and plucking it out of midair.

"Some kind of capsule thing," Eric repeats dully, not bothering to turn to look. "Is that something we have to worry about?"

"Vocks, what is this?"

*A telemetry transceiver capsule.*

"A telemetry transceiver capsule," Emily says to Eric. "Telemetry is something with communications, isn't it?"

"I don't really know," Eric says dismissively, his attention on the stars outside the cockpit window. "But I'm looking outside the window and I'm wondering why we're floating in outer space when we were supposed to wake up on the moon. I'd really like an answer to that."

"You don't think this transceiver thing—?"

"I don't know," Eric interrupts impatiently. "But first things first. Why aren't we on the moon?"

Emily huffs, reading Eric's frustration. "You know, I don't really want to be middleman here any more than you want me to. Just because I have Vocks and you don't—"

"Can we not—?" Eric interrupts again, his voice tired. "Just—where is the moon?"

Emily capitulates. "Vocks, where's the moon?" she asks, her voice measured, falsely calm.

*Approximately 82 million kilometers aft.*

"Eighty! Two! Million!" Emily shrieks, absently releasing the capsule and instantly forgetting about it.

Her anguish startles Eric. He is now more alarmed than frustrated by his inability to hear Vocks, and turns back to look at Emily.

Emily, as usual, waves him to silence while she tries to learn more. "Vocks, why are we not on the moon anymore?"

*Lunar Orbiter Selene was in flyby proximity to map the southern lunar pole. To prevent possible exposure, the ship enacted emergency protocols and moved into a heliocentric orbit equidistant between Earth and Mars.*

"We had to leave the moon," Emily explains, "to prevent being discovered by a lunar orbiter. I'd have figured we'd've had a zero percent chance of being discovered on the moon."

"So where are we?" Eric asks.

"Between Earth and Mars. Vocks, *when* are we?"

*In the Jovian year—*

"Gregorian! Vocks, give me dates in Gregorian standard."

*In the Gregorian year 2016, October.*

"October, 2016!" Emily yells out. "What day?"

*Determination of calendar day is dependent upon specific Earth coordinates.*

Emily thinks of making Eric go through the process of finding Chicago on the projected map again, but then she has a better idea. "What about Central Standard Time?"

*10 October, 08:33.*

"Oh no!" she exclaims, turning to Eric. "It's today! Today's the day we left! Left Earth!"

"What happened to waking up in 2012?" Eric asks.

"I don't know! Do you remember what time everything happened?"

"A little bit after nine, I think," Eric answers. "Like nine-thirty...ish."

"Dammit! Vocks, how long will it take to get back to Earth?"

*Approximately 12 hours utilizing standard propulsion.*

Emily drops her head into her hand. When the tears threaten to flow, she folds her other arm over her, as if trying to envelop herself. "We can't do this," she whimpers, defeated.

"Em," Eric says softly, trying to get her back to her senses, "what did Vocks say? How long?"

"Tw...tw...twelve...hours..." she sobs.

Eric sits back. He feels a momentary numbness but forces it aside, deciding to reflect on options. "Twelve hours," he murmurs absently.

Emily lifts her head suddenly and sniffles. She wipes her flooded eyes with her palms, then exhales deeply. "Utilizing standard propulsion."

"What?" Eric asks.

"Hold on a sec," Emily says, regaining her composure in the light of an idea. She pulls herself into the co-pilot's seat and straps herself in. "Vocks, what do you mean standard propulsion? What's standard propulsion?"

*Standard propulsion utilizes a gravity-wave engine capable of warping space such that duration of travel is the equivalent of 1/150 light-second per minute of travel.*

"And...?"

"And what?" Eric asks.

"And is there a non-standard propulsion?" Emily tells him, gesturing to her ear. "As smart as this thing claims to be, it doesn't want to give me complete information. Vocks, is there a non-standard propulsion?"

*Exigent propulsion utilizes a gravity-wave engine capable of warping space such that duration of travel is the equivalent of 1/8 light-second per minute of travel.*

"I don't quite know what that means."

"What what means?" Eric asks.

"Something about exigent propulsion and a gravity-wave engine. Sounds like a warp drive?"

"So, *Star Trek*. Let's do it!" Eric says eagerly.

"Vocks," Emily asks, an intentional note of caution in

her voice, "if we travel with the warp drive—" she pauses, a disgusted look on her face, to which Eric gives an eager thumbs up "—the wave engine?—how long will it take to get to Earth?"

*Approximately 35 minutes.*

She tells Eric.

"That's damn close. We'd better do it now."

"Vocks," Emily commands, "how do we—?"

"Already took care of it," Eric interrupts, his finger pointing to a glowing button on the windshield that says 'Engage Wave Engine.' "Just have to read what's right in front of you. Hold on."

"Wait, wait!" Emily screams, "Did you—!"

She doesn't get to finish. The stars in front of them suddenly appear to stretch and twirl and meld together like streams of light swirling down a drain. Instant and acute dizziness turns their field of vision completely black. When the dizziness finally subsides and their sight returns along with consciousness, they see before them an ominous, dark chasm surrounded by what appears to be a fountain of extremely slow moving sparks.

"What the hell is that?" Eric mumbles as if his tongue were too big for his mouth.

"Gravity," Emily answers breathlessly, "warping the light around it. Where are we headed?"

"Earth! Where else would we be going?" Eric says.

"Did you even set coordinates?"

"Yes, I even set coordinates!" he answers haughtily. "If you'd have been paying attention, you'd have seen me doing it!"

"How did you know?"

"*Halo*, remember?" He grins. "I'm a pilot, dammit!"

————

Thirty-three minutes later, the dark chasm begins to collapse, and the sparks fall in on themselves, forming again into a vast, twinkling ocean of stars. The chasm then retreats to an infinitesimal dot, revealing a small, pale blue water droplet of a planet. Soon the Earth sits in front of them, taking up the majority of their field of vision. They are in a geosynchronous orbit, oriented such that their view out the front portal is of Eastern Europe.

Eric points to an undulating wave of glowing green and orange hanging over the North Pole. "That's the glow we saw the day we left."

"The aurora borealis," Emily clarifies. "It's really active." She looks down toward the equator. She can't quite see the southern tip of Africa from their position, but she does see a gauzy glow peeking over the horizon. "The aurora australis looks active too."

"Then we've got to get our asses in gear," Eric says. He calls up the global map and begins manipulating it to find their high school again. When he finds it, he again pushes the flashing button below the map. The ship begins to move laterally, the features of Earth rolling sideways beneath them. Eastern Europe gives way to Western Europe. Portugal gives way to the Atlantic Ocean, which gives way to the southern tip of Greenland. Nova Scotia. New York. Lake Ontario, Erie, and finally the distinct thumb shape of Lake Michigan.

But as they approach their destination, they see filaments of auroral light snake downward from the borealis, a glowing waterfall filtering to rivulets, carving jagged paths like spectral tears rolling down a loamy cheek. Finer, wispier fibers work their way north from australis, ghostly fingers reaching up hungrily, growing brighter as they mix and coalesce over...

"Chicago!" Emily says, "They're moving onto Chicago!"

"Why do I have this bad feeling that it has something to do with us?" Eric asks.

"Why would it have anything to do with us?"

"Well, gee, I don't know," Eric says tartly. "Maybe the fact that there are people capable of travelling through time in an invisible spaceship who just happen to be right below that glowing spot is just a simple coincidence?"

"You mean us?"

"Yes us! The us down there!"

Emily glares at him. "Okay, I get your point. You don't have to be nasty."

"I'm not being nasty. I'm being—"

An intense, unworldly flash of green explodes right in front of them. They barely have time to register it before the ship begins tumbling violently, scrambling their equilibrium, twisting their stomachs, and savagely throwing aside any other rational thoughts. They are buffeted violently back and forth and side-to-side, their seatbelts straining to keep them in place. The electrical system begins to flicker and the lights strobe, turning the experience into a carnival horror ride.

"Oh-kay," Emily says, drawing the word out slowly, breathlessly, absently. She's trying to regain equilibrium, recognizing that she should be able to see stars or something out of the front portal. Eventually, she regains a sense of them, strings of light streaking in a haphazard fashion, a visual clue to the ship's erratic spin.

"Okay, yeah. Can you stop it?" she asks Eric, but gets no answer other than a tapping on her arm and a faint 'Em, Em!' The ship, it seems, has already stopped spinning. "What, what? Why are you tapping me?"

"You passed out," Eric says. He stops tapping her.

"I didn't pass out," she says matter-of-factly, trying to maintain a sense of dignity.

"You did. I'm not sure for how long. You asked me if I could stop the ship and then I didn't hear a word out of you."

"Obviously, you stopped the ship."

"Stopped it from rolling, anyway. Got us away from the shockwave, but then something flashed and the power went out again. And, um…"

Something in Eric's hesitation shakes Emily. She turns to Eric. "What?"

In answer, Eric points with his chin, indicating something outside the ship. Emily turns back and looks. Beneath them and slightly ahead, barely visible in the low light, she sees. . .

Another timeship.

"Oh crap," Emily says. "That's us, isn't it?"

"I'm guessing, yeah."

"Is that bad?"

"I don't know," Eric says, the sarcasm unmistakable. "I've never travelled through time before."

Suddenly the other ship becomes illuminated, its portals luminous balls of light, casting a feeble glow within their cockpit, punctured with mechanical regularity by splashes of Christmas color, the traditional red and green strobes flashing from opposite wings.

As they watch, a figure appears momentarily in the portal closest to them. Backlit, they see only a silhouette, but there is no question of who it is.

"That's Ms. Crana," Eric says excitedly. "We need to call…" But she is gone as suddenly as she'd appeared, leaving the portal a luminous white bubble again.

"We can't call her," Emily says, "she's from…she's…we need to get away from her!"

"Why?"

"Because she's from the past. She can't know we're here."

"I think she knows we're here. I'm pretty sure she just looked right at us."

"Then we need to move away!"

"Are you kidding me? We can't move away! We have no power!"

"Well, can you fix it?"

Eric stares at her, incredulous. "Really?" he asks with derision. When Emily doesn't answer, he unstraps himself from his seat and pushes up, preparing to move. "Sure," he scoffs, "I'll go fix it!" He kicks away and floats to the back of the ship.

Emily sits and stares at the other timeship, trying to remember the events occurring within it. But that's just an exercise to keep her mind away from the knowledge that they've lost again. They've lost their mother, lost their planet. Lost their way. They've tried but lost.

And the tears come silently.

No whimpering this time, no blubbering or trying to fold in on herself. No retreating but no moving forward. Nothing new but nothing old. Neither light nor darkness. Heaviness, yes. The dull ache of remorse. Self-pity and self-loathing. Fear. Regret. The past and the future both equally unknown and unknowable, converging, drifting away. Everything extraordinary and everything mundane, the entire universe, all matter, energy, feeling, thought sucked into a massive black cavity.

In the portal, an ephemeral reflection appears. Her mother. The young mother she never knew. The one from the picture, but without joy. Just plenty of judgment. Plenty of withering criticism.

She turns and see her father. The young one from the picture, but without the whimsical effervescence that she barely ever saw. The one with the worry lines and the tear streaks down his cheeks. The one who says to her, "Here's your capsule."

Emily furrows her brow, wondering about the context for that statement. Just as she comes to the realization that the voice is not actually her father's but is her brother's calling from the back of the ship, the white capsule floats past her head. The rounded end rebounds off the windshield with a barely perceptible clink, the concave shape of the glass redirecting it right at Emily. She unstraps herself from her seat and rises up, reaches forward and grabs the capsule, and tucks it under her arm. Then she turns and pushes herself toward the back of the cabin.

"I don't know what anything is back there!" Eric says from the shadows. "Not that I can see it anyway," he adds, suddenly appearing right in front of Emily. "This is way beyond *Halo*. We need Geordi LaForge to come and fix this."

"Who?" Emily spies what appears to be a locker situated between the cryo-chambers and the exit hatch. She opens it and stuffs the capsule inside, then closes it, listening for Eric's answer.

"Geordi. From *Star Trek*. The engineer?"

Emily sighs heavily and tries to dry her tears without Eric seeing. "Will you stop with the *Star Trek* already?"

"No," he says, "no, I won't!"

"We've got to figure out a way to get the ship fixed," Emily says unnecessarily. She turns and floats back to the cockpit. "Vocks, how can we fix the ship?"

*Please specify the system that is not functioning.*

"Uh...the entire ship."

*Begin by running a full diagnostic on all systems.*

"Do you know how to run a full diagnostic on all systems?" she asks Eric.

"Of course I do," he lies, lowering himself into the pilot's seat. "Except, you know, there's no power!"

Emily groans. "How do we get out of this?"

"Ms. Crana," Eric says.

"No. No Ms. Crana. I don't think that's a good idea."

"No," Eric says firmly, suddenly illuminated, pointing out the front, "Ms. Crana!"

Emily follows his finger, looking out into a direct spotlight that she had completely missed while in the midst of her pensive reverie. The other timeship is facing them, almost touching nose-to-nose. Ms. Crana sits in the cockpit staring at them with a fervent curiosity.

Emily and Eric wave feebly, abashedly.

Ms. Crana begins, for some strange reason, to roll upside down. Emily stares off in dazed wonder, while Eric twists his head to follow Ms. Crana's roll. It takes a few seconds, but they both orient to the idea that Ms. Crana is actually rolling her ship.

"What is she doing?" he asks.

When Ms. Crana's ship is completely upside down, it begins to slide sideways and disappear around the side of their ship.

"I think she's coming aboard."

"How?"

The answer comes in the form of a gentle thud to the side of the ship. A few scraping sounds, the hiss of the airlock, and

Ms. Crana is floating urgently into the cabin of the ship. "Do not speak," she says sternly, then turns and floats to the back of the ship.

"Are we supposed to go back there?" Eric asks in a whisper.

"I don't think so."

Within seconds the ship flares back to life. Momentarily, Ms. Crana comes floating back into the cabin.

"We're out of—" Eric starts to say, but his words drift off as Ms. Crana floats out of the ship again, back into her own.

Emily and Eric sit and stare at each other, unsure of what to do. Just as the moment is about to become uncomfortable, a bright flash turns the cabin completely white, and fades to darkness. The power on the ship is now out again. Only the pale emergency lights provide any illumination.

"What is that?" Eric asks. "Why does that keep happening?"

A large plastic, fluid-filled container, like a double-sized beer keg, floats into the cabin from the airlock, followed by Ms. Crana. She steadies and releases the container, leaving it floating in place, then turns and heads back into the airlock.

"Ms.—!"

"Shhh!"

After another long moment Ms. Crana returns with another, identical container and swings it forward toward the cryo-chambers. Opening a door above one of the chambers, she pulls out an empty container, casts it off to float on its own toward the back of the chamber, then lifts the new one into place. She does the same thing to the next chamber. After shutting the hatch above that cryo-chamber, she turns and floats back to retrieve the empty containers, then disappears again back into her ship.

A long moment of silence follows.

"So—" Eric says, letting the word drift off.

Then Ms. Crana reappears and stops just outside the airlock she's entered. She looks from Eric to Emily, her lips pressed together. Whether it is in anger or concentration, Emily is sure she is about to find out.

Emily stammers a bit. "It's been a complicated day."

"To say the least," Ms. Crana says. "Indeed, say the least: I already know too much. It is not appropriate for you to be both there—" she gestures to indicate her own ship docked just to the side of theirs, "—and here at the same time."

"How did you know it was us?" Eric asks.

"I looked out the window."

"Yeah but, how did you know we needed fluid?"

"I didn't until I got the power restored. How is it that you come to need fluid?"

Eric shrugs. "We don't know. Why is the power out again?"

Ms. Crana shrugs. "I don't know." She floats forward and grabs Emily's chin, turns her head, and bends her ear back to see Vocks. She screws her face and shakes her head, though whether it is in anger, curiosity, or frustration, Emily cannot tell. "It is against my better judgment to be speaking to you," Ms. Crana says. "It is, in fact, a serious violation of protocol. But then, so is your being here."

"We were—" Emily starts, but is interrupted.

"We do not know the consequences of foreknowledge," Ms. Crana explains further. "That is why there are multiple failsafes put in place to prevent any timeship encountering another. Fortunately for you they are easily overridden as necessity may dictate. It is just not wise to do so.

"Now, as to why you were floating in space between Earth and Mars even though you went into cryo-sleep on the moon. The answer is: I don't know."

"Why...?" Eric starts to ask, but is interrupted yet again.

"No," Ms. Crana says definitively. "No more. Answers will come in time. Time now to sleep." She waves them to her.

They both unstrap and float to the cryo-chambers, Emily entering hers and Eric entering his.

"The ship's chronometers will wake you when you have passed a duration of twelve hours after your time of departure from the station. You will be approximately five million kilometers from Caelestis. Expect to have to answer to the

Prime Minister immediately upon docking. I suspect she will not be happy."

She closes the chamber doors and looks at Eric with a crooked grin. "I guess I'm going to have to teach you to fly it, aren't I?" The chambers begin to fill, and then Emily and Eric are asleep.

———

Emily finds herself suddenly delighted that Deacon has joined the Prime Minister's welcoming committee. It wasn't the case at first—she was indifferent at best—but the Prime Minister's instantaneous accusations and forceful rhetoric had triggered a fit of pique, even if what the Prime Minister said was indeed accurate. Emily had stolen a timeship. Emily had travelled back in time illegally (though Emily didn't actually know it was illegal, she suspected it wouldn't exactly be a welcome act). Emily didn't know what she was doing.

It was a shock, at first, when, upon docking, the ship's door swung open and the Prime Minister, flanked by Deacon and Ms. Crana, immediately began venting. Angrily. Emily hadn't expected to be warmly welcomed, exactly, but her previous encounter with the Prime Minister left her with the impression that her initial greeting would be a slow-burn glare and a condescending lecture. The reality was a splash of ice water in the face. The Prime Minister's measured demeanor was absent. What stood before her was an uncaged beast spouting fire about paradoxes and the unknown and danger and recklessness and ignorance. Emily's ignorance. Emily's dangerous ignorance.

And it had a curious effect. Over the past several days, after encountering gunfire, rockets, the destruction of life on Earth, the loss of her mother, space stations, time travel, killer farming machinery, being drowned on several occasions, being told untruths, half-truths, and unbelievable truths, and failing to roll it all back, Emily wasn't about to be demure in the face of some stranger's self-important and patronizing accusations. She had done that all her life. Faded into the background, merged with the wallpaper, accepted invisibility even while fantasizing about acceptance and importance and some small measure of popularity. She wasn't just a fourteen-year-old girl anymore. (An instantaneous wry observation flitted through her mind at that: she was actually an eight- or nine-hundred-and-fourteen-year-old girl now!)

Drawing on her new-found sense of defiance, she looks at Deacon, squares up her shoulders, channels every valorous speech she's ever seen, heard, or read, and prepares herself to do something that she finds at once both distasteful and necessary:

Be their messiah.

"You don't get to yell at us like that," she says firmly, cutting off the Prime Minister's conveyed sentence.

The Prime Minister, clearly unused to being spoken to in that manner, stares daggers at the impudent young girl. But she ceases her communications. Even Eric gasps, though it is barely audible. Deacon betrays no emotion whatsoever, which Emily had expected. And Ms. Crana stands stock still, silent, her hands clasped behind her. The expression on her face unknowable.

Or is it? Emily, her eyes flitting to the imposter science teacher, searching for strength, sees a slight twitch of the lip. So minute it barely registers. But it was there, fleetingly, and Emily recognizes it for what it was: her mother's smile. Her mother's grin. A sign of defiant encouragement. Of pride.

"We didn't ask to come here," she continues, trading on her momentum, "We didn't ask to be your saviors. You did that. You made us that. And now you're complaining about us trying to do what you expected us to do? For trying to actually fix things? Sorry, no. If you want us to be your saviors, we will be."

A flash of concern crosses Ms. Crana's features. Something in that last sentence apparently didn't sit right.

Emily continues. "But we're going to do what we feel is the right thing to do. You don't get to yell at us for doing the very thing you want us to do."

A long, tense silence falls over the docking bay. Even the whirring and motorized hustle and bustle of the automated machinery has stopped, making the dead air even heavier. The echo of Emily's last word is allowed to die down before anybody speaks.

"I will speak to you alone," the Prime Minister finally croaks, her unpracticed speech slow and crackly. Her eyes flit between Emily and Eric. "Both of you."

Eric swallows hard.

Emily seems unperturbed.

————

The Prime Minister opens the door of her office and steps aside, beckoning Emily and Eric through. As Ms. Crana steps forward, the Prime Minister spins and raises a hand. They exchange words silently. Even Emily doesn't hear what is being conveyed.

"No," Ms. Crana eventually verbalizes, "I am their guardian. I will be present."

"Guardian is not your official capacity," the Prime Minister conveys. "You have no—"

"I claim familial right. They are my sister's children. They have no other family here."

"Your claim is registered and accepted. Nonetheless, I will speak with them alone."

"It's okay," Emily says to Ms. Crana, cutting off her response. "We'll be fine."

Ms. Crana frowns. "I will speak to her alone for a moment," she says to the Prime Minister. She waves Emily to her and pulls her away further into the hallway. She places her hands firmly around Emily's neck, as if cupping her skull, and gently touches Emily's forehead to her own.

It is an intimate embrace, and Emily is surprised to welcome it. Then she feels a slight tap behind her ear.

"I can listen to your conversation," Ms. Crana conveys, "if you allow it."

"Why do you..." Emily looks around sheepishly. "You don't need to listen! I can handle myself!"

"I know you can, but I have concerns about your willingness to play the role of savior."

Emily thought to argue, but she decided that she didn't want to fight on two fronts. She wasn't even sure she wanted to fight on one front, but she was still feeling the momentum of anger, though it was already waning. She needed to concentrate on the devil she didn't know. "How do I allow it?"

"Just tell it to listen. Do so before you enter the Prime Minister's office. She does not know about this—" she double taps behind Emily's ear, "—so be discreet."

Emily nods.

Ms. Crana releases her hold. "You will be fine; there's nothing to worry about. Just don't make promises you're not sure you can keep. You've learned much about Caelestis, but you still have a lot more to learn."

"Okay." Emily turns and enters the Prime Minister's office without first telling Vocks to listen.

The Prime Minister closes the door behind her. "You two have had quite the adventure," she conveys as she takes her place in her singular chair. Emily and Eric stand back, barely moved from their positions when they'd first entered the room. The Prime Minister smiles. "You may approach," she conveys.

Emily takes a few steps forward, then stops when Eric lags. He looks at her, his face a mask of frustration. With great hesitation, he steps forward to align with her, and they take a few more steps together toward the Prime Minister.

The Prime Minister, for her part, keeps smiling, but it somehow becomes more sardonic. "The distance you keep is telling," she conveys.

Emily does not respond. She's not sure how to. She had prepared herself for a confrontation, but the Prime Minister seems to have pivoted. The aggression and anger the woman had displayed only minutes earlier seem to have disappeared completely, as if a switch had been flipped, and replaced with a calm, deferential demeanor that felt, to Emily, vaguely duplicitous.

Emily's own adrenaline seems to be evaporating quickly. Her body suddenly feels heavy, shaky, and the anger she'd cultivated in the docking bay is beginning to wither into dusty exhaustion.

The quiet lag clues Eric in to what is happening and he just shakes his head in frustration. "Is this how this conversation is going to go?" he asks Emily.

Emily looks at the Prime Minister. "We'd appreciate it if you spoke to us. Verbally. My brother is unable to follow."

"Please offer my apologies to your brother," she conveys, "I am unpracticed in verbal communication. A vocal conversation would render me...inarticulate. I think it best we continue in this manner. I would be obliged if you would translate for him."

Emily turns to Eric. "I'll translate," she says, empathetic to his frustration.

"Okay, you know what?" he says, throwing up his arms. "I'm so frickin' tired of this! I'm out! You won't talk to me, why should I talk to you!" And before Emily can react, he turns and storms out of the room, purposely slamming the door behind him.

The Prime Minister raises an eyebrow. "A fit of pique," she conveys, then appears to become contrite. "I apologize for being unable to accommodate Mr. Clocke. I was unaware of the strength of his discontent. I did not mean to insult him."

"It's not you," Emily says, wondering why she's suddenly finding herself needing to apologize. "Well, it's not just you. And I guess it's not just him."

"I gathered that from your reaction in the docking bay."

Emily says the only thing she can think to say: "Yeah, I'm sorry for that."

The Prime Minister smiles mirthlessly. "Whatever for?"

"I don't actually know," Emily answers, embarrassed by how quickly she's losing the sense of control and authority she had only minutes ago. She feels strangely disarmed, unsure of herself again. She's not entirely sure if she meant what she said in the docking bay, nor whether she's really sorry she said it.

Was her bravado temporary, the result of circumstance and no longer needed now that the immediate danger had subsided? Or was it conviction? Was it long term? Was it who she was now?

"Did you not mean what you said?"

"No, I—I mean, yes, I meant it. But—"

"You're learning to express yourself. There's no shame in that. Never apologize for an honest opinion. We both could have been less aggressive in stating our convictions. It is rare that my emotions get the better of me, and I regret pushing you to that reaction. But such is my concern for your welfare. "

Emily nods.

"I have to express that you and your brother have—I believe it would be said in your parlance—boxed me into a corner. It is dangerous to have you stealing timeships."

"Okay," Emily replies, just to have something to say.

"Even beyond concern for your safety, time travel is a complex process which requires years of learning before we can allow you to attempt it."

"Yes," Emily says, "Ms. Crana told us about—" She realizes too late what she said.

"I am sure she did. Quite sure she did." The Prime Minister nods knowingly. "However, she couldn't possibly encapsulate all of the nuances involved in such a short amount of time. It is a dangerous activity and should not be attempted by those who are untrained in its complexities." There is a quality to her conveyance of the last sentence that suggests that the subject is now closed. A subtle implication—expectation? threat?—that no further attempts to steal a timeship will be tolerated.

The Prime Minister then softens. "May I tell you something in confidence?" It is conveyed under a strange aura of political appeasement.

Emily shrugs. "Sure."

"I am not a believer in the prophecy. Not like Deacon or your friend Brin, or many of the people on Caelestis. I do not cling to the idea of Saviors or of Reunification. I rather find the prophecy to be nonsense. How do you call it in the colloquial? Gobbledygook?

"But I am nothing if not practical. People *do* believe—not all, but the majority—and as administrator of this station I must account for them. So regardless of what I believe I play the role. I make appearances now and again at the sacellum in order to assure the people of Caelestis that I am a trustworthy, unifying leader. That I have their interests at heart. There is no sense of disunity here; the people on Caelestis are generally happy and productive. There may be disagreements on occasion, but overall it is peaceful.

"But the prophecy is wound inextricably into the cultural fabric of this station. People believe that they need to believe, whether or not it goes against their sense of logic or even their self interest. And when that belief is challenged, there is discord. I cannot have discord."

The Prime Minister's conveyed message stops. It becomes so quiet that Emily can hear her own pulse. 'Is she expecting a response again?' she wonders. She swallows hard.

"Do you understand?" the Prime Minister asks.

"Yes," Emily responds weakly. Then, "Well, actually, no. I don't really get what you're asking. I can't really tell whether you want me to be the Savior or not."

"I have no preference either way. I merely want you to be comfortable being who you are. Who you are is shaped in large part by who you want to be, so I caution you to think long and hard about that before you speak again of your willingness to be the Savior of Prophecy. Can you indeed be Savior if you don't have the strength of your convictions?"

"I guess not." Emily answers with a note of defeat creeping in, yet it's not defeat she feels. It's confusion. She's not sure what the Prime Minister is saying—or asking—so she's clutching at straws to give an answer she thinks the Prime Minister wants.

'Why can't I just be honest?' she thinks. 'Do I even know my own truth?'

"I will ask you that question again soon. Think on it. You

will receive plenty of counsel on the matter, I'm sure. But I would like *your* answer."

Seconds later, Ms. Crana bursts through the door. At first, Emily thinks she's come to save her, but after a moment she realizes that her aunt was merely called in by the Prime Minister to retrieve her.

"Thank you, Ms. Clocke, for granting me an audience," the Prime Minister conveys as the last word.

Ms. Crana then draws Emily by the elbow and guides her to the door. But Emily stops and turns. "Why are you asking me this?" she asks the Prime Minister.

"As I said, I cannot have discord."

Ms. Crana gently pulls her from the room. "You didn't cyte-cast the conversation," Ms. Crana scolds after the door is closed.

"I didn't have a chance to turn it on."

"What was said?"

"I'm not really sure, to be honest. She said she doesn't believe in the prophecy."

At that, Ms. Crana pulls her away from the closed door and ushers Emily down the hallway. "I am aware of her beliefs on the subject," she says, lowering her voice to a loud whisper, even though there is nobody else around. "I suggest you say nothing more of that."

"She told me to think about whether I really wanted to be the Savior or not."

"Do you?"

"Of course not!"

"Then you need to be more careful with your comments."

"Yeah. I think that's what she was trying to tell me." Emily stops walking, confusion drawing itself on her face. "I don't get it. Does she want me to be or not?"

"To her, it doesn't matter," Ms. Crana says. "What matters is knowing your intentions."

"I don't have any intentions. Why does that matter?"

"Because the future—*your* future—depends on it."

# :12 resolve

Ms. Crana looks past Emily, to the distant door of the Prime Minister's office. Her voice becomes quiet again, conspiratorial—equal parts admiring and scornful—as she pulls Emily into motion again. "She wants to know what her next steps should be. If you and Eric are going to be the Saviors, she'll need to strengthen her alliance with Deacon and align herself more closely to you. If you decide to reject it, she'll need to handle the fallout and message a path forward without you."

"Is that good or bad?"

"The Prime Minister is the Prime Minister for a reason. She is a politician. It is both good and bad."

"What do you think I should do?"

"I was under the impression that you'd already made up your mind."

"I guess I have. I mean, I don't know about Eric..." Emily grows pensive. "Do you think we're the Saviors?"

"No." It is said without inflection. Concise, to the point.

Emily is unsure how to react. She feels almost offended, as if stung by a lack of faith.

Ms. Crana sees it instantly. "Emily, you do not need that to be validated. Prophecy anoints whoever is best positioned to exploit it. We are time travellers, you and I. Prophecy is our effect, not our cause. It is certainly not our currency. I leave that to the politicians. But your fate and her fate are intertwined. The decisions you make on this matter will have repercussions on your relationship with her."

They continue to walk, silently for awhile.

"I'm not sure I trust her." Emily asks.

"That may be very wise of you. Do you trust me?"

Emily stops. "I do," she says.

Ms. Crana grabs Emily's arm and tugs it lightly to encourage her to begin walking again. "Good. Then tell me what you're still not telling me." When Emily fakes a look of curiosity, Ms. Crana continues. "I've sensed a reticence ever since you've returned. Something's weighing heavily."

Ms. Crana leans in closer to Emily, their shoulders almost touching as they walk. "Emily, whether you want it or not, you now have a responsibility to this station. For its future...and its past! The question of your being Savior may not be yours to answer."

"What do you mean?"

"There is no dispute over the fact that when we left Earth we were hit by a massive shockwave. The ship's log corroborates my report. But even though I stopped far short of ascribing the shockwave to humanity's destruction, many people, including the Prime Minister, believe that it was, in fact, the cataclysm."

"The one you've been looking for."

"Yes, the cataclysm, the one we've been looking for. But there is no evidence. Something drained our power, preventing us from probing the surface for signs of life."

"So how do they know it was the cataclysm?"

"They don't. They just want it to be. As indeed I wanted it to be at the time. But my reasons wre selfish and personal; theirs are selfish and political. And they perceive a link between you, the cataclysm, and the prophecy. If they learn and believe that humanity was still intact after the shockwave, the expectation will be that its salvation was a direct result of your intervention during this last trip. You and Eric will be the Saviors whether you want to be or not. The choice will not be yours. And then you will be pressed upon to deliver reunification."

"How do I do that? I still don't even know what reunification even is."

Ms. Crana throws up her arms. "Nobody knows what reunification is! There has never been agreement its meaning."

"So what do we do?"

"Nothing."

"Nothing?"

"Do nothing. In the absence of absolute certainty and verifiable proof, we must work under the assumption that the Earth was indeed destroyed, and that we were unable to prevent it. We will work surreptitiously to compile facts, and I will petition the Prime Minister to travel back to that era to confirm."

"Wait! You can do that?"

"Yes, though we've never done it before. Primarily because it's not been necessary, but also because of the fear of unintentionally creating paradoxes. The fact that you've already travelled back and crossed your timeline will complicate matters a bit, but considering their probable belief that it was the cataclysm, I'm sure the council will agree to it. It does need to be confirmed and investigated."

"And what if it's not true? What if humanity wasn't destroyed?"

"Then you stay behind. Live your life. You won't have to come back, so you won't have to play Savior to us."

"But what if it is true?"

"Then we have one piece of the puzzle. You live with us on Caelestis, and help us get the other pieces of the puzzle: how did the Remnant come to be, and how did we lose our history?"

"I won't have to be Savior?"

"It will likely still be expected, but it will be up to you. You'll be free of the pressure of reunification. You'll have options."

Emily stops again, finally noticing an absence. "Where's Eric?" Emily asks.

"Deacon accompanied him back to your quarters."

"Deacon did?" Emily asks, incredulous that Eric would agree to that.

"Yes. Though I suppose it is more appropriate to suggest that Deacon followed him to ensure that he did, in fact, return to your quarters. Your brother's temperament upon exiting the Prime Minister's office suggested that he was not of a mind amenable to reason."

"Yeah, and I have a bad feeling about that," Emily says with thick concern. She quickens her pace, running ahead of Ms. Crana's naturally long stride. "We have to go find him!"

————

Emily bursts into their quarters, yelling for her brother. She is met by the dull echo of her own voice. She does a quick survey of the room. The pong game is still on the couch where Eric dropped it. The photograph is still on the side table where she left it. From what she can see of the bedrooms, they appear empty. Eric had never even been here.

"Where is he?" she asks herself.

Ms. Crana, standing in the doorway, answers: "We have no way of knowing."

"Why can't you track him?"

Ms. Crana replies slowly. "As you recall, the station does not even know you're here."

Something about her response irks Emily, but she stops herself from administering a sharp reply. A thought occurs to her. "Cytes. He went to get cytes. Where are cytes implanted?"

"The nursery. But he can't get cytes—wait. Response to query: Nursery 4. A discrete cyte umbilical has discharged. Root cause undetermined."

"What does that mean?"

"A cyte umbilical is what is attached to newborns to stabilize the cytes in their systems. A discrete umbilical is one that is not in use. It has apparently discharged despite being unattached."

"That's him," Emily says definitively.

Ms. Crana is in a rage.

After arriving at Nursery 4 to discover that Eric was not to be found, she sent out a query to determine the whereabouts of Deacon and discovered that he was in the infirmary. A query directly to Deacon netted information that he was overseeing Eric's recovery.

"I can't believe this," she fumes. She is so agitated she is pacing in the monorail car in which she and Emily are riding. "I shouldn't have had to ask him. He should have informed me the instant he knew."

"Maybe we should have cytes," Emily says, a bit defiantly. "I mean—"

"You can't have cytes," Ms. Crana responds peevishly. "They cannot be added to an adult. Your systems are already too mature to accept the nanocytes as anything but a foreign substance. Your bodies will reject them. That's why he's in the infirmary. He poisoned his system."

"You make it sound like it's his fault." Emily says. She instinctively defends him, though in the back of her mind she agrees, at least, that this is the result of his impulsiveness.

"No, it is not," Ms. Crana admits, and she softens a little. "I do not blame Eric. I blame myself. I have been unable to fashion a telemetry unit for him, though I know it was a priority for him. I should have made it a priority."

"He'll be okay, though, right?"

Ms. Crana looks at Emily, formulating an opinion as to how much truth to tell. She decides that caution will do more harm than good. "I don't know. I don't know," she says. "We assume there have been incidents of cyte poisoning in the past, hence the newborn therapy protocols. But there is no recorded incident in our files. If it happened, it happened in Caelestis' prehistory."

Emily had stopped listening after 'I don't know.' All that is running through her mind as she sits there, seeing the blur of the station as the monorail speeds silently through it, is 'I can't lose him too.'

---

Ms. Crana had suppressed her rage for Emily's sake...and for Eric's. But as she enters the infirmary and sees Deacon leaning over Eric's inert body, the rage returns. She pounces forward and grabs Deacon by the shoulders and spins him around. It is a strange, animated, silent puppet show. The two stand there arguing, gesturing, their faces shooting blood and fireworks, their bodies tensing and releasing and tensing and releasing, but no noise emerges. Neither Emily nor Vocks hear a thing.

But Eric.

He's lying prone on the table, mostly submerged in the curative fluid that had restored him once before, his damp head lifted out in what appears to be an uncomfortable position, various tubes streaming from his arms and chest. Emily hesitates, afraid to upset the delicate arrangement, as if it were a paper mache Eric that would somehow wither and dissolve into wet strips of newsprint as a result of her mere presence.

She moves to his side anyway, turning her back to the absurd pantomime. Except for the tubes, Eric looks as though he could be happily relaxing in a bath. As if sensing her presence, he opens his eyes and shifts them to her without moving his head. His lips tremble, prompting Emily to lean over and put her ear within inches of them.

"What is he saying?" Ms. Crana asks, startling Emily, who immediately springs upright. She turns to see both Ms. Crana and Deacon standing uncomfortably close, their faces barely managing to mask a certain eagerness. To what? Learn of his condition? Ensure his survival? Saviors can't die before they fulfill the prophecy, can they?

'Oh, I guess they can, yeah.' Emily thinks darkly.

"I think he said he feels like crap," Emily answers Ms. Crana.

"Whaaat eees craaap?" Deacon asks thickly, relieving Emily of her dark thought and replacing it with genuine amusement.

"Fecal matter," Ms. Crana answers, her disdain still showing.

"Will he be all right?" Emily asks.

"He should be," Ms. Crana reassures her unconvincingly. "His condition appears to be similar to that of contracting influenza. We believe it is what you would call a small bout. He will be feverish and inert until his system completely flushes out the cytes. You will find that he will be mostly unconscious during that period."

"How long does it usually take to flush them out?"

"As I explained earlier, we have never before encountered cyte poisoning, so we have no way of determining that. But given his condition's similarity to influenza, it could be 24 to 48 hours until his health is fully restored."

The fluid slushes a bit, distracting Emily from her conversation and bringing her attention back to Eric. He is still looking at her with a sideways glance. His lips are trembling again and the fingers of the hand closest to Emily are flexing rapidly, stirring up the fluid.

"What? What?" Emily says, then leans in close again. Eric's eyes move off hers and glance downward, taking in the room and the tubes and the fluid he's immersed in. She leans her ear close again.

"Don't make me a Cyberman," she says for Ms. Crana's benefit. "I think."

Eric nods slightly.

"Whaaaat eeess…" Deacon starts.

"A Cyberman. It's from a TV show. *Doctor Who*. That and *Halo* and *Star Trek*—he keeps bringing them up. It's driving me nuts!"

"They are cultural references from your period? Fictional science?"

"Science fiction, yeah. He likes it."

Ms. Crana nods. "They were—are—the filters through which he makes sense of everything he's going through.

There are, I believe, fictional precedents for this station in the entertainments of your era. You have the benefit of Vocks. He has the benefit of those precedents. And indeed they have served him well: He did pilot the ship."

"Yeah, I guess he did." She turns to Eric. "They're not going to turn you into a Cyberman." She says this louder than she means to, as if she were speaking to someone who is hard of hearing.

More lip trembling. Emily leans in. "Joke."

"Yeah, well...you should have worried about that before trying to turn yourself into a Cyberman, you idiot. Remind me to kill you when you're better."

"Why keeel him?" Deacon's expression is one of alarmed curiosity.

"Joke!" Emily says abruptly, pointing her nose directly at Deacon and firing the word off like a bullet.

———

Emily's eyes flick open. She doesn't even know how long they've been closed. Her head is slumped uncomfortably backwards, and muscles in the back of her neck protest painfully as she slowly raises her head to take in her surroundings. She gasps and groans and instinctively puts a hand behind her head as if giving herself necessary leverage just to get it into an upright position. Obviously she's been asleep for awhile.

She's lounging lazily in an oddly shaped chair, one she suspects is meant to conform to her body but obviously offers little in the way of head support. Despite that, she can't decide if it's comfortable or not. Her feet are propped up on a small, white plastic stool. Or plastic-*like* stool. She's beside Eric's bed, or medical table, or whatever it should be called. Eric is still half submerged in fluid, his glazed, sleepy eyes, blinking at Emily.

"Go home," he says breathlessly.

"I don't have a home." Emily stands, the pain in her neck now transferring to her back and legs, which suddenly begin to tingle. She looks at Eric, preparing to ask him a question, but his eyes are closed again. "Are you asleep?"

"Yes," he says, and it is apparent to Emily that he may indeed not be lying.

She lifts her left foot and shakes it, then drops it and follows suit with the other foot. She follows that pattern several times until the tingling becomes a dull heaviness. That she just waits out.

"Are you okay if I leave for awhile? I guess I will go back to the room."

Eric does not answer.

"You're okay, right? You're going to be okay, I mean?"

Still no answer. Despite the position of his head, Eric's face is a portrait of serenity. She wonders where his mind is taking him. A few minutes of ignorant bliss would be quite welcome just now.

She turns and makes it as far as the glass door to the nursery before being stopped by a feeble, mumbling voice.

"Sorry," Eric says.

"For what?" Emily asks. She moves back to his table but sees that his eyes are still closed and he is clearly asleep. "It's okay," she says quietly, "I get it. I just don't think it matters. I can hear but I still don't understand what's going on."

"Mission failed." Eric opens his eyes again, but clearly sees nothing. His heavy lids force themselves closed again.

"That wasn't your fault. And none of this—" she gingerly lifts one of the tubes that is running from his arm, "—would have helped. All we have is us."

She waits a moment to see if he will respond. When he doesn't, she leaves the room.

She finds Brin sitting cross-legged on the floor, propped upright against the wall opposite the nursery door. His hands are folded in his lap, and he has the beatific look of one in a deep meditation. Yet Emily knows better. He is fast asleep.

She walks up to him and gently nudges his knee with her foot. "Brin," she says, "wake up."

His eyes spring open and he dips slightly to the side, his balance interrupted by sudden and unexpected consciousness. His red-rimmed eyes dart around before looking up at the familiar face of Emily. "Ms. Clocke—I mean Emily. I must have—"

"Go home, Brin."

"I am concerned about Mr... Eric."

"So am I. But he's fine. I'm going home myself. If I can actually figure out where home is."

"May I accompany you? I know where your quarters are."

"I think I'll let you." She holds her hand out to help him to his feet.

He takes her hand, shakes it, and says, "Hi, I'm Brin."

Emily lets out a long, hard belly laugh.

Brin stares at her, and despite his not understanding the source of her laughter, nonetheless begins to form a smile, delighted by her mirth. "What is humorous?"

"Oh, I'm sorry," Emily says, trying to wind down her giggle. "I just wasn't expecting you to shake my hand."

"Is that not the appropriate response?"

"It is, if I were introducing myself. But we've already met. I was holding my hand out to help you up." She holds her hand out again.

Instead of taking it, Brin tucks his legs into a low crouch and jumps to his feet. It is a surprisingly spry move for someone who only moments ago recognized that he was awake. "Forgiveness, Emily. I find that I am still confused by some of the norms of your culture. But I am pleased you have accepted my offer."

He holds his arm out. Emily stares at it.

"Does a woman who is escorted by a man not traditionally take the man's arm?"

"Oh," Emily says, finally recognizing the gesture. "Yeah, we really don't do that anymore."

Brin drops his arm. He's less disappointed than curious about his miscalculation.

"Hold on," Emily scolds, suddenly realizing that she

should not pass up chivalrous attention, "just because we don't doesn't mean we shouldn't." She grabs his arm and lifts it again, sliding her free arm under and around it. Then she takes a step forward, tugging on him to follow. But he remains firmly in place, pulling her back to his side. She frowns at him.

"It's this way," Brin says, then gently turns her to face the other direction before setting off.

They walk in silence for a while, Emily discovering that it's not particularly comfortable to have her arm in Brin's, but also not comfortable with the idea of removing it, either. Would he be offended? Is it chivalry or just a database reading of customs? She realizes that she is unaccustomed to relating at all to a boy who is not her brother. Add to that the fact that it is a boy from five-hundred years in her future with very few cultural similarities. How to relate? They sink into the nervous tension of their encounter in the temple, neither sure what to say, both thinking the other will eventually break the uncomfortable silence.

And it turns out that Brin was right in that regard.

"Have you ever traveled?" Emily asks.

"Through time, you mean?"

"Yes."

"I have never. It is expressly forbidden," he says. "Only the chronographers are allowed."

"Chronographers?"

"The teams who travel back to reconstruct our past. Like Crana."

"So would that make me a chronographer? I travelled. Twice."

"I do not possess information pertaining to the council's intent in that regard. Adolescents have never travelled."

Emily mutters, "Adolescents?" but Brin does not hear.

"Chronographers require years of learning before they are allowed to travel. However, you and Eric are unusual in that, as you say, you have already travelled. And you are a Savior."

"I haven't made that decision yet," Emily says, annoyed.

"Forgiveness. I neglected to consider your position in the matter. I do understand you have yet to make the choice."

"Yeah," Emily sighs. She gets the feeling that Brin is humoring her. "Do I really have a choice?" she asks. The question is both rhetorical and begging for an answer.

"To a certain extent it is a choice, yes. You should understand that we will always believe that you are the Saviors ordained by Prophecy. You have the choice to embrace that or disregard it. Your decision will define how you are treated by the populace, and in turn define your actions and your self-identity."

"You think I'm the Savior?"

"*A* Savior, yes, of course," Brin answers earnestly. "Your brother would be the other referred to by Prophecy."

She stops, removes her arm from Brin's and takes a step back. "Wouldn't this be...isn't this a bit...familiar? If I'm the Savior?"

"There was no expectation as to when or how the Saviors would arrive, or who they might be, thus there is no protocol for how to behave amongst them. Deacon has cautioned me against such familiarity, as you call it, but you have made it clear through action and temperament that you do not wish to be overly venerated."

"No," Emily responds absently. Brin's truth disappoints her, but she only vaguely understands why. She suddenly feels like walking the rest of the way alone. "You know, I think I'm going to just head home."

"That is where I am taking you."

"No, I mean by myself."

"I thought you did not know the route."

"Vocks can guide me."

"I see. May I ask: have I said anything to distress you?"

"No," Emily answers with phony enthusiasm. "Why would you ask that?"

"You seem...distracted."

"I'm just tired. It's been a long day. I'd just like to walk alone for awhile. Clear my head."

"I understand," Brin says. "May I have your permission to check in on Eric?"

"Sure."

"Thank you. Goodnight Emily." Brin spins and begins walking back in the direction of the infirmary. She watches him for a moment, waiting. After another moment, he pauses and looks back over his shoulder at her. He throws up a little wave then turns and continues on.

"Good night," Emily says, satisfied.

———

Emily steps out on the balcony. It is the dusk equivalent; the lights throughout the module have shifted to a pale, amber color, mimicking, as best as artificial light can, the moment day is folded away and covered by the blanket of night. She can feel rather than see the upturned eyes of the people on the sidewalks below, gazing up at her, their curiosity piqued by the girl whose thoughts and actions can't be read, can't be anticipated. She doesn't know how she knows, but somehow she knows that her presence brings them not fear but reverence. Those who believe she is the Savior, the unifier, the answer to prophecy harbor no anger, no hatred, no mistrust. To those who don't believe, she is a harmless curiosity, a cyte-less cipher, the ward of Crana, formerly Maren.

She is not the new kid in a new town rushing into a new school, surrounded by dozens of new friends who sidle up to her to bask in her exotic aura of newness. That fantasy cannot exist here. They are separated by the distance between Earth and Jupiter; the distance between thought and language. And by time.

She looks at her mother in the picture again. And at her father. The two of them, reckless and happy, as she never knew them. Seeing their mood gives her the glimmer of an idea, a realization of a cathartic need.

She leans slightly over the edge of the balcony, turns her

head to look over at Ms. Crana's balcony, searching for any sign that Ms. Crana is present. A movement, a sliver of light, a sound. But her quarters are empty. She turns and looks at the balcony on the other side. Nothing. She leans over just a bit further and looks out across the manufactured vista in the waning amber light.

And she screams.

"I!"

"Am not!"

"Your savior!"

She enjoys the warm embrace of the silence that follows.

———

Emily sits beside Eric's bed staring vacantly out of the glass wall of the infirmary into the white hallway, her elbow propped on the arm of the chair and her chin propped on her closed fist. She's lost track of time sitting there, and has eventually lost track of her thoughts. She realizes she hasn't really slept much in the previous 48 hours (give or take 500 years), so when her thoughts turned to white noise, it basically constituted sleep.

Eric is in a real bed now. No submersion in therapeutic fluids, no tubes or wires hanging off him. A thin sheen of sweat covers his forehead. During the night, he'd alternated between throwing his covers off and stripping down to cool off and layering up and cocooning himself under blankets to rid himself of the uncontrollable shivers. His symptoms did mimic those of the flu, as Ms. Crana said. It meant he was on the mend.

'This mission will succeed,' she thinks, 'and all of this will be wiped from history. The history yet to be.'

"What mission?" he asks.

"What?" Emily says, startled. "I didn't realize you were awake."

"I'm not," Eric retorts, his eyes half open and glazed. His

voice has the long, faraway, thick-tongued quality of a sloppy drunk. "I didn't realize you talked to yourself."

"I didn't either," she says, her face a shade of scarlet. "What did I say?"

"A mission. Or something. I don't know, I'm really tired."

"Then go back to sleep."

"Hoe-kay," he says lazily, then allows his eyes to close again.

On the mend but not mended, which is what Emily had hoped would be the case. She'd hoped to be able to call upon his strength and decisiveness, hoped to rely on him to do what needed to be done. What she'd hoped to do. Instead she has to sit there and will herself to have his confidence.

"It doesn't matter," he'd say, "when the mission succeeds, all of this will be wiped from history. The history yet to be."

"You said that before," she'd reply, "and it didn't work."

"Because we played it too safe," he'd inevitably argue.

"Yeah, well, I'm not you. I don't know how to play it less safe."

"Jump the apple cart."

"What?"

"The conveyor. The harvester thing. With the apples. You jumped it. It wasn't the safe thing to do. But you did it."

"Because I had to. I had to get to you!"

"Well, now you have to save the world."

"You're being melodramatic," she'd say.

"No, you're being melodramatic. Adversity brings out the best in you."

Wait, who said that?

She lifts her head off her fist and slowly opens her cramped fingers. They resist, but she fights it, and eventually she wiggles them, attempting to regain some blood flow. She looks at Eric, his eyes closed, his breathing soft and shallow.

He wouldn't just sit here and ponder, she thinks. He'd just go. And maybe that's not always a bad thing.

She stands and looks down at him. "All right, I'm going to go. Don't try to talk me out of it."

"Hoe-kay," he mumbles, never opening his eyes.

She laughs silently.

"Shut up," she says quietly, unwilling to let him have the last word, even if he didn't know he'd had it.

————

There is one *Star Trek* door—thick and heavy with a small triangular portal window—that leads into the docking bay where the timeship impatiently waits. It's gears whrrrr breathlessly as the door slides as Emily approaches. She wonders how it opened if the station doesn't recognize her, but abandons the thought entirely when the doors reveal Brin standing between her and the timeship. He stands in a defiant pose, arms behind his back, legs spread as if anchored to the floor. But he betrays an apprehension. He is not fully confident in what he is doing.

"Brin," she says. It is neither a greeting nor a question. It is an exclamation of surprise. "What are you doing here?"

"Ms. Clocke, I ask you to reconsider your actions," he says.

"Emily," Emily corrects.

"Excuse me?"

"I told you to call me Emily."

"I think that would be inappropriate. I am here in an official capacity."

"You're guarding the ship?" It is an exclamation of surprise.

"I am asking you to reconsider your actions," he repeats.

"Yeah, you said that. Why?"

"What you are doing is wrong."

"How is it wrong? And how do you even know what I'm doing?"

"It is a logical supposition. Your behaviors dictate impatience with life on Caelestis; a strong desire to return to your home. Given that you attempted it once, it was logical to conclude that you would attempt it again."

"And why is it wrong to want to go home?"

"It is not. It is understandable given your circumstances. However, the risks are too great."

"I'm the one taking the risk. I'm okay with it."

"But you're not just risking yourself. You're risking all of Caelestis." It is Deacon, entering the docking bay. He is followed by Ms. Crana, who wears a sheepish look on her face. Deacon is as melodramatic as usual, delivering grand gestures and flourishes in sync with words that do not actually exit his mouth.

At his appearance, Brin seems to deflate slightly.

"What you are doing is wrong," Brin adds, repeating himself again. He says it with more force, with the strength of false conviction. It is more for Deacon's sake than hers.

"How can I be wrong? I'm the Savior." Emily says it with neither malice nor conviction. She is not throwing it in his face; she is testing his logic.

"You are untrained," Deacon answers, "You are unaware of the potential consequences of your actions."

"You rejected the obligation!" Brin blurts out, cutting off his mentor. There is a note of bitterness in his response. This is not for Deacon's sake, it is for his own. He sighs heavily and adds in a low, cheerless voice: "You were heard last evening. You screamed your repudiation."

"And you said it didn't matter. I would be the Savior whether I wanted to be or not."

"But you rejected it!" Brin is very forceful now, spitting the last two words out like bullets.

Emily is unprepared for the venom. Is this the same calm, even keeled Brin? The quiet gentleman? "So? Why does it matter whether I want it or not?"

"He is conflicted," Deacon interjects unhelpfully. "You are testing his faith."

"How am I...?" She begins responding to Deacon, but turns to Brin. "How am I testing your faith? You either believe it or you don't. "

"You were supposed to be the Savior!" Brin says, anguished.

"And why does it matter that I'm not? Or that I don't want it? Is that all I am?"

Brin does not answer. That he doesn't infuriates Emily. She steps to her right and makes to walk past him, but he counters her move and blocks her.

"Please move," she says.

"I cannot." Brin looks momentarily at Deacon. Whether it is for strength or approval, Emily can't tell.

"He won't resist," Ms. Crana conveys to Emily.

Emily growls. "Please. Move."

"Do not let her pass," Deacon conveys. "It is too dangerous."

"I guess you have to decide if I'm the Savior," Emily says to Brin.

"Don't play that card Emily," Ms. Crana warns.

"It's not my card to play," Emily answers, still looking at Brin. "*He* has to decide. It doesn't matter if I believe, it matters if *he* believes." She turns and points to Deacon. "And him! If they believe, then they will let me pass."

"How does that stand to reason?" Brin asks.

"Because," Ms. Crana explains, suddenly understanding the strategy herself, "if you believe her to be the Savior, if you believe that that is her destiny, you'll believe that every action she takes will be in fulfillment of Prophecy. If you don't let her pass, you'll repudiate your own faith." She looks at Emily. "You're right. It doesn't matter what we think."

Deacon merely reiterates: "Do not let her pass!"

Brin looks at Deacon, imploring. "But—"

"It is not a repudiation. Prophecy dictates that TWO shall arrive. They must be together."

"Two shall *arrive*," Ms. Crana says, a subtle note of satisfaction in her voice. "And two did arrive. It says nothing about two leaving."

"Either it's my destiny...or my choice," Emily says to Brin.

Brin drops his head, tortured and defeated. He steps aside.

Deacon does nothing.

"The Prime Minister is approximately one minute away," Ms. Crana tells Emily. "I think it best you leave before she arrives."

"Can she stop me?" Emily asks. She hates that she has to verbalize her question for all to hear.

"Possibly," Ms. Crana answers. "She probably won't at first. But she can make it unnecessarily complicated."

Emily turns and looks at Ms. Crana. As subtly as she can, she rolls her eyes to indicate the presence of Deacon and Brin.

"They can't stop you. They have no experience at true resistance."

Emily steps to the other side of Brin and walks past him, to the ship. He makes no move to stop her. She pulls open the outer hatch.

Brin, not turning or looking up, calls out: "Emily!"

Emily turns.

Brin continues, in an exhausted voice: "I do not believe you are the Savior."

Emily pauses, looks at her hand on the latch of the ship's hatch. After a moment, she looks back at Ms. Crana, who simply nods, her lips arranged into a slight but nonetheless victorious smile. Emily passes into the ship and closes the hatch behind her, just as the Prime Minister enters the docking bay.

Emily settles into the pilot's seat and follows through preparations as she had on her previous trip. The steps for launch take longer because she doesn't have Eric's help, and because she is often distracted by the movements of Ms. Crana, Deacon, and the Prime Minister that occur to the side of the ship, in her peripheral vision. Whatever argument is occurring is occurring silently—to Emily at least. They are not casting their words to her.

She sneaks a look at the commotion. It is less animated than previous discussions among the three have been, but Emily is sure it is no less passionate. She steals a glance at Brin, who stands still and silent, looking directly at her. She looks away quickly, ashamed or embarrassed (or both), unable to judge what he is feeling or thinking.

Turning back to set coordinates, she wonders why she is able to get this far, why she is able to continue with her preparations.

She sets her return date to one day before the cataclysm. She is almost set for launch. Surely the Prime Minister can override the ship's systems to prevent her from leaving. But preparations continue, and she only needs now to push the launch button and put herself into stasis.

She looks again to Ms. Crana, who turns away from her argument to look back and nod. Then she looks once again at Brin, who is still looking at her. 'Conflicted is right,' she thinks. It is written all over his face. Deacon turns away from his participation in the argument and stands behind Brin, resting his hand on his acolyte's shoulder. It is almost parental. Brin flinches slightly at the mentor's touch, jarred, perhaps, by his apparent disobedience. Does he fear reprisal? Does he feel guilt? Or perhaps neither? Brin looks back to Emily and raises his hand in a slight wave.

Emily pushes the button.

# :13 velocity

Emily wakes to the strangely familiar and strangely welcoming blue orb that is Earth, which is once again staring her in the face. But she has little time to wonder at it: she's barely in the pilot's seat when a shrill blare pierces her eardrums, the same one she'd heard once before.

"Vocks, turn off the proximity alarm!"

The sound mercifully stops.

"Why...? Dammit! I'm tired of having to say 'Vocks' every time I need to ask you a question. Vocks, until I tell you otherwise, I am speaking to you, okay?"

*Understood.*

"Why did the proximity alarm go off?"

*There are five other timeships within three thousand kilometers of yours. Both bear telemetry signals identical to this ship.*

"FIVE!?" Emily asks, shocked. "Five? How could there be fi...wait a minute! Why? What is the current date and time? In Gregorian, central standard time."

*In the Gregorian year 2016, 10 October, 09:16.*

She instantly forgets the other timeships. "Shit! I set it to arrive yesterday!" She seethes with frustration, but leans back and exhales, having figured out instantly how she missed the correct date. "The Prime Minister reset the coordinates," she says as if she had a companion who needed it all explained. "That's how I got to leave in the first place."

*I do not understand.*

"Never mind. I wasn't actually talking to you."

*Does that terminate your directive?*

"Does that what? Oh, no. No, just assume I'm still talking to you. I'll let you know when I'm not."

*Understood.*

Emily leans back to think. She stares out at Earth, teeming with life and constantly churning with activity. But from 150 kilometers over the East coast of the United States, it is none of those. It is a temple, a symbol of hope and home. It is peace and silence and comfort.

She leans forward. "Vocks," she says, noticing something approaching. A dot, a black dot floating over Indiana, getting larger, fast. "What is…?"

She can't finish. The blaring wracks her head again, the proximity alarm. She can barely think to tell Vocks to turn it off when a green flash explodes in front of her and all she feels is the entire universe spinning. And spinning. And wailing. It is all Emily can do to think over the sensory overload. "Vocks!" she screams, forgetting her earlier directive. "Turn off the alarm!"

The alarm ceases. One issue down, one to go. "Vocks, how do I stop the ship from spinning?"

*Initialize stabilizer thrusters.*

"How do I do that?"

*Depress the glowing green circle on the manual control panel.*

"Where is the…? Never mind!" Through unfocused eyes she finds the glowing circle on the windshield and strains to get her hand to it, the wild spin of the ship jerking her this way and that, making a mockery of hand-eye coordination.

"I can't reach it! Can't you just initiate the thrusters?"

*I can read and transmit information only. I do not have command access. If you are physically unable to perform a function, you can initiate voice command.*

Furious, Emily lets out a loud, long, throat-searing primal scream. "Ship! Can you hear me?"

*Voice command engaged.*

"Initiate stabilizer thrusters!"

Within seconds, the ship stops spinning. But Emily's head does not. She is lurched forward in her seat, head lolling against her chest, her body straining against the restraints.

"Vaaaahhhh....Vaaaaaxxxxx…" Her voice trails off. There is blackness, then the pale glow of emergency lighting.

Her head jerks up at a familiar voice.

*Do you wish to initiate emergency return procedures?*

"I doone liiike duh shpinning."

*Do you wish to initiate emergency return procedures?*

"Nnnnoooo." She lifts her head slowly, painstakingly. Her skull is pounding and her neck cracks at the effort. She regains, however, a semblance of voice. "Why didn't you tell me about voice command earlier?"

*You did not inquire.*

"I hate you." She gulps air and pushes it slowly from her lungs. It helps clear her head a bit. "What do I do now?"

*Please clarify.*

"Vocksaaaa," Emily whines impatiently, "just tell me what to do!"

*Please provide context for the directive. What is it that you would like to do?*

"I just want to go home."

*Coordinates for home are not currently in the ship's records.*

"Yeah, I know," Emily says tiredly. "That's the definition of my life."

*Do you wish to initiate return procedures?*

Emily leans her head back into the soft, curved support of the chair and stares out at the sea of stars in front of her. She can hear the crunchy swooshing sound of her blood flowing through her veins, timed to the throbbing of her head. In between pounding beats she draws herself a dire picture: she missed her chance again. Eric is gone, Ms. Crana is gone, her mother is gone. They're all gone again. Again.

"Are you trying to tell me that Caelestis is home?" she asks. She's not sure if she's asking Vocks or herself. But it sparks a thought. Is home gone? Is Earth gone?

"Vocks—"

Before she can get the next word of her question out, a blinding, white flash disrupts her train of thought. "Vocks," Emily asks when her eyes have sufficiently recovered, "what was that flash?"

*Unknown.*

"Figures," Emily huffs. "Can you at least tell me whether the Earth is out there or not?"

*Ship systems are down. Energy stores are drained. Only emergency return protocols can be activated.*

Emily suddenly noyices that she is bathed in darkness. Power to the ship has been lost. "Shit. So I don't have a choice."

*Correct.*

She tries to generate options, but knows she's out of her depth. She speaks reluctantly: "Ship, initiate return procedures."

*You have 75 seconds to enter the cryo-chambers before the ship enters hibernation.*

Emily unstraps, floats to the cryo-chambers, enters, and wearily shuts herself inside. Her thoughts are blank as the fluid rushes in and consumes her. For some reason, as the fluid touches her chin, a precise, angry resolve rises with it, and the germ of a thought forms in her head. Then her mouth opens and the fluid rushes in...

———

...and then out again in wave after wave. And then as she makes her way back to the cockpit, the thought continues where it left off 525 years previous. A plan. A new plan. A—

"Emily!"

"Ms. Crana?"

"Yes. Welcome back."

"How do I hear you?"

"I'm cyte communicating with the ship. The ship is relaying the communication to your device."

Emily positions herself back into the pilot's seat and straps in, noting happily that the pounding in her head has stopped. From the cockpit she can see the pale dot of Europa, a glint of Caelestis haloing it.

"Did you confirm the destruction of Earth?"

Emily swallows. She didn't even think to look. She almost wishes the pounding in her head was back; suddenly she feels deserving of it.

"I didn't. I was a little...distracted."

"That is disappointing," Ms. Crana conveys. There is something in her words, though, a careful delivery that makes it clear that she is disappointed in the outcome but not in Emily.

"I'll go again."

"That is not necessary, Emily. I don't blame you. I'll petition again for a formal return mission."

"No. This is my mission. I'm going back."

"I'm not sure that will be possible, Emily. The Prime Minister only grudgingly let you go this time. Your Savior argument won't work on her. "

"How long does it take to recharge the ship after I dock?"

"Emily—"

Europa is now the primary object in her field of view. Caelestis now looks as large as a hula hoop. This isn't an academic discussion. Emily reiterates slowly, deliberately. "How long. Does it take. To recharge the ship. After I dock?"

There is a long pause. Emily imagines Ms. Crana releasing a frustrated sigh, fighting to give the answer she wants rather than the answer she must. "Just come and dock. We'll think of something."

———

The ship slides into the docking bay, and Emily immediately sees Ms. Crana, the Prime Minister, Deacon, and Brin framed behind the glass partition separating the docking bay from the control room, the same place the Prime Minister was when Emily saw her for the first time. She wears the same enigmatic scowl.

"Have you completed your endeavor?" the Prime Minister asks, looking at Emily through the cockpit windshield. She tips her head as if she'd actually said the words out loud.

Emily stares back, making no move to unstrap her seat belts. "No."

"I am sorry to hear that. I had capitulated to your impetuous behavior on the chance that you might return with some useful information. As you have not, I return to my original disposition: I cannot permit you to launch again."

"Emily," Ms. Crana cuts in, "Listen. Your chief advantage right now is that the Prime Minister, while unusually circumspect for a Caelestisian, has very little experience with dissention. You may have done this twice, but she's still more conditioned to believe in your obedience than she is in the possibility of insurrection."

"So what do I do?"

"You disembark," the Prime Minister conveys in answer. Circumspect? Try tough and wily: it was definitely a command.

Emily winces. She didn't realize that anybody but Ms. Crana could hear.

"First of all," Ms. Crana conveys, "don't speak. The Prime Minister is tapping into the ship's voice recognition system so she can hear you. So don't respond to me. Just listen. The ship will reconfigure to the launch position in 10 seconds. When the ship spins the cockpit out of the Prime Minister's line of sight, find the coordinates from the last trip and select them. Don't use voice commands, do it manually. When I give you the command, launch the ship."

"She won't—" Emily says then realizes what's she's done.

"She won't...what?" The Prime Minister asks with a slight note of suspicion.

Emily looks down, desperate for inspiration to finish

251

her sentence. Something she can use to divert the line of the conversation. She sees the convoluted buckling system of her seat belt and begins tugging at them with theatrical exaggeration. "Let me go. The ship. I can't get the seat belts loose."

"I'll have a technician help you as soon as the ship finishes the reorientation process."

'She actually bought it?' Emily thinks. 'That old TV cliche?' "I guess it's not a cliche here," she says, forgetting again that she's not just speaking to herself.

"Emily!" Ms. Crana scolds. "You're out of our line of sight now. Find the coordinates!"

Emily begins pressing her fingers to the windshield, pushing furiously on the various buttons that appear on it, hoping she's pressing the right ones. She assumes the navigation systems work like the GPS of a smart phone and she can find her past coordinates listed somewhere. Thankfully, her assumption is correct: she finds a list of previous coordinates and recognizes some of the numbers that Vocks had dictated to her. She realizes, though, that she doesn't know how to alter them.

"Emily, when you've found the coordinates, just select them. Don't try to change them, just select them."

Emily presses the last coordinates in the list.

"Okay, now initiate launch!"

"But…"

"Don't speak! Push the button!"

Emily pushes the button. Almost instantly, she notices that some coordinate numbers change. Then they change back. She moves toward the cryo-chamber, but takes a last glance at the coordinates. They've changed again. She scurries into the cryo-chamber, but looks once more before closing the door. The coordinate numbers are changing furiously, flip-flopping between what they were originally and what they became when Emily initiated the launch. She realizes that she's witnessing a battle of wills between Ms. Crana and the Prime Minister.

She closes the chamber door knowing that very shortly she'll know who won.

She wakes to the familiar and welcoming blue orb that is Earth, which is once again staring her in the face. She has little time to wonder at it—she's barely in the pilot's seat when a shrill blare pierces her eardrums, the same one she'd heard before.

"Vocks, turn off the proximity alarm!"

The sound mercifully stops.

"This is like really bad deja vu. Vocks, where are we? I mean, when are we? In Gregorian, central standard time."

*In the Gregorian year 2016, 10 October, 09:14.*

"Dammit! It didn't work." Emily is now too frustrated for tears. She really wants to hit something. Unfortunately, something hits her first: The shockwave. The rolling and rocking and shaking takes over her senses again, and she can barely think to shout out commands to the ship in her increasingly sloshy voice.

"Shhhhshhhhhshshhhh-iiiiiiiii-pppp! Staaaayyy-bulll-zashun. Stay-bull-zashun ssshhhrrruuussshhhttteeerrrzzzzz!"

She blinks and sees only the ceiling (At least she hopes it's the ceiling!). Miraculously, the ship has stopped rolling. Emily, utterly exhausted, realizes that she sees the ceiling because her head is draped against the back of her chair. She knows now that she had indeed passed out. For the first time, she longs to put herself at the mercy of the cryo-fluid.

"Where are we?"

*Three point three million kilometers beyond Earth's orbit.*

"How did we not lose power?"

*Unknown.*

"You're very helpful. What are my options?"

*Please provide context for query. Options for what?*

"Where can I go?"

*Earth and Caelestis offer the best probability of long-term survival.*

"Earth? Really? It's there? It hasn't been destroyed?" Suddenly, the arduous trip may have been worth it.

*The Earth is presently intact in the spatial coordinates of record, its orbital location consistent with that predicted by the laws of motion.*

Emily could swear that there was a slightly mocking tone in Vocks's response, although it may have merely been her own filter of disbelief. "That's not what I meant," she vents, "I know the planet is there... Oh, just show me!"

*Orient the ship to .30501 by .94876.*

Emily repeats the coordinates out loud, and the ship spins and flips again, making Emily regret asking to see her home planet. But presently the ship stops and Earth, smaller and more fragile-looking than she remembers, appears in the center of the cockpit windshield.

Emily stares at it in disbelief. "It's there," she says quietly, afraid she'll scare it away. It wasn't destroyed: it is blue and white and seemingly intact. She plops her head back again, but positions it so that she can stare at the planet. "I have to think this through. What do I do now?"

*Presenting such options is beyond my...*

"Okay, shut up. I need to think."

Her eyes suddenly flick open and she sits forward, her heart beating just a bit faster. She doesn't even remember closing her eyes.

"Vocks, how long was I—? Oh, never mind. Let's...let's go down." She brings up the map of Earth on the windshield. She spins it and enlarges it and enlarges it some more until she finds the spot she wants to go. She presses the spot, then presses the launch button and is instantly thrown back into her seat as the ship propels itself toward Earth.

Cleveland, Detroit, Lake Michigan. They blur past as the ship zeroes in on a tiny patch of green just beyond the edge of Chicago, where the city sprawl begins to slowly taper off to slightly less coagulated highways and less dense crops of houses. An oddly triangular cement building comes into focus, kind of like an unhinged 'A,' contrasting with the wide area of flat green grasses that surround it.

Fermilab, the U.S. Department of Energy's high-energy physics lab, and her mother's employer.

The ship doesn't have to get close for Emily to know that she will not find what she'd hoped. In stark contrast to the dull cement building, the flashing lights of the dozens of police and emergency vehicles surround a smoldering crater a few hundred meters to the east of the building. Emily points to a location and touches the windshield, deciding to land, deciding to trust but verify.

But if she's honest with herself, she's deciding to hope against hope. "This is a mistake, isn't it?" she asks herself, watching the crater as the ship glides over it.

Emily ignores Vocks's inevitable request for clarification. She concentrates on the scene outside. The people surrounding the crater seem mostly unperturbed by the ship though some look up and around blindly. Emily realizes that the ship is invisible but not silent. They all hear it but can't see it.

The ship lands near the crater in a clearing thickly ringed by trees. Emily, not bothering to make the ship invisible, climbs down the gangplank and into the grass. She makes her way through the thicket, pushing her way through dense webs of reedy branches to emerge facing the crater much closer than she'd expected. The distances from above always seem longer than they do on the ground, she realizes.

She instantly sees something that makes her stop in her tracks: peppered among the emergency first responders and regular police are SWAT tactical officers. Fully armored and even more fully armed, they form a tight cordon around the crater, projecting an attitude of nonchalant intimidation.

The swishy crunching of Emily's footsteps over dried leaves attracts the attention of a solid, husky brick of a man carrying a fully automatic weapon at the ready, barrel pointed downward. He doesn't make a move to raise his weapon, but instead stares curiously at her.

"How did you get here?" he asks, and steps forward to approach her. "You shouldn't be here."

Emily stands stock still for a moment, her eyes wide and her left leg jittering. The one thing she hadn't expected from all of this is getting shot.

The officer twists his chin toward his shoulder and begins talking, presumably making an announcement of Emily's presence into his communication device. This is confirmed when the head of nearly every tactical officer within view suddenly snaps in her direction.

"Girlie," he says, "we need to get you out of here." He begins advancing on Emily.

Before he's taken a half dozen steps, a voice from the crowd shouts, "Hey, it's her! That's the girl!" A short, narrow woman with jet back hair in a ruler-straight bowl cut steps forward, pointing straight at Emily. She repeats her yell, her voice high and accusatory.

Emily freezes a moment to process the situation. Some of the SWAT officers raise their weapons and suddenly Emily can think of nothing else to do but turn and run back into the trees. Back to the ship. She hears shouting from behind her, but it is nothing but vague and unformed commands, a white noise soundtrack to the violent whipping of branches and the scraping of coarse bark that she endures as she runs.

Scraped and bruised, with tiny beads of blood dotting her face and arms, she reenters the clearing and is up the plank and in the ship, slamming the door behind her, just as three SWAT officers burst into the clearing. Emily plops into the pilot's seat and watches them slowly work their way in toward the ship, their manner more curious than guarded. All three begin to spin on their heels, searching all around them for some sign of Emily. Then one of them spots something in the grass, pointing to an area just below the ship, out of Emily's line of sight.

"Look how the grass is crushed flat," Emily hears the officer say. All three of them begin walking toward the ship.

"The feet!" Emily says to herself, realizing what they're looking at. "The...what are they? The landing skids!"

*Please provide—*

"They can see the indentations of the landing skids in the grass! They'll find the ship!"

Without a second thought about a destination, Emily presses the blinking launch button on the windshield. The officers are instantly shot backward, propelled by an invisible force, launched as if from a cannon into the safety net of the webbed thicket of trees.

The ship rockets upward, whipping through clouds into an increasingly blue sky. As the blue turns slowly to a shade of indigo, Emily croaks out through gritted teeth: "Where are we going?"

*The ship is on a trajectory for lunar orbit.*

Emily does not respond to this information. The edges of the Earth bend away beneath her, wiping away any sense of the existence of flat, even ground. It's only when the forces of acceleration wane that she can exhale fully and take normal breaths again.

But as soon as she takes that first satisfying breath, a familiar shrill tone pierces her skull.

"Vocks, kill the proximity…!"

FLASH!

She is momentarily blinded, and when her sight recovers, she sees no grid on the windshield, only stars and the dull reflection of a dull yellow emergency light.

"How long do I have to keep doing this?" Emily asks herself, her voice weak and gravelly.

*Unknown.*

"What happened?"

*Unknown.*

"Is Earth there?"

*Unknown. Power is depleted. Emergency power is engaged.*

Emily sighs. She doesn't even ponder another option. "Ship, initiate emergency return procedures."

*You have 75 seconds to enter the cryo-chambers before the ships enters hibernation.*

"How long do I have to keep doing this?"

*Unknown.*

"So...as long as I have to, I guess." She makes her way wearily to the cryo-chamber.

———

"There is a slight problem with that plan," Ms. Crana conveys as Emily's ship drifts towards the docking bay, "in that you have only enough cryo-fluid left for one more two-way trip."

"Damn!" Emily exclaims. "And I sincerely doubt they'll just let me fill up on cryo-fluid and leave again."

"We absolutely will not," the Prime Minister breaks in, her disembodied voice very severe in Emily's head. "So I hope your mission was a success this time."

The ship pulls into the docking bay and clamps its landing skids to the deck.

"It was not," Emily says. "At least, I don't think it was." She looks directly at the Prime Minister—who is again standing in the control room. She continues: "Earth was there this time but...then it wasn't."

"I don't understand."

"I keep approaching just as the shockwave hits. It pushes me away and damages the ship so I can't control my direction. But...this time I landed. Earth was there...but then there was another shockwave. And then it wasn't there. I think. The ship was damaged again. I couldn't turn and try to find Earth to make a visual identification."

"I am sincerely sorry to hear that," the Prime Minister conveys insincerely. "But I am afraid that I cannot allow you to leave again. We cannot trust that you have left the chronology untainted."

"Emily, secure the hatch!" Ms. Crana conveys.

"What do you mean?" Emily asks. "You mean lock it? There's a lock?"

"And don't talk!" Ms. Crana conveys. There is no 26th

century cultural equivalent for a facepalm, but it's apparent in Ms. Crana's conveyed tone. "Just hurry and lock the hatch!"

The Prime Minister breaks in again. "Ms. Clocke! Allow us to board!"

This last conveyance panics Emily. She immediately unstraps from her seat and rushes to the hatch at the back of the ship. She finds a latch that she hopes is the lock and presses it downward. The hatch suddenly flies open to reveal the Prime Minister and a contingent of other citizens standing at the bottom of the gangplank. A man and a woman immediately break from the group and rush toward the hatch. Emily quickly grabs for the hatch handle, pulls, and slams it shut before they can reach it. Then she lifts the latch upward until she hears a click. She immediately hears the snapping sound of the outer latch being depressed, but nothing happens. The door stays shut.

"Thank god for manual latches," Emily says, despite Ms. Crana's warning not to speak.

"Indeed," Ms. Crana conveys. "And your brother questioned their utility."

"So what do I do now?"

"You disembark!" The Prime Minister demands.

"Same thing as last time," Ms. Crana conveys immediately afterward.

"I shut up and listen," Emily says sagely.

"You will not be allowed to launch again, Ms. Clocke!" The Prime Minister conveys. This is followed by a harsh pounding on the hatch.

"In truth, it doesn't really matter if you remain silent," Ms. Crana says. "We do not have the element of surprise this time. She won't be fooled twice."

Emily can feel the ship shudder. She runs back to the cockpit and looks out at Ms. Crana, still behind the protective shield of the control room. The Prime Minister and the others she saw are out of sight, at the back of the ship.

"What's happening? Why is the ship shaking?"

"The Prime Minister is preventing the ship from returning to launch position. I am attempting to countermand her order."

"Against three of them?"

"They are unused to insurrection."

"But won't you to get into trouble…?"

"There is no constabulary on Caelestis, Emily. My punishment will not be oppressive."

"So then what's the plan?"

"This is the plan. This is all we have. Brute force."

"No offense, but that's not much of a plan."

The ship continues to shudder but Emily sees that it is slowly rotating into launch position.

"Ms. Clocke, are you certain that you wish to continue?" It is Deacon. He enters the control room and takes a position right next to Ms. Crana.

"Absolutely," Emily answers defiantly.

"Then I shall assist."

The shuddering decreases slightly and the ship begins to rotate a little faster. It is now halfway into launch position.

"Wait, why?" Emily asks. "A few minutes ago…"

"Emily, don't pursue the matter," Ms. Crana conveys. "Just say thank you."

"Thank you," Emily says. It is as much a question as a statement. She peeks along the edge of the windshield, sees both Ms. Crana and Deacon standing beside each other. Before they pass completely out of sight, she catches a glimpse of three figures rushing from the docking bay into the control room, taking positions among the two strange bedfellows who are fighting to launch her.

'What a strange war,' she thinks. Then the ship stops shuddering and smoothly locks into position.

"Emily," a voice conveys, "are you in a cryo-chamber?"

"Brin?" Emily asks, shocked. And pleased. "Why…?"

"We don't have time, Emily!" Ms. Crana interrupts. "Are you in a cryo-chamber?"

"Not yet," she answers, then asks "Whose side are you on?"

"Never mind! Hurry up!"

She takes a step back toward the chambers, but is suddenly lifted off her feet and forcefully shot to the back of the ship, a bolt of pain shooting from her left shoulder down to her hand as she slams violently into the wall. She spins instantly, her whole body now pinned to the bulkhead.

Just as suddenly she is thrown forward and lands face down on the deck, instinctively rolling to her right as she falls to avoid more trauma to her left arm. She flops down, a gravelly burn running across her cheek as she scrapes it against the rough treads of the floor. She lies prone right in front of a cryo-chamber.

"What the hell happened?" she groans.

"Get in a cryochamber!" two voices convey in chorus.

Emily pushes herself stiffly up off the floor, panting and groaning as she tries to stand upright, the joints and muscles of her arms and and legs abandoning their friendly rapport with the rest of her body. "But—am I launched? How can I travel back...?"

"Just get into a cryo-chamber while we still have control of the ship!"

She strains against shoulder pain to pull open a chamber door. As she swings it open, another forceful lurch of the ship pushes her face first into the curved back of the chamber door.

And then there is only blackness.

————

Sight returns accompanied by the retching of fluid and the immediate knowledge that she was not exactly properly positioned within the cryo-chamber. Emily is sufficiently used to reviving from 500-year comas at this point to actually be able to think relatively coherently within seconds of waking. Thus, the first thought through her head is: why am I wedged like a pretzel into the lower portion of the chamber? The second is: how did I even get here? The last thing she remembers is wrenching open the door—then nothing.

"How...what happened?" she says out loud, trying to spit out the remaining fluid that coats the inside of her mouth.

*Please provide context for query. How what happened?*

"Okay, wait, when am I? When is it?"

*In the Gregorian year 2016, 10 October, 09:15.*

Emily shakes her head, whipping droplets of fluid all around her. She has to shimmy to unwedge herself and straighten out. When she is upright she lets out a deep breath and gathers her thoughts.

It's the same time she's always arrived, just before the shockwave hits. Just before the Earth is destroyed. Or maybe destroyed. She's disappointed, but not surprised enough to curse or cry, or even be that upset. Not anymore. In fact, the only thing she gives voice to is her original query: "How did I get here? How did I end up in stasis and travelling through time? I don't remember making it into the cryo-chamber."

*The following is conjecture extrapolated from external conversations: You were rendered unconscious after being thrust into the cryo-chamber door. The door recoiled with sufficient force to carry you into the chamber and seal you in. Commander Crana then initiated stasis remotely.*

Emily floats to the cockpit, not stopping to bask in the blue glow of home. "But how was I able to travel back to now?" she asks, strapping herself into the seat in preparation for the shockwave she is now conditioned to expect. "I thought the ship needed energy from the station to launch."

*According to mission logs, the ship received a $9.4 \times 10^{19}$ joule energy burst from the station power grid before exceeding the 10 kilometer distance limit.*

"I have no idea—"

She can't finish her sentence. It is lost in the instantaneous nausea brought about by uncontrollable rolling and tumbling that no amount of conditioning or expectation can overcome.

Emily wakes to discover that the ship is stabilized. Either she was able to command the ship to initialize the thrusters or the ship has gotten used to her, cytes or no cytes. She hopes it's the latter. Closing her eyes, she leans back and breathes deeply, trying to stop her head from spinning. She feels likes she's done this same thing a million times now, and she's not entirely certain that's not an exaggeration. When she opens her eyes again it slowly dawns on her that the cockpit is different. The entire windshield is lit up with full instrumentation.

"Vocks, are we on emergency power?"

*Negative.*

"Why not?"

*Connection to main power reestablished.*

"Really? How?"

*Connection to main power reestablished.*

"You said that already. But how—you know what? Never mind." Emily gnaws a thumbnail, staring absently at the speckled blackness outside. Her vision slowly adjusts to the darkness and the stars become more pronounced, some coalescing into a cloudy ribbon. Several brighter points of light move slowly across her field of vision, like stray bubbles of carbonation in a dark cola. There is another flutter at the back of her mind. "Vocks, what are those moving points of light I see outside?"

*Conjecture: there are four other iterations of this timeship within a three-thousand kilometer radius. It is possible you perceive them visually.*

Threads of an idea tickle the back of her mind. She's not entirely sure where the threads came from, but she's sure the manner in which she is weaving them together is ridiculous in the extreme. Except...

"Vocks, how much power does the ship currently have?"

*$4.5 \times 10^{19}$ joules.*

"Okay," Emily says, suppressing her first instinct to ask what that means. She knows that the explanation will not provide a clear answer. "What would that be in whole numbers?"

*45 exajoules.*

"45 exajoules," she says as if the whole number somehow made it understandable. "How much power does it take to reverse time? In whole numbers."

*90 exajoules.*

"90 exajoules. And you'd have to release the 90 exajoules twice, right? Once to reverse time to go backwards, then once again to re-reverse or make it go back forward or whatever?"

*Correct.*

"And the ship can store how much energy?"

*Ship storage limit is 175 exajoules.*

The idea flutters again. "Ok, let me talk this through and make sure I got it straight. The ship really needs 90 exajoules of energy for a single trip. So that means that a round trip requires 180 exajoules of energy, but the ship can only store 175, which means it needs to get energy from somewhere else. That somewhere else is the station, which gives the ship a boost as it launches, which means it doesn't have to use a full 90 exajoules from storage on the first trip. So then that leaves more than 90 in storage for the return trip. Right?"

*Correct.*

"But right now we don't have 90."

*Correct.*

"Do the timeships have the same ability as Caelestis? To transfer energy?"

*Affirmative, but unlike Caelestis the effective transfer distance is less than 1 kilometer.*

"But I can get the other 45 I need..." she tapers off, answering her own question in her head.

The idea that tickled the back of her mind suddenly grows and solidifies before Emily can even curve her lips into a satisfied smile. She works through each detail out loud, her fingers flying and sliding across the windshield, pressing letters and numbers and buttons as Vocks answers her volley of questions. When she finishes she rolls her head to work out the kinks in her neck and sighs deeply. And then she pushes the glowing button that had presented itself on the windshield and finds herself once again pressed back against her seat, the ship's thrusters pushing her through the star-spattered ocean of night.

Toward, inexplicably, herself.

*20 kilometers to first target,* Vocks announces.

Through the front portal, she sees a dot of bright white drawing closer, a mote of shining dust. After mere seconds the dot seems to puff up to the size of a grain of rice, but that is a trick of the eyes, another illusion of her motion toward it looking like its motion toward her. As she moves closer still, the grain morphs into the distinct and recognizable shape of a timeship.

It draws nearer and nearer, faster and faster, looming larger in her field of vision, until Emily squirms in her seat and begins desperately pressing on an imaginary brake pedal to try to stop the ship.

But it doesn't stop.

# :14 crash

"Uh, Vocks…?"

  *Yes, Ms. Clocke?*

"When do we pull away?"

  *At .15 kilometer.*

"That's awfully…!"

And the timeship is in front of her, a stark, luminous sheen, approaching as fast as a bullet train, about to strike, then SWOOSH! A bright flash and a quick sinking of her stomach and the other ship is gone. A gauzy incandescence envelopes the windshield like a thin film of radioactive milk. Somehow, her tongue tastes it, acrid and metallic, and it sets her hairs on end, making her whole body feel fizzy, like a colony of ants is walking all over her. Then both the feeling and the milky film dissipate in swirls and strands and Emily is looking at empty space again, her eyes still too accustomed to the flash to see stars.

"Did we do it?"

  *Affirmative.*

"How much did we get?"

  *34.33431 exajoules.*

"So that's what?" She does the math in her head. "About…80 exajoules we have stored now?"

*80.30987 exajoules.*

Emily smiles. She takes a deep breath and lets it out in a deep, long sigh. She's confident about her plan, almost giddy, even, now that she's proven its worth. But she's nonetheless leery of what it's going to take out of her. She takes another breath and lets it out, then she raises her hand again, ready to push the glowing virtual button on the windshield.

But first she decides to check her success so far against her plan to make sure she's hit every angle. There are still three chances for this to go wrong, and she doesn't want to end up a hot mist of microscopic debris if her timing or trajectories or off.

"Vocks, confirm the rest of our plan and determine its probability of success, please."

*The trajectories to the remaining iterations of your timeship are confirmed. This ship will, when in proximity, automatically take command control of each trajectory for the purpose of discharging its batteries when you are within .15 kilometers. This will serve to recharge this ship's energy store. Estimate the first three timeships will charge your batteries to approximately 150 exajoules. The fourth timeship will provide a 35 exajoule boost which, combined with the stored charge, will be sufficient to turn time. A stored charge of approximately 95 exajoules will suffice to return time after an appropriate duration of travel, leaving a stored charge of 3 exajoules.

*Proximity failsafes are circumvented; repulsive measures will not be implemented when you approach the other timeships. Energy discharge will only be possible within the first five seconds of the respective crews having reestablished power to their ships, the exact times of which are recorded in this ship's database. Thus, this ship will need to maintain a constant acceleration in order to reach each ship within those windows of opportunity.

*Probability of success is currently 68%.*

Emily scratches her head. "What do you mean *currently?*"

*Every two seconds of delay decreases the chances of

success by a percentage point. This figure is determined by the proportional increase of acceleration necessary to reach each ship before it initiates emergency return procedures.*

She mulls over that statement, trying to make sense of it. Suddenly realizing that every second of delay drives her closer to failure, she presses her hand to the windshield and the button glows green under her touch.

Her head, not quite set straight after the last burst, is twirled around again by the tight turn the ship makes toward its next target. Then her breath is squeezed out of her, her lungs compressed by the force of instant and rapid acceleration as the ship pushes forward on a straight path. She wishes she'd gone on more roller coasters when she was younger, but the thought is pushed aside by the rapid approach of another timeship.

As with the last one, it approaches at an alarming speed. Emily swallows hard, intellectually aware of what is coming, but not ready to trust that it will. She pushes down on her arm rests, sliding her body up the back of the chair, irrationally hoping the action will somehow control the ship to move. But it doesn't. The ship presses forward toward the other ship, on a path toward collision, until FWOOSH!, another bright flash and a fluttering of her heart.

Then the ship spins again, continuing to gain speed, directing itself toward yet another distance speck.

"Aaalleeeggggssss—!"

*33.97634 exajoules.*

The speck seems to split like a fertilized egg and then there are two. Two dots piercing the night. One if by land, two if by—

The two dots float side by side, tethered by a retractable umbilical. Emily wonders if Ms. Crana is floating through it right now, on her way to the duplicate Emily and Eric. The thought is short lived. Before she can barely even recognize that it is the two tethered ships, her own ship shifts up to avoid a collision and... Flash!

And blackness.

And then the buzzing. The annoying buzzing that only she can hear.

And then there's a strobe. A light strobe. Red, directly in front of her, pulsing in unison with the grating alarm.

"Vaahhhggs," she says, her head lolling back and forth against her headrest, "whass dat?"

*You have 60 seconds to enter stasis.*

A vague numerical truth pierces the fog in her mind, but doesn't slice it open enough to fully illuminate the inside. "Da wassiss?" she says, quite certain that she is no longer alive. "Stop alarum."

*You have 45 seconds to enter stasis,* Vocks announces, its 'voice' supplanting the buzzing.

Her eyes snap open. Before her, another dot. It too suddenly splits into two.

"Vahggs—two ship. Toooo ships. Only neee un."

*We are approaching a lone ship.*

Emily realizes she's seeing double. She shuts her eyes tight and then opens them again wide. There is indeed only one ship in front of her, and it is now considerably closer than before she closed her eyes.

"Oh hell!" she yells, the fog lifting. "It's the last one!" She starts clawing at her straps, trying to tug them loose. Gathering her senses, she unbuckles them methodically and strains to push herself up off her chair. She's up only a few inches when she's lifted over the back and tumbles head over heels, then jerks to an instant stop, her arm yanked painfully forward by a restraint strap twisted around her wrist. She's stuck fast, and the dot is now distinctly a time ship, and it is within seconds of discharging its power.

She loosens the restraint into a slight noose and slips her fingers through. Holding tight to the noose, straining her hand to keep it from knotting shut, she twists her legs under her and slips the noose onto the tip of her foot, then lets go. She is shot back head first, wincing from the hot pain of her leg feeling as if it had been torn loose from her hip. But it worked: she finds herself within arm's reach of the closest cryo-chamber door. She grabs hold of the latch and kicks her leg to break her foot free of the restraint. Except it doesn't let go—it is wrapped tight around her toes.

*You have 30 seconds to enter stasis.*

Emily grips the door handle with both hands and begins kicking violently, hoping the continuing strain on the tightened loop with essentially squeeze her toes out. It works. Her body spins around and she's pulled feet first toward the back of the ship, swinging the chamber door wide open. She slams into the other chambers and loses the grip of her right hand.

*You have 25 seconds to enter stasis.*

"I KNOW!" Emily reaches her right hand forward again and latches onto the chamber handle. With little more than brute force and iron will, she pulls herself toward the open chamber and grabs hold of the door frame. She is able to pull herself forward even more, her head breaching the frame so that she can see the inside of the chamber.

*You have 20 seconds to enter stasis.*

She lifts an arm and hooks it over the edge, pulling herself forward, her arm jittery from the strain, until she hooks her other arm over the edge too. Using both arms she hefts herself forward even more until the frame hits her waist and she is able to bend her upper body into the chamber.

*You have 15 seconds to enter stasis.*

With nothing else to grab onto, Emily can only swing her legs to try to whip the lower half of her body into the chamber. Three tries and she's in, her awkward position pushing her against the side wall into a crumpled fetal ball. Flailing wildly to stretch out, she succeeds in arranging herself upright but still plastered to the side wall, still needing to close the door and fill the chamber.

*You have 10 seconds to enter stasis.*

She rolls slightly and reaches out of the chamber as far as she can, fishing for the door handle. After several pats, she feels the door edge and runs her hand up and down until her wrist hits the handle. She grabs it and pulls with all her might, lifting the door and swinging it toward her, slamming it shut. Fluid begins to pool around her feet.

*You have 5 seconds to enter stasis.*

"I'M IN!" she yells, knowing full well that it means nothing to either the ship or to Vocks.

The fluid is up to her waist when the cabin is suddenly whitewashed, flooded with a blinding, pulsating, pearly shimmer. After a long fade out, she suddenly feels a disorientation unlike anything she's felt in all of her experiences since leaving Earth. It is as if each part of her body is being separated and spun around, muscle by muscle, bone by bone, only to be reassembled facing in the other direction—yet her mind had stayed put, cemented into place and unmoveable. There is no pain, only vague kaleidoscopic visions and merry-go-round sensations, like she's a two-sided puzzle being flipped over piece by piece.

She finds herself swallowing fluid and regurgitating it at the same time, like she's two people, twins conjoined at every body part, occupying the same space at the same time, two bodies for one disjointed mind. The cryo-chamber door is opening and closing, not in succession, but in unison. The fluid is filling and emptying, filling and emptying. The ship is flying toward and away from the other ships, flooding with both blinding light and blinding dark.

And then dark.

Emily regurgitates fluid again. Not swallows and regurgitates, it just streams from her mouth and lungs and stomach like it has done countless times before, sucked into the drainage vacuum and sent who knows where. Probably into outer space to reduce the ship's mass. There is light and the cryo-chamber is empty of fluid, and Emily is once again unmoored by gravity. Is it over or is it yet to begin? She pushes on the chamber door and it swings open. She pulls herself out tentatively, not sure if she's really coming or going, and peers around to the cockpit.

Outside: Earth. But when?

"Vocks, when are we?"

*In the Gregorian year 2016, 10 October, 08:29.*

"20—? October? Wait, when were we before, again?

*In the Gregorian year 2016, 10 October, 09:15.*

"So we only went back, like...forty-five minutes?" Emily's eyes go wet and blurry. She shuts them tight and drops her head, replaying everything over in her head. Everything she's done, everything she's endured. All the planning, all the pain, all the heartache. The anger and the frustration and the tears and—and—all she has to show for it is forty-five minutes.

Rage wells within her and she grips the sides of the frame of the cryo-chamber door so tightly her hands turn white and the insides of her fingers feel like they're being sliced open. No. NO! She refuses to shed tears again, refuses to let circumstance dictate terms of surrender. This anger won't be wasted. It will be shaped and planed and polished into action. Come what may she's going to make use of the time. She has forty-five minutes to save her mother, and dammit, she's going to save her mother.

Emily pulls herself out of the chamber and swings around toward the cockpit, launching—perhaps a bit too forcefully—toward the pilot's chair. Strapping in, she takes stock of the glowing data on the windshield and finds the map. She taps the map button and a globe zooms forward, wiping all of the other windows and applications away. It's a bit disorienting ('But what about space and time travel isn't?' she thinks) to spin and zoom the map while the real Earth sits directly behind it, imposing in its apparent passivity.

"Why can't there be a favorites list?" she mumbles to herself as she zooms in on the Chicago suburb that is her destination. Without delay, she presses the launch button and suddenly she is zooming through clouds and into open sky, toward a spiderweb of streets and highways.

The alarm blares again, making Emily wince as Vocks conducts the the harsh metallic scraping directly into Emily's skull.

"Vocks, stop the proximity alarm."

*That is not the proximity alarm. Battery stores are low.*

"How low?"

*.47564 exajoule is remaining in battery store.*

"Point four seven—! What the hell! I thought we were going to have 3 exajoules left!"

*Ship was unable to extract full charges from each timeship.*

A cracked patchwork of green and brown and gray seems to zoom up beneath her, the familiar upside-down Y of the main Fermilab building bearing up toward her like a concrete knife. But unlike the timeships from which she stole energy, there is no empty space to escape to if she even manages to evade the building. The only safety net to catch her is the hard surface of Earth.

"Vocks, stop!" she screams, unconsciously pushing her foot down again on the imaginary brake pedal.

*Ship's guidance is on emergency protocols. Manual controls are disengaged.*

The ship comes to a sudden, violent stop, as if attached to an elastic cord that finally reached its tension limit and is about to recoil.

Emily sits panting, slung low in her chair, her eyes squeezed shut so tight she sees paisley patterns zooming at her. After a moment she begins the pantomime of checking herself for signs of life, opening her eyes slowly and peering out the cockpit, expecting to see herself surrounded by smoking debris. Instead, she sees beneath her a turbulent ballet of tallgrass fluttering beneath her ship, whipped to and fro by the air displaced by engines keeping the ship aloft.

The ship floats next to a small outbuilding—a cinder-block shack, really—several hundred yards away from the main building. When the few people who are out on the Fermilab campus appear to be drawn to the discordant, mousy squeak of the rusty weather vane atop this small building, spinning like a befuddled helicopter blade, Emily realizes that despite the ship's invisibility, it is distinctly noticeable. Maneuvering the ship up, she glides it over to the tree-ringed clearing she'd landed in the last time she was here and makes a rough landing.

She unstraps herself, unseals the airlock hatch, and steps into the sunlight, noticing instantly that the ship must still have enough power to maintain invisibility. All she can see beneath her feet are the crushed grasses beneath the unseen landing skids.

She makes her way through the thicket of trees and emerges into the glade in which the small outbuilding is situated. She has hardly taken a step when a gray, steel fire-door in the side of the building swings open and clanks against the cinder blocks. A woman emerges, her demeanor confused and curious. She looks around and then up as if looking for something, though not quite sure what.

Emily recognizes her instantly.

"MOM!" Tears well up in her eyes and she begins running full throttle toward Sarah, whose curiosity only grows more pronounced.

"Em?" Sarah says, though she can say little more as Emily smacks into her with such force that Sarah is propelled backwards against the building.

Emily squeezes herself into Sarah, arms wrapped so tightly, sobbing so loudly and breathlessly that neither of them can get much air. Sarah, more inquisitive than alarmed, tries to pry Emily away so she can get a look at her daughter.

"Emily, what's the matter?"

Her inquiry is met by unintelligible sobs masquerading as sentences. Sarah can feel the wetness of tears seeping into her shirt, damp against her skin. She raises her hands and places them on either side of Emily's face, trying to pry her head away, but is struck suddenly by something she feels behind her daughter's right ear. She folds Emily's ear back and sees the little metal dot attached just under the lobe.

"Emily, what is that?"

There is no intelligible answer. But there's something about that metal dot. Something familiar...

"Emily, look at me. What's the matter? Why are you here?"

The answers are wet and cottony, but Sarah is able to extract some meaning from them.

"You missed me? Em, it's only been 45 minutes. You came all the way here because— Wait, how did you even get here?"

Emily finally lifts her head away from Sarah's chest and lifts it to look at her mother. Her eyes are tired and wet, shimmering ponds rimmed in red. Sarah is startled by how much older they are than when Sarah last saw her.

"Emily," Sarah says, enunciating slowly and clearly, her concern unmistakeable, "what is going on?"

Emily takes a step backwards and wipes her eyes with her sleeves. She sniffles loudly then looks at Sarah again. After only a second, her face contorts with emotion again and tears begin to roll. She looks down, slightly ashamed, slightly embarrassed.

Sarah grabs Emily gently under the chin and lifts her head so her daughter's face meets her own. "Emily tell me what's happening." Sarah's voice is commanding but gentle.

Emily stammers, pushing out seemingly random words in a gibberish sequence.

"Okay, slow down," Sarah says. "Relax and start at the beginning."

With effort, Emily finally says, "I don't even know what the beginning is."

Sarah chuckles despite herself. "Okay, well, first of all, how did you get here? I dropped you off at school 45 minutes ago. It'd take you way longer than that to walk here."

"Ms. Crana—"

"Ms. Crana what?" Sarah's face darkens. "Ms. Crana shouldn't be anywhere near you."

"No," Emily protests, "she's not—just—hold on..." She wipes her eyes again and takes a breath. She looks straight into Sarah's eyes. "Maybe you should just follow me." She grabs Sarah's hand, then turns and moves back toward the treeline.

Sarah is hesitant for no other reason than that she's confused. She remains in place for a moment, but then submits to Emily's gentle tug and starts following. When they reach the treeline, Sarah pulls her hand from Emily's and stops. "What's going on with you?" she asks. "Where are you taking me?"

"Mom, I can't explain this," Emily says. "It won't make any sense. I have to show you."

"You're making me nervous," Sarah replies. "You're acting weird."

"Yeah, well, prepare to be really weirded out." Emily crosses into the thicket and works her way a few yards in. She turns to see if Sarah is following, then stops when she discovers that her mother is still at the edge, staring at her. "What?"

"What do you mean 'what?'" Sarah laughs. "What do you think? It's been a weird couple of days, and this isn't capping it off well. This has something to do with that Ms. Crana? Has she contacted you?"

Emily sighs. "If I say no you won't believe me and if I say yes you're going to run and call the school or the cops or something. I just need you to follow me so I can show you what I need to show you. It's the only way I can possibly begin to explain this."

Sarah just stares back at Emily, a wry skepticism written on her face. Her mouth curves into a tight smile, like she's expecting a punchline, but after a moment she steps into the thicket. "You know," she says, trailing Emily, who has turned and resumed her trek through the foliage, "there's something different about you. I mean, even beyond the fact that you're acting weird. It's like you're—"

"Like I'm what?" Emily asks after a moment of silence. She turns again to see if Sarah is still following, and discovers her stopped again, her head turned slightly aside, looking back at Emily with thin, probing eyes. "What?" Emily finally says after an awkward moment.

"How did you get here, Em?" Sarah asks, her tone grave and troubled. "There's no way you could have walked here in 45 minutes. And I know you didn't pass through security. They would have called me."

"I'm trying to show you," Emily says, bouncing with impatient excitement. She turns and again starts walking toward the clearing.

Sarah follows. Her steps are halting and tentative. She moves forward, not taking her eyes off Emily. After about a half dozen steps, she stops again and begins looking around her as if she's being buzzed by gnats. Then she collapses into the bramble.

"I'm okay," she yells to Emily, putting up her hand to stop Emily from coming forward. "The blood rushed to my head..." She climbs to her feet and brushes herself off. Then she looks forward, past Emily. "Oh my god!" she exclaims excitedly.

She takes off running, catches up with Emily and grabs her by the arm. "Em, how...!" Then she's off again, through the thicket and into the clearing, up the ship's ramp to the hatch, pulling the handle. The hatch opens then she suddenly regains control of her senses. She lets go then runs back down the ramp.

"You can see it?" Emily asks.

"Of course I can see it!" Sarah exclaims, a big grin pushing her cheeks out. "It's my ship! Well, not *mine*, but... Oh my god, Em! Oh my god!" Then she stops again, turns to look back at the ship, then swings almost immediately back to Emily, the grin wiped from her face, replaced by a look somewhere between parental concern and horror. "Oh my god," she says again, quietly this time, then grabs Emily into a tight hug.

"You see it?" Emily asks again, not so much for confirmation but as an expression of gratitude.

"I see it," Sarah says, her voice cracking as her rejuvenated cytes download the ship's logs. "I see it. Everything. Everything that happened to you. My little girl—" She starts crying. "I'm sorry."

"It's okay, Mom," Emily says, trying to gently push herself away, suddenly embarrassed despite her own behavior only a minute ago.

"I'm sorry," Sarah says again, though Emily suddenly realizes that she didn't actually say it.

"I know," she tells Sarah. "We should probably get moving here."

Sarah smiles and wipes her own eyes. "So that's how you're different," she conveys.

The irony of the situation is not lost on Emily. Only seconds ago she was a blubbering mess herself, and now she's taking command. That's been her life lately: an emotional yo-yo, dropped by circumstance, yanked up by necessity. She wonders if the only thing she really wants is stability.

Sarah grabs her head and turns it, lifting her ear to see Vocks. "Did Crana give that to you?"

"Yes."

"That's very clever. I wouldn't expect something like that from her. She's resourceful, of course, but—"

Emily pulls away from her mother. "Mom, we don't have time. We really have to go and I can't see the ramp. Vocks—"

Suddenly, the entire ship is visible.

"You may not be little anymore, but that doesn't mean I'm old and useless," Sarah says with a wink. She walks up the ramp. "We're not going anywhere in this thing," she says, patting the side of the ship, "it's out of gas."

"So what do we do?" Emily asks.

Sarah pulls open the hatch. "Fill 'er up," she says then steps inside.

"Um...how?" Emily asks, following her mother into the ship.

Sarah strides right up to the pilot's seat, sits, then thinks better of it and stands back up, motioning for Emily to take the seat. "This is your ship. You're the captain."

"I'm perfectly okay with not being the captain," Emily says, plopping herself in the co-pilot's seat.

Sarah takes the pilot's seat again and straps in. "We have more than enough power to get over to the Tevatron access building." Before she even finishes her sentence, the ship powers up and begins rising above the treeline, even though Sarah didn't touch a thing.

Emily is stunned. "It would have been so much easier if I could have done that," she says.

"You did quite well, my dear." As the ship lands in the clearing next to the outbuilding, Sarah unstraps herself and spins in her seat to face Emily. "Em...I am very proud of you."

Emily blushes. "Thanks," is all she can squeak out.

"And you're right, we should get moving!" Sarah slaps Emily's knee and is up out of her chair and striding to the hatch before Emily can get herself unbuckled. But she stops suddenly and turns to look at one of the passenger seats. She reaches down and picks up an object, holding it out to Emily to show her.

It is the small white cylinder.

"Where did you find this?"

"It found me. Well, us."

Sarah looks at her quizzically, then turns her attention back to the capsule. She rolls it around in her hands. "It's cyte shielded so I can't access it," Sarah says. "Though this one looks like it's been tampered with. Interesting."

"What does that mean?"

"These are beacons," Sarah explains, shaking the capsule in front of Emily. "You could probably call them time capsules. They hold our mission arrival data. When we emerge into forward time, they download the mission log, launch away from the ship, then scurry home and deliver it to Caelestis. If something happens to us, Caelestis will at least have a record of when and where we last were."

"So why didn't it go back to Caelestis?"

"I don't know. Could be any number of reasons. These things basically just float in outer space for five-hundred years. Anything could happen to them. I'm actually surprised they don't get lost more often."

"Okay, so it's tamper proof. What are we going to do?"

"Tamper with it," Sarah answers, a small grin forming. "It's cyte-shielded, not exactly tamper proof, as evidenced by the fact that it has been tampered with. We can take it apart and see what's what. When we have time, that is." She hands the capsule to Emily and strides back out of the ship.

Emily tosses the capsule back onto the passenger seat and walks out onto the ramp—which is invisible again—but sees nothing but the clearing and the outbuilding.

"Mom?"

Sarah's head suddenly appears from behind the gray door of the outbuilding. "I'll be right back," she says. "I have to figure out how this is going to work—" She slips behind the door.

Emily stands there, unsure of what to do. Noting movement in her peripheral vision, she turns and sees, of all things, an immense knotty-haired brown bison grazing about a dozen feet away. She stares at it a moment before remembering that Fermilab hosts herds of bison on its campus. She wonders how it got so close to her, then notices a ten-foot tall chain-link fence running along the clearing. It dips low, almost running down into the ground, about twenty feet behind her, then abruptly angles back up to its full ten-foot height and continues further along the clearing. The ship, apparently, had landed on it, crushing a fifteen-foot section beneath it, inviting the bison to move to new pastures.

Not knowing that to do, she simply says, "hello," and continues to stand there.

The bison looks up at her, its large black eyes staring impassively. It approaches slowly, stepping toward the crushed gap in the fence, then stops suddenly, a dull thud bouncing off it head. It backs up, then approaches again, and just as suddenly stops, eliciting another thud. It tilts its head, gazing quizzically at her, then tries once more to approach. Thud! It backs up and stares again.

"Hey!" she hears from behind her, and turns to see two Fermilab employees, a man and a woman, in the distance, about a hundred or so meters away, closer to the main building, both glaring at her. "Get away from it!" one of them yells.

Suddenly aware of the more problematic aspect her predicament, she looks down and sees the tall grass waving six feet beneath her. Looking back up, she gives the two employees a small wave—which they return tentatively—then walks slowly and carefully down the ramp, trying to be as nonchalant as possible.

It didn't matter. The two employees are trotting toward her now, a purpose clear in their stride.

"Mom…" Emily mutters through gritted teeth, almost afraid that the two people will overhear her. "We might have a problem."

At just that moment, Sarah emerges from the doorway, pulling a thick, heavy-looking black cable. A complicated metal attachment at the end makes the whole thing look like a fire hose.

"Mom, look!" Emily points with her chin.

Sarah turns and, seeing the two employees approaching, drops the cable. "Stay here. And do not touch that," she says, pointing to the cable. She starts to trot toward the two people.

Emily turns to look back at the bison and sees that it has wandered off, away from the fence. 'One problem solved,' she thinks. Turning back she sees Sarah about fifty yards away, talking animatedly to the two employees, her body language telegraphing a forced friendliness. Even without hearing the conversation, she can tell that Sarah is failing to explain away the situation; the two employees are insisting on continuing on toward Emily.

The woman, trying to make some sort of point, begins gesturing at Emily, then the two begin to walk around Sarah. Sarah backs up at their advance, her hands up in friendly insistence. But the two don't stop, and as they get closer she hears the woman say, "She can't be here!" Her voice is directed at Sarah, but it floats lazily over the glade and reaches Emily's ears with surprising clarity. "This is a restricted area!"

The two advance past Sarah, their pace increasing. Sarah, clearly frustrated, turns and watches them walk away. Her posture conveys conflict: there is determination in her face, but hesitancy as well. But then she acts. She steps forward and races up behind the two employees and places her hands on the back of their heads. They stiffen for a moment, then collapse into two heaps, their bodies disappearing into the grass.

Emily is struck by a sudden and intense terror. Did her mother just kill two people?

Sarah jogs back to the outbuilding and is about to zoom through the gray door when she stops in her tracks, raising a small cloud of white dust as she skids on the gravel path. She sees the alarm is Emily's face.

"Mom, did you just—?"

"No, of course not," Sarah says, having anticipated the question. "They're just unconscious. Which may be a mercy: according to the ship's log we've only got about fifteen minutes."

Emily exhales, her relief palpable. "So I've been wondering about that. Do we even need to do this?"

"Do we—? What do you mean?" Sarah is about to let Emily answer when she thinks better of it and immediately adds, "Hold that thought. We don't have time to debate. You'd better come with me." She beckons Emily to follow her, then walks through the door into the outbuilding.

Emily follows expectantly but stops almost immediately after passing through the doorway, her eyes needing to adjust to the sudden darkness. She's in a small vestibule, dimly lit by dull, fluorescent strip lights, some of which are strobing in a dank horror movie kind of way. Before her is another door, next to a wall of grimy tempered glass. Beyond that is a cinderblock and concrete stairwell, like an industrial fire exit. Sarah is already down half a flight of stairs, dancing over the cable that snakes upward from shadows. Emily pulls open the door and starts running down, taking the stairs two at a time, attempting to catch up with her mother.

"So why shouldn't we do this?" Sarah asks, her voice echoing up the stairwell.

"I didn't say we shouldn't," Emily answers. "Just maybe that we don't have to. The last trip I took, I saw Earth. Intact. After the time when we all thought it was destroyed."

This stops Sarah in her tracks on a landing just below Emily, who jumps the last few stairs to land right next to her mother. Panting heavily, she watches Sarah stare down the stairwell, looking at nothing, lost in her thoughts.

"Mom?"

"Yes," Sarah says absently. "I mean, wait. You saw Earth?"

"Yes."

"On the last trip?"

"Yes."

"Not on the others?"

"No."

Sarah thinks another moment, then shakes her head. "No, we can't trust it. We don't know if it's a true future or a potential future. We don't even know if it was truly the future." She starts down the stairs again at a brisk pace. "Time travel does cause hallucinations from time to time. It's even happened to me and your father. We have to work under the assumption that the Earth will be destroyed in thirteen minutes and that we have to get the hell out of here before then!"

Emily gives chase again. "But it was here! It was right here, there was a big crater!"

Sarah is not hearing. She is on a mission. At the bottom of the stairs, she exits through another doorway into a long, curved tunnel. The wall of the tunnel is lined with piping—bundles of metal tubes, large and small, secured to the wall with thick, metal clasps, disappearing after about a hundred yards, arcing around with the wall. The cable Sarah brought to the surface runs into a large electrical closet housing a junction connecting the cable to the metal piping. Emily turns and follows the piping in the other direction, watching it curve around in another long arc.

They're in the Tevatron, the vast particle-accelerator ring buried under the Fermilab campus.

Sarah runs forward another fifty feet and disappears through another doorway. Emily follows, entering what appears to be some sort of control room. Sarah pulls some smaller cables, tools, and bits of equipment and dumps them into Emily's arms. Then she turns and pulls some sort of bulky control box off a shelf. When it is free of the shelf, the box swings down with tremendous force, making Sarah step backward and twist her legs to keep the heavy box from bashing her knee caps.

Dropping the box gently on the floor, she stands up straight. "It's been awhile," she says to herself, then grasps the box again by a handle and lifts it effortlessly.

"Okay, let's go," she says to Emily, passing her to exit the room.

When Emily follows, Sarah stops at the doorway to the stairwell and beckons Emily to go first.

Emily's lungs and legs burn as she tries to outpace her mother up the stairs. Sarah is nipping at Emily's heels, moving up with minimal exertion, breathing normally. At the top, Emily stops to catch her breath, and Sarah zips past. "Gotta keep up!" Sarah says, cheerful despite the imminent destruction of the entire planet.

"Hoe-kay," Emily grunts. She straightens her back and steps out into the sunlight. When her eyes adjust, she sees Sarah standing with her arms up, the control box rocking in the gravel at her feet.

"What's the matter?" Emily asks, then turns to follow Sarah's eyeline.

Police.

Police she recognizes. Several of them pointing guns at her.

# :15 counterclockwise

Emily drops her equipment and raises her hands.

"You are trespassing at a restricted Department of Energy facility," one of the officers says.

"Actually, I work here," Sarah says, lowering her hands and raising the ID card that dangles from a lanyard around her neck.

"But *she* doesn't," the officer says, pointing to Emily. "*She* is in a restricted area."

"*She* is my daughter," Sarah responds, provocatively.

"She's not supposed to be here."

"It's take you daughter to work day," Sarah says, not disguising her sarcasm. She says to Emily, "You can lower your hands."

Emily just looks at Sarah, who nods. She looks back at the officer, who is holstering his gun. She lowers her hands.

The officer reaches behind him and pulls out a pair of handcuffs. "I'm afraid I'm going to have to ask you to come with me," he says. He steps forward and stops suddenly, rebounding a few feet from where he stopped, a dull thud announcing a collision between his forehead and...something. He looks stunned, eyes locked on Emily but his focus clearly on a point only two feet in front of him. He steps forward again and comes to a stop, reaching up now to feel for some sort of barrier.

Emily thinks of the Bison and chuckles.

"Pick that stuff up," Sarah commands Emily. "We have nine minutes. We've got to get a move on."

"But what about them?" Emily asks, gesturing toward the police. Other officers have moved forward, attempting—with no luck—to pass the invisible barrier that is preventing them from approaching. They are a strange sight, hands up and out, gesturing like uncoordinated mimes trying to unbox themselves.

"They'll be busy for awhile." Sarah reaches down and picks up the control box. She carries it over to where she dropped the cable. "I extended the ship's shield out about 10 yards. But we only have a couple of minutes of power to keep it up. They'll be calling for backup any second now, military backup, and when it comes we may not have the power to keep them away anymore. We've got to get this set up."

Emily carries her load over to her mother and places everything down beside her. Sarah begins taking pieces and fitting them onto the control box.

"But no," Emily says, distress creeping into her voice. "I mean, what about them? And those other people, the ones you knocked out. Isn't there anything we can do?"

"About what?" Getting no answer, Sarah looks up at Emily, squinting through one eye to make Emily out over the glare of the sun that peeks over her shoulder. When she finally sees Emily's face, the anxiety written on it, she looks back down and continues building her control box.

"Ah" she says, acknowledging Emily's distress. She sits back and wipes her brow with the back of her hand. "Your father and I...we've spent our lives looking for this day. *The* day. I hoped I'd never find it, actually, for the very reason you're asking."

She gives Emily a quick glance to check her mood. Emily just stares back, her eyes listening. Sarah leans forward and starts working on the control box again. "What can we do? Probably nothing. At least not right now."

"So all these people—?"

"Are going to die, yes." It came out cold and direct, more so than Sarah intended.

Emily is shocked. "So just like that we leave them to their fates?"

Sarah looks up at Emily. "No! Not fate! We leave them to circumstance. Never fate! Fate is for Deacon. Fate is for those who sit around waiting for deliverance, for prophecy and destiny to carry them along.

"I'm not cruel, Em, even if you think I'm being so now. It would be cruel to accept this as their fate. It would be cruel to see this as the fulfillment of prophecy and to relish that because it suits my goal. But you have to understand that this is also history to me. This is as real to me as...the destruction of Pompeii is to you."

"So you leave it as a foregone conclusion? And do nothing? That sounds like you're accepting fate!"

"No," Sarah answers, picking up the cable. "Emily, we don't have time to save them. But we do have *time*! And we can exploit that to their benefit. You, of all people, should understand that." As if to end any argument, she slides the mechanism at the end of the cable into a large port on the side of the control box. It connects with an aggressive click.

"And now I have to go," Sarah says, turning toward the door.

"Wait, what?" Emily squeals in a sudden panic. "Where are you going?"

Sarah raises her palms to Emily as a reassuring gesture. "I'm just going down to turn on the power! I'll be right back up!"

She disappears into the outbuilding, leaving Emily standing next to the control box, self-consciously trying to ignore the increasingly aggressive threats of the police officers.

She jumps with a start at a sudden explosive pop. She turns and sees one of the police officers, his gun drawn, aimed at too slight an angle away from her to be comfortable. She refocuses her eyes and sees a bullet floating in mid air, a barely perceptible ribbon of smoke curling up to disappear into the ether.

"What the hell is going on?" The officer yells.

Sarah emerges from the outbuilding, breathless, her cell phone pressed to her ear. "Em," she says, "You need to go find Eric."

"What?" Emily asks, for the millionth time confused.

Sarah looks at Emily and shakes her head, pointing to her cell phone. She drops to her knees at the control panel and flips a switch. A red button lights up. "They're here too!" she says into the phone, turning to look at the police as she says it. Spotting the floating bullet, she points a finger at it and the bullet drops, lost in the tall grass.

The officers merely stare in disbelief.

"You need to go find Eric and the both of you need to..." she pushes the red button and a jittery, piercing bright beam of white, like a miniature, perpetual bolt of lightning, shoots out of a turret at the front of the control panel.

"Emily!" Sarah pulls her cell phone away from her ear and looks at it. "Ah, dammit!" She presses the red button on the control panel again, and the beam stops, leaving a crackling, milky glow rushing over the ship. "Emily," she yells into the cell phone again. "I can't hold the frequency, so just listen!"

"Emily stares at her mother, dumbfounded, realizing suddenly who she's talking to. "You're talking to me!" she mutters. "I mean...me."

"You need to go find Eric then find Ms. Crana. Emily, did you hear that? Emily?" Sarah looks at her phone again. "Damn call dropped!"

She dials again. "Emily!" she yells into it. "Emily, listen to me. Listen to me! Is Eric there? Dammit!" Disgusted, she looks at her phone again. Then she looks up at Emily. 'Circumstance,' she says.

Emily nods. "Effect and cause," she says. "I remember everything you're saying. I'm here because of it. But why are you saying it if I'm here?"

"First of all, she—you—called me!" Sarah argues. "Second of all, we don't have time to argue this." She pushes the red button again and the beam crackles back to life, splashing energy against the ship like a firehouse dousing a flame. "Get in. We won't have time to fully charge for a standard launch before the zero moment. We're going to have take our chances launching directly into FTL."

"What does that mean?"

"It means we're going to go really really fast," she says, walking up the platform. The electrical beam shifts away from her as she rises. "Don't worry about the beam. The ship will direct the contact point away from you." She disappears inside the ship.

Emily follows. "But why—?" Her voice betrays the need to argue a point.

Sarah senses this and turns abruptly to face Emily, her stance unintentionally confrontational. "I don't know, Em!" she yells, frustrated. "I don't know! I don't know what any of this means! I don't know what will happen if I do something differently! Nobody does! We have protocols to prevent us from doing exactly what we're doing because we don't know what happens if we use effect to alter cause. But my instinct is to protect you! You're my primary focus here! And if I can do anything to prevent what I expect you're about to go through, I'll do everything in my power to do that. To keep you whole and safe. Now strap in, we're going for a ride!"

Emily straps into the co-pilot's seat, Sarah into the pilot's. A high-pitched whirring pierces the cockpit, and the ship begins to rise. To Emily's surprise it doesn't actually lift off, but instead arcs up so that the cockpit is pointed up to the sky, and she is leaning back in her seat like an astronaut waiting for launch.

As she watches the thin gauze of clouds veil the blue sky, she sees a black dot form about twenty meters straight out from the cockpit. From her perspective, is is about the size of a pea, but it quickly grows in size, distorting the sky around it, like waves rippling out from a stone thrown in a pond. She realizes suddenly what it is, and says so:

"That's the gravity wave engine!"

"It is," Sarah says.

"We can do this while we're on land?"

"We'll find out!" Sarah flashes Emily a crooked grin.

The pea quickly grows to the size of a bowling ball, and Emily notices thin, wispy hairs of green gas begin to grow on it, like electrically charged hair.

And then it disappears.

"What happened?" Emily asks.

"We lost power." Sarah unbuckles herself and leans forward to peer out the windshield. "Damn! The shield retreated."

Emily unbuckles and leans forward too. She spies more police milling around, closer to the ship. They surround the ship in a wide arc, ending at each edge of the crushed gap in the fence. Weapons drawn, they nervously shift their weight from foot to foot, clearly trying to determine whether to move any closer. Trying to determine, for that matter, what it is they aren't seeing.

Emily spots one of the Fermilab employees, the man, fully awake, leaning over the control box. At that moment the woman emerges from the outbuilding and says something to the man. This prompts him to disconnect the cable.

"Stay here," Sarah says, and exits the ship, shutting the hatch behind her.

Emily sees the police turn their weapons and scramble to surround Sarah as she emerges. Many of them bump into or trip over invisible portions of the ship, forcing them to navigate with one hand out in front of them as if the lights had just been turned out. All of them show conflicting expressions of fear and wonder and the sight of Sarah standing in mid-air.

Sarah pauses a moment after closing the hatch to look down at them, slowly turning her head to assess them as if they were children. Then she pushes her hands out and all of them— all of the officers and the two Fermilab employees—go flying away from the ship, lifted a few feet into the air, spinning end over end like rag dolls, landing about thirty meters away from the ship.

Sarah bolts down the ramp, plugs the cable back into the control box, then runs into the access outbuilding.

Emily maneuvers herself into a standing position, her feet resting on the support bar of the co-pilot's chair. She now has a better vantage of the grounds around the ship.

Within seconds, the control panel is again shooting out thick, jagged bolts of electrical current at the ship. A milky-white film washes over the cockpit windshield, slightly washing out the pulsating black orb that has resumed its position over the cockpit. The orb grows considerably faster than it had before the power went out, the strings of green gas that emanate from it stretching out further, rising up toward the sky.

This vision brings a disquieting thought, a simple arithmetic, one that Emily is ashamed she hadn't considered earlier, and is almost afraid to contemplate now. She unconsciously turns to look at the treeline of the glade she had originally landed in, suddenly understanding the adage about 'seeing the forest for the trees.' To her dismay, she discovers that she can't block the thought from continuing on its path. Once an idea enters her head...

All she can do now is follow it and see what forest it leads her to.

She looks down the aisle of the ship stretching unnaturally beneath her, at the cryo-chambers and the few passenger seats and finally at the back of the ship that is currently serving as the bottom. She judges that it's too far to jump all the way down, so she aims for the closest passenger seat and leaps off her perch, pushing off just enough to arc toward the seat closest to her. She lands hard against it, the armrest jabbing right into her stomach and knocking the wind out of her, and dangles, half on, half off the seat. She grasps at the wall of the ship, trying to find something she can hold onto to pull herself up. Finding nothing, she begins wiggling backwards off the armrest, grabbing hold of it just in time to slip off and dangle beneath it, the muscles of her arms and fingers feeling a burning strain almost instantly.

She lets go, landing an instant later in a crumpled heap against the back wall. Quickly checking herself and detecting no serious injuries, she jumps to her feet. With the door latch now facing downward, she has to push it upward and out to open the hatch. But it's heaver than she expected for what she thought was a plastic door, and the exertion again strains her already burning muscles. She pushes it up just enough to crawl under and out, then lets the hatch fall to clank shut, its echo giving the already edgy officers another reason to point their weapons at her.

Most of the police officers have by now gotten back on their feet, though they have not moved any closer to the ship than where they were thrown. Emily scans their faces and realizes that, as much as she hoped she wouldn't, she's seen several of them before. At the crater.

Behind the officers, in the distance, others approach, other she's seen before, too. The heavily armed ones. And the three who, in their future—her past—will chase her into the thicket of trees and into the very ship she's standing next to now. She looks up at the dark, round artifact produced by the gravity engine. The sky around it is warped and distorted, like she's watching a solar eclipse through the bottom of a glass. Despite this, she can see clearly that what she thought were ribbons of green stretching off the orb are, in fact, ribbons of green being captured by the orb. The ionized flux of electrons and protons from the magnetosphere.

An aurora.

A disquieting thought, a simple arithmetic. Tree plus tree equals forest.

She spots the tactical officers running through the tall grass, their automatic weapons raised and aimed at her.

Just then, Sarah bursts from the outbuilding, her phone once again jammed to her ear. "Emily, honey, she didn't—" she says into the phone before her voice is drowned out, both by Emily's pleas and by the cacophony of commands being yelled to her by the approaching tactical officers.

"Mom! Mom, mom, listen! We're not in any danger!"

Sarah spots Emily standing on the ramp. She cups her hand over the phone and with her other waves Emily into the ship. "You and I have a slightly different ideas on that," she says with an acerbic calm. "Go back and strap in, I'm right behind you!"

"But no, I mean—!"

"GO!" Sarah turns away, removing her hand from her phone's mouthpiece and putting it over her ear. "I'm here, honey!" she says into the phone, then steps further away.

Emily runs up the ramp, hauls open the hatch, and slips back into the ship. With surprising speed she hops up on the side of a set of cryo-chambers and grabs hold of the closest passenger seat, pulling herself up the first, then the second seat, climbing them like a ladder. Perched on the topmost seat, she stretches out and is able to grab hold of the copilot's seat, which she climbs into by holding tight to it and leveraging its position to allow her to essentially run up the wall.

As soon as she's strapped in again, she hears her mother's voice behind her. "Okay, good. I need you to go with Eric and find Ms. Crana. Can you do that?"

Emily is about to respond, but realizes that Sarah is talking into the phone. Emily shakes her head in disbelief. 'Deja vu,' she thinks. But her train of thought is interrupted by a loud, staccato tapping sound, which she recognizes as gunfire.

Seconds later, the glow of the energy beam dissipates, its sun-like bath of luminescence fading to the neon-green glow of the energetic ions being attracted to and absorbed by the black orb, which itself begins to slowly shrink in size.

"Dammit!" Sarah yells, peeking over the rim of the windshield. She sees the cable lying next to the control panel, the connector coupling shattered into shards of sharp metal. "They shot out the coupling! Stay here!" She wags a finger at Emily. "And I mean it this time: stay here!"

Emily begins to protest, ripping at her straps but unable to pull them from the buckles. She's stuck hard to her seat.

"Emily, Emily! It's okay!" Sarah says, the phone propped

on her shoulder. She's speaking into it but looking directly at Emily. "It's going to be okay. And Emily?"

"Yeah?"

"I love you. You know that, right?"

Sarah doesn't wait for an answer. She jumps and lands on the back wall with a clank, her phone slipping from her shoulder to land and skid into a corner. She lifts the hatch, scurries under and through, and races down the ramp.

Emily twists in her chair in an attempt to wiggle out of her restraints. But she's stuck fast. Groaning in misery, she abandons the idea and instead maneuvers into a position that will allow her to see as much of what is happening outside as possible.

She cannot see her mother. She can, however, see the tactical officers slowly approach the area where the control panel is, which is likely where her mother is too. Then she sees the tactical officers flying through the air and landing near to where the other officers are standing.

Then the power goes back on and the black orb above the ship pulsates, the ripples around it swirling the green vapors.

"Emily," Sarah conveys.

Emily tries to will silence throughout the ship. She can hear her own heart beating.

"Mom?"

"Emily, listen. We've gotten ourselves into a bit of a pickle here."

"Mom, no, you just have to stop—"

"I'd love to, Em, but I can't stop. The coupling is in pieces. I have to hold the cable in place here to give the ship a charge. If I don't hold it in place, the ship doesn't charge and we'll both be arrested and the ship will be discovered. What'll they make of that, huh?"

"But you can't be arrested! You have—!"

"I can, Em. Just listen, listen. The ship's power was pretty drained and it'll take this facility about an hour to charge the batteries enough for a launch and sustained lift to a distance where momentum will keep us out of Earth's gravity. And we don't even have minutes at this point. Even building the gravity wave means the ship's shields had to be deactivated. The only reason the police are staying back is because they don't realize it."

"But I saw the police—"

"I did that," Sarah says. "That wasn't the shields, that was me. I can't keep the shields on and create a gravity wave at the same time. It'll take too long. And reinforcements are coming, and when they do, they'll converge and shut it down. After they do that, they'll try to arrest us. I can prevent that for a few hours, but with the ship out of power, my cytes will eventually go dormant again. Then we will be arrested and the ship impounded."

"So?" Emily says. "What are they going to arrest us for?"

"Em, really?" Sarah conveys, disappointment sneaking into her mind. "Do I need to paint you a picture?"

Emily doesn't. She paints it herself. She's sitting in an invisible spaceship, there's a small, black ball hovering five meters above her attracting auroral particles with such force that the entire sky is green, and a small control panel is syphoning energy off one of the premiere particle accelerators in the country and shooting it at an invisible spaceship.

Then she turns and looks at the police. They look positively alien, lit as the are by the green sky and the strobing white of the energy beam. They are so dumbstruck at the sights before them that they're not even bothering to hold their weapons up anymore.

"It takes more power to sustain a gravity wave than to create one, so I can give the ship enough power for a two-second trip, enough to get you roughly twice as far away as the moon, maybe a little bit beyond. You'll have more than enough power for emergency return."

Emily tries again to unbuckle her restraints. She growls in frustration. "But—!"

"No buts. I love you. You know that, right?"

Emily does not answer. She can't. She is struck mute by the crushing sensation that weighs upon her body. The next two seconds unfold as the proverbial life before her eyes, but she sees instead the events that play out before her, and she doesn't even try to think about why she perceives them so clearly.

The windshield filters through the green, rolling it aside like a breath in a ghostly fog and revealing the soft glow of a moon far off to her right and the backlit blues and greens and tans of the planet behind her. The stars ahead of her are like tiny strings wiggling before her eyes.

The ship approaches a stubby, pulsating wedge of light, and she sees that it is trailing a brighter object that on close inspection looks not unlike the very ship in which she is riding. It's one of her duplicates, trailing propulsion exhaust as it struggles to break free of Earth's gravity. The ripples around the black hole in front of her seem to extinguish the trailing wedge, then the bright object—the ship itself—bounces away, spinning frantically off at a slight angle from her own path.

The wriggling strings of stars seem to shift slightly, then another wedge and a partner object appear, and the process happens again: extinguish, bounce, spin, continue.

There was no cataclysm. No explosion. No destruction. There was only...

Emily, swatting the other ships aside like a hand shooing gnats.

The cause. And the effect.

The ship pushes past two more duplicates of itself, then the strings stop wriggling and retreat into themselves, becoming the familiar shapes of stars dotted across the universe that she now sees from her portal.

It was a glorious two seconds. Slow and languid, a complete absorption of the visual, free from thought and feeling. Nothing to do but just watch time unfold in slow motion. Free of the crushing knowledge that would impact her with the force of a meteor milliseconds after the gravity drive ceased operation.

But it does end. And that end brought with it the knowledge

that she had found her mother and lost her again. It brought the numb sensation of getting everything she'd ever wanted in life and having it snatched from her fingers before she could even fully grasp it. There is no consolation in having it in the first place; there is only the unfillable void left by its loss.

Emily spasms, like a bolt of the energy that powered her flight has suddenly leapt into and animated her. She shifts herself up, frustrated in her attempt to rise by the straps that hold her to her seat. No matter, she still has a mouth. "Mom!" she yells, hoping the ship is somehow still linked to her mother. "Mom, can you hear me? Mom? Mom!"

There is no answer.

"Vocks, can she still hear me?"

*Negative. There is insufficient proximity for an aprocyte link.*

She waves wildly at the windshield, searching for an action, a command, an application that would do...something. Frustration wells within her and her hands began to shake. "Vocks! How do we go back?"

*Please clarify? Back to where?*

"Earth! How do we go back to Earth?"

*There is insufficient power to safely return the ship to Earth.*

"Ship! Set a course back to Earth! Now!"

*There is insufficient power to safely return the ship to Earth.*

"Not you! I'm not talking to you! I'm talking to the ship!"

*I am relaying the ship's response.*

"Then what—?" Emily suddenly stops waving at the windshield. The truth—the final, irrevocable truth—hits her. "Moooooooom!" she wails, and tears gush forth in full waterfalls. Tears she didn't even know she could shed anymore; tears she thought had dried up after so many missed opportunities.

And then there is just the weeping. The loud, long, unabashed, unconstrained wailing, swallowed up by the soundless vacuum of outer space.

Momentum carried her far and she drifted for a considerably long time. Where two seconds seemed like a lifetime, an hour felt like an eternity. But only when she actually felt it. She had no real sense of it. It could indeed have been only two seconds that had passed for all she thought and cared. She sat the entire time and thought nothing, heard nothing, saw nothing.

But then her eyes draw unconsciously to two small spots of light; binary orbs locked at arms length, twirling freely to a waltz only they can hear. Eventually, she can no longer ignore what is before her, and she recognizes the two orbs as two timeships, locked in that dance she'd briefly seen them do before. One rotated 180° from the other, their airlocks connected by a short, flexible corridor.

The sight brings her to her senses, and she engages what's left of the forward thrusters to stop her ship about one-hundred meters from the other two. She sits for a few minutes thinking about the circumstances of the two ships being linked. It brings to mind the emergency return procedure, which she suddenly realizes that she can't engage because...

"Vocks, confirm the amount of cryo-fluid available."

*Cryo-fluid stores register empty.*

"Well, I guess we'll have to do that again, too," she says, eyeing the two linked timeships and the unused fluid aboard them.

She makes no move, though, to maneuver the ship any closer to the others. She just sits and watches the ships float, the solar currents pushing them across the sea of stars, thinking about the people inside these two ships. Four of them at rest: two crew and herself and her brother, dreaming. Another is trying to calm two others, also herself and her brother, who are awake and jittery and confused. Ms. Crana is probably right now telling them a bedtime story, trying to tuck them in for a long night's sleep.

She feels something like jealousy towards them, both the

two asleep and the two awake. Jealousy for their naivety, for their innocent optimism. They're certainly not happy about their respective circumstances, but they haven't bitterly accepted defeat, either, like she has.

Indeed, she wonders whether she even wants to bother getting more cryo-fluid. Perhaps she'll just stay right where she is, floating quietly, peacefully, staring at the two ships, locked together, arm in arm, like...mother and daughter.

Or sister and brother.

She wipes her hand down her face as if wiping off a mask and sighs deeply. In all of this she forgot who she'd be leaving behind if she just gave up.

"Vocks, is there a way to link my ship to the others?"

*There is an emergency access hatch situated between the primary thrusters. It is not a multi-door airlock system so its use will decompress the ship.*

She quizzes Vocks further and is able to formulate a plan. Like the last plan she concocted, it's not one she's particularly gung-ho about, but if it works it will get her a return ticket to her brother. On the other hand, if it doesn't work...

She fires up the windshield display and silently thanks her mother for charging the ship enough to allow her to put her plan into action. She slowly and methodically positions her ship so that its tail is butted up against the tail of one of the other ships, thrusters touching thrusters. Unstrapping herself (with ease, she notes bitterly), she floats to the back of the cabin, grabbing hold of a latch to a storage locker just past the cryo-chamber and using it to stop herself.

She opens the locker, pulls out a pressure suit, and stretches it on over her regular clothes. 'Seems a bit thin,' she thinks. It fits like a compression tracksuit, tight to her body, exaggerating the lines and wrinkles of the clothes she wears underneath so that she looks like an unpolished sculpture. Next she pulls out the helmet and slides it onto her head. As soon as she's able to force the opening past her ears, it pops into place, feeling tight and slightly claustrophobic, like an *Iron Man* mask but with a clear faceplate. The suit's collar reaches up and grabs onto the helmet, clinging to it as if the entire thing were magnetized.

She hears a hiss and Vocks then announces, *Suit pressurized. You have twenty-five minutes of oxygen.*

Emily walks past the airlock hatch, wishing she could have configured the ships so that she could safely exit her ship's airlock to reach the emergency hatch of the other ship. But aligning one escape hatch to the other escape hatch is what Vocks ultimately advised. Emily wasn't so sure, but who was she to argue? A few days ago—relatively speaking—she was just an average high-school freshman.

She gets on her hands and knees and unspools a thin, stranded cord from a small pouch on the back of her suit. Capped by a surprisingly light carabiner, the cord's delicacy does not inspire confidence, but Emily has learned not to judge the resilience of the objects she's encountered lately based solely on how they look or feel. She clips the carabiner to a hook on the ship's back wall, then proceeds to crawl through a tight tunnel left by the tubing and wiring coming from the engine enclosures. She feels like she's crawling through a thicket of brambles and trees roots. Although the light from her face mask is the only illumination in the tunnel, the small, rounded hatch before her is white, so she is able to see the handle and locking wheel clearly enough. With great difficulty she maneuvers her hands up and starts to spin the locking wheel. Within a few seconds, there is a hiss and the hatch explodes outwards, swinging violently on its hinges. Emily feels the pull of the vacuum, but the cord and carabiner hold steady, so she's only pulled a few inches forward. As the air from the ship rushes past her, its pressure makes her feel as if she is momentarily caught in a water current.

And then something hits the back of her suit and trails up to her head, thudding against the back of her helmet and wedging itself between her and the rim of the open hatch. She tries to reach up and grab a hold of it, but the motion frees the object and it zooms past her faceplate to slam against the back of the other ship, then scramble up between its engines and into outer space. From the fleeting glimpse she caught she recognizes the object as the beacon she carelessly tossed onto the passenger seat after her mother's brief examination.

No matter. Emily looks at the hatch of the other ship, about ten meters in front of her, past two sets of engine exhaust ports. She notes that the exhaust ports seem almost perfectly locked together, as if the rims were magnetized. That, Emily realizes, is probably why Vocks indicated this configuration: the decompression that occurs when the hatches open would essentially create thrust, which could separate the ships. Locked together in this configuration, the decompression has no appreciable effect. The ships are still together.

"Thank you, Vocks," Emily says absently, pulling herself back into her own ship.

*You are welcome, Ms. Clocke.*

Emily unclips her tether and crawls back through the tunnel. She pulls herself through the hatch up to her armpits, scissoring her legs out against the tunnel walls to create tension and provide a sense of security while she looks for something outside the ship to clip the carabiner to.

Against her better judgment, she looks down through the gap between the two ships. "Yep, shouldn't have done that," she says, looking back up to focus on the other ship's hatch. She clips her tether to the hatch handle, then pulls herself completely out. She slides onto the narrow platform between the other ship's exhaust ports, untethers herself, and quickly clips herself to a hook on the other ship's hatch.

Then she begins turning the release wheel of the hatch, but after two spins, she stops. "Vocks, are you sure there's no activity on the other ships?"

*Ships' systems confirm no activity. A total of seven cryo-chambers are currently occupied.*

"And the ships are decompressed?"

*Affirmative. As per emergency return procedures.*

Emily spins the hatch release again, and she feels a click. She pulls the hatch open and eases herself in.

Glancing around, she can hardly believe that she is in the exact same ship that she'd just left. Yet everything appears the same, save for the occupants of the four cryo-chambers. She peers in curiously. Mr. Algate. Next to him is Mr. Verton. She turns to check out the occupants of the two chambers across from the two pilots.

She barely recognizes the first occupant she spots, shocked to see herself.

"That's what I look like?" she exclaims. "Eeuuww."

She looks away, to the next occupant.

Eric.

"I'm coming," she says to his frozen face.

She moves on, floating through the flexible corridor that connects one ship to the other. She sees the occupants of those cryo-chambers. Herself again, Eric.

And Ms. Crana.

There's a comfortable familiarity to her now. She hadn't noticed the resemblance to her mother before, but it's there, hidden in the curve of her thin lips and the high, rounded cheeks. And they both possess a slightly weathered look that the residents of Caelestis lacked, the look of a child of Earth.

"Wait a minute, why are you here?" she asks the frozen Ms. Crana. "Aren't you—?" Then it dawns on her: there are only four cryo-chambers on the ship. Ms. Crana had brought Emily and Eric on board that first time knowing that, with two extra people on board, someone couldn't go into stasis. "I guess it's a good thing we showed up again, then, huh?" she says, wondering what the woman would have done if she and Eric hadn't unintentionally crossed paths with their own first flight. But they had, and Ms. Crana had loaded them up with precious cryo-fluid and then taken advantage of the serendipitous meeting to put herself into stasis.

Emily shakes her head, trying to untie the complexities. She's been back and forth so many times now that she has to stop and roll the whens, the hows, the whos, and the whys of this whole twisted adventure through her mind. She ponders the events that, to the people in stasis, are still to unfold. She can't seem to fully wrap her head around the idea that everything in their future is all in her past.

She looks at herself again, frozen in the chamber across the aisle, crystalline cracks in the frozen liquid that encases her. She is less judgmental. "I'm sorry," she says to her.

She retrieves a cryo-fluid canister from above the empty chamber, then works her way back with it through the emergency hatches, careful to ensure that both are sealed and locked tight. She orders the ship to restore life support and, when air and heat are restored, pulls off her helmet, and strips off her icy suit.

After popping the cryo-fluid canister into a slot above the first chamber, she instructs the ship to begin emergency return procedures. Then, at Vocks's prompt, she floats back to the chamber, enters it, and hears a hiss as the door closes. Within moments the familiar watery pressure starts to creep up her legs.

Eventually, she is completely submerged in it, and after the requisite holding of breath, she blows out the remaining air in her lungs and succumbs to the liquid.

———

Ms. Crana is staring straight into Emily's eyes, horizontal across her field of vision, her shoulders and torso disappearing to her right periphery.

"She's awake," Ms. Crana says.

Another familiar face darts into view, horizontal from the left.

"Wake the hell up, Dorothy," Eric says, mightily repressing a smile.

"Dorothy?" Emily asks, confused. "Where am I?"

"It's not Kansas, I can tell you that," Eric answers, "but Toto's here." He looks up across the room.

Emily lifts her head and peers in the same direction as Eric. She sees Brin standing against the door of what she now recognizes as the infirmary. She props herself up on her elbows. "Hi," she says, blushing.

"Hi," Brin responds.

"He gets a 'hi' and I get nothing?" Eric says with fake disgust. "So much for blood being thicker than water."

"Why am I in the infirmary?"

"Your ship didn't actually have enough power left to wake you up," Ms. Crana explains. "You're lucky it stayed on course."

"We had to defrost you," Eric adds. "Like a popsicle."

Emily says, "The Prime Minister probably has—"

"The Prime Minister can wait," Ms. Crana interrupts gently. "You take all the time you need to get your sea legs back. She's been briefed."

"How—?"

"We have access to the ship's logs. We knew everything that happened the moment you were within cytecast range of the station."

"Well, some of us knew," Eric says, throwing a provocative look at Ms. Crana. "Others had to ask questions."

"That has since been rectified," Ms. Crana says.

Eric leans toward Emily, turning his head away from her and bending his ear back. She sees a small metallic disk attached directly behind the lobe.

"Are you happy now?" Emily asks indifferently.

"It's the coolest thing ever!" he gushes. "It's like it's in my head."

"Trust me, there's nothing in that head," Emily says.

Ms. Crana stands upright, shaking her head. She turns and shuffles toward the door. "Come, Mr. Brin. Let's away. These two have much to fight about."

"Fight?" Brin asks, alarmed. "Why would—?"

Ms. Crana takes him gently by the arm and guides him out of the infirmary, attempting to explain to the confused young man how some cultures express love through humorous banter.

Left alone, Eric tenses up and backs away from Emily, as if in subtle retreat.

"What's the matter?" Emily asks.

"Nothing," Eric says unconvincingly.

"What?"

"Nothing!" He knows Emily is not buying it. He crosses his arms and looks down at his feet, hiding behind an attitude.

"You don't have to get pouty," Emily huffs.

Eric turns red and throws his arms down rigidly. He turns to storm out, but stops after two steps, spinning back to Emily, his face disconsolate and contrite. If Emily didn't know better, she'd have thought he was about to cry.

"Look, I'm sorry, okay?" he blurts out. "I'm sorry I couldn't go with you."

Emily is blindsided by this. For a split second, her attitude veers toward feminine fury at the idea that only he—the big, pompous, man—could have saved their mother. But she just as instantly realizes that he's being sincere, and it's not a masculine mask. It's genuine regret. "I don't think...you could have done anything different," she says tentatively, hoping she judged correctly.

"No, I know. Ms. Crana told me. You know, it's not—I'm not saying that I could have done anything, like, differently. I just think about how you had to handle it alone. Just the weight of it all."

"I'm okay," Emily reassures him.

A long silence falls between them.

Emily lowers herself off her elbows, resting her head on the bed again. Her mouth begins to slowly contort into a twisted frown. She covers her eyes with her hand. "I'm sorry," she says quietly, tears welling up. God, please, no more tears. "About mom. I tried."

"No, no, Em, it wasn't your fault," Eric says, forcefully. "That's what I'm saying. This wasn't your fault!"

"It was. She did this because of me! If I'd have just left it alone—!"

"I wouldn't have let you leave it alone. I'd have done exactly the same things as you. And she would have done exactly the same thing for me, too! This isn't anyone's fault. We all just got caught up in circumstance."

Emily understands. She knows what Eric is saying is true, and she hopes that someday it will all feel true. She wipes her eyes with the back of her hands and props herself up again. "So you got an Vocks."

"I call mine Siri."

"Really?"

"No. I'm going to figure a name out. Something easy and original. Maybe Fred."

"Why do I talk to you?"

"Because I'm awesome!"

"Oh jeez," Emily says, swinging her legs over the edge of the bed and sitting upright. "Poor Caelestis. It went from utopia to dystopia the instant you arrived."

"I don't think it's either," Eric answers, suddenly serious. "I guess it's home."

"I guess."

Another long silence follows. Emily sits quietly, unsure of what to say. Eric looks at Emily, unsure he should say what he thinks he should.

And then he does.

"Em," Eric says soberly, "I'm glad you're here."

Emily considers this for a moment, expecting a punchline. When none comes, she replies: "I'm glad you're here too."

"You big dufus."

# epilogue

Emily feels a slight pang when she thinks of that first flight. Ms. Crana thought she was saving them, thought that the Earth was going to be destroyed. Was deadly certain of it. Was as certain of it as Emily herself was certain that she could save her mother.

But ultimately none of it had to happen. If their respective beliefs had simply been ignored, Ms. Crana would not have felt compelled to 'save' Emily and Eric, to bring them on board her ship and transport them 500 years into the future.

To separate them from her mother...

"I don't blame you," she says to Ms. Crana, having run the spectrum of thoughts and feelings on the subject. The forgiveness was genuine but hard fought.

"Thank you," Ms. Crana says, flatly but sincerely.

It is three days since Emily's return. She is standing with Ms. Crana and Eric on the wide balcony of Eric's and her apartment, leaning on the railing, gazing at the cityscape that spans the width of the station. It is quiet, seemingly inert. A slight, warm, artificial breeze brushes Emily's cheek. An occasional bird (she'll have to learn the species) zooms across her field of vision. If it isn't quite home, it's home enough.

"So you think it's destiny, then?" Emily asks.

Ms. Crana throws her an admonishing look. "You should know me better than that."

"Then what is it? My mother—"

"Your mother made choices. As did I. As did you. Choices born of circumstance. This moment was not preordained, and I know you know that. I know this because ever since you've gotten back, you've been holding me accountable for the circumstance, and beating yourself up for the choices. Now you've forgiven me for the circumstance. When will you forgive yourself for the choices?" Ms. Crana asks.

Emily shrugs. She'd wanted to blame destiny—prophecy—consumed as she was by the sad irony that the events of the past few days (centuries) seemed to be their own cause. But Ms. Crana was right: what looked like predestination was just choice and result.

Aka: life.

Her former science teacher was herself consumed, dealing with the aftermath of Emily's adventures, meeting with and explaining to the Prime Minister all of the permutations of Emily's actions. Defending her own actions.

"So were you censured?" Eric asks.

Ms. Crana shakes her head. "Yes, but no. The Prime Minister made it clear that she was not pleased, but I did some perverse semantical gymnastics—Is that the word? Gymnastics?—and satisfied the council that no harm was done." She turns to Emily. "And it should be noted that Deacon argued in your defense as well."

"Why? He was against my leaving!" Emily says.

"Like I said: perverse. It doesn't change the fact that he believes that you two are the saviors of prophecy. He just thinks you're reckless saviors."

Emily snorts. The prophecy is a sore subject. "All this talk about prophecy. This whole thing was predicated on a prophecy. A self-fulfilling prophecy."

"No," Ms. Crana corrects, "It was predicated on the simple fact that at some point in the past a cataclysmic event destroyed life on Earth. That same event, or one similar, had also wiped away the cultural history of Caelestis. Those were our truths, and we clung to them." She remains silent awhile, a painful truth welling up. She sighs, her tone becoming quiet and confessional: "I clung to them."

"What do you mean?" Emily asks.

"I spent my adult life railing at the irrational belief in prophecy, yet coveted my own truths just as desperately. But truth is malleable; it is biased and individualized. It is not fact, it is the result of a tenuous interpretation of facts...and expectations and beliefs. It is, therefore, easily manipulated. Remove a fact and the truth changes. Add a fact and the truth changes. Ignore facts and the truth remains comfortably right where you want it.

"I clung to my truth to the exclusion of new facts. I believed that when we had found you, we had also found the moment of cataclysm. I was so certain that I had found what I was looking for that I stopped looking for it. But the missing variable was right in front of me, and I chose not to see it. That is my great regret."

"Ours too," Eric says. There is no malice in the statement, but he immediately realizes what he's said and regrets it. "Sorry," he says sheepishly.

"What was the variable?" Emily asks. "I don't understand."

"You," Ms. Crana answers. "The two of you. And your mother. The entire time it wasn't a cataclysm; it was you and your mother. But I didn't even think to look for that."

"I guess you do need our forgiveness, then," Emily says. There is no malice in this statement either, just sincerity.

"I guess I do," Ms. Crana conveys.

"This is just too cool!" Eric suddenly blurts out, beaming. "I'm never going to get used to that!"

"What?" Emily asks.

"This thing," he answers, bending his ear back to show the metal dot. "Vocks. Siri. Fred. Whatever. I haven't named it yet." He turns to Ms. Crana. "I can hear so much! Why didn't you give me this sooner? It would have saved me a lot of pain."

"I had to construct it."

"You built it? You mean they don't just, like, make them?" Eric asks.

"The station's infrastructure, as you know, is built around cytes. And since all of the residents of Caelestis have cytes, we have no use for external transmitters such as those."

"Well then, why didn't you just build two when you built mine?" Emily asks.

"I didn't build yours."

"What do you mean you didn't build mine? Who did?"

"I don't know."

"How could you not know?" Emily's confusion is drawing out an argumentative tone. "You had Vocks on the timeship. The one you brought us here on. You gave it to me before we got off when we docked."

"Yes," Ms. Crana nods. "But I didn't create it. I found it. On your timeship after I put you and Eric to sleep. It would not download data to me other than a message to give it to you. I brought it with me onto my ship. I had to determine what it was and why it was made. Someone knew you were coming."

Emily looks at Eric, who looks back and shrugs. "And you say there's no prophecy?"

Ms. Crana sighs. "We are time travellers," she says firmly. "We don't follow prophecy, we trade in it. It is a result of what we do, not the cause. Whoever knew you were coming is probably the same person who moved you off the moon."

"What are you talking about? Nobody moved us off the moon," Emily says, "the ship did it itself. There was some lunar orbiter—"

"There was no lunar orbiter," Ms. Crana announces. "You were on the moon in 1997. Selene, which was the first lunar orbiter with instrumentation capable of discovereing you, was not launched until 2007."

"Then why—?" Emily is suddenly alarmed. "Is someone manipulating us?"

"Perhaps," Ms. Crana calmly answers. "There are a number of possibilities. We shall explore them all."

Emily is suddenly energized, anxious. "We need to investigate!"

"Be patient," Ms. Crana says. "Do not let this trouble you. We have nothing but time."

"But—!"

"But!" Ms. Crana interrupts, the word spilling out with firm authority, like it's an exclamation point on what Emily didn't say. "The council may not have censured us but we will not have access to the timeships for the foreseeable future. There is little we can do right now to investigate other than review the logs of your trips. We may find clues in them as to what exactly happened. And why. But in the meantime, I caution patience. Any reactionary or incendiary behaviors will only hamper your cause. You are not exactly in high standing with the Prime Minister at the moment."

The punch of this information is followed by silence. All three of them turn to gaze out again at the waning light on the cityscape, each with different threads of thought running through their heads.

Emily forces herself to be calm. Or at least to make a reasonable attempt at calmness. In reality, her mind is racing.

Eric feels the tension. "You know," he says after a time, "I guess I could get to like it here."

Emily does not respond. She can't like it here. There are still too many unanswered questions.

———

The next morning, Emily is startled awake by a pressure on her shoulders. Her eyes focus on a figure leaning over her. Eric.

"You make it sound medieval," he laughs. 'Brin the acolyte. Benedict the blacksmith. Martin the minstrel.'"

"What are you talking about?" Emily asks her brother in a gravelly morning voice. She can barely crack open a crusty eye to see that she's entombed herself under a blanket on the couch in the living room.

"You, muttering about Brin the acolyte in your sleep,"

Eric answers, releasing her shoulders and stepping back. "I'm surprised you weren't kissing your pillow. Why are you sleeping out here anyway?"

"I must have—" she starts to answer, but suddenly stops and perks up, like a cat hearing a mouse across a room.

"Must have what?"

She shushes him. *Brin the acolyte is paying a call.*

"He must be outside," she says.

"Who?"

"Brin."

"Brin? The acolyte?" Eric teases. "How do you know?"

"Vocks," she says in answer. "You don't hear it?"

"No. But he's not calling me, is he?" Eric says, plopping on the couch.

"Well, aren't you going to answer the door?"

"I repeat: he's not calling *me*!"

"Oh for...!" Emily kicks off her covers and jumps off the couch in a huff and stomps to the door.

*Brin the acolyte is—*

"I know!" she says as she whips the door open.

Brin stands before her, hands clasped unpretentiously before him. He is not wearing his robes but is instead wearing a less austere outfit more in keeping with public fashion. But she barely notices that; her focus is on his short, jet-black hair brushed forward and up in a style that is to Emily considerably modern (relatively speaking) and not at all unassuming. His eyes, unhidden by the shadows of a dark cowl, are a modest, earthy golden brown.

"Wow. Did they engineer...those?"

"Engineer what?" Brin asks.

Emily flushes, her face a burning rose.

"I presume by the vasodilation of your facial capillaries," Brin says softly, "that you did not intend to verbalize that thought."

Emily slams the door and retreats back into the room.

"What did you do that for?" Eric asks. He stands and strides across to the door. When he opens it, Brin begins speaking immediately.

"I give you no cause for embarrassment," he says, then stops when he recognizes Eric. "I did not know to what she was referring."

"Oh boy," Eric says, nudging Brin back as he steps out and closes the door behind him. "So she obviously said something that got her—wait, you know what? Never mind. I don't want to get involved. Just do me a favor and pretend that whatever she said and whatever you said was never said, okay?"

"I don't understand."

"Exactly!" Eric reenters the apartment and closes the door behind him. "Get back out there," he commands to Emily, who is standing in the doorway to her room.

"No, I don't want to." She vigorously shakes her head.

Eric rubs his head in frustration. "I really don't want to be in the middle of this," he mutters, then turns back to the door and opens it. He disappears through it and Brin enters suddenly, lurching forward as if pushed in. The door slams behind him.

Brin stands there, looking across the room at Emily, who has retreated further into her room, only half her face peeking out from behind the doorway. He shuffles nervously, then looks down at his feet. "I'm calling...er...I'm inquiring as to...I mean, I'm hoping you are well?"

"I'm yes. I mean, yes," she answers nervously. "I am. Thanks."

"Why do you stand in the shadows?"

"I probably look frightening."

"I do not notice such things," Brin says. It is no attempt at a compliment.

"Oh," Emily says, not entirely registering his words. "Thanks?"

Brin shuffles some more, gazing around the room as if admiring the decorations. At once, he straightens up and announces, "Well. I did not mean to disturb you. I merely wanted to pay my respects. I shall take my leave."

As he turns and reaches to the door, Emily jumps out of her room and into the living room. "Wait!" she yells, her curiosity lowering her defenses.

"Yes?" Brin says, slightly startled by the abrupt change in tone.

"I just...I just wanted to ask. I'm curious. What made you decide that I wasn't the Savior?"

Brin looks away. For a mere whisper of a moment, he takes on the appearance of a scared animal trapped in a corner. It was a question he was not expecting and clearly does not want to answer. But he does, very quietly. "I did not actually make that determination."

"Wait, you lied? You think I'm the savior?"

"I did not make that determination."

"Then why did you tell me you didn't believe?"

Brin nods nervously, as if words are logding in his throat and making his head jitter. He finally mutters something breathlessly, then exhales loudly with relief.

"What?" Emily says.

"Did you not hear?"

"No."

"I did not wish you to be," he whispers.

Without conscious effort, Emily moves forward, toward him. "I don't understand."

Brin struggles again to answer. He composes himself, then looks Emily in the eye, answering as a gentleman would. "I must confess, when I tried to stop you from leaving, it was not in an official capacity. I was not sent by father...by Deacon. Nor was I sent by the Prime Minister. I went there of my own accord."

She steps closer again. "Why?"

He looks at his shoes. "I did not wish you to leave."

"Obviously," she says dryly.

"No. You misunderstand. I didn't..."

Emily is sure she feels her heart skip. She finds herself hoping that the conversation is actually going the way she suddenly wants it to go. Nonetheless, she responds with a curious, "You didn't what?"

"I didn't..."

"You didn't what?" Emily asks again, then smiles. Without her even realizing it, she has moved to within a meter of him.

"I didn't—" Brin pauses. The pause lingers as he makes a decision on his next words. "Perhaps it is best to postpone this conversation," he exhorts, his face turning red.

"Judging by the vaso...whatever, of your facial...or whatever it is you said. Anyway, your face is turning red." She smiles.

"You know," Emily says, "you learn a few things after a few thousand years."

"Indeed?" Brin says, her irony lost on him.

She leans over and kisses him. After a few moments, he withdraws, clearly uncomfortable.

"I've become a little bolder in my old age," she says, his discomfort lost on her.

Brin smiles. It is a curious, polite smile, full of guilt and jumbled emotions. "Yes," he says flatly. "Will you excuse me, please?" He turns and bids a hasty retreat.

Her eyes follow him. The smile drops from her face and she realizes that her newfound confidence may take some getting used to.

When Brin is about thirty meters away, his pace slows, and he turns shyly around and glances back at Emily. But when he sees her watching him, he instantly turns back and continues on.

'You know,' Emily thinks, her smile coming back, 'I guess I could learn to like it here.'

CPSIA information can be obtained
at www.ICGtesting.com
Printed in the USA
FFOW02n0835050418
46130991-47195FF